What readers and reviewers are saying about
The Temptation...

"Nancy Moser deftly melds page-turning suspense with engaging characters and solid biblical truth. Along with the two prequels, *The Temptation* deserves shelf space with spiritual warfare classics like those of Frank Peretti!"

CINDY SWANSON

PRODUCER/HOST OF *WEEKEND MAGAZINE* RADIO SHOW, ROCKFORD, ILL.

"Nancy Moser pulls off an astonishing feats—a book of remarkable spiritual depth that entertains as well. Combining scenes of high drama and characters pulsating with human emotion, *The Temptation* is a tremendous addition to The Mustard Seed series."

JAMES SCOTT BELL

AUTHOR OF *FINAL WITNESS* AND *BLIND JUSTICE*

"Unusual plot and varied characters...and God works in the midst of them all."

LISA SAMSON

BESTSELLING AUTHOR OF *THE HIGHLANDER* AND *HIS LADY AND THE CRIMSON SKIES*

Readers love the Mustard Seed series!
The Invitation

"*The Invitation* is a fascinating tale of four different people who are called together for a mysterious purpose. Through their intriguing story and the suspenseful ending, Nancy Moser sends her own invitation to the reader, asking us to consider how God can use us—and all ordinary people—in the most extraordinary ways."

FLORENCE LITTAUER

SPEAKER AND AUTHOR OF OVER 25 BOOKS, INCLUDING *PERSONALITY PLUS*, *SILVER BOXES*, AND *GETTING ALONG WITH ALMOST ANYBODY*

"Nancy Moser clearly has a knack for mixing humor, inspiration, and faith."

LINCOLN (NEBRASKA) JOURNAL STAR

"Few novels in the marketplace are quite as inspirational or offer as a background such real-life relationships, danger, and intrigue. *The Invitation* is fiction, but its message of hope is real for us all."

READER FROM NASHVILLE, TENNESSEE

The Quest

"Nancy Moser has again written a page-turner as she takes the reader to the next level of faith and commitment to God. As usual, the story line holds the reader's interest as the well-rounded characters face life-changing decisions. The characters are ordinary enough that readers can find a bit of themselves within the flaws and strengths revealed. Filled with challenging Scriptures, *The Quest* mirrors a bit of Frank Peretti's books as we see the battle for good and evil come to the forefront."

MARY MCKINNEY
CHRISTIAN LIBRARY JOURNAL

"Nancy weaves a fascinating story showing how God uses ordinary people in extraordinary ways. Get ready for a page-turner!"

KAREN KINGSBURY
AUTHOR OF *WHERE YESTERDAY LIVES* AND *WAITING FOR MORNING*

"Nancy Moser is a woman of style and substance as a writer and as a person. Whatever she does, she does well and with a heart for God."

GAYLE ROPER
AUTHOR OF *THE DOCUMENT*, *THE KEY*, AND *THE DECISION*

THE TEMPTATION

NANCY MOSER

Multnomah®Publishers *Sisters, Oregon*

THE TEMPTATION
published by Multnomah Publishers, Inc.
© 2000 by Nancy Moser

International Standard Book Number: 1-57673-734-9

Cover illustration by Peter Fiore/Artworks

For information:
Multnomah Publishers, Inc.
Post Office Box 1720
Sisters, OR 97759

Library of Congress Cataloging-in-Publication Data
Moser, Nancy.
The temptation/by Nancy Moser.
    p. cm.
  (The mustard seed; 3)
ISBN 1-57673-734-9

I. Title
PS3563. 088417 T46 2000
813'.54—dc21
        00-008508

00 01 02 03 04 05 — 10 9 8 7 6 5 4 3 2 1 0

To my husband, Mark…
for twenty-five years you've helped me through temptation…
and been my temptation.

I have great confidence in you;
I take great pride in you.
I am greatly encouraged; in all our troubles
my joy knows no bounds.

2 CORINTHIANS 7:4

OUR STORY SO FAR

In *The Invitation,* four ordinary people were mysteriously summoned to a small town. They had little in common other than a vague dissatisfaction with their lives and a small white invitation that seemingly came out of nowhere. "Come to Haven, Nebraska…*If you have faith as small as a mustard seed, you can say to this mountain, 'Move from here to there' and it will move. Nothing will be impossible for you.*" None of them knew what the invitation was about or who sent it; all dismissed it as a practical joke. Yet strange things happened; and soon, they found themselves in Haven, assigned to mysterious mentors—angelic mentors. Before it was over, all discovered that they were called for a purpose—to *find* their purpose. After experiencing the terror and miraculous aftermath of four tornadoes, they dedicated their lives and their talents to God. They left Haven with a new determination to change their lives, and a mustard seed pin to remind them of their faith.

Two years later, in *The Quest,* the people who visited the mysterious Haven continued to implement the promises they made there. This was their quest. It was not an easy process, for they struggled against their own egos, fears, and doubts. And something more…As they made progress fulfilling their unique purposes, they drew the attention of the evil forces in the world. One of their group was taken hostage. Confused and afraid, they were forced to face evil head on. But through prayer and the deepening of their faith, they found that God had given each of them the power to prevail if only they stopped depending on themselves, and depended on Him.

Julia Carson: When she received the mysterious invitation, she was the former governor of Minnesota. While visiting Haven, she was kidnapped by a young robber (Art Graham). Not one to lose control of any situation, Julia ran the kidnapping—her way—and in the process helped Art turn his life around. In Haven, she dedicated her leadership abilities to God—and He led her to run for president (*The Quest*). During her campaign many people of faith started receiving anonymous mustard seed pins like the ones the Havenites had received. God was definitely at work, getting the attention of the nation. Julia is now the president of the United States, and she shares an enviable marriage with Edward, who tries (often unsuccessfully) to contain her passion to change the world.

Walter Prescott: Walter was a single television news producer when the invitation arrived. He was a reluctant, skeptical Havenite. Spiritual issues do not sit easily with Walter, and he occasionally tells God no. He's glad God is patient—and thanks Him for giving him a wonderful family in Bette and their daughter, two-year-old Addy. Having found that there can be integrity in the media, he now works at a TV station in Minneapolis, producing a program called *Good News*.

Natalie Pasternak: Natalie was an unwed, pregnant teenager living in Estes Park, Colorado, when she was invited to Haven. There she dedicated her writing talents to God and made a decision against abortion. She eventually gave up her baby for adoption. In *The Quest*, Natalie left Estes Park and moved to Lincoln, Nebraska, to start over. She felt the need to break with Sam (the father of her baby) and concentrate on her writing. In Lincoln, she was drawn to a handsome man named Beau who fed her bruised ego. Yet Beau was not who or what he seemed—he was a demon who wanted to keep her from writing about her experiences in Haven, thus preventing her from sharing with the world God's amazing ways. In Lincoln, Natalie also met Jack, a plain man whose faith helped sustain her—and save her from Beau. All the Havenites banded together in Eureka Springs, Arkansas, and battled it out with Beau, using the omnipotent power of Jesus' name. Once freed from Beau's influence, Natalie moved back to Estes Park, confused, but determined to make yet another new beginning. She felt very lucky to be alive.

Father Antonio Delatondo: A homeless man by an act of self-imposed penance, Del stowed away in Walter's van as he was heading to Haven. Shot in Haven (by Art), Del's wound was miraculously healed. Although he couldn't pinpoint any great talent to dedicate to God, he dedicated himself, just as he was, flaws and all. It was enough. Father Del is open to God's direction—and therefore, receives it. He is currently a priest attached to St. Stephen's Church in Lincoln, Nebraska.

Kathy Bauer: Kathy was the young mother of a two- and four-year-old living in Eureka Springs, Arkansas, when she received the invitation. Although she knew her unfaithful husband, Lenny, would not approve, she felt compelled to take the kids to Haven. Angry, Lenny followed but obstinately refused to be touched by Haven's extraordinary opportunities. Stubborn to the end, he was swept away by tornadoes. Suddenly a widow, Kathy struggled to fend for her family. She pursued her hobby of painting portraits of children and worked at the pro-life clinic, A Mother's Love. In *The Quest,* Kathy was stunned when Lenny reappeared in her life, especially when she discovered he was working for the demon, Beau. But during the spiritual battle for their lives, Lenny finally rejected the evil and accepted the goodness and forgiveness of the Lord. He was killed, but Kathy took solace in knowing that he was spiritually saved. She also found comfort in the sustaining love of a doctor, Roy Bauer, who had attended a Haven in California. Roy is a former abortionist who is now pro-life. Roy and Kathy are now married.

Ben Cranois: Ben was Julia's campaign manager when she ran for governor and president. He did not approve of the changes that came with her Haven experience, nor did he agree with her determination to share her faith with the country. Bitter that she listened to God more than him, he quit before the election.

Art Graham: Art kidnapped Julia in Haven, and his life was never the same. Julia led him to the Lord; his own actions led him to jail. He has been there ever since.

It's been four years since they received the invitation. Now it's time for *The Temptation*...

PROLOGUE

> *Because he himself suffered when he was tempted,*
> *he is able to help those who are being tempted.*

HEBREWS 2:18

"They try hard."

　　"But they will be tempted…"

CHAPTER ONE

*The LORD looks down from heaven on the sons of men to
see if there are any who understand, any who seek God.*

PSALM 14:2

THE WHITE HOUSE DREW BEN CRANOIS across the street like a
sorceress with graceful, mesmerizing hands luring a victim
close.

Ben shook his head, wanting to stay back, keep his distance. He had not planned to come here on his day off. He'd
tried to resist. *This does me no good. This makes things worse. I
hate her. And I hate Him.*

President Julia Carson. And God. Two enemies that made
Ben's mind rebel, his heart battle, and his gut threaten mutiny.
Two enemies who wanted to claim his soul. But they wouldn't.
They couldn't. Ben wouldn't let them. He'd erected a door
against them that he kept shut, locked, and guarded. Nothing
got in, nothing got out. Not them…and not the *other.*

Ben stepped onto the sidewalk. The White House grounds
were dead. The leafless trees reached to a gray sky, creating a
stark backdrop to Ben's black mood. He raised his shoulders
and dug his hands deeper into his pockets. He kept himself
separate from the line of tourists waiting for the tour, from
Julia's gullible fan club, braving the cold to enter this palace of
Pollyannas. This castle of Christianity. He let out a soft snicker.
Even the windows of the White House should be rose-colored.

Hope, faith, love. Julia was destroying the country with
such mindless—

Ben did a double take. A figure stood at a window. He
grabbed hold of the wrought iron fence and stared between the

posts. Was that her? Was that the president?

His hand began to wave. *Hey, Julia! It's me, Ben! Remember me?*

With a violent jerk Ben's hand retreated to its grip on the fence. The knuckles whitened as the energy that lived inside took control. His body tightened, bracing against the inner rush. He had not been able to identify the cause of this new intensity—this *other* power—but he found it fascinating. And just a bit dangerous…

It was an urging. A push from the inside out. A feeling that something important might happen at any minute. And he liked it. If his gut wrenched a bit too hard sometimes, so what? It was a small price to pay for living on the edge of expectancy.

Ben closed his eyes and tried to take a deep breath, but the presence was heavy…demanding. He stopped resisting—resistance only made the urgency tighten its grip until it got its way. It was best to surrender willingly, sooner rather than later. He had known he would get punished for coming here, for giving in to his desire to be close to—

Move on, you weak fool! Get away from the sickening hypocrisy of this place. You have work to do. You must show the world the truth.

Ben nodded, then opened his eyes, letting the command settle into his pores. He released his grip on the fence, relieved that he'd been given the strength to leave, while at the same time, reluctant to go. He shrugged his overcoat into place and walked away.

He had work to do. Important work. He was on a mission.

—⁓⁓—

Julia inched the sheer curtain aside. Her eyes zeroed in on a dark figure along the White House fence. He raised a hand as if to wave, then suddenly gripped the fence like a prisoner on the wrong side of the jail cell. He stared at her; she took a step back.

Edward looked up from his morning paper. "What's wrong?"

Julia returned for a second look. This time she did not draw the curtain aside. "There's a man out there."

"There are always men out there." Edward snapped the paper front to back. "We happen to live smack dab in the middle of a tourist attraction. You asked for it, missy. And now you've got it."

"But this is...different. He's not sightseeing. He's staring me down. It's like he can see me, like he's tossed a rope around me and wants to rein me in." A shiver coursed down her spine.

Edward joined her at the window, just in time to see the man walk away. "See? I'm such a strong influence, he's leaving. Never fear, Edward's here."

"There you go again, taking credit where it isn't due."

Edward returned to the couch. "Hey, I've got to take it anywhere I can. Being the husband of the president is a tough job. The thanks I *don't* get are astonishing."

"Is the First Man feeling neglected today?"

"Completely and absolutely. And don't call me that. You know I detest that title."

"You picked it."

"A lot of choice I had. *First Gentleman* sounds like I'm a baron who wants first dibs on a polo pony; *First Guy* makes me sound like I'm sitting around in a stained T-shirt chugging beer and sprinkling crackers on my gut. And *you* didn't like *First Master.*"

"Imagine that."

"I could have been like Queen Victoria's husband: Albert, Prince Consort of the queen. Edward, Consort of the president."

"*Consort* sounds too much like *escort*—like I picked you up at one of those buy-a-date services."

"You'd never be able to afford me."

"No doubt."

"I'm priceless."

"Whatever you say."

Edward sighed. "Anyway, this First Man is feeling terribly, fearfully neglected." He looked up, his eyes hopeful, and extended a hand.

"I don't have time for cuddling today, Edward. I have to—"

"So I've already used up my five-second allotment?"

"It's not that bad."

He patted the seat beside him. "It is. And you can take a few moments to sit with me. The world will wait. Call it preventative medicine."

"I'm not sick, and neither are you."

"But I *am* on the verge of a mutiny."

"Oh, pooh." She plunked on the couch beside him, and he wrapped his arm around her shoulders. But she couldn't relax. Her mind swam with the to-dos of the day. She popped up. "Sorry, Edward. I can't. I have to—"

"It's not *can't,* missy. It's *won't.*"

"That's not—" She saw a picture of herself in the newspaper on his lap and plucked it from him. "This one is cute. I wonder if they try to catch me with my mouth open?"

"They have contests."

Julia studied the photo. "It looks like I'm saying, *banana.* I don't remember saying *banana* this week."

"An oversight, I'm sure." Edward glanced at the picture. "It's a good one of Senator Varney."

"That's because Varney the Vain has learned to live life in a constant pose."

"The big cheese can say *cheese.*"

Julia tossed the paper onto the coffee table. "Pooh to Varney and all the rest. I can't believe Congress didn't pass my education bill. If we continue to let everyone sit on their duffs, saying it's someone else's responsibility…if we don't spur the citizens of this country to stand up and make a difference, we are all going to drown in a sea of lukewarm nothingness. People support my bill. I know it." She lifted her coffee cup, took a sip, made a face, and put it down. "Speaking of lukewarm…"

"Either Congress isn't listening to their constituents or your instincts are wrong about what the people want."

She poked him in the side. "My instincts are never wrong."

"Did you take your cocky pill this morning?"

She faced him. "When was the last time my instincts were anything other than brilliant? I dare you to even think of such a time."

Edward looked to the ceiling, then pointed toward the window. "That man you saw outside. Your instincts said he was up to something. He wasn't. He walked away."

"You discount him because he didn't throw rocks at the window? I know what I felt, and it was…evil."

"*Evil's* a harsh word, Julia."

She glanced at her watch. She needed to get dressed. "Evil is out there whether we want to admit it or not, dear one. Come on, Edward…after what we experienced in Eureka Springs, even you can't tell me evil is merely a vague feeling. It's real. And more often than not, it has two legs and a five o'clock shadow."

"That was one occurrence, Julia. One demon defeated by good people."

"With the help of prayer. And Scripture, and our Haven friends, and the protection of a few angels—" she held up a finger—"my verse from the battle is still appropriate: 'Put on the full armor of God, so that when the day of evil comes, you may be able to stand your ground, and after you have done everything, to stand.'"

Edward shrugged. "I'm certainly not diminishing our experience, but it's not right for you to see evil around every corner, in every frown or dirty look."

"I don't. But God *has* given me the gift of good instinct and He expects me to tune into it. So when I get a gut feeling about someone or something—"

"You spill your guts."

"Only figuratively."

"Thank God for that."

She leaned over to kiss the top of his head. Edward was like a cup of hot chocolate she could savor while dealing with the cold and slow government—even if it was for only a few sips at a time. She felt the clock ticking on her day, and on her presidency. She only had so much time to accomplish what God had called her to do. She only had so much time to change the world. If only the world would cooperate. "Now, dear one, I must get back to the salt mines."

"Ah, yes. Julia, the salt of the earth. Always ready to spice things up."

She pointed a finger at him. "You betcha. But watch out for my pepper."

———

"Pass me the pepper, hon." Walter salted his scrambled eggs.

Bette spooned a few eggs into a bowl for their daughter, Addy. "No pepper today, Walter. We've misplaced it."

"Misplaced?"

"It's been misappropriated by a third party who has gotten in the habit of taking what doesn't belong to her." She cast a glance at their two-year-old.

"Stop with the double talk," Walter said. "If Addy's taking things that aren't hers, just ask her, point-blank."

"That doesn't work. That's what she wants us to do. Play the g-a-m-e."

Walter tossed his fork onto his plate. "This is ridiculous." He flashed Addy his father look. "Addy, did you take the pepper?"

The toddler grinned and giggled. "Pepper!"

"Go get it. Right this minute."

Addy's face changed to a pout and she crossed her chubby arms. "No!"

Walter's jaw dropped. "No?"

"Told ya." Bette got up from the table and returned with the tin of black pepper from the spice shelf. "You push, and she pushes back. It will turn up when she decides it's time."

In the business world, Walter rarely heard the word no. In the world of a toddler, he rarely *didn't* hear it. He poured some pepper into his hand and sprinkled it on his eggs. He took a bite and made a face. "Ugh. Lukewarm." He pointed his fork at his daughter. "How did you get so stubborn?"

Addy giggled. Bette shook her head. "She takes after someone very close to her."

Walter crossed his arms. "I am *not* stubborn."

He was appalled when Addy mimicked his stance. "Subborn."

Bette laughed. "I rest my case."

Walter shoveled the rest of his eggs into his mouth and got up, still chewing. "Lucky for both of you, I have to get to work." He grabbed his overcoat off the rack. The Minneapolis autumn had turned permanently cold.

"What time will you be home?"

"Late." Walter dug his keys out of a pocket.

"Not late tonight, Walter. You promised to go with us to the Harvest Dinner at church."

"I don't know, Bette. I really should—"

"You really shouldn't have to work evenings. You need an assistant."

"I'm doing fine. Though I am aware that if *Good News* were a talk show about cross-dressing aliens on welfare, I'd have two assistants, my own dressing room, and a six-figure salary. You can't be proud of me for dedicating my expertise to God and then gripe about me following through."

"Actually…I can."

"The show's syndicated now, with more markets signing on every day. I thought you'd be proud of me."

"I am proud of you." Bette helped Addy drink some juice.

Walter took his briefcase from the back hall. "Rolf promised me a huge bonus—"

"Huge?"

"Well…I assume it will be huge—in direct proportion to my abilities."

"And equally huge pride…"

"Can I help it if I'm proud of my talents?"

"Whatever you say, Walter."

"Don't be negative. Please don't."

She sighed. "A bonus will definitely come in handy. We're three months overdue on the house payments and you promised—"

Walter didn't want to talk about it. The subject made his stomach grab. He'd never been one to get behind on bills, but then again, he'd never had a house or a family before. "I'll get to it. The bank's getting enough of our money. They can be patient."

"But you shouldn't spend—"

"Money on nice things for my family?"

"You shouldn't spend money we don't have. The credit card bills are way too—"

"I'm getting a bonus, Bette. I told you. Where's your faith in me?"

"It has nothing to do with you. It has to do with other people. Besides, the size of the bonus is an unknown. It would be prudent to cut back and—"

"That's no fun. I only want the best for my girls."

"Then you need to understand that the best is not always the biggest and most expensive."

He put on a shocked face. "It isn't?" When she didn't answer, he bent down and kissed her forehead. "Ease up a little. I enjoy buying things for you and Addy. I want to give you *everything*."

"But we don't want every—"

"Gotta go. See you tonight." He kissed them and opened the door.

Bette sighed and finished her sentence. "But I don't want

everything, Walter. I just want you."

He shut the door so he wouldn't have to answer her.

———∞———

"I just want you, Natty." Sam ran a finger under Natalie's chin. "But you can't give me you because you're obsessed with this book. You won't even go to a movie with me."

Natalie Pasternak escaped to the computer in the corner of her living room. Her fiancé followed, taking a position next to the monitor. "Talk to me!"

She glanced up at him, then back at the computer screen. "What do you want me to say, Sam? You've got me."

"Do I?"

It was an old argument; one she was tired of rehashing. "We'll get married as soon as my writing takes off."

"What if that's never?"

Her throat tightened as his words echoed her own fears. "Thanks for the vote of confidence."

He tossed an apple paperweight from hand to hand. "You know what I mean, Natty. You're delaying our entire lives for something that might never—"

"Don't say it."

"For something that might not happen for a long time."

She rescued the paperweight and set it down—though heaving it across the room would have made her feel better. Why couldn't Sam be more like Jack? Although Natalie's months living in Lincoln, Nebraska, had been stressful in other ways, befriending Jack Cummings had been a balm to her soul—and her self-confidence. He had believed in her dream even when she hadn't. *He'd* understand what she was trying to do. If only she'd hear from him again. It had been a while...

"Natty, you're not even listening to me."

She shook her memories away. "I can't give everything I've got to the writing God wants me to do *and* a husband. At least not until I get established."

21

Sam stuffed his hands in his pockets and looked at the floor. She'd hurt him again, but it was his own fault. She couldn't plan a wedding until the book was accepted. In fact, until then, even going out to a movie was a distraction.

That's not the real reason you don't want to leave your apartment...

No, it wasn't. But could she tell Sam? She looked up at him, then took a deep breath. "Besides, I'd rather stay home because...today's the fifteenth."

Sam shook his head. "You are a certified wacko. On the fifteenth of every month, you sit here, glued to the phone, waiting for this...this hallucination of yours to come true. It's nuts."

Natalie had no defense except her gut feelings. Since dedicating her writing to God in Haven, she'd gone through huge adjustments in her work. Her first step had been to stop writing the drivel that she'd been sure would bring her stardom and big bucks. After Haven, cardboard characters, predictable plots, and swooning heroines had given way to more believable novels written about life and God and truth.

But there had been roadblocks. And diversions, including being seduced away from her work—and nearly her life—by a demon. Two years ago, after being rescued from the demon's influence, she had finally figured it out. She was supposed to write about *her* experiences, not someone else's. She was to write about Haven and the invitation God had sent her and many others. She was supposed to spread the message that God was inviting everyone to know Him. If people accepted that invitation, He would use them in extraordinary ways. Even if they were as ordinary as Natalie Pasternak.

Natalie *knew* this book was right. This was it. She had written *Seeking Haven* in two months. Once it was complete, she'd sent query letters and sample chapters to publishers. She'd gotten rejections, but had persisted. This *was* going to happen. It was a certainty that gnawed from a place deep inside.

At least she *hoped* it was certainty doing the gnawing...

Then, finally, she'd gotten a call from an editor at Capstone Publications. "I love *Seeking Haven!* I usually scan through these sample chapters, but I couldn't put yours down. Send me the rest of the manuscript."

That had been over thirteen months ago. What Natalie had thought would be a quick process of weeks had grown into interminable time—when hope battled with doubt and tension.

But she hadn't wasted the waiting time. She'd written a second book about her experiences battling the demon in Arkansas: *Battling Evil.* But the second book was of no use until the first book was accepted.

She nearly laughed when she remembered the desperation she'd felt after waiting only five months. On one morning when she'd been particularly discouraged, she'd made a tearful plea to God: "Please show me when *Seeking Haven* will be accepted. Please!" Her prayers had worn her out and she had stretched out for a nap on the couch. During that nap she had received her answer. Her "vision." From a high vantage point she had looked down on the couch where she lay—an empty couch except for the throw pillows at each end. Then suddenly, a shaft of light had illuminated a pillow. A glowing number appeared. Fifteen.

Natalie had awakened, astounded by the clarity of her dream. Fifteen! She would hear from the publisher on the fifteenth! When the fifteenth had arrived, she'd stuck close to the phone, even holding it on her lap, waiting for it to ring. It didn't. When the fifteenth of the following month came around, she repeated the process. After all, God hadn't specified *which* fifteenth.

During the fourth month of the fifteenth ritual, Sam had caught her in the midst of it. Reluctantly, she had explained it to him, and his reaction was as she feared: He laughed.

Now it was the fifteenth again.

Sam grabbed his coat. "Are you coming with me? The early movie starts in a half hour."

Natalie glanced at the phone. Logic told her to go, but her ambition said different. "Can't we rent a video?"

He put his hand on the doorknob. "I don't understand you, Natty. One minute you say that this book business is out of your control and all the worrying in the world won't help, and the next you think you can make something happen by…by believing some hocus-pocus vision. Either you trust your God or you don't."

Natalie went to his side and took his arm. "Quit calling Him *my* God. And I do trust Him. I feel with my entire being this is going to happen—with *this* publisher. If I thought differently, I would have withdrawn the manuscript from them long ago and tried someone else. I trust Him, but sometimes I wish…I wish God would hurry up."

"I wish you'd hurry up. I want to marry you, Natty. Or at least live together."

Living together was not an option. She accepted his kiss to ward off any further discussion, then turned away. If only he would leave her alone so she could wait in peace.

Sam zipped his jacket with extra force. "Maybe there's more faith stuff you have to do. Stuff you have to start believing." He ran a hand through his hair. "You know more about this than I do, Natty. I wouldn't know squat about God if it weren't for you."

She ran a hand up and down his arm. She was so grateful that she and Sam were learning about God together, still…her spiritual progress wasn't as fast as she'd like. As for Sam's—it was downright sluggish. She knew a lot of what he said and did was for her benefit. If only he'd really try believing, she would know she had accomplished something for God in the four years since Haven. If only she could shake the nagging feeling that there was something more to Sam's reluctance… something that couldn't be explained away by his casual nature.

"Let's go, Natty. We're going to be late."

She looked at him. How she loved his hazel eyes. They could make her do anything—almost. She sighed. The vision wasn't real. Sam was. She had to remember that.

"I'm coming."

———❧———

Del rubbed his eyes to clear his vision. He was tired of grading tests. Twenty-five maps of the United States, labeled with the states and capitals. An easy quiz for most of his ninth graders, but there were still some students who thought New York City was the capital of New York, and Los Angeles, the capital of California.

He looked at his watch. He'd come to the classroom early to grade the papers and only had a couple minutes until class started. Just a few more…

He got back to work, pleased that the next map was Carrie Peterson's. She was a good student—and an amazing child. Ever since her mother died, Carrie had been forced to handle extra responsibilities around the house for her father. Yet she still managed to get good grades. Her test would be easy to grade. She wouldn't mismark North and South Dakota. Del placed his red pen in the upper left corner of the map, ready to sweep down and across to check it, when he noticed that Carrie had put Haven as the capital of Washington.

Del shook his head. "Come on, Carrie. I know you're interested in my experiences in Haven, but—"

Del's eyes scanned the rest of the map and went back again. There was not one Haven, but fifty. Albany and Albuquerque and Atlanta were all marked Haven. This was not like Carrie at all. She certainly wouldn't sabotage a quiz to play a practical joke.

Del heard the bell and looked up as the kids began to flow into the room. He set Carrie's map aside so he could ask her about it, then finished grading the final two quizzes as the last student came in.

"How'd we do, Father?"

Del tapped the stack of maps against the desk. "Most of you did great, though there are a few of you who should stay away from navigating a car on a cross-country trip. And one of you was a little obsessed with my Haven experience." He glanced at Carrie but her face was merely curious. "Josh, would you hand these back, please?"

As Josh stood to take the maps, Del moved to Carrie's desk. "Carrie, would you come out in the hall with me a moment?"

The room filled with whoops and laughter. Del regretted the look of unease on Carrie's face. They went out in the hall, and Del closed the door.

"Did I do something wrong, Father Del?"

"Not exactly…" He pulled her map from behind his back. "Can you explain this?"

She took the map and stared at it. Then she looked up at him. "I don't understand…I don't see anything wrong with it."

Del raised an eyebrow. "Nothing wrong with it?"

She looked again. "Maybe I could have moved Jackson, Mississippi, a little further south, but the rest of it looks—"

Del grabbed the map away. It contained the fifty capitals— and not one Haven. He turned the page over. He looked again. *What's going on? I saw fifty Havens!*

"Father?"

Del ran a hand across his face. "I'm sorry, Carrie. I thought…I saw…the map is fine. One hundred percent." He felt like a fool. Again. "Come on. We'd better go back inside. It's time for class."

———— ∙∾∙ ————

"It's time, Kath."

Kathy looked up from the clothes strewn across their bed. Her husband Roy stood in the doorway, handsome—and ready to go—in his suit.

Their daughter Lisa appeared by his side. "Come on, Mommy."

"I know, I know. I'm hurrying. Where's Ryan?"

"Cleanin'." Lisa stuck her head under Roy's arm. "He called me a disgusting pig."

"Oink, oink," Roy said.

"You *are* a messy girl, Lisa."

"I'm only messy compared to Ryan."

"Everyone's messy compared to Ryan."

Kathy had no idea where her eight-year-old son got that particular character trait. From the looks of the master bedroom, she knew it wasn't from her.

Roy pinched Lisa's nose. "You and your brother get in the car. We'll be there in a minute." Lisa left them. Roy leaned against the door jamb, studying his wife. "Though I personally find the slip and bare feet appealing, if you go to the showing like that, they will forget all about your paintings."

"Is that a compliment?"

"It is. And make sure you put it on my tally sheet. I want to get full credit." He came over to the bed and chose a royal blue silk suit. "I thought you bought this one for today."

"I did, but then I was wondering if the color was too bright. So yesterday I bought this dress." She held it in front of her. "What do you think?"

"I think you should take it back."

She tossed it on the bed. "No…I'll use it some time. But how about this one?" She draped a gray sheath under her chin.

Roy reached for the tags hanging from the sleeve. She pulled it away before he could check the price, but he simply detoured to the other three outfits on the bed. All had the price tags attached. His jaw dropped. "What did you do, Kath? Buy out Eureka Springs?"

"That wouldn't be hard. Actually, I got most of these in Springfield."

"I make a good living as a doctor, and your paintings are starting to take off, but these are expensive. Who are you trying to impress?"

She stepped into the blue silk skirt. "No one." She shrugged. "Everyone. I don't know."

Roy took her face in his hands. "You don't need pricey clothes to prove your worth to the world, Kath."

But it proves it to me… "I need to play the part, don't I?"

He let go of her face. "The part of what?"

"A successful artist."

"This is your first real showing."

She slipped on the matching blouse. "But Sandra says this will lead to more and more and—"

"I support you in all your work, Kath, and I do think your time has come. But don't get ahead of yourself or let the fame and fortune go to your noggin."

She gave him her best smile. "How about just the fortune part?"

His eyes revealed his hurt. "We have a nice life. Or I thought we—"

"We do, Roy. We do." She kissed him on the cheek. "You've taken us from the edge of poverty to a very comfortable life."

"You make *comfortable* sound mediocre."

"I don't mean to. You know money's been an issue with me my entire life. I didn't have a new dress until Lenny and I got married, and then I was careful to get one that I could wear to church every Sunday. In fact, I still wear it. I wore it to the Bartell's anniversary party last August. Do you want me to show—?" She started for the closet.

"That was your wedding dress?"

She backtracked and took his hands. "J.C. Penney. On the clearance rack for $39.95. So you see? Buying expensive clothes…well, it makes me feel like I've come beyond all that. Like I'm safe."

"Clothes make you feel safe?"

She considered this a moment. "Being able to buy or not buy without worrying if I have enough money for food…yes, that makes me feel safe."

He waved a hand toward the bed. "Then keep them. Keep them all."

"The shoes too?"

He raised an eyebrow, then lowered it, shaking his head. "I don't want to know."

She squealed and gave him a better kiss. On the lips.

CHAPTER TWO

———⌘———

Listen to advice and accept instruction, and in the end you will be wise. Many are the plans in a man's heart, but it is the LORD's purpose that prevails.

PROVERBS 19:20–21

FATHER ANTONIO DELATONDO KNELT in the sanctuary of St. Stephen's. He was alone except for Lionel, the parish handyman, who was replacing candles near the altar. Just Del, Lionel—and God.

Del adjusted his knees on the kneeler. He rested his elbows on the pew in front of him and closed his eyes. *Father. Lord. You've blessed me with this impression regarding Haven. A map. Many Havens. What does it mean? I'm not a brilliant man. Make it clear. Show me—*

"Excuse me? Father?"

Del opened his eyes to see the handyman in the center aisle. "What is it, Lionel?"

"Sorry to disturb you, Father, but I wanted to tell you that we need more reunion candles. These are nearly burnt out and I only have—"

"Reunion candles?"

Lionel looked at him. "Reunion? I didn't say reunion. I said communion."

Reunion. Haven. A Haven reunion!

"Father? You all right?"

Del bowed his head. *Thank You for the quick answer, Lord!* He got to his feet and brushed past Lionel. He had to talk to the monsignor.

"Father? The candles?"

Del turned as he reached the narthex, taking the last few steps backward. "Don't worry about the candles, Lionel. The candles aren't important! You've just been used by God!"

At Lionel's stare, Del knew another story would be added to the legend of crazy Father Del.

It couldn't be helped. He had work to do.

Monsignor Vibrowsky sat at his desk and shook his head. "A disappearing map, you say? And then Lionel heard you say *reunion?*"

"No, I heard Lionel say it."

"But he didn't actually say *reunion?*"

"Well…maybe. He claims he said *communion* but I heard *reunion*. The point is, I believe I'm supposed to organize a reunion of the Havenites."

"Uh-huh."

Del squirmed in his chair. For the umpteenth time he wondered why God had placed him under the direction of a superior who didn't believe in the physical evidence of divine guidance. Hadn't the monsignor ever received any? Del pushed such rude thoughts away.

"I can only tell you what I believe to be true, Monsignor. We can choose to ignore such promptings or follow through. But I don't see how we dare—"

"Ignore God?"

Del felt himself redden.

Monsignor tented his fingers. "I know you've had some unique experiences, Father Del. And during the two years you've been here in Lincoln, I—we—have come to appreciate the essence of your experiences, even if we haven't fully understood them."

"They're not that hard to understand. God reaches different people in different ways. He wouldn't speak to you in the same way He speaks to me."

"Uh-huh."

"He wouldn't." *He'd have to shout!*

Monsignor held up a finger. "The point is, He isn't speaking to me; He is only speaking to you."

Del looked past him, out the window. This was not going well. "Actually, He's not *speaking* to me at all. Not in words said out loud."

"So He speaks without words?"

"Well, yes…"

"He speaks in mystical signs. And…?"

Del couldn't miss Monsignor's smirk. "He has given me various…urgings."

"Which you've interpreted using your vast experience in such matters."

Del wondered if there would be any advantage to going out and coming in again, beginning this conversation fresh. Probably not. He settled for starting with a fresh breath. "I believe many of our ideas come from somewhere beyond our own limited imaginings. And when something comes up like this—out of nowhere, with no prior inkling or clue—I tend to believe it's the prompting of the Holy Spirit, wanting us to join Him in His work." He looked at his lap. "This idea of a reunion didn't come from me, Monsignor. In fact I'm rather intimidated by the very thought of it. I mean…how do I pull it off? I guarantee you, this isn't a grand scheme I've cooked up to get out of my duties around the parish."

"Which will not happen no matter who gave you the idea." The monsignor cleared his throat. "And as far as it being a prompting from the Holy Spirit…" He leaned forward, and Del had the impression the monsignor would have been in his face if the desk had not spanned the space between them. "All I want to know is, who do you think you are?"

Del blinked. "Excuse me?"

Monsignor stood and paced behind his desk. "Believe it or not, Father Delatondo, you are not important enough for the

Holy Spirit to give you special guidance. You are no better—"

"I'm not saying I'm better than anyone. And you don't understand...and I think you're mistaken about the Holy Spirit."

Monsignor stopped pacing and raised an eyebrow.

Should I stay quiet? Or speak the truth whether he wants to hear it or not?

"You have something to say?" It was clear the monsignor expected him to say no.

Del pushed his back against the chair, finding comfort in the support of the cushion against his backbone. He thought of a familiar verse: *Then you will know the truth, and the truth will set you free.* It was imperative that Monsignor, being a man of high appointment, be told the truth. It was also amazing that he was so obviously misinformed.

"In all deference to your position, Monsignor, the Holy Spirit comes to all believers, not just those we deem important. At Pentecost Christ gave us His Spirit, to live in us and work through us. The Spirit is a gift for all—"

"Are you preaching at me, Father?"

Seeing Monsignor's jaw tighten, Del was quick to add, "Of course, I, being one of the least important people, feel highly honored at the Holy Spirit's attention—and yours."

"False modesty does not become you, Father."

Nor does pompous ignorance become you.

Del wisely let a moment of silence pass between them. *Lord, if this is Your will, open the door. If it is my own misguided notion, shut it.*

The monsignor glanced out the window, then suddenly turned to face Del. He cocked his head, his eyes sparking. His wrinkles deepened and his muscles twitched. "I...I suppose you can look into this reunion idea. In your free time."

Del sat in a moment of shocked silence. Then he said, "Thank you, sir," and left before the monsignor could change his mind.

It was true. The Holy Spirit did speak to all believers. Even the monsignor.

The door had swung open.

After dinner, Del retired to his room to do some heavy thinking about the reunion. There were so many questions: Where should it be held? When? How would he ever contact the Haven alumni? What would happen when they got together? And most important, why should they reunite in the first place? What did God have in mind?

Del changed into sweatpants and a sweatshirt and sat at his desk. He pulled a yellow pad forward and found a pen. He began to write "Haven Reunion" at the top of the page, but the pen didn't work. He rummaged through a drawer…no pens, but he did find a nail clipper. He proceeded to give himself a manicure.

A few minutes later, he stopped himself. *What was I looking for?* "A pen. I need a pen."

He went into the rectory living room and found one by the phone.

Father Caspian held up a deck of cards. "Want to play Hearts, Del?"

"Not tonight. I've got business."

"Ooh, sounds important."

Del shrugged. "Could be."

Back in his room, he heard a tree branch scrape against the window. It made him cold. Hot chocolate. That's what he needed. He left his room a second time and went to the kitchen where he heated a mug of water in the microwave. Looking through the cupboard for a packet of hot chocolate, he felt a sudden craving for marshmallows. It took him nearly five minutes to find some on a top shelf behind the cake mixes.

By then his water was tepid, so he had to reheat it. On the way out of the kitchen, he grabbed two oatmeal raisin cookies.

When he passed Caspian a second time, he received a raised eyebrow, asking a silent question.

Del raised his mug. "Cocoa."

Finally settling in, Del placed his hands flat on his desk. "Now…let's get start—" He suddenly found himself standing. He needed to go to the bathroom. He was halfway there when he stopped himself.

"Enough!" He glanced around the room, looking past the furniture. "I've had enough of you, Satan. If you think you're going to distract me one more minute…I see what you're up to. You're trying to keep me from doing what the Lord has instructed me to do. But I won't let you. Not any more."

With new determination, Del took a seat at his desk, picked up his pen, and started jotting down ideas for the Haven reunion.

He was only slightly surprised to find that he no longer had to go to the bathroom.

—◆—

Walter Prescott's boss at KMPS paused in the doorway to Walter's office, one hand in the sleeve of his overcoat. "Working late?"

"I've got work to do, Rolf. You know that on-site interview we're doing with Habitat for Humanity? These interview questions Christine put together are lame."

"Then have her change them. That's her job."

"But I can do it faster."

Rolf took a step into the office. "Faster is not always better. Sometimes by butting in on other people's work, you're depriving them of the chance to do what they've been called to do."

"I'm only doing what *I've* been called to do."

"And you're doing it very well, but there has to be balance. You can't drown yourself in your work—in other people's work. God first, family second, job third…"

Walter sighed. It was nice to have someone at his workplace

36

to talk to about God things, even if Rolf often told him things he didn't want to hear. He leaned back in his chair. "You should talk. You work harder than anyone I know. And you're still here."

"Only because I'm going to an out-of-town meeting later this week."

Walter glanced at his watch. Six-thirty. The Harvest Dinner Bette had wanted him to attend had started. He felt a twinge of guilt but shoved it away. Certainly his work for God on *Good News* was more important than a potluck dinner of goulash and apple crisp.

"Job third, Walter." Rolf buttoned his coat. "Seems to me you've got your job right up there at number one."

Walter slammed a desk drawer shut. "God's up there too. After all, I'm doing it for Him. I have special work to do."

Rolf ran a hand across his chin. "God doesn't call us to work, He calls us to Himself."

"So we're not supposed to work?"

"Of course we are. But work is secondary to the relationship with Him." Rolf looked to the ceiling. "I read somewhere that we slander God by our very eagerness to work for Him without knowing Him."

"I know Him."

Rolf raised his shoulders and held them there.

"I do. I was in Haven. I wear one of His mustard seed pins. I talk to Him all the—" Walter stopped his own thought. "I talk to Him."

Rolf let his shoulders drop and pulled on his gloves. "Slow down, Walter. You're talking, but you're not listening."

"I heard every word you said."

Rolf paused in the door. "Don't listen to me. Listen to God. The quieter you become the more you can hear."

When he left, Walter found the office very quiet indeed.

Walter was just taking off his tie when Bette and Addy came in from the church dinner. "How was it?"

Bette gave no answer.

Great. "You going to talk to me?"

She shook her head.

"I had to work, Bette. They needed me."

Her eyes flashed as she took off Addy's coat. "We needed you. Emma spoke tonight. She told the entire audience how you were instrumental in her faith."

"She told the story about us buying the house from her and the pin and…she said that?"

"And you weren't there to hear it."

"Wow. Why would she do that?"

"Because—though at the moment I find it hard to believe—it's true."

"All *I* did was tell her about my mustard seed pin."

"Which was enough to get her to open up to God. You don't have to be Billy Graham to affect people's faith, Walter." She hung up Addy's coat. Her voice softened, and Walter remembered yet another reason he loved her: Bette was not one to hold a grudge, no matter how much he deserved it. "How was work?"

"I'm hot stuff. Things are going great. If it weren't for me—"

"Whoa there, buddy."

"What?"

"You're doing it again. Taking all the credit."

He rolled his eyes. He knew what was coming. "Ah, come on, Bette. Every time I get a compliment, do you really expect me to say, 'Don't compliment me, compliment God'?"

"Maybe not those exact words, but something like that."

"Saying I owe everything to God is not an easy thing to express in polite conversation, especially not at work."

"Why not?"

He gaped at her. "Because it's just not done. If I brought God into every conversation, people would think I was a fanatic or something. Weird."

"You're taking it to the extreme. I was just pointing out that you seem to think everything you've accomplished comes from your own efforts."

"It has."

"Walter!"

"Well…I know God's given me my talents, and He invited me to Haven and gave me direction, but once He got me going, I took over. I'm handling things just fine."

"Without Him?"

"No, not without Him, Bette." He ran a hand through his thinning hair, wishing he could find the words. "You're twisting things around."

"I merely want you to get your priorities straight. God first, family second, and job—"

"Have you been talking to Rolf?"

"No—"

"You guys are a broken record. I know God's there when I need Him, but that doesn't mean I have to go running to Him over every little thing. He did give me a brain, you know."

"A brain that is His. Talents that are His. Opportunities He created. There's a bigger picture here, Walter. Your work, my work, Emma's work, it all fits together into a larger plan. The only way our work will find its place is if we give our work— our lives—completely over to God so He can put the puzzle pieces together. But if we hoard our work, thinking it's our own doing…that puzzle piece will be missing from the big plan. He can't use you if you hold on to the piece too tightly. Don't make Him pry it out of your hands."

Walter suppressed the urge to open his hand to see if there was a puzzle piece there. Bette was so good at painting a picture with her words…He wiped his palms against his pants. "So we're supposed to let go and do nothing?"

"No, no…" Bette's voice trumpeted her frustration. "I've heard a saying, 'Pray to God; row to shore.'"

"Huh?"

"First, we give everything to Him in prayer, then we do our part. We row to shore."

"That's what I'm doing." But even as he said it he knew it wasn't true.

"No, Walter. You're rowing, but you aren't praying."

She left to give Addy a bath.

———

Sam shoved his hands in his pockets as they walked away from the theater.

"I'm sorry we missed the movie, Sam." Natalie slipped a hand around his arm. "There's another one in two hours. Or maybe we can do something else."

He shrugged and kicked a pebble. It clattered to a stop. "Forget it. I might as well get you back to your place so you can wait by the phone for destiny to call."

"That's not very nice."

"I don't feel very nice. I'm ticked off."

"I can see that."

She had to make amends. She looked north, to the top of the hill that crowned Estes Park. There stood the Bishop Hotel where Sam worked as a desk clerk. She was always impressed at how its white columns spoke of a more elegant time. "Didn't you tell me there was a new singer starting tonight? We could—"

Sam looked toward the hotel. "Sure, why not? What can it hurt?"

The featured singer at the Bishop Hotel went by a single name—Lila. Natalie found herself regretting that her own hair didn't curve in luxurious waves that were so intensely black that blues came and went with the play of the light. And though Sam had never requested Natalie wear more makeup than her quick flick of mascara and lip gloss, she couldn't help but note how he seemed enraptured by Lila's lined eyes and the deep recesses of her eyelids where shadows lurked behind promises of things done in the dark.

As Lila offered the usual preshow banter, Natalie watched Sam watch Lila. His eyes did not stay on the singer's face, but roamed south to her body—which was displayed like goods in a store window, hoping to entice lookers to buy. Sam's eyes were wide and sparkling, like a kid who'd just discovered a toy he couldn't do without.

I'll bet she can't carry a tune. Natalie knew the uncharitable thought wasn't fair, but she didn't care. Unfortunately, Lila's voice was the perfect match for her image: mellow, smooth, seductive.

Sam barely looked up when their order of root beer and mozzarella sticks was delivered to the table. Natalie popped one of the sticks into her mouth and chewed on the fried cheese—and her fried emotions. The space between Lila and Sam all but vibrated with electricity. When Lila sang her songs of love directly to Natalie's fiancé, Natalie had had enough. She pinched Sam's arm.

"Oww!" He looked at her for the first time since they'd sat down. "Why'd you do that?"

"To remind you I'm here."

"Shh! She's singing."

"And you're drooling."

He glanced at the stage, then back at her. "I am not."

"I should get you a bib."

"Don't be rude."

"Me? Rude?" She leaned toward him, lowering her voice. "Don't you think it's rude to flirt with another woman when you're sitting with your fiancée?"

"I'm not flirting."

41

"Ogling profusely with the intention of seduction. Does that sound better?"

"You're making too much of this. She's an attractive woman. She sings great. Can't I appreciate her talents?"

"It depends on which talents you're appreciating."

Sam took a sip of his drink, his eyes remaining on Natalie—but she could see they struggled to remain there. "You know you have me, Natty. Didn't you just say that to me an hour ago when I was jealous of your writing?"

"This is different."

"Only because *I* mean it."

"Sam!"

He held up a hand. "Quiet. We'll talk about it later."

He could count on it.

Natalie, who loved to eat out, was ready to go home after the appetizers. She'd lost her appetite watching Sam enjoy the visual and audible dessert of Lila.

When Sam foiled her plan to leave early by ordering a burger, she suffered through his meal foodless. Her sacrifice was lost on him. He ate every bite, though she wasn't sure how much he tasted. He didn't even notice the mustard on his chin—and Natalie wasn't about to tell him.

When Lila finished her last set and the audience applauded, Natalie managed one clap to Sam's two.

Finally. Now they could leave.

Not quite.

When Natalie stood to get her jacket, she noticed Sam remained seated. "Come on, let's go. We've spent enough time—"

She watched as Sam's eyes lit up like he'd won the lottery. He wiped the mustard off his chin, then stood. But he didn't reach for his jacket. Instead, he extended his hand across the table...

"Lila."

The woman placed her hand in Sam's and let him shake it profusely. Close up, her allure was tactile. She smelled of earth and spice.

"I thought I'd come and meet my biggest fan." She nodded to Sam. "You stayed for every set. That doesn't happen very often. People have busy lives."

Sam grinned like a groupie. "Not too busy to listen to good music."

Lila looked to Natalie, and Sam was forced to remember her. "Lila—can I call you Lila?—this is my...this is Natalie Pasternak."

Lila nodded at Natalie, but did not offer her hand. She turned her attention back to Sam. "And you are?"

He put a hand to his forehead and blushed. "Gee, I'm sorry, I'm Sam Erickson. I work here...well, not *here*...I'm a desk clerk."

"Then we'll be seeing a lot of each other, won't we?"

"Yeah...sure."

When Lila walked away, Sam headed for the exit, then back-tracked to grab his jacket. As he put a hand on Natalie's shoulder to guide her through the door, she sidled out of his reach.

"What—?"

She waited until they got outside. "Don't *what* me, Samuel Erickson. You made a fool of yourself, and it makes me sick."

"I did not." He got in his truck. She stood outside the passenger door, waiting for him to open it for her. He started the engine, and she got in by herself.

He would have opened the door for Lila.

※

Kathy walked into the gallery. Eyes turned her way and she stood taller, glad she'd decided to wear the blue suit instead of the pale gray dress. Tonight was not a night to blend into the crowd.

Sandra Perkins, her friend and instigator of the showing, rushed toward her. Sandra slung an arm around Kathy's shoulders and squeezed. "You are a hit, Kathy dear. A bona fide hit."

Kathy looked around the room at the two dozen people who stood before her paintings. They studied and discussed them with a pointed finger, a nod of the head, a pensive hand to a mouth. It was rather disconcerting having people judge her work, good or bad.

How dare they? It's my work—work God chose me to do.

The fire of her thoughts startled her.

"Don't frown, woman. This is great stuff happening here."

Kathy nodded. "Who'd have thought?"

"I thought." Sandra waved an arm to encompass the room. "If I have my way, the name Kathy Bauer is going to be known nationwide."

Roy popped his head between them after checking their coats. He put a finger to his lips. "Shh! Don't tell her such things."

"Why not?"

Kathy rolled her eyes and answered for him. "Because he thinks I'll turn into an egotistical snob."

"A bit overstated, my dear. I merely think it's best if we keep fame and fortune in perspective and remember where it's coming from."

Sandra hooked her thumbs into her blouse. "That's the ticket. You can thank me now *and* later."

Kathy spoke behind her hand. "He's talking about God."

Sandra pretended to pout. "A person can't even gloat properly anymore."

Roy shook his head. "I'll leave you two to practice gloating. The kids need punch."

He'd said the words amicably enough, but Kathy knew there was substance behind the teasing. She watched as Roy helped Ryan and Lisa get some punch and cookies. He settled them into a corner, letting them sit on the floor rather than trying to balance a plate and glass on their laps. Lisa's lavender lace dress made her look so grown up, though she did find it hard to sit ladylike on the floor. Ryan was ever the big brother, holding Lisa's punch until she got comfortable.

They are what's important. I mustn't forget—

"Excuse me, but are you the artist?"

Sandra and Kathy turned toward the voice. Sandra answered for her. "Why Randolph, how good of you to come. Indeed she is. Randolph, this is Kathy Bauer, the artist of the hour. Kathy, this is Randolph Sears, the biggest real estate developer in northern Arkansas."

Kathy could tell by his grip that the man was used to shaking hands. "I sure like what I see, Ms. Bauer. And so does my wife."

He indicated a silver-haired woman across the room wearing an elegant dress that hung on an emaciated frame. She looked like one of those country club women who played too much tennis and ate too little in an attempt to wear a one-digit dress size.

"We've dabbled in art the last few years, Ms. Bauer. We especially like to get in on new talent." He smirked. "Before the price gets too high."

"Is there a particular painting you're interested in?" Sandra asked.

"Ask the wife. She's the one who makes all the executive decisions." He smirked again. "Or at least I like her to think so."

Sandra left them alone to go speak to Mrs. Sears. Kathy was unsure what to say. If this man was as successful as Sandra implied, he had power and clout. He certainly looked the part. His impeccable grooming made her question her own. Randolph Sears had made it. He had climbed the ladder and was at the top where he could look down at the rest of them.

But maybe she wasn't a part of *the rest* anymore. Wasn't her foot firmly placed on the bottom rung, climbing upward?

Randolph sipped his drink and raised the glass to encompass

the room. "It appears you're doing real well for yourself."

"Thank you. I—"

"I would guess you're in the market for a new home."

"Well, no…we've never really thought about—"

He flicked her comment away. "Of course you have. It's the American dream. Big, bigger, biggest." He leaned closer, and she caught a whiff of musk. "I don't mean to disparage your current home, Ms. Bauer, but I must confess I've seen it. I drove past after all that turmoil two years ago, with President Carson in town, and your first husband showing up out of nowhere and dying again." He fingered his tie clip. "The papers never divulged much. Would you care to tell me how that really happened?"

"No!" Kathy lowered her voice when heads turned. "That's private, Mr. Sears."

He shrugged.

"Actually, the home you saw is not our present home. After Dr. Bauer and I got married, we purchased a nice three bed-room with a family room and—"

He raised a hand, stopping her short. "I'm sure it's lovely. But the point is, Ms. Bauer, you're on your way up. You and your family deserve a house befitting your hard work and your new position in the community."

Kathy enjoyed a wave of pride.

"I have a new development starting up just outside the city limits. Nice houses. Big houses. If you'd like to come by tomor-row I could show you…"

She let him ramble on, relishing his talk of formal dining rooms, breakfast nooks, and whirlpool tubs. That was the life. Maybe if they got a house like the ones Randolph Sears described she could finally leave her past behind. Maybe then she'd never again feel like Scarlett O'Hara, raising a mental fist in the air to proclaim to the world, "As God is my witness, I will never be hungry again!"

And she wouldn't. Not if she could help it.

President Julia Carson leaned back in her chair in the Oval Office and closed her eyes. She had five minutes before her next appointment, and she planned to make the best of it with a nap.

Those who knew of her ability to nap and wake at will were in awe. It was something Julia had perfected during her college days, when sleep at night was scarce. She took a cleansing breath and repeated the prayer that was forever linked with her naps: *Lord, if there's something You want to tell me, here I am.*

She let herself slip into the deep, floating in the peaceful waters, as a veil covered the harsh sun. Her breathing slowed. She was renewed. Then, as the nap neared an end, she let her thoughts wander. She dreamed…

Julia stood before a group of people. Calling to them. She couldn't hear what she said. Only one word slipped into her mind: *Laodicean.*

The veil was lifted and the sun told her it was time to return. Julia's mind swam back to the solidity of shore. She lifted herself out of the deep, blinked her eyes, and wrote the word down.

Laodicean. How odd. What does it mean?

Julia aimed the shower's spray to the far corner of the stall until it got hot. Her hand gauged the temperature. It remained barely warm.

"Edward!"

He stuck his head in the bathroom. "You shrieked?"

"I didn't shriek. I called. There is a difference."

"Which we don't have time to discuss. The Harvest Service starts in an hour. Get your shower done."

"That's why I shrieked. There's no hot water."

"That's absurd. I had a shower an hour ago and steamed up the place."

"But now it's lukewarm. Feel for yourself."

Edward rolled up a sleeve and stuck his arm in the shower. "Hmm, that's odd."

"What are you going to do about it?" She shivered in the corner.

"Think good thoughts?"

"Call maintenance. Tell Nick to get it fixed. Pronto."

"That's all fine and dandy, but in the meantime, you either need to brave the lukewarm or get out. Nick might find it a bit cozy in the shower with you in it. This may well be a government 'by the people,' but I'll be jibbed if I let any people get by my lady of the government when she's nekkid."

"I suppose I should be flattered you're willing to defend my honor."

"Honor has nothing to do with it. I'm a selfish man who wants to keep you all to myself. So…do you want a towel or are you going to be a courageous president and brave the agony of lukewarm?"

She sighed. "It's such a pain being courageous after a hard day at the office." She took a deep breath. "But here goes."

Edward left the bathroom, shaking his head. "That's my president."

"Good evening, Madam President." The chauffeur opened the door to their limousine.

Julia stopped. "So you're the gentleman taking over for Oscar. I do hope his mother feels better soon."

"Me too, ma'am."

Edward put a hand on her back. "We have to go, missy."

Julia ignored him and kept her eyes on the driver. "What's your name?"

"Luke Warm."

"Luke Warm?"

"No, no," Luke chuckled. "Not lukewarm, Luke Warren."

She nodded and got in the car. As they pulled away, Edward patted her knee. "You've got lukewarm on the brain, Julia. The driver; the shower; and this morning, you complained your coffee was lukewarm."

"Mere coincidence."

She was wrong.

The congregation that had gathered for the Harvest Service stood and sang "Fairest Lord Jesus," one of Julia's favorites. She sang full voice, although common sense—and a lack of vocal talent—often told her to take it down a notch. But as the nation had found out, Julia was not one to approach her Lord with less than 100 percent effort, no matter how off-key she was.

As they sat down, Edward whispered in her ear, "Too bad they weren't doing the Hallelujah Chorus, they could have given you a solo."

"You're just jealous." She turned toward the pulpit, ignoring his soft laugh. She took out her pad of paper and pen. She'd always taken notes in church and wasn't about to stop now that she was president.

The minister's sermon was on a subject Julia cared a lot about: taking a stand. She found more affirmation of her own beliefs than new ideas until the pastor mentioned a certain word.

"There was one town that was singled out in the New Testament for not taking a stand. This town was Laodicea."

Laodicea? Laodicean...the word from my dream.

Julia sat up straighter in the pew. Edward noticed and gave her a questioning look. She shook his attention away, focusing on the pastor.

"The town of Laodicea was probably started by one of the apostle Paul's converts. It sat on what is now the Turkish peninsula. It was very wealthy and was known for its banking industry, its medical school, and its wool industry. It had every-thing going for it, much as we do today. It had no excuse not to be a vital church, but it was lukewarm."

Lukewarm! Julia nearly climbed over the pew railing so she could get closer to the words. *Explain it to me, Lord. Let me know what You've been trying to tell me!*

The minister looked down at the president and noticed her increased interest. He stammered and fumbled his notes.

Calm down, Julia. Don't scare him off. She felt Edward's steady hand on her arm and drew in a deep breath.

"There was an aqueduct that brought water to the city from a hot springs. Yet, by the time the water got to the city, it had cooled and was neither hot nor cold. It was lukewarm."

Yes, yes…but what does it mean?

"We all know that a lukewarm drink is unpleasant. But what of a lukewarm personality? The spiritual lives of the people of Laodicea were also lukewarm, and therefore just as unpleasant and distasteful as the lukewarm temperature of their water. They didn't take a stand for anything. They were indifferent. Idle. Tepid. There is the lesson. Let us not in our satisfaction with our lives turn lukewarm about Christ. We must take a stand and boil over with our enthusiasm for Him. God said, 'I know your deeds, that you are neither cold nor hot. I wish you were either one or the other! So, because you are lukewarm—neither hot nor cold—I am about to spit you out of my mouth.'"

Julia wrote as fast as she could. When she ripped off a page to use the back, the sound resonated throughout the sanctuary.

"Assign someone to look it up for me, Edward." She pulled back the bedspread, ready to crawl under the snug sheets.

"Perhaps we should get a government grant to study Laodicea?"

"Don't tease." She walked over to the dresser and picked up

the note she'd made upon waking from her nap. "Here."

He read it. "Laodicean?"

She pointed toward the bathroom. "All the lukewarms, Edward. Add to that this word that comes to me right before I wake up from a nap. You must admit it's an odd word."

"It's an odd word."

"Have you ever heard it before?"

"Nope. Though I must have read it in the Bible. I've read the book of Revelation where those verses originate."

"Me too, but I didn't remember it. And that part about luke-warm. It's just what I needed."

"For what?"

"To get people in this country fired up."

"This is a priority?"

"Yes." She got under the covers, then swung her legs out again. "I think it is. As of this moment it is."

"Your supposed to be getting *in* bed, Julia, not *out.*"

She grabbed her robe and headed for her desk in the den. "I have work to do."

With a sigh he followed after her, pulling on her nightgown to make her stop. "Work tomorrow. You don't have to do it now. It's nearly midnight. Even you have to sleep, missy. You may be president, but you are not superhuman."

She swung to face him. "Is that a cut?"

He slipped his arm through hers and tried to lead her back to the bedroom. "Not necessarily, although you do have a tendency to think that only *you* can fix the world and only *you* can do the work and only *you* have this direct line to God's will."

She shrugged his arm away. "I don't think that." *Do I?* She shook her head. "I don't."

"Then why do you pretend you only need three hours of sleep? Why do you insist on taking on every project when other people could do the work just as well? Why do you…" He hesitated. "Why do you think you're so *right* all the time?"

She turned her back on him and strode to her desk.

51

"Because I am." She sat down. A moment later she felt his hand on her shoulder and both loved and hated its calming presence.

"Are you sure? Do you have time to consult God any more to find out? Or has Julia Carson taken on the role of God's proxy?"

Her fire began to extinguish with doubt. Was he right? But in the time it took to turn around in her chair, the fire reignited. She had too much to do to waste time arguing. "You're just jealous, Edward. You're jealous because I'm president and you're not."

His jaw dropped and his eyebrows dipped in pain.

Julia clamped a hand over her mouth. *What have I done?*

Edward turned to leave, and she wanted to go after him. But for some reason she couldn't. Her hand reached for him, but the words of apology remained unspoken.

When she turned toward her desk, she felt very alone. Right, but alone.

After a fitful hour, in which she accomplished little, Julia slipped into bed. She did not wake Edward, but put a hand on his shoulder. He stirred, and she willed him to accept her apology.

They slept beside each other as they had done for thirty-seven years.

CHAPTER THREE

"My grace is sufficient for you, for my power is made perfect in weakness."

2 CORINTHIANS 12:9

"THIS IS FOR YOU." Rolf handed Walter an envelope.

"Is this what I hope it is?"

"I've learned never to guess another person's hopes."

"Is it a bonus?"

Rolf touched the tip of his own nose. "Enjoy, Walter. Good work on *Good News.*"

Rolf left Walter alone to open the envelope. Walter was afraid to look. He'd been nursing Rolf's hint that he might get a bonus, but he had never let himself get too specific about the amount. Perhaps the amount didn't matter? Perhaps just getting the recognition that the check represented was enough?

Nah.

Walter slipped a finger under the envelope's flap, then stopped before breaking the seal. The amount did matter. If it was fifty bucks he would be upset. If it was a hundred? No go. He wanted a check with at least three zeros.

"Money doesn't matter, Walter," he said to himself. But with a chuckle he added, "You are such a liar."

He set the envelope on his desk and stared at it. If only Bette were here.

He grabbed the envelope, walked across the room, and stuffed it into the pocket of his overcoat. He gave the envelope a pat. "Later, when I'm home with Bette."

Walter heaved a pencil across his office just as Rolf walked in. It ricocheted off the wall by Rolf's head.

"Whoa! Incoming missiles. How rude of you to declare war and not tell me."

Walter opened a file and pretended to work.

Rolf took a seat. "Having a hard day? I thought you'd be flying after getting that bonus."

It must be big! I've got to look—

"I wouldn't know." He glared at his overcoat.

Rolf turned around to see the object of Walter's annoyance. "You're giving your coat dirty looks and throwing pencils at it because...?"

"Because of my bonus."

Rolf shook his head. "Two plus two is coming up five. You need to help me here."

Walter strode across the room and pulled the envelope from the coat's pocket. "This is driving me crazy."

"If you don't think it's enough, I'm sure something can—"

"I don't *know* if it's enough because I haven't looked at it." He fingered the edges, hoping the flap would pop open.

"I know a simple way to remedy this turmoil."

Walter shook his head. "I want to wait until Bette is with me."

"I'm sure she wouldn't mind, especially since *not* opening it is affecting your mental health."

"No." Walter stuffed the envelope back in his coat pocket. "I've gone this long. Now it's a matter of pride." He returned to his seat and laid his hands on his desk. He took a cleansing breath. "I can do this."

Rolf rose to leave. "Go for it, Walter. 'Lead us not into temptation...'"

"But deliver us from evil."

Walter rubbed his temples. Who would have thought receiving a bonus would cause him such pain and torment?

When two o'clock rolled around, he thought he was going to burst with the stress and pull of it. Finally, he closed the door of his office, turned his chair toward the window, and bowed his head.

"God, help me. I don't know what You're trying to prove by putting me through this. I suppose I started it by not opening the envelope right away. But now…I feel like You're testing me. What am I supposed to be learning here? Not to be greedy?" He had to laugh. Funny how God zeroed in on what Walter *didn't* want to deal with.

He leaned forward on the windowsill and looked at the street below. His eyes were drawn to a sleek silver car. *Now that, I could handle.* Would the bonus be enough to buy it? They sure wouldn't get anything for trading in Walter's rusty Chevy van. He glanced back at his overcoat. Surely the bonus wasn't big enough to pay for a new car? But maybe…*Good News* was climbing in its time slot and the sales department had just snagged two sizable sponsors who wanted to be listed on the Honor Roll—his previous project.

"You're crazy, Walter Prescott. You've gone from thinking it might be fifty bucks to tens of thousands. You are two bushels short of a load."

"I'll agree to that."

He turned to see Bette come through the door. "You heard that from out there?"

"I have very good hearing when it concerns my husband's mental health." She walked around the desk and kissed his cheek. "What's up?"

"I'll ask you the same question. You never pop in like this. Where's Addy?"

"Addy's with Emma. Actually, I was going out anyway. It's my day to volunteer at the Liberty Shelter down the street. I helped distribute some newly donated coats and blankets. It's getting cold out there. We've had to turn people away. And—" she pulled out a ticket—"I bought us this raffle ticket for their fund-raiser. Who knows? Maybe we'll be the big winner." She ran a hand over his thinning hairline. "Plus, I'm here because you need me."

"Who says?"

"Excuse me?"

Walter waved his awkward words away. His wave turned to a pointed finger. "Did Rolf call you?"

Bette stood by the window. "Could be."

Walter slapped his hands together. "He had no right. I don't need you to come all the way down here—"

"He said you haven't been able to concentrate. He said you're 'battling temptation.' That sounded serious enough for me to take a detour to your office."

"I'm not battling…well, maybe I'm wrestling a little." He went to his overcoat, pulled out the envelope, and handed it to her.

"What's this?"

"My bonus."

She turned the envelope over. "It hasn't been opened."

"I know."

"Why don't you open it?"

"I was waiting for you."

"I'm here." She held it out to him. He took a step back. "Walter? Open it."

He shook his head.

"Then I'll—" She put a finger under the flap.

"No!" He took the envelope away from her.

"You're not making any sense, hon. Rolf says you aren't getting any work done because you want to open the bonus when I'm here. Now I'm here, and you don't want to open the bonus? You have to make up your mind. Do ya or don't ya?"

Walter ran a finger over his name on the front of the envelope. This was his money. He'd earned it. He looked at Bette. "This is mine. I earned it, right?"

Bette looked at him a long time. "It's not your money, Walter. It's—"

"Of course it's my money." He returned to his desk and placed the envelope in front of him.

Bette walked to his side and spoke softly. "Of course it's yours, Walter. But from whom did it originate?"

"Rolf brought it into me this morning."

"Before Rolf."

Walter shrugged. "The accounting department, I suppose."

"Before that."

He read the look in her eyes. He knew what she wanted him to say. "You're trying to get me to say this bonus belongs to God."

"So…?"

"I just said it."

"No, you just said what you thought *I* wanted you to say. You need to say what *you* want to say. What you know in your heart to be true."

Walter ran a hand over his face. "I hate it when you try to get me to be a good man."

"I know it's tough for you, Walter." She smiled but he took her seriously.

"You'll never know."

"So, are you going to say it?"

"Arghhh! I hope God realizes what a team player you are. You are constantly pitching me what's right, forcing me to hit a home run or strike out."

"I try to pitch 'em to you easy, hon."

"I'd hate to see your fast ball."

She ran a hand across his shoulders. "I hereby promise not to bean you with it."

57

"So…am I supposed to say it now?"

"Now is always a good choice."

He picked up the envelope. "All right. Here goes. I admit that this bonus—no matter how many zeroes it contains—comes from God."

"And belongs to…"

"God."

She nodded twice as if sealing a bargain. "'Every good and perfect gift is from above, coming down from the Father of the heavenly lights, who does not change like shifting shadows.'"

"With the Bible quoted and me properly humbled, am I allowed to open it?"

Bette hesitated. "I have a better idea."

Walter threw his hands in the air. "I am doomed to be tortured."

"Such an attitude."

He put a hand over his eyes. "Go ahead. Tell me your better idea."

Bette took the envelope and moved to the window. "Let's give this bonus to the shelter."

Walter peeked over his hand. "But we don't even know how much it is."

"Exactly."

He rolled his chair toward her and grabbed the envelope away. "You're crazy. It's one thing admitting that God is responsible for me getting this bonus in the first place, but quite another to give it all away. Don't you think He'd want us to enjoy it?"

"We would enjoy it—by giving it away."

"But we need the money. We're behind in house payments."

"Only because you keep buying—" She sighed. "A new TV was delivered this afternoon. What was wrong with our old one?"

"It doesn't have picture-in-a-picture."

"We *are* deprived."

The envelope felt heavy. "I got a good deal on it. You know I always get good deals."

"A good deal on something we don't need is wasted money."

He looked away. "Not that again."

"The shelter needs the money more than we do, hon." She pointed to the street below where the homeless were ever present shadows amid the commotion of everyday business.

"But I was thinking of getting rid of the van. Buying a car."

Bette turned to look at him. She swallowed. "The bonus is that much?"

"I don't know. It could be a dollar or thousands of dollars. I don't know."

Bette started pacing. "Thousands of dollars. A new car. We could use a new car."

"Exactly." He held back a smile. She was finally seeing things his way.

"But…"

Don't falter on me, Bette. Be selfish just a few minutes longer. Don't leave me alone in this. "But what?"

She stopped pacing. "The van has lasted this long. And my car's fine. I know you'd—we'd—like a new vehicle, but we really don't need one. Want and need are rarely synonymous."

"We don't *need* anything, Bette."

"But *they* do."

Walter slumped in his chair, closed his eyes, and sighed. "Things were so much simpler before God got involved in my life. It was easy to please myself. But trying to please Him…it's not fair." Bette opened her mouth to speak but he stopped her with a hand. "Don't you dare say, 'But life isn't fair.' I hate that."

"Hate what?"

The truth? "Why can't life be fair?"

"Why don't you ask the homeless people I saw today."

"Now *you're* not being fair."

She shrugged. "The money is yours, Walter. You can do with it as you please."

"I thought you said it was God's?"

"It is. But He's put it in your hands. He's giving you the choice. And the chance."

"The chance?"

"To do a really great thing."

She kissed him and left him alone with his conscience.

The ache in Walter's temples migrated to the space above his eyes, where it zapped what was left of his energy. He wanted to slip out early and go home. Go home to Bette who would ask him what choice he had made.

There was a knock on his opened door. Cassandra, the hostess of *Good News,* flashed him a smile. "What are you going to do with your bonus, Walter? Take a week in Hawaii?"

It's that much? "I don't know. What are you going to do with yours?"

"There's a dining room set I've been drooling over. We're having my family down for Christmas, and I really don't want to serve my mother on a card table and folding chairs."

A dining room set? That costs a few thousand. If Cassandra got that much, then surely I got more...

"You make pecan pie, Bette and I will show up for dessert."

"It's a deal. Enjoy!"

"That's exactly what I plan to do." Without thinking about it a moment longer, Walter opened the envelope that contained his bonus. A check for ten thousand dollars grinned back at him.

He held it to his lips and gave it a kiss.

———⟳———

Monsignor Vibrowsky looked at the schedule for the food bank volunteers. He disliked the administrative duties of collecting, cataloging, and distributing. It had been fine when the food bank was small and ineffective, but now that it was successfully reaching a lot of people—he didn't have the time or the patience for it.

Finding volunteers was the worst. Calling people, begging for their time. It was so demeaning. Far below his station—

The monsignor smiled with a new thought. He pushed the intercom button for his secretary. "Get me Father Delatondo."

He leaned back in his chair, clasped his hands in his lap, and smirked. This would take care of two problems at once: the food bank and the saintly Father Del who wanted to change the world in his spare time.

If Monsignor Vibrowsky had his way, Del wouldn't *have* any free time.

———

"I think the responsibilities suit your talents, Father."

Del blinked at the monsignor's suggestion. Considering Del had no experience with food distribution and would rather eat lima beans than do paperwork, his radar zipped to high.

"But what about the Haven reunion?" Del shook his head. "You promised I could work on it during my free time. And now…I'm not going to have any—"

"We all have to make sacrifices, Father."

Some more than others.

Del collapsed on the couch.

Father Caspian laughed. "I heard. All hail the new king of the food bank."

"I hereby abdicate."

"And give up the perks of royalty?"

"Tired feet and a frenzied mind."

Caspian tossed him the remote. "Here. Drown in the babble of nothingness a while."

"Is it good for the soul?"

Caspian pushed an ottoman close and lifted Del's feet on

top of it. "Probably not, but *this* is good for the sole." He slapped the bottom of Del's feet and left the living room.

Del scooted down so his head rested on a cushion. He aimed the remote at the television and flipped channels. The fragments of sound and picture suited him, a running commentary of his thoughts. A scream, a whisper, a shout, a song—all in three-second bites. When he'd first gone to the food bank after his classes were finished, he'd thought it might be a good place to do some quiet brainstorming about the reunion. He'd imagined stocking shelves and letting his mind wander. It didn't work that way. Paperwork, people, and packing had devoured four hours of his day.

Del closed his eyes while his thumb kept the progression going. Suddenly he recognized a voice, but by the time he realized it, he was two channels past. He sat up and backtracked.

"Walter!"

He turned up the sound and let his friend's voice fill the room. Walter wasn't on screen, but he was the voice-over for the introduction to a news magazine program.

"Good News! I forgot about *Good News!"* Del's mind raced as he fit Walter's TV show into his plans for the reunion.

He laughed and slapped the remote against his leg. "Walter!"

It was a beginning.

—◦∿∿◦—

Ben Cranois stood in the hallway outside the hotel ballroom. He adjusted his name tag: *Hello! My name is…* According to all who saw him, his name was John Brown. A fitting name. An abolitionist. Ben fought against slavery of a different sort. Slavery of the mind. Death of the individual. He was tired of being a slave to Julia Carson's good-will-prevail-if-we-all-think-alike philosophy.

He had a job to do: destroy Julia Carson and all she stood for. He would do it, too, for the sake of truth and the sanctity of the individual. No more people stumbling through life like zombies, buckling to a God who demanded their utter obedience. It was absurd. People had to see what she was doing. They had to stop being the blind being led by the blind.

Which brought him to his plan for today…

He paused, hoping the energy that resided within would confirm his plan. But it remained disappointingly silent. *Oh well, the thrill will come after the job is done.*

Like most of the convention participants, Ben carried a briefcase. But his didn't contain a laptop or a notebook crammed with multicolored handouts. His contained a bowl full of pins—very special pins.

Ben nodded and smiled as people filed into the ballroom to hear the keynote speaker. When someone's eyes held his a moment too long—as if expecting conversation—he looked away. He would come and he would go, and no one would see him again.

But just to be safe…he slipped into the rest room to wait.

The restroom was finally empty. Ben stood before the mirror and adjusted his tie.

It was time.

He peered into the hotel hallway. The last two conventioneers entered the ballroom, and the door shut with a muffled thud. The corridor was abandoned and the tables of free pamphlets, buttons, pens, and key chains sat unmanned. Ben opened his briefcase and pulled out the basket of mustard seed pins. He walked past the displays and set it front and center. He adjusted the sign that said, Take One. *Or better yet two…*

He walked toward the hotel exit, whistling. Surely the thrill would grab hold and affirm the grand gesture he'd just made for the cause. But nothing happened. He hesitated at the door and stopped whistling to concentrate. He waited to feel it. Feel something. A tug. A swelling inside. A shiver. He'd even take a bite. Something.

Nothing.

What do you want from me?

He burst onto the street and let the sting of the October air snap his senses to attention, masking the silence within.

Quickening his step, he willed the energy to take over. After all, he had many more stops to make, many more opportunities to triumph. The city was full of conventions. Before the day was over thousands of people would have in their possession a mustard seed pin.

He was brilliant.

Wasn't he?

—◦◦◦—

Natalie sat at her desk, sifting through her mail. Her eyes were ever watchful for the return address of the publisher who held the fate of her book in its hands. But there was nothing from Capstone. Another day, another disappointment.

Then another return address caught her eye; her own.

She flipped the letter to the top of the stack and saw that it was addressed to Jack Cummings. *Return to sender, forwarding address expired.* She stared at the letter, unbelieving. "I've lost contact and it's all my fault."

She had been negligent in keeping in touch with her friend from Lincoln. He had been her rock against the seductive pull of the demon who'd called itself Beau Tenebri. Jack had literally saved her life. And then proposed to her. Although she'd been flattered, she had not been ready for marriage, and had run back to her Estes Park roots to sort things through.

But what had she sorted? She'd taken up with Sam Erickson again—her first love and the father of the baby she'd given up for adoption. Grace was three and a half now. Natalie had plunged into her old life, only showing gumption with the act of moving away from her parents' resort complex and into her own apartment. There, she had written the book.

But Jack…

He was the sweetest, kindest, most spiritual man she had ever met. So what if he wasn't flashy and handsome? Why *had* she ignored his many letters; answered one to his every five? No wonder he had given up. And now he had moved beyond her reach. Natalie held her returned letter to her lips. *Oh, Jack. I'm so, so sorry. I've wasted our friendship.*

She set the mail aside and turned on her computer. Maybe if she immersed herself in her writing she would forget her past mistakes and be able to think positively about the future.

But what future? Sam was attracted to Lila. The memory of Sam's goo-goo eyes haunted her. If she married him now, would he stop looking? Natalie shook her head violently, then stopped when she realized the vehemence of her reaction. Why was she so against marrying him?

She wanted to be a published writer before they got married.

Her gaze drifted back to Jack's letter. Or was there another reason?

Natalie tried to write, but the words wouldn't come. Her entire body vibrated with unrest, as if no two cells agreed. She needed to know something, *anything* concrete in her life's plan. The need grew like a hunger that tore through her, making her fear she'd never be satisfied again. She had to appease it or die.

But nothing was concrete. Nothing. Her relationship with Sam was rocky; Jack had moved who knows where; and the fate of her writing was, as always, up in the air.

Although Capstone had shown interest in *Seeking Haven,* although they had offered up bits of encouragement in the thirteen months since she'd sent them the completed manuscript, they hadn't offered her a contract. And without a contract, their interest meant nothing. Which meant her act of dedicating her writing to God meant nothing. What good did it do to write if no one read what she'd written? Wasted hours. Wasted hopes. Wasted promises.

It was ridiculous she'd had to wait thirteen months. She deserved an answer. Now! *Call them. Insist on a yes or no.*

Natalie pushed her chair away from the keyboard. "I *do* deserve an answer. It's not fair. It's not right. They're torturing me."

She needed to call and get it over with. That, or give up her ridiculous dream. She needed to move on with her life.

Natalie pulled the phone into her lap. She stared at it. *Do it!*

Her heart raced. Her breathing became heavy. She put her hand on the receiver...*Pick it up! Call!*

Wait!

A sudden shiver shot through her. The intensity of her doubt sickened her like the smell of sour milk. This feeling was wrong. Alien. She was usually an optimistic person. How else could she have waited so long? This obsessive need to know was strange.

She took a deep breath, trying to calm her pulse and her stomach. She set the phone on the desk. "Help me, Lord. Guide me through this."

On impulse, she grabbed her Bible and opened it to the bookmark. Just that morning she had read the story in 1 Samuel, where Samuel the prophet had told King Saul to wait for seven days at Gilgal with his army. At that time, Samuel would come and make a sacrifice and tell Saul what God wanted him to do next. Seven days passed and the soldiers around Saul got antsy because the army of the enemy amassed close by. Saul figured since he'd waited the right amount of time it was up to him to offer the sacrifice himself. But just as he finished, Samuel arrived and said, "What have you done? The Lord told you to wait. He would have established your kingdom for all time, but now—because you insisted on taking matters into your own hands—your kingdom will not endure."

Natalie read the story again and was struck by the lesson—which just that morning, she had not taken past the obvious. Now she saw that it applied to her. Saul had done the right thing, but in the wrong way—in his own way. His true spiritual character was revealed under pressure, and he had failed. He trusted himself more than he trusted God. He had become impatient with God's timing, because he was afraid of failure.

Like she was afraid of failure.

You can do things your way in your time, or do things the right way in God's time.

Natalie closed her eyes and let the thought take hold. It made sense, but still she fought against it. Certainly God would understand if she called the publisher? The normal response time was two or three months. She'd been more than patient. All she wanted was to have her work seen by others. What good was a book if no one read it? *After all, Lord, I'm doing it for You.*

Natalie's eyes sprang open at the thought, and she put a hand to her mouth. She bowed her head as the lie hit home. "I'm sorry, Lord. But You already know my true motives, don't You? I want it so bad I eat, breathe, and sleep it. For me. I want it for me. So I'll feel good about myself. Good about Haven. Good about You. I'm so sorry…"

I know. And I forgive you. Now obey Me.

Natalie nodded and shut the Bible. She glanced at the phone. The desire to call Capstone faded. If nothing else, she would obey the Lord.

She would go on waiting—waiting for Samuel.

———

"You going somewhere?" Roy flipped over the morning paper. "I thought you'd be basking in last night's praise or busy at work, creating another painting for your next showing."

Kathy sat on a kitchen chair, putting on her shoes. "I do have a life outside this house, you know."

"I thought you got the day off from A Mother's Love—"

"I did." She put both feet on the floor. "In fact…since you've brought it up, I was thinking I might quit my pro-life work."

"Why?"

She avoided his eyes, not wanting what she saw there to reinforce the inner voice that told her she was wrong to even think such a thing. "You heard Sandra. She told me I need to concentrate on my painting. I'm in demand. I can't let my public down."

"But you can let unwed mothers down? What about Marcie? She gave you the job at A Mother's Love when you needed it to survive. Now you want to abandon her?"

"She's got plenty of people to help. She doesn't need me."

"But in Haven...you promised—"

"To preserve the sanctity of children. I know, I know." Kathy had been afraid he would bring that up, and as yet, she didn't have a good rebuttal. It was time to change the subject. She stood and poked her head in the living room. "Come on, kids. Shoes. Jackets. Now. I'll drop you off at school on my way."

"Where you going, Mommy?" Lisa pulled at her socks, which had the habit of sneaking down into her shoes.

Ryan turned off the TV. "She's going to look at fancy houses, don't you remember?"

Roy put the paper down. "What fancy houses?"

Kathy walked past him to gather the kids' jackets. "I met a real estate developer last night at my showing. Mr. Sears is going to—"

"Randolph Sears?"

"That's him."

"He's a greedy shyster."

"Just because he's made a good living doesn't mean—"

"I don't begrudge the man his money, just the way he made it—overcharging people, making them equate high cost with high quality even though—"

"He builds nice houses."

"How do you know?"

She helped Lisa zip up her jacket. "We could use a new house, Roy. One in a better neighborhood."

"What's wrong with this neighborhood? We have friends here. The kids have friends—"

"We'd all make new friends. Better—" She caught herself. "We've got the money now."

Roy put a hand on her shoulder so she had to look at him. "I'm a doctor, Kathy. I earn plenty for us to live on. More than enough."

"I know, I know, and I don't mean to diminish your hard work."

"Then don't."

She slipped a hand around his arm and pulled him close. She'd hurt his ego. "I'm bringing in some big bucks now, Roy. Don't you think it's time we lived up to our image?"

"Oh. Right. The image of a successful artist and her family." He pulled away from her. "Success and snobbery don't *have* to go together."

Kathy glared at him. Why did he always put a damper on things? Her success made her feel special, as if she had something unique to contribute to the world. She wasn't some unwed teenager who had to get married. She wasn't the wife of Lenny, a man who thought so little of her work and their marriage that he had slashed all her paintings and slept with who knew how many women in seedy motels.

She was Kathleen Bauer: artist, painter. *Artiste-peintre.* People looked at her creations and approved. They paid money for her work. Her name was associated with something good and worthwhile and high class.

Roy's voice broke into her thoughts. "…not like you, Kath, acting so high and—"

She shucked off her shoes, sending them bouncing off the lower cupboards. "Fine! I'll stay home. You take the kids to—"

"Kath—"

She opened the door to the stairs that led to her basement studio. Even in this house she was still relegated to the dungeon. True, the room wasn't exposed to bare pipes, open studs, or dead bugs in the corner, as the basement in her other house had been. No, this basement was a step up. But not enough. "You'll have to excuse me while I go back to work to make us more money which you won't spend."

"I didn't say we couldn't spend—"

She shut the door in his face.

CHAPTER FOUR

―――⚬⚭⚬―――

"When I called, they did not listen; so when they called, I would not listen," says the LORD *Almighty.*

ZECHARIAH 7:13

"CALL ON LINE TWO, Mr. Prescott. It's your father?"

Walter was yanked out of his thoughts. Pop was dead. He'd died just before Walter moved to Minneapolis. "Run that by me again?"

"Call on line two. He said something about father…he's calling from Lincoln, Nebraska?"

Del! "Father Del?"

"Maybe that's—"

Walter didn't let her finish. He grabbed the phone. "Hey, priest, defeated any demons lately?"

"All the time, Walter, all the time. If you have an extra one hanging around, I'd be glad to ride shotgun."

Walter laughed. "So good to hear from you, Del old boy. I meant to stay in touch, but one day leads to a month, leads to a—"

"Funny you should bring up staying in touch."

"Uh-oh. The good father has something up the sleeve of his vestment?"

"Sort of."

"Out with it. I knew you wouldn't be calling me after all this time if you didn't want something."

"Rude as ever. What makes you think I wouldn't call you if I didn't—"

"*Do* you want something?"

There was a pause. "Actually…yes."

"Ha! Guilty as charged."

"I hereby make a full confession. Although it is nice hearing your grumbling rumble, I have called for a favor."

"Batten down the hatches, here it comes."

Walter heard Del take a deep breath. *This must be serious.*

"I'm organizing a reunion of the Havenites."

"Why?"

"I don't know."

"Where?"

"I don't know."

"When?"

"I don't know."

Walter hesitated. "You're three for three. All that's left is the 'how.'"

"I hoped you could help me on that one."

Walter wasn't sure he wanted to hear any more. Although he loved his Haven friends, every time they got together there was a crisis…or was there a crisis *because* they got together? "Did Julia ask you to organize this? It sounds like something she'd dream up."

"Nope. This is my idea…or rather, I got my instructions from a higher source."

"Edward?"

"Don't let Julia hear you say that. Actually, I believe God wants me to organize it."

"Did you get another invitation?"

"Not a paper one."

Although Walter had experienced many interesting and miraculous things since receiving the invitation to Haven four years earlier, he still wasn't used to them. "You'll have to explain this to me, Del. I'm a facts man. Give it to me straight."

"I think God put the idea in my head. And it won't go away."

"Did God tell you how to do it?"

"Not yet."

"Did God tell you to call me?"

"Sort of."

Walter shook his head. "You're waffling on me, Del. Next, you'll be pouring on the maple syrup. God told you one thing and sort of told you another?"

"I didn't hear a voice or anything, if that's what you're waiting for me to say."

"It would make things easier." Walter drummed a pencil on his desk. "So what's supposed to happen at this reunion—and don't say, 'I don't know.'"

There was silence on the line.

"Del? Speak to me, buddy."

"You told me I couldn't say, 'I don't know,' and the truth is, I don't know."

"Great."

"What I *do* know, is that the only way to reach the Haven alumni is to make an announcement. On television."

"Ah, the plot thickens."

"You're in the television business, Walter."

"So I've heard."

"You have your own show."

"I'm seeing a pattern here."

"You could interview me on the air, and I could offer an open invitation for Haven people to contact me."

"Uh-huh."

"You could do this, Walter, but *will* you?"

A crisis. He knew it. Wasn't he suffering enough of those on his own? Like the situation with his bonus—

"It would be a real bonus if you helped—"

"Bonus? Who said anything about bonus?"

"What?"

"It was *my* money. I earned it."

"Mmm-hmm...someone has a guilty conscience."

Walter snapped his mouth shut, embarrassed that he'd blurted out his latest act of disobedience.

"Walter? Out with it. I'm used to hearing confessions. I'm a priest."

"But I'm Presbyterian."

"Then forget the priest part. I'm your friend."

To confess his shortcoming—his act of greed, or lack of charity—to anyone, would make it more real. Although he knew it didn't make sense, Walter hoped by never speaking of it—or even thinking of it—God wouldn't notice. The image of a child covering his eyes and saying, "You can't see me" floated into his mind. He shoved it aside. "Forget I said anything. Let's get back to the subject. The reunion."

"Chicken."

"I'll accept that. When can you come on the air with me?"

"You'll do it? You'll interview me?"

"The hostess, Cassandra, might grumble a bit...but it's about time the world saw my handsome mug. And yours. When do you want to do it?"

"When?" Del laughed. "I don't know. I haven't even figured out where the reunion's supposed to be held. What city? What facility to hold how many people? I don't even know how many people originally went to the different Havens, do you?"

"Not a clue."

"And how am I going to get Monsignor to agree to send me to Minneapolis?"

"Sounds like you have a few details to work out, priest man."

"Just a few."

"Need some help?" Walter hoped Del wouldn't take him up on the offer.

"If I can get the Monsignor to spring for a plane ticket...no, first I need to figure out where and when to have the reunion."

"Yoo-hoo? Earth to Del?"

"Sorry. My brain is turning right while my mind is turning left."

The answer came to Walter in a flash, yet he still found it hard to say out loud. *But this is Del. He's a priest. He was in Haven with you...*

"Pray, Del."

"Of course! I got so caught up in the logistics I forgot who's in charge."

"Me?"

Del laughed. "You wish."

"No, I *don't* wish. But I know it'll come off."

"If it's supposed to come off."

"What happened to God telling you to do it?"

"Maybe I misunderstood?"

"You're not getting off that easy." Foreign as the feeling was, Walter wanted to offer encouragement. He couldn't let Del give up. Del was one of those special people who always seemed to walk the right road—God's road. "Just do it, Del. Pray to God, then row to shore."

"Where'd you hear that gem?"

Where had he heard it? Oh, yeah. "My wise wife gave me the same instructions."

"Tell Bette thanks. Gotta go. I've got some praying to do— and a lot of rowing."

<hr />

Pray to God; row to shore.

Del couldn't get Walter's advice out of his mind. He had a lot of work to do, spiritually and physically. He walked through the halls of St. Stephen's school, his head down, his hands behind his back. His prayers intertwined with the practical questions. *First off, I need a date. When—*

Del didn't see the student's feet in his path until they were quickly pulled out of his way. At the sudden movement, Del stumbled.

"Sorry, Father." Jason looked up from his seat on the floor. He sat alone outside his seventh grade classroom. Through the closed door, Del could hear Father Lucas going over some Bible verses.

Del stooped to Jason's level. "What are you doing out here?"

"Learning stuff."

"Wouldn't you do better learning stuff in the classroom with the others?"

Jason shook his head. "Memorizing stuff. Homework stuff. I didn't do it when I should've."

Del looked at the notebook in the boy's lap and read a few lines. "Philippians?"

"Uh-huh. A whole verse."

"It is a long one."

"Tons of words. I can't do it."

"It's a good verse." Jason shrugged.

Del sat beside him, leaning his back against a cold locker. He looked over Jason's shoulder at the familiar verse. "Recite what you've got so far."

Jason nodded, closed his eyes, and began the ton of words. "Do not be anxious about…something or other, but everything…something…" He sighed from his diaphragm. "See? I can't get it."

"Hmm." Del read the verse a second time. "Maybe you haven't applied the stickum properly."

"The what?"

"The stickum. If you don't understand *what* you're saying the words won't stick to your brain."

Jason made a disbelieving face. Del raised his right hand. "Honest."

"You're just trying to get me to do more work. Understanding it and everything."

"Isn't that why Father Lucas wants you to memorize it? So you understand it?"

"I suppose."

Del pointed to the verse. "Tell me what it says in your own words."

Jason held the notebook closer to his face. "'Don't be anxious'…don't worry about stuff."

"Good."

"'But in everything, by prayer and petition'—" He turned to Del. "What's petition?"

"Asking."

"So…we're supposed to ask and pray about everything."

"Right."

Jason sighed, as if the effort drained him. "'With thanksgiving, present your requests to God.'" He looked at Del. "Say thanks, and then ask?"

"You got it. Now say the whole thing in your own words."

Jason studied the page a moment. "Don't worry about stuff. Thank God for what you have, then pray about the rest."

"Couldn't have said it better myself."

"But those are my words, not the Bible words."

Del pushed himself to his feet. "Try it again, Jason. I bet the Bible words are ready to stick."

Del walked away accompanied by Jason's mumbling. Halfway down the hall he heard, "Hey, Father! I remembered the first part!"

"Good boy."

Del went into his history classroom with a lighter heart. He repeated the words of the verse, the stickum working in his own brain: *Do not be anxious about anything, but in everything, by prayer and petition, with thanksgiving, present your requests to God.*

He sat at his desk, relishing the quiet. He had five minutes before the room would be filled with students. Just time enough to do a little *petitioning.*

"With thanksgiving," he reminded himself.

Thanksgiving.

Suddenly the verb became a noun. A holiday. A date.

"Thanksgiving!"

It was perfect. What better day to have a Haven reunion

than on a day designated for giving thanks? Wasn't that why they were getting together? To give thanks for their experience? To encourage each other, nourish each other? Pray together?

Thanksgiving was a holiday of families. The Havenites could bring their families. And friends. If each one reached one…

The school bell rang.

Del shook his head at the thought of whole families coming to the reunion. *Is this thing getting too big?* But as his first student came in the classroom, forcing his mind to think other thoughts, he shook his head in resignation.

If God could think big, so could he.

Del's day was far from over. He still had some rowing to do.

Although he'd had a conversation with Walter, figured out the date and the reason for the reunion, he couldn't sit back and ignore his duties. He had a wedding rehearsal to officiate.

Weddings could be a tedious job, but he approached this particular event with joy. It was the uniting of two friends: Stevie Wellington and Hayley Spotsman. A few years earlier, when Stevie's wife, Gloria, had committed suicide while under the influence of a demon, Stevie had been devastated. Not only had he lost a wife, he had lost the mother of his baby girl, Tasha. But then, through a "chance" meeting, Stevie had met Hayley Spotsman, the owner of Hayley's Antiques. Hayley approached life as if it were her grandmother's attic, full of treasures waiting to be discovered. The love between Hayley and Stevie had become a treasure that would be polished and displayed at tomorrow's wedding.

As soon as Del entered the sanctuary, Hayley pounced, linking her arm in his. "Father! You simply have to meet my very best friend in the world."

A woman was drawn forward in Hayley's wake. "Now, if that title isn't hard to live up to…" The woman extended her hand to Del. He was immediately impressed by her confident presence. "Ellen Richardson, best friend *extraordinare.*"

He shook her hand. "Father Antonio Delatondo. Priest quite ordinare."

"Not from what I've heard."

Del turned to Hayley. "Have you been telling my secrets again?"

"Every one, Father. If I know them, they're not secrets anymore."

Ellen laughed. "That's for sure."

Hayley pointed a finger at her friend. "You, be nice, or I won't let you wear that luscious bridesmaid dress."

"Promise?"

Hayley ignored her. "Ellen works for a hotel's convention bureau in Kansas City, Father. Luring people to the city of hot barbecue and spicy jazz. Or is that spicy barbecue and hot jazz?"

"If you ever have a wayward convention you need booked, Father, just let me—"

"Kansas City?" Del's stomach did a three-sixty.

Ellen and Hayley exchanged a look, reacting to Del's odd expression.

"You have convention facilities? For a lot of people?"

"Yes, of course…" Ellen cocked her head. "Father? Do you have something in mind?"

Del grinned. "Yes, I think I do."

After the rehearsal was completed, Father Delatondo commandeered Ellen Richardson in a corner of the narthex. He filled her in on what little he knew about the Haven reunion.

Ellen took out her planner. It overflowed with notes and papers. She noticed his look. "You have your Bible, Father, and I have mine. If I lost this, *I'd* be lost."

"Ditto with my Bible."

She opened the planner and clicked a pen into action. "What dates did you have in mind?"

Del started to say "Thanksgiving" but stopped himself. *Let's see if this is the right day...*

"November."

She raised an eyebrow. "Of this year? That's next month! Sorry, Father, but I'm used to people planning *years* in advance."

"I realize that. But I get the feeling time is essential here. Sooner is better."

She turned to November and scanned through the dates. "Ooh, this is going to be a tough one. I'm not sure we have any—" She sighed. "Just as I thought. The only dates open are right around Thanksgiving."

Del lifted his face upward and closed his eyes. "You're amazing."

"Excuse me?"

"We'll take it."

"No."

"But, everything's falling into place, Monsignor." Del leaned forward in his chair. "We have a date, a place, and a vehicle for spreading the news. But in order to do it properly I have to fly to Minneapolis. I'll get the cheapest ticket possible. I promise."

The monsignor adjusted his bony posterior in the cushion of his chair. "I believe this could safely be judged an extracurricular activity, Father. Well outside the realm of the parish's responsibilities. Certainly you understand why I can't give my approval of a monetary outlay. It wouldn't be fair to the parishioners. When they give their offerings, they don't want it used for plane tickets to promote a private function."

"But it's not private. It's a convention of people who were in Haven and their families—and anyone else who wants to come." He hesitated. "Even you could come."

"Don't do me any favors."

Del sucked in a breath, along with the monsignor's bitter words.

"The plane ticket is a part of God's will—"

Monsignor frowned. "I'm still not convinced of that, Father. Are you sure you're not achieving your own will?"

"I want what He wants."

"A handy defense."

Del shrugged. "You said I could pursue the reunion in my spare time. I'll use my vacation days. The parish won't be out any of my time."

"But you do want them to be out the money for the plane ticket? And the hotel, I suppose."

"I'll stay with my friend, Walter. All I'm asking for is the plane ticket. Get me there, and I'll take care of the rest."

"I'm sure you will."

Del knew he was losing the battle. Where could he get the money? The fare was 482 dollars. He didn't have that much in his own savings. He was such a sucker for books, most of his earnings went to stock his library…maybe if he sold some of them…he could handle the 82 dollars, but the 400 dollars… *Please, Lord. Don't shut the door on me. Help me get to Minneapolis.*

Monsignor's intercom buzzed. "Yes, Mildred?"

"Mrs. Greenway would like to see you, Monsignor. She says she has a…a gift."

Monsignor and Del exchanged a look. Mrs. Greenway was a familiar presence at St. Stephen's. She was a joiner—especially since her husband had died the previous Christmas. She was a Friend of the Food Bank; on the altar guild, the wedding committee, leader of the prayer chain; plus she made a cherry cobbler that could be assigned its own food group.

"Send her in." The men stood to greet her.

The door opened, and Mrs. Greenway burst in the room, her eyes shining. When she saw Del, she gasped. "You're here too!"

"Yes." Del fidgeted at the intensity in her voice.

She put a hand to her ample bosom. "Oh, this is just too, too miraculous."

Del guided her to a chair. "You'll have to explain yourself, Mrs. Greenway. It's rare my presence garners such a greeting."

She nodded, taking calming breaths. She fingered the clasp of her purse. "Perhaps I should start at the beginning."

"A good place." Monsignor clasped his hands across his middle.

"It all started this morning when I was going through Al's desk. Since his death, little by little, I've gone through his things, sorting, crying, remembering…" She looked at her lap. "I've found the nicest treasures. Notes. It's like Al knew he would be gone soon and wanted to leave me little messages. Some notes are instructional and some…he was quite romantic." She blushed. "I'd put off going through his desk. It was the last bastion of *him*. But lately I've felt stronger. Today when I passed the desk, I suddenly found myself sitting in front of it. Before I knew what I was doing, I was going through all those cubbyholes, nooks, and drawers." She opened her purse and pulled out a note. "In a little drawer with nothing else in it, I found this." She handed it to Del.

Del read it aloud. "'Give this to Father Del when he needs it.'" Del turned the note over, looking for more. "Give me the note when I need it? I'm afraid I don't understand."

Mrs. Greenway beamed. "There was something else paper-clipped to the note, Father." She pulled some money from her purse, started to hand it to Del, then changed her mind and put it on the monsignor's desk.

The monsignor picked up the stack of bills. The top showed a fifty.

"It's 400 dollars. Eight fifty-dollar bills."

Del's stomach rose to his throat. "Thank you, Lord!"

"What?" Mrs. Greenway looked from Del to the monsignor, then back again.

Although Del wanted to blurt out the explanation, he extended a hand toward his superior, letting—making—him do it.

The monsignor ruffled through the bills once. Twice. He looked at Mrs. Greenway, his face stern. "Has Father Delatondo contacted you in the last few days?"

She looked confused. "No, no…why do you ask?"

The monsignor tossed the money on his desk and tented his fingers. He rocked in his chair, staring at the bills.

"Monsignor? Is there something wrong? I realize it's rather odd assigning money to a specific priest but I'm sure Father Delatondo can be trusted to use it wisely. My husband was a big fan of Father Del's."

"I'm sure he was."

Del wanted to smack him. This poor woman had entered his office overflowing with generosity and the joy of giving, and he had quenched her fire, like water on a flame. Why couldn't the monsignor admit the money was a gift from God? Was his need to be in control so great that he would negate this woman's offering?

Del was on the verge of speaking, extending his thanks and explaining the miracle to Mrs. Greenway, when the monsignor sat upright in his chair. He placed a hand on the money and nodded. "Thank you, Mrs. Greenway." His voice was soft. "'I know that God can do all things; no plan of His can be thwarted.'"

Did this mean…?

Monsignor took a deep breath and turned to Del. "When do you leave?"

CHAPTER FIVE

Those who are wise will shine like the brightness of the heavens, and those who lead many to righteousness, like the stars for ever and ever.

DANIEL 12:3

"Have a seat."

Ben positioned a chair for his colleague Hamm Spurgeon. He felt like a kid, eager to show his father an A on a test.

Hamm wedged himself in the living room chair, his hips skimming the upholstered sides. He pushed against the arms, getting comfortable. "Why did you ask me over?"

Ben smiled and stood between Hamm and the television. "Be patient. I have something to show you. A surprise." He turned on the set.

"I'm not in the mood, Ben. I have things to do."

"Just a few more minutes." This was going to be great. Perfect. Ben had been tipped off by a contact that Channel 11 would be airing a report on the mustard seed pins. Hamm would be impressed by Ben's insight and initiative. Ben's position in the organization would soar and he would finally get the recognition and authority he deserved.

Hamm Spurgeon was the self-elected head of TAI: Truth for American Individuals. TAI was an organization intent on opening the eyes of the inane masses who were devoted to a God no one had ever seen. Where was the power in that? Power came from within oneself, by trusting *only* oneself, by using one's intellect. It did not come from mindlessly depending on a God who couldn't even control the world. God the Creator of all things? What a joke. *If* any being created the world, it would

85

be powerful enough to control it. And one only had to look at the rampage of world chaos to see that no one was in control. No one.

The only answer was in the power of individuals, of those willing to look within themselves for the answers. "Look within and win" was a motto Ben lived by. TAI didn't believe in the power of the people, but in the power of the *person*. Individuals had the ability—and the responsibility—to change things.

He'd discovered TAI on the Internet. Ben had never met any of the other members except Hamm, but he *had* been an active part of their chat room and reveled in the fact that he was not alone in his hatred and distrust of a God bent on weakening mankind. He felt honored to have met Hamm, the founder and leader of TAI.

Actually, Hamm had found *him*. Soon after Julia had been elected president, Ben had moved to D.C. with no job, no place to live, and no goals except an absurd need to be near the woman who had ignited—and extinguished—his political career.

Hamm had found Ben sitting on a park bench, looking through the want ads. The man had sat down, laid an arm across the back of the bench and asked, "Hoping to change your life?"

Ben had looked at the older man, trying to assess if he was a mugger with a strange sense of humor or maybe a wayward investment banker, hoping to corral Ben's meager savings into stocks and bonds. But Hamm didn't look like either. He looked like a schoolteacher caught in the sixties. He wore a bow tie, a white short-sleeved shirt, and Hush Puppies that were scuffed at the toes. He was balding and had a nick on his chin from shaving. He looked like an older version of a fat kid Ben might have shoved into a locker in high school. Hamm's smile and soft-spoken ways had won Ben's trust.

After their initial meeting, Hamm had even found Ben a job

delivering for a freight company. Then he'd helped him find an apartment. And a purpose.

Hamm hadn't mentioned TAI until their fourth meeting, after Ben had aired his bitter views on President Carson and what was wrong with the country.

"You're all talk and no action, aren't you?"

Ben had taken offense, even though he knew it was true.

"Would you be interested in an organization that can silence Julia Carson and her Scripture-spouting, freedom-bashing philosophy?"

He would.

TAI's actions were clandestine and small scale and were focused on Christians. What had their Jesus called them? Sheep? It was an apt analogy. Few things were more stupid than sheep or more willing to follow blindly than Christians. TAI's activities were simple: Members plastered photocopied posters outside the doorways of Christian offices, vandalized statues and pictures of religious figures, sent out mass mailings, and issued anti-Christian press releases which, typically, the press ignored.

At first, Ben had been content with TAI's low profile. But soon it had grown boring. His discontent was directly related to the appearance of the energy in his life. Its arrival had been sudden and life changing. The morning after he had joined TAI, he had awakened with a feeling that something new had been added to who he was. He felt stirred up inside. More alive. Ready to burst with anticipation. He found himself thinking in ways that would appease the energy—even feed it. Somewhere, in the back of his mind, a small voice warned that he was acting like some kind of alcoholic who took one drink, thinking it would be enough, when it only made him want—and need—more.

But he'd pushed the voice away. He wasn't like that. Not at all. Besides, today Ben's hard work would be validated in front of the head honcho. After this victory, maybe Hamm would be willing to let Ben take over the reins of TAI. It was a logical progression. After all, Ben was used to running huge political campaigns. He was a dynamic, confident man. What was Hamm? A bookish blotto who rarely spoke loud enough for Ben to hear. TAI was ripe for a coup. And Ben was ready to step in.

The intro to the news started, highlighting the topics to come. Ben turned up the sound. *"Fake mustard seed pins inundate area conventions…"*

Ben pumped a fist in the air. He pointed to the set. "You watch. This is the surprise I was telling you about. I planted fake mustard seed pins all over the city at conventions. They will—"

Hamm shrugged. "May I have a glass of milk, please?"

Ben blinked. "What?"

Hamm pinched a piece of lint off the arm of the chair. He cocked his head and rubbed the fabric. "A large glass. Skim, if you have it."

What was with this bizarre little man? *I'm about to show him how I'm willing to change the world, and he wants a glass of milk?* Ben shook his head, but got up. He poured. Two percent. He held the glass a moment before handing it over. "I suppose you want some cookies with this?"

For a moment—just a moment—something flashed in Hamm's eyes. Then it was gone. "The milk is satisfactory, thank you." He downed half, balanced the glass on his knee, and dispensed of the milk mustache with his index finger. Only then did he look at Ben and smile. His words were slow, carefully articulated. "You, Benjamin Cranois, are an idiot."

Ben's elation deflated like a slashed tire. He swung his arm toward the TV. "The fake pins are on TV. They'll dilute the effect of the real pins. They—"

The news report started. A reporter stood front and center. "Dozens of mustard seed pins were distributed to convention-goers across Washington today. These pins are reminiscent of the mustard seed pins that began appearing two years ago during President Carson's campaign. Although the distributor of the original pins was never determined, recipients are reported to believe that they received the pins due to godly living. It has been a hard explanation to discredit. Yet the appearance of these new pins seems to bring the entire explanation into question."

"Yes!"

Hamm took another sip of milk.

Some people wearing convention name tags came onto the screen, their eyes skittish. Ben held back a sneer. He'd bet they liked the idea of being interviewed more than the reality of it. The reporter held the microphone in front of them. "What do you think of the pins?"

The woman held one between her fingers, as though it were as fragile—and repulsive—as a dead sparrow. "At first I was excited, but then, when I realized they weren't the real thing, I was disappointed. I mean, who wants something that has no meaning?" She sighed. "It's like getting a trophy with someone else's name on it." She turned to her companion. "Now, Jim, here, he got the real thing a year ago."

The camera took in a fiftyish man with a wide smile. He held a lapel that sported what was obviously one of the original mustard seed pins.

"Your copies aren't very good," Hamm said.

Ben didn't want to hear it. "I did the best I could. Nobody in our crowd has one, you know."

"These pins are special," the man said. "When I got it in the mail, I was shocked—and thrilled. Plus, the Bible verse that was included was very meaningful to me. I've memorized it. Do you want to hear it?"

The reporter looked taken aback, but nodded. "Sure."

Jim cleared his throat. "'The Lord watches over you—the Lord is your shade at your right hand; the sun will not harm you by day, nor the moon by night.' Isn't that perfect?"

The reporter cleared his throat. "So you're saying the fake pins don't mean anything because they didn't come with a Bible verse?"

Jim looked right at the camera. "I'm saying these fake pins don't mean anything because they didn't come from God."

Ben clicked the TV off. This was terrible. How could things have gone so wrong? "I...I never thought—"

"An understatement."

Ben moved to the refrigerator and grabbed a beer. He snapped the top open. "It wasn't that bad. At least I—"

Hamm lowered his multiple chins and raised an eyebrow. "Not that bad? You managed to get the Bible quoted *and* God's name mentioned on national television. Whose side are you on, anyway?"

Ben felt himself redden and threw back a swig of beer. "That's not fair."

"I didn't hear your answer."

"I didn't think your accusation deserved one."

Hamm held one of the bogus pins to the light, rolling it between his thumb and forefinger. "Did you actually think distributing fake pins would dilute the power of the real thing?"

"Doesn't counterfeit money dilute the power of the real thing?"

"You *are* a fool!" With a sudden explosion of movement, Hamm heaved the pin against the wall. A few drops of milk escaped the glass and stained his pants.

Ben backed up until he ran into the refrigerator. "Hey, no need to—"

Hamm stood and set the milk on top of the television. When he swung around, Ben could see the muscles in the older man's neck twitch. Ben's confidence withered; he wished he were alone.

"Don't you understand, you imbecile? The counterfeit only makes the genuine more valuable. Cubic zirconia is good enough until you see a real diamond. The false makes the truth

90

shine brighter. *Their* truth. Not ours."

The false makes the truth shine brighter. Something deep inside Ben—something he didn't fully understand—seized on this fresh idea and pulled it to a safe place, out of the line of Hamm's fire. In the next instant, a string of thoughts scurried through his mind. *The falseness of the energy you've been feeling only makes the truth of the Lord's energy shine brighter. If Christ is a glittering diamond, then the world apart from Him is cubic zirconia. A paltry replica. Man-made. Weak. Flawed. Cheap. The diamond of Christ's truth is formed by the very powers of the earth, converging together in an awesome unity to create such a gem of beauty as could never be created by man—*

Hamm snapped his fingers in front of Ben's face, and Ben wondered when he had come so close. "Snap out of it, boy. I don't like the stupified look in your eyes."

The new ideas faded. The fact Ben wanted to grab them back was troubling.

Hamm reclaimed his milk and his seat, and emptied the glass with a satisfied ahhh. His anger seemed to have dissipated, and Ben found himself wondering if the outburst had really happened.

"If you're interested—" Hamm's voice was mild—"there *is* something coming that will call us to action in a way that will make a difference."

Ben wasn't sure he wanted to hear. "What kind of action?"

Hamm smiled. "The kind that goes beyond pamphlets and posters. The kind that will test your loyalty."

"*My* loyalty? What about yours?"

Hamm looked past Ben, out the window. His forehead tightened and his voice softened. "I've already been tested." His focus came back to Ben. "And *I* passed. Will you be able to say as much?"

"Of course." Ben walked to the sink, setting his beer on the counter. He washed his hands though they didn't need washing. He didn't want Hamm to see his doubt, to sense the fear that had sparked to life with Hamm's words. He spoke above the running water. "Haven't I proved myself already? Didn't the pins do that? Whether things turned out as I planned or not, I did do *something*. I had them made at my own expense."

Hamm applauded, and the muscles in Ben's back tensed.

"Bravo! What are you out? A few hundred dollars and a couple hours of your time?"

Ben shivered at the sarcasm. He'd really blown it. So much for the coup. He turned slowly. "I'm willing to do more—"

Hamm stood. "Good. Because the time is coming." Putting a beefy hand to his chest, Hamm sucked in a breath slowly, deliberately. He closed his eyes and let the breath ease out. When he spoke, his voice quivered with an eerie intensity. "I feel a sense of urgency. Something's brewing. Something huge." When he opened his eyes, they flashed a challenge. "I assume you feel it too?"

Ben nodded. So Hamm felt the urgency too? Ben wasn't alone in feeling this energy inside? *I'm not crazy?*

Hamm headed toward the door. He turned one last time, his gaze boring into Ben. "It's going to happen." He pointed a finger into the space between them. "The time of destruction is coming! The time is coming to stop them all!"

The tenor of Hamm's voice, the fire in his eyes, sent a chill skittering down Ben's spine. Maybe the source of their urgency wasn't the same after all?

Without another word, Hamm left. Only then did Ben realize his wet hands were dripping on the floor, and the faucet was still running.

CHAPTER SIX

*[The Lord] will bring to light what is hidden in darkness
and will expose the motives of men's hearts. At that time
each will receive his praise from God.*

1 CORINTHIANS 4:5

OTHER THAN THE DRIVER, Jack Cummings was the only one
awake in the van. His traveling companions slept, some with
their heads propped against windows, others slumped in their
seats, their heads lolling back and forth with each twist of the
mountain road. The flight to Denver had been uneventful but
exhausting, and the hour-long drive to Estes Park was the perfect time for a nap. But Jack couldn't sleep. Not when he was
getting so close to Natalie.

He'd never been in the Rocky Mountains before—normally
that in itself would have kept him awake. He was fascinated
with the way the scrub desert gave way to sheer cliffs towering
hundreds of feet above the road, and then opened up to a
fairyland of pines, orange aspens, wildflowers, and a rushing
stream that followed the highway up to the tourist village of
Estes Park.

He saw the driver look at him. "First-timer, huh?"

"I think it would affect me the same way the hundredth
time."

"You're probably right." The driver pointed to Jack's window. "Crack the window and take a whiff."

Jack did as he was told. "Pines." He rubbed his nose. "It's so
clean it hurts."

The driver laughed. "You're coming for a teacher's convention, right?"

"Right. I teach English. I wasn't supposed to come, but someone got sick and bowed out, so here I am." To himself he added, "By an act of God."

"What?"

Jack had to share with someone. "God wanted me here."

The driver shook his head. "If you say so."

"Actually, the convention is only one reason I'm being brought here."

"Ahh." The driver smirked. "A woman."

"Why do you say that?"

"Whenever there's another reason, it has to do with a dame. Nine times out of ten." He glanced at Jack. "So? Am I right?"

"You're right. She lives here."

"Bingo!" The driver hit his hand on the steering wheel.

"She doesn't know I'm coming."

"Which you can remedy within five minutes of getting—"

"I'm not sure I will call her."

"Why not?"

"We haven't seen each other for two years. We wrote…actually, I wrote more than she did." He looked out the side window. "She's probably forgotten about me."

"Now, now. What happened to your act of God?"

Jack had to smile. "I guess you're right."

"I always am."

The lobby of the Bishop Hotel swarmed with teachers and their luggage. There were lines everywhere—at the convention registration desk to pick up their packets and name tags, and at the hotel registration desk to check into their rooms.

"Next."

Jack stepped to the front desk. "Jack Cummings."

The clerk looked down at the list, then up at Jack. "From Lincoln?"

How did he know that? "Yes." The clerk didn't look familiar.

Was it on the sheet in front of him? Nope. Frowning slightly, Jack let his eyes wander to the man's name tag. He read the name twice, trying to make sense of it. Then it hit him. Jack met the other man's stare—or was it a glare? "You're Sam Erickson! You're Natalie's—"

"Fiancé."

That one word struck Jack square in the chest, like a malicious sledgehammer. "Fiancé?"

"Yeah." Sam pulled a card for Jack to sign. "We're going to be married. Soon."

"When?"

"Uh…soon." He handed Jack a pen. "She told me about you. How you went to Eureka Springs after her and…helped her with that Beau guy."

That Beau guy? That Beau guy had been a demon. "I haven't heard from Natalie in a while. How is—"

"Well, yeah…why should you? She's engaged to me."

"We're just friends, Sam."

"I know. She's marrying *me.*"

A bit testy, aren't you? "Will you tell Natalie I'm in town? I'd love to see her again."

"She's busy." He handed Jack his key. "And you will be too. Right?"

"Yeah…right."

How dare he try to imply I shouldn't see Natalie? She's my friend. God brought me here.

Jack sat in his room and looked out the window across Estes Park. Natalie was out there somewhere. He had every right to call her and see—

But she was engaged. She was taken. She was gone.

Jack bowed his head. "Oh, Lord, I was so sure you brought me here to see her. But I can't pursue a woman who's engaged, especially not when her fiancé has all but warned me to stay away." He sighed at his own confusion. "Give me peace, Lord. Give me peace."

———⟨∿⟩———

Sam's coworker pinged him on the arm. "What's wrong with you?"

"Nothing."

"The computer keyboard doesn't like to be pounded on. Take it easy."

But Sam couldn't take it easy. Jack Cummings was in town.

———⟨∿⟩———

Roy handed Kathy the phone. "Kath, you'll never believe it. It's Del!"

Kathy was tongue-tied. Antonio Delatondo was one of the last people she expected to call. She took the phone, feeling a rush of adrenaline. "Del?"

"Hi ya, Kathy. I know it's been too long. None of us have stayed in touch like we should have."

A wave of guilt took hold. "How are you?"

"Fine, fine, but that's not why I'm calling. Or actually a calling is why I'm calling."

"You lost me."

He laughed and explained about his plans for a Haven reunion. She loved the thought of it—especially since she'd be going back as a successful painter…

"That sounds wonderful. Roy will love the idea too."

"What will Roy love?" her husband whispered.

Kathy covered the receiver. "A Haven reunion."

Roy spoke loud enough for Del to hear. "She's right. Roy loves the idea."

Kathy smiled and turned her attention back to Del. "Did you hear that?"

"Loud and clear. I'd forgotten that your new husband went to a Haven in California."

"He's definitely one of us."

"That's great. But this won't be an exclusive reunion. Anyone who wants to rededicate his or her life to God can come. Havenites, people who've received mustard seed pins…anyone."

"But Thanksgiving…it's coming so quickly. How are you ever—"

Del explained how he was going to be on Walter's show.

"But will that reach everyone?"

"We'll have to trust God to do the rest."

"It's nice to hear from you, Del, and you can count on Roy and me being—"

"Actually, there's something else. Are you still painting?"

So he hadn't heard about her success. Nebraska wasn't *that* far away. Kathy squelched the disappointment. "Yes, I'm painting. Quite a lot. In fact, I had a showing the night before last and sold a lot—"

"Good, good. I wondered if you would paint a piece for us, something we could use as a symbol of the reunion. Something we could reproduce on the program, and then maybe raffle off?"

"Paint something for the reunion? For a raffle?"

"Sure. I've seen the painting you gave Julia back in Haven."

"That was some of my early work. I've gotten better since then."

"He wants a painting?" Roy asked.

Kathy shushed him. "How much—"

"I'm not sure how much we could raise through a raffle, but they are usually good money makers for charity."

"I mean, how much would I get paid?"

Silence.

Roy waved his hands at her, shaking his head.

She covered the receiver. "What?"

Roy's eyes were wide. "You don't charge him!"

Kathy's mind swam with the reprimand. Her paintings

brought in hundreds of dollars, even thousands. She couldn't afford to give them away for nothing…

Pride goes before destruction, a haughty spirit before a fall.

Oh, fine. Where had *that* verse come from?

Del was still talking. "I'll…well, I'll see what we can manage. Will you do it?"

Roy's face was a brewing storm cloud, and Kathy wished she could replay the last minute of her life. It was so embarrassing to be caught being greedy. "Del, listen, I'd be happy to help. And…and, I'd like to donate the painting. For free."

Kathy was sickened—and shamed—by Del's sigh of relief. "That's so good of you, Kathy."

Hardly. Barely. "What would you like the painting to look like?"

"I trust you completely."

Maybe you shouldn't.

They said their good-byes, and Kathy hung up the phone, wishing Del had picked a time when she was alone to call. Then again, maybe not. If Roy hadn't been around to push her into doing the right thing, she might have blown it. She hated that she hadn't thought about donating the painting. She didn't like what it said about her character. Had she really changed so much?

She walked out of the room, a hand covering her face. As she feared, Roy followed her. "Don't say it."

"But I have to—"

She stopped short and faced him. "Fine. Tell me what a greedy, egotistical, prideful snob I am. Tell me how disappointed you are that I even asked how much I'd get paid. Say that you're mad and disgusted and you wonder why you ever married me."

He rubbed a hand across his chin. "Actually…you've covered the points quite well."

"At least I do that right." He extended a hand toward her waist, and she let him pull her close. She buried her face in his shirt. "What's happening to me?"

He kissed her nose. "'For they loved praise from men more than praise from God.'"

"Is that what I'm doing?"

Roy shook his head no, but said, "Maybe. Getting paid for your work is a form of praise, isn't it?"

"But after all the years of getting next to nothing...*having* next to nothing, I'm finally earning—"

"What you deserve?"

"That sounds like a trick question."

"The trickiest."

She moved to the couch and slumped into the cushions. "Being almost rich and nearly famous is hard work."

Roy slumped down beside her. "The hardest."

—✿—

Walter worked late, trying to catch up on the work he had neglected while pondering his bonus. At eight he finally closed up shop, his guilt appeased. He ventured into a freezing rain, pulled his collar up, and ducked his head against the wind. His balding pate tightened at the cold lick of the raindrops, and he experienced a wave of nostalgia, wishing it were the 1950s when no adult ever ventured outside without a hat. He tugged his leather gloves to cover his wrists, then held his collar tight against his mouth. The sidewalk was puddled. Walter watched his footing, not wanting to slip and—

"Ugh!"

He'd bumped into a woman. Her satchel fell to the ground. She picked it up, holding it close to her chest.

"Sorry. I didn't see—" The woman gave him one intense look before gathering a child under her arm and scurrying away. Walter watched her go. The child looked back at him, her stocking hat brushing her eyebrows, her long hair heavy with rain. He noticed the lining hanging from the back of the woman's coat, how her too-long jeans dragged on the wet pavement. He noticed the girl's navy ski coat. A boy's coat. Where was the purple and pink little girls craved? She had no gloves, much less matching gloves and a stocking hat like Addy wore. The woman and child turned into the alley behind the television station.

They're homeless.

Although Bette volunteered at the homeless shelter, Walter had never met one of their kind face to face. Never seen their eyes. Watched where they went. Never cared.

Until now.

They can't stay outside! It's freezing out here. Why don't they go to the shelter?

Then he remembered. Bette had said the shelter didn't have enough room or funding. If only more people would give—

Walter blinked at the thought. *My bonus. If only I'd given my bonus—*

A car horn honked.

The spell was broken. Walter hurried to his van, leaving his guilt to puddle in the frigid rain.

Walter lunged for the phone, knocking it off the nightstand. He pulled the receiver onto the bed by its coiled cord. "Hello?" Rolf's words ripped the last vestiges of sleep from his mind. "I'll be right there."

The flashing lights of police and fire vehicles marked the spot. Walter scanned the KMPS building, trying to gauge the damage. The alley side of the station was blackened. A portion of the first floor was open to the world, and smoke billowed out of the crater carved by the fire. Firefighters sprayed a stream into the black hole. A charred chair was silhouetted against the light of the final flames.

"Walter!"

Walter saw Rolf Wingow running toward him. Rolf's plaid pajama bottoms stuck out from beneath his topcoat.

"How much damage?"

Rolf shook his head. "It's too soon to say, but from the location…I'd guess it got your set."

"My set?"

Rolf pointed. "The *Good News* set sits on the far end of the first floor, Walter."

He'd never thought about his set's location in the building. The studio was without windows, so he'd always considered it a room without a north, south, east, or west.

Walter took a step toward the main doors. "Let's go in and—"

Rolf pulled him back before a policeman barred his way. "We can't go in yet. It's unsafe. We have to wait until they're—"

"But we *have* to go in. The set. *My* set. All my hard work!" Walter stared at the black hole that had suddenly opened in his career. He swung toward Rolf. "What started it?"

Rolf pointed across the street to some people talking to police. "Witnesses saw a homeless woman and child in the alley. Saw a flame on the ground like they'd started a fire."

"They started the fire? Arson?"

"No, no. Apparently, they started the fire to get warm. It's a nasty night, Walter."

"Was anyone hurt?"

"No, thank God. I'm sure they got out of there pretty quickly when it started. And everyone inside escaped."

Walter looked toward the alley, half expecting to see the woman staring at him, the little girl huddled under her arm. Condemning him. Accusing him.

He shook his head. He didn't need to see them. They were forever etched in his mind.

CHAPTER SEVEN

Therefore do not let sin reign in your mortal body so that you obey its evil desires.

ROMANS 6:12

BETTE HANDED WALTER A CUP OF TEA. She sat on the couch beside him, tucking her feet into the warmth of her robe. She listened to him rant, knowing that even if she were not in the room, the same words of anger and frustration would spill from her husband's mouth. Walter was not one to stay silent in a crisis.

She'd heard him describe the fire twice. He was just starting into rendition number three when she finally found the courage to break into his monologue.

"What did you do with your bonus money, hon?"

Walter blinked as though he'd just realized he had an audience. "What does that have to do—"

Bette inched closer and combed a strand of wayward hair behind his ears. "Did you give it to the homeless shelter?"

"That's none of your—"

She pinched his ear. "If you finish that sentence, you'll experience another kind of fire, mister."

He wouldn't meet her eyes. "I thought about it a lot and—"

Oh, Walter. Don't say it. Please don't tell me—

"I kept it."

Bette felt a twinge of disappointment—coupled with another of greed, as if an angel and the devil sat on her shoulders, bickering.

It would be nice to have the money…

She mentally swiped the devil to the floor. "I was afraid of that."

"Don't mess with me, Bette. I'm not up to it. We both agreed it was my money."

Bette traced the quilting of her robe. *How do I say this to him? It's just a thought; it may not be true. Who am I to say—*

You're his wife. Speak to him.

Bette took a sip of her tea, hoping the warmth would make her next words less cold.

"If you had given the bonus to the homeless shelter, maybe they would have had enough room to house the little girl and her mother. And maybe they wouldn't have had to sleep in the alley. They wouldn't have been cold. They wouldn't have made a fire that spread to the station, burning your set. *Just* your set, Walter."

Walter pushed himself to the next cushion. "Because I was greedy, God destroyed my set?"

With difficulty, Bette kept her eyes on his. "Basically."

He slammed his mug on the table and tea splashed over the top. "How dare you!"

Bette moved close, her hands prepared to comfort and soothe. "Maybe I'm wrong—"

"You *bet* you're wrong!" Walter pointed a finger at his chest. "It was *my* money! God has no right to punish me just because I didn't do some high and mighty good deed. He gave me a choice, and I made it."

"I'm merely suggesting that it was—"

"The wrong choice?" He began pacing, and Bette glanced toward Addy's room, afraid his rising voice would wake her. Walter noticed her look and lowered his volume, though not his intensity. "Even if I'd given the check to the shelter today, that wouldn't have helped that particular mom and kid. It might have helped somebody days from now, but last night? My check wouldn't have made diddly difference."

Bette knew he was right, but that didn't stop the gnawing feeling that somehow, if Walter would have given freely, his work would not have been destroyed. She went to the kitchen to get a towel to clean up the spilled tea.

Walter grabbed his coat. "I come home to get support, Bette. Not criticism."

"But, hon, I—"

He left, slamming the door behind him. Addy woke and began to cry. Bette joined her.

———✦———

Walter stood at Rolf's office window and watched a truck full of debris drive away from the building. "It's not fair." He heard Rolf take a breath and turned to face him. "Don't say it."

"Say what?"

"Life's not fair."

"That's not what I was going to say."

"Good." Walter took a seat in the guest chair in front of Rolf's desk.

"I was going to say, so what?"

"Huh?"

"The fire isn't fair. So what?"

Walter threw his hands into the air, popped up, and began to pace. "So what? We've got a big hole in our building, or didn't you notice? And though I love my job as well as the next person, it's Saturday. I have better things to do on my weekends then start from square one."

"Don't be snide, Walter."

"Me, snide? You're the one who's acting like the destruction of the *Good News* set doesn't matter."

"I didn't say that."

"*So what* said that."

Rolf gave Walter a calm stare and sighed.

Walter jerked to a halt. "A sigh? That's all you're going to give me? What do you do if there's an earthquake? Clear your throat?"

"Watch it."

Walter swallowed and felt his face redden. He raked a hand over his head, trying to press some common sense through his skull.

"That's better."

Walter sank into the chair. "I'm sorry. It's just that I've worked so hard. I've given this show everything I've got. I've put in tons of hours, slogged through a slew of ideas to get just the right one. I've babied this thing every step of the way, only to have it go up in flames."

Rolf studied him a moment.

"What?"

"There were an awful lot of *I*s in there, Walter."

"But *I* did it. Not all by myself, that's for sure, but *Good News* is my baby. It's what God assigned me to do."

Rolf did not react.

"It *is*." He looked away. "Why would God ruin my hard work—my hard work for Him? It doesn't make sense." He decided not to mention Bette's theory that his greed was a viable factor in the fire. It was too preposterous.

Rolf shook his head and studied his hands, which were clasped across his stomach.

"You're too quiet."

Rolf opened his mouth to answer, closed it, then with a blink, opened it again. "You know my son, Kevin."

"Sure, nice kid."

"Did you know he's great at yard work? Not just good, really great."

Walter made a face. *What did this have to do with anything?* "That's nice, Rolf. Have him come over and do mine. I hate doing it."

"He could, you know. He's that good. And best of all, he loves it. It's like he was meant to mow lawns, prune trees, and grow gardens."

"Maybe he should start a business some day."

"Hmm."

"What's going on, Rolf? Not that I don't want to hear about Kevin, but…"

"But…"

"Is there something wrong?"

Rolf nodded and tapped his fingertips together. "When I come home from work, Kevin doesn't talk to me anymore. He's working outside or up in his room, making plans for next spring's growth. He used to ask for my advice and confide in me." Rolf looked at Walter. "I was the one who taught him how to do yard work in the first place, and now he barely acknowledges I'm alive. He never has time for me."

"That's the pits."

"He makes me sad—and mad. I wanted him to have a goal and to find something he could be passionate about. But this isn't what I had in mind. What do you think I should do with him?"

Walter pursed his lips, expelling a mouthful of air. "None of this sounds like the Kevin I know."

"He's changed. I encouraged his enthusiasm, assuming he'd let me be a part of it. I didn't expect him to shut me out."

Walter slapped his hands on the armrests of the chair and stood. "Take the yard duties away from him." He took two steps, then spun to face Rolf. "Tell him you don't care about the yard anymore and you're going to hire someone else to do it. Tell him you want to talk with him again. You want him to come to you. You want to spend time together." Walter nodded, satisfied. "Do that."

"You want me to tell him that his work *for* me isn't as important as his relationship *with* me, is that it?"

"You bet tha——" Walter snapped his mouth shut. *Uh-oh.* Walking back to his chair, he tapped a finger against his mouth. "I think I've just been had."

Rolf tapped his fingertips together. "I don't know what you're talking——"

Walter wagged a finger at him. "You and Kevin aren't having any problems, are you?"

Rolf rocked in his chair and grinned. "Not a one."

"Kevin represents me, the obsessed worker. And your

character in the story—the neglected father figure who taught him everything he knows—represents God."

Rolf tapped the end of his nose. "You are more important to God than your work *for* Him, Walter. God just proved that by letting your work burn. Maybe to teach you something."

"And that something is...?"

"He wants you, Walter, not your work. He misses you. Sometimes in our enthusiasm to produce results for God—and for ourselves—we forget that our main work is to produce a close relationship with Him. If we stray too far from the relationship, God sometimes puts a stop to our work to get our attention. God calls us to Himself, not to work. Jesus said, 'Come *to* Me,' not 'Work *for* Me.'"

Walter's shoulders slumped. "So the work's not important?"

"The work *is* important, but the relationship must come first. Just like a parent-child relationship. I care about Kevin's talents and accomplishments, but the most important thing is how he and I love each other. *Your* Father, God, wants to talk with and spend time with you. Your work is the evidence of your faith, not the cause of it."

When Walter didn't say anything, Rolf opened a drawer and pulled out a Bible. He ruffled through the pages, then took a red pen and marked in the middle of a page. Slipping the ribbon marker in place, he handed the book to Walter. "Go back to your office and ponder this a while."

"But I have work to do."

Rolf pointed to the Bible. "Yes, you do."

Walter hurried to his office, holding the Bible away from the prying eyes of his coworkers; they'd also been called into emergency service on Saturday. He was just feeling relief that he had made it without being seen when he entered his office and found Harriet Lane standing over his desk. Harriet was Rolf's counterpart. She handled such consumer-oriented shows as

Buyer Beware, Cooking with Kate, and *Fixer-Upper.*

"Harriet."

"Oh, hi, Walter." She looked up from a note she was writing, then crumpled it. "Rolf mentioned *Good News* is going to share the *Buyer Beware* set and I wanted—" Her eyes dropped to his hands. "Is that a Bible?" From the sneer in her voice, he might as well be carrying a porn magazine.

Walter looked down at Rolf's Bible and thought of pretending he hadn't seen it before—but knew that wouldn't work. "Yes." Then he passed the buck. "Actually, it's Rolf's."

"What do the higher-ups think of you two pushing your religion at work?"

Walter brushed past her and took a seat at his desk. "Rolf and I do not *push* our religion. We simply believe in God and choose not to hide it."

"I can see that." She pointed to the way he held the Bible under his desk.

He set the Bible in front of him and looked up at her. "I appreciate you sharing your set with *Good News.* I'll try to make the experience as painless as possible."

"No problem." She walked toward the door. She hesitated. "By the way, I've been hearing some complaints about *Good News.*"

"What kind of complaints?"

Harriet shuffled her shoulders. "That it's getting too goody-goody, too preachy, too…religious." She smirked.

"I'd like to know exactly who has made these complaints because I haven't heard a thing."

She turned to the door. "Just…people. I thought you'd want to know. The higher-ups are always watching, you know."

"They watch *all* of us, Harriet."

She pursed her lips. "Hmm. See you later, Walter."

He resisted the urge to scream. Sometimes he wished he could stand on a desk in the main office, spread his arms wide, and make a declaration, once and for all: "Listen up, people! I believe in God. I believe in Jesus, the Holy Spirit, the cross, Easter morning, the whole shebang. Personally, I think those of you who don't believe are making a huge mistake, and your ignorance and stubbornness is amazing to behold. As for the rest of you who do believe but want to keep it hush-hush, I don't begrudge you your silence—I've been there. But the least you could do is not fight against me. Those that ain't for me are against me. Just lay off and let me do my job."

He'd get applause from a few: Cassandra, Oscar, Tim, Doug. But mostly he'd get blank stares—at least in his presence. Behind office doors, the gossip would scorch him. *I thought Walter was weird before, but now…he's gone over the edge.*

Walter breathed slowly until his heartbeat returned to normal. No use getting worked up over something he could never say. He pulled the Bible in his lap—easier that way to hide it if someone came in—and opened to the page Rolf had marked.

"For no one can lay any foundation other than the one already laid, which is Jesus Christ. If any man builds on this foundation using gold, silver, costly stones, wood, hay or straw, his work will be shown for what it is, because the day will bring it to light. It will be revealed with fire, and the fire will test the quality of each man's work. If what he has built survives, he will receive his reward. If it is burned up, he will suffer loss; he himself will be saved, but only as one escaping through the flames."

Walter read it twice, closed the book, and was quiet a long time. Would he ever be able to escape the flames? For four years he'd been struggling to follow God, and for four years, he thought he'd done all right. But now…

Rolf, Bette, and the Bible were telling him that the quality of his work was lacking? Not worth saving?

He wasn't worth saving?

Am I saved?

He shook his head. He didn't deserve to be saved. He was selfish, arrogant, egotistical, cowardly, impatient, obnoxious…

At this last character trait, he smiled in spite of his doubt. He couldn't remember ever reading in the Bible, "Thou shalt not be obnoxious." He picked up a pencil and began to doodle, trying to push the convicting thoughts away. He drew an *O* for obnoxious.

Maybe it did say such a thing in the Bible. How would he know? He'd read little and studied even less. He humored Bette when she wanted to have quiet time together, and he heard verses quoted in church—and from Rolf—but he wasn't into it like they were. He didn't thirst for the Bible. Was there something wrong with him? Why didn't he thirst for it?

You don't need it.

Walter shook his head again. He drew a capital *B* for Bible.

He *did* need the Bible, but it was a fact he chose to ignore. Yet, shouldn't it come easily? Shouldn't he wake up in the morning and run to it, *eager* to see what God wanted to teach him? He drew an *E* for eager.

Shouldn't he *yearn* for it?

He drew a *Y*, then did a double take when he realized what he'd spelled. *Obey.*

Walter dropped the pencil. He stared at the word, pushed his chair back, and stood. Rolf's Bible slid to the floor, and a paper came out of it. When Walter bent to pick it up, the word written across the top in bold, block letters called to him: *OBEDIENCE.*

"Oh, Lord…"

Walter studied the paper as if its presence in his hand was a miracle. Maybe it was.

Below the word *OBEDIENCE* was a verse: "If… you seek the LORD your God, you will find him if you look for him with all your heart and with all your soul. When you are in distress and all these things have happened to you, then in later days you will return to the LORD your God and obey him."

Obey Him.

Rolf had been right. Walter did have work to do. He fell to his knees—not caring who saw him. He obeyed.

Walter was not in a normal state: He was calm. As he dealt with the chaos of setting up a temporary set and figuring out what had been lost and what was salvageable, he felt peace. He actually smiled.

People noticed. His uncharacteristic attitude in a time of crisis was the newest subject to weave its way through the office grapevine. His attitude became the true good news about *Good News*. There were even bets on how long it would last.

The pessimists lost.

Walter went through the entire day without blowing up, sounding off, yelling, snapping, or being a grouch. Even when Bette called to tell him not to bother to pick up the dry cleaning—that she'd pick it up, to be nice—he said no, he'd do it. It was no problem. He'd pick it up on his way home.

"You feeling all right, hon?"

Walter grinned. "I feel spiffy."

"Spiffy? This is not a Walter word."

It felt good to laugh.

"What happened? Did I dream the fire?"

"Nope. The set is a total loss."

"And you're happy about it?"

"Wrong word. I'm…relieved." He cleared his throat and pulled a notepad close. He read part of the verse he'd jotted down. "'When you are in distress and all these things have happened to you, then in later days you will return to the LORD your God and obey him.'"

"Is that a Bible verse coming out of your mouth?" He heard her tapping the phone as though they had a bad connection. "Are you sure I'm speaking to Walter Prescott?"

"Oh, ye of little faith!"

"What turned you from spitting nails to spurting verses?"

"It has to do with a four-letter word." He grinned again. "Isn't it strange that we think four-letter words have to be negative?

This is a very positive word."

"Love?"

"Nope. Though that's a good one."

"Hope?"

"Bette! You're taking away my thunder."

"Then tell me."

"Obey."

"You obeyed?"

"I obeyed."

"Whom did you obey?"

"God."

Walter heard her gasp, then whisper. "You obeyed God?"

"Yup."

"What did you do?"

"I did a little confessing, a little thanking, and a little asking. I've been ignoring Him, Bette. But no more."

"Oh, Walter, that's wonderful. I'm so proud—"

"Got to go. I've got some dry cleaning to pick up. Be home soon."

Walter grinned. Obedience had its rewards.

Walter left the office to go to his car with a spring in his step—until he saw a homeless person huddled against a building. He slowed his pace, his mind racing.

Obey.

Before he could talk himself out of it, he pulled out his wallet. He was shocked to find he only had eleven dollars.

This hardly seems like anything. If only I hadn't spent nine dollars on that huge lunch.

Obey.

Walter pulled out the bills and handed them to the man. "Here. I know it isn't much but—"

The man held Walter's eyes. "Bless you."

Walter dipped his head and hurried away. The vigor of his

step returned. He grinned like a fool.

An obedient fool.

Walter stood at the counter at the dry cleaners. "Can I write you a check?" When he'd given his last bills to the homeless man, he'd forgotten he still had to pay for dry cleaning.

"No problem." The clerk held the hangers while Walter paid. As she handed the bag to Walter, she removed an envelope that was taped to it. "I almost forgot. We found some money in one of the inside pockets of the man's suit. It's in here."

Walter took the envelope and ripped it open. He took out the bills.

"It's not much but—"

Walter laughed. "Bless you!" He stuffed the eleven dollars in his pocket and left, absolutely giddy.

———✽———

Del studied his plane ticket from Lincoln to Minneapolis. It left at noon tomorrow, right after mass. "Ready, set…it's a go, God. Let's do it." He picked up the phone and dialed Walter's home number.

"Prescott here. What can I do you for?"

"Walter? Can that happy voice be yours?"

"Del?"

"What's fired you up?"

Walter laughed. "Funny you should mention fire." Del listened carefully as Walter explained that the set for his show had gone up in flames. Literally.

"I know it seems weird for me not to be going crazy over this, but even though the fire was bad, good came from it. It put me in my place. It made me get my priorities straight. You know, God first, family second, job third."

Del wanted to share Walter's elation but… "But your fire is stopping *me*." He fingered the ticket. "Everything fell into place for me to come. I was so sure I was supposed to be on your show. I was really trying to obey—"

"Hey! Obey...that's my lesson." Walter laughed.

"But how do I obey if your set—"

"Don't give up so easily, priest man. We've already moved the production of *Good News* to another studio. The show will go on."

"It will?"

"A little fire will not deter the likes of Walter and Del! Right?"

"Hey, I like this new Walter. He's quite...upbeat."

"I'll have to admit upbeat is better than downtrodden. And I came cheap. Eleven dollars."

"You lost me."

"I'll tell you the whole story when you get here."

"I'm on my way."

Their God was an amazing God.

—⁓—

Rolf swung his briefcase as he walked out of his office. He paused at the elevator, but since it was floors away, he detoured to the stairs. He took the steps with a rhythm matching the song he hummed, the taps echoing in the vertical chamber. He felt upbeat in spite of the fire. A charred building could be rebuilt, but a charred soul...

Walter was on the right track, and it felt good that he'd been able to help. Rolf knew that everyone could use a push now and then to remind them to—

The lights dimmed like a cloud shrouding the sun. Rolf stopped. His skin prickled. Hesitating, he looked around. No one else was in the stairwell, yet he had the distinct impression of another presence...

Lord—

He felt a sharp push on his back. His feet faltered, and then he was falling. He felt pain.

Then he felt nothing at all.

It just wasn't fair.

Harriet Lane put her full weight against the push bar of the door. It clanged open and the sound echoed in the stairwell.

Why should she have to share her set with *Good News?* Work on Saturday? Bow down to the can-do-no-wrong Rolf Wingow? She was a better producer than he was. If only the bosses would open their eyes.

Harriet turned the corner on a landing and stopped. Rolf lay at the bottom of the stairs, unmoving.

Take that, you meddling do-gooder. That's what you get for interfering with my work. Maybe now you'll leave—

She shook the thought away, pulled out her cell phone, and called 911.

Yet she couldn't help but smile…maybe life was fair after all.

—◦◦◦—

Walter paused in the doorway of the hospital room. His eyes were drawn to Rolf's bed. Standing beside the bed was Rolf's wife, Marion. "How is he?"

Marion did not look up, but continued to stroke her husband's hand. "He's in a coma."

Walter stumbled toward the bed. "Coma? As in not-wake-up, not-hear-us coma?"

She looked at Walter for the first time. Her reddened eyes blazed. "He *will* wake up."

"Of course he will…I'm sorry…I didn't mean…"

Marion reached across the bed and touched Walter's arm. "I know. I'm just so thankful Harriet found—"

"Harriet Lane found him?"

While Marion explained what had happened, Walter fumed. If only he'd been the one to find Rolf. But as he noticed

Rolf's bandaged head and bruised face, he set the selfish thought aside. As much as he disliked Harriet, apparently she was good for something.

CHAPTER EIGHT

For where your treasure is, there your heart will be also.

MATTHEW 6:21

KATHY LAY IN BED, unable to get back to sleep. The pressure was on to create. Del needed a painting, and he needed it now.

She looked at the bedside clock for the forth time: 4:33. She could sleep for two more hours.

She could, but she couldn't.

She slipped out of bed, put on a robe and socks, then tiptoed downstairs to her studio. Positioning her stool in the middle of the room, she studied the paintings leaning against the wall, the ones she and Sandra had determined weren't good enough for the showing. Maybe she could give Del one of them...

That didn't feel right.

Maybe she should donate one of the paintings Sandra still had hanging in her gallery? Those were already finished; it would certainly save time.

She shook the thought away. Those paintings were her best work. They earned good money. Kathy didn't want to waste one of those by *giving* it away.

The bottom line was, she needed inspiration. Now.

Maybe if she just began, the inspiration would follow? Sure, the inspiration usually had to come first. It was the fuel for her work, and without it, she was like an out-of-gas car pulled to the side of the road, waiting for someone to come along to fill her up.

She needed to feel something before she could paint something. Feel good...

Speaking of which…Kathy glanced at the closet. *No, don't be dumb. You need to work. You need to produce. You don't have time to—*

Without realizing she'd made the decision to move, Kathy found herself in front of the walk-in closet. She opened the door, flipped on the light, and stepped inside her personal domain. No admittance. Stay out! The kids had been warned that this closet was off limits. And she didn't need to worry about Roy stumbling across her stash. He didn't know what was in half the closets in their house. If he needed something he simply asked her where it was. No, this was her stuff. *Mine.*

To her right were her painting supplies and boxes of the kids' old toys and clothes. Nothing to rouse any suspicion. But behind the door…

Kathy went deeper inside and shut the door enough to look at her treasures. Shelves full of boxes. Boxes of things.

She bypassed the food processor, the electric can opener, and the Fry Daddy. She disregarded the complete works of Shakespeare and Jane Austen. She ignored the white towels with the embroidered satin edging and the matching sheet set. Her hands brushed past the boxes of Bavarian mints and truffles until her fingers found their quarry. A gold box. The big, fancy, gold box.

She placed it on the floor and knelt in front of it, running her hand over its smooth goldness. Smiling, she opened the lid.

It was filled with items wrapped in white tissue printed with gold stars. Fancy stores did that. Fancy stores knew how to make her feel special. She carefully unwrapped the first item and held it up to the light. It was a silver creamer with intricately detailed feet. The inside was brushed gold. She set it aside and chose the next bundle. A sugar bowl with a lid. The coffee pot was next, its handle a sleek *S* ending in a burst of rosettes. At the bottom of the box was a tray, etched with curlicues. Kathy held it up, seeing her form in the reflection.

Beautiful things. Special things. Things she'd never seen growing up.

She placed the tray on the floor and carefully set each piece on top, polishing away her fingerprints with the edge of her robe.

There. All done. A silver coffee service fit for a—

"Mom? Are you in there?"

Kathy whipped toward Ryan's voice. She lunged for the door, but it was too late. He walked in.

His eyes found the silver, then moved over the shelves behind the door, bottom to top to bottom again. Kathy had the urge to leap in front of them, spreading her robe in an attempt to hide her booty.

His eyes finished their inventory and found hers. "What's all this stuff?"

It's mine! You can't have it!

She wrapped the creamer in tissue, trying to act nonchalant. "Just some things I've bought."

"For who?"

"Whom."

"Whom."

Her English lesson was a ploy to buy time. Time to think of a good excuse. "They were on sale." Pitiful.

Ryan pointed to the food processor. "Don't we have one of those?"

But this one is new and improved. It has extra attachments and—

He touched a box of hand-dipped chocolates. "Now I know why you don't want us in here. If Lisa saw all this candy…"

She stood and shooed him out. "I don't want you in here because there may be presents for you in here. Christmas is just a few months away, you know. What are you doing up so early anyway?"

"I heard—"

She nudged him up the stairs, following behind to make

121

sure he went. "You get to bed. You have school in a few hours."

"But—"

"No buts."

Kathy tucked him in and kissed his forehead. Then she returned to the basement and put away her treasures. She closed the door carefully, trying not to think about the fact that among all the boxes, all the beautiful things, there wasn't a Christmas present in the lot. Nothing for Ryan. Nothing for anyone. Except Kathy.

She turned the light out in her studio and went upstairs. Any hope for inspiration was gone.

CHAPTER NINE

No temptation has seized you except what is common to man. And God is faithful; he will not let you be tempted beyond what you can bear. But when you are tempted, he will also provide a way out so that you can stand up under it.

1 CORINTHIANS 10:13

THE TEACHERS GATHERED IN THE LOBBY. They'd spent the day in meetings, and they were ready for some fun.

Sam's lip lifted in a sneer. They were pitiful. Men and women milling around, laughing and talking like kids free from their parents' control. Most likely some of them would go downtown to shop for souvenirs, others would take in a movie, while others would hang around the hotel—and listen to Lila sing.

In the midst of it all, Sam watched Jack. Every so often, their eyes would meet and both would look away. Jack stood on the fringe of the crowd, his hands in his pockets. Sam had seen his type before: the loner who wasn't interested in laughing too loud or gathering cronies to go out. He'd probably be content to stroll the streets of Estes alone.

But Sam couldn't allow that. He couldn't let Jack run into Natalie. She was working at Bill and Tiny's pizza tonight, so Sam had to keep Jack at the hotel.

Stepping out from behind the desk, he approached the group. "You looking for some good entertainment?"

He got a flurry of affirmative replies.

"We've got a great singer. Li-la." He gave her name an extra stroke.

One of the men grinned. "You make her sound sexy. Is she?"

Sam glanced at Jack, hoping the question wouldn't scare him away. "She's a good singer. You'd like her, Jack."

There were a few catcalls and slaps on Jack's back. Then the teachers drew Jack into Lila's lair.

Good. Now Sam could go back to work.

Jack sipped his tonic water and tried to concentrate on Lila's music. She *was* a good singer, but he grew weary of all the suggestive comments his tablemates shared behind their hands.

He looked at his watch. Wasn't an hour enough time to have himself deemed one of the gang? Couldn't he slip up to his room now?

He saw Lila look toward the doorway to the lounge, and suddenly her song was sung in one direction. He turned to see the recipient of such special attention.

Sam.

She's singing to me!

Sam's stomach danced. He lifted a hand, acknowledging Lila's attention, then glanced at Jack. The jerk's eyes were full of questions—and accusations.

He thinks there's something going on between me and—

Sam was appalled when Lila walked off the stage toward him. He'd seen her do the same in other shows, draping an arm around the neck of some unsuspecting man, sitting on his lap, making him think thoughts...

But now, she came toward him.

No! Not now. Don't choose me with him *watching!*

Lila kept coming. The only way Sam would be able to avoid her was to run from the room. And he couldn't do that. He had his pride.

She slithered to his side, singing her sultry song. She ran a hand up his chest, eliciting cheers from the audience. Her fingers found the back of his neck, and she paused in the song long enough to kiss him on the lips.

For a brief moment, Sam allowed himself to enjoy the kiss. If Jack hadn't been in the room, he might have kissed her back.

She released him, and he gasped for air. Her smile said he'd given her the reaction she'd wanted. She locked her eyes to his and backed away, finishing her song.

Sam took advantage of the applause and escaped to the safety of the front desk.

Sam didn't feel like counting the receipts anymore. He leaned his head against his hand, closed his eyes, and thought about Lila. He imagined her sitting next to him, leaning close enough so he could see the color of her eyes and smell the musk of her perfume. She'd hold out one red-painted nail and draw curlicues on his arm, sending undeniable signals up and down his body. Her words would make his insides melt. When a stray curl would fall into her eyes, he would brush it away, finally touching her velvety skin—

"Excuse me?"

Sam opened his eyes; Jack stood before him.

"Hi."

Sam grabbed a pen and looked down at his papers. "How did you like Lila?"

"I think the question might be, how did *you* like Lila?"

Sam felt himself redden. He risked a glance. "It didn't mean anything. We're coworkers."

Jack nodded, but Sam could see he was unconvinced. And why shouldn't he be? *Sam* was unconvinced.

He tossed the pen aside. "Did you need something?"

"We have some free time tomorrow morning. Could you recommend a hike? I'd like to get away. Have some time to myself."

Fine with me.

Sam found a map of the most popular trailheads. "Mill Lake is a good one." And steep enough to give Jack's city legs a workout they wouldn't soon forget.

Jack took the map. "Thanks. I'll try it."

The smell of musk was unmistakable.

Sam looked up. Lila stood at the desk. She put on her coat and flipped her hair from under the collar. "Going home soon?"

He glanced at the clock. It was five minutes to one in the morning. He looked at Lou, the other desk clerk. Lou looked at Sam, then Lila, then Sam again. Then he grinned. "Go on. I won't tell."

Lila ran a hand along the top of the counter. "Seems you're free."

"Seems so." Sam got his coat from the back office and slid his arms into it so fast they got tangled.

"Eager, are we?" Lila led the way to the front door.

He scrambled to get the door for her. When her coat brushed against his, he panicked. What was he doing? Lila was ten years older. He was out of his league. And what about Natalie?

"Walk me to my car?"

Sam was flooded with relief. She just wanted an escort. That was it. No big deal. He could do—

Sam sucked in a breath when she slipped her hand around his elbow. A wisp of her hair blew against his shoulder.

"How did you like my song tonight?"

"It was fine. You're a good sing—"

She stopped beside a dark car and turned to face him. "No, Sam. How did you *like* it?"

His cheeks grew hot and he was glad she couldn't see his blush in the dark. "You embarrassed me."

"Which is still not an answer to my question." She ran a finger along the open zipper of his jacket. "If no one else had been around, how would you have liked…my attention?"

"I—"

She looked to the left, and then to the right. "Like now. When no one's around. How do you like my attention?" Her hand crept behind his neck, just as it had done during the song. He knew what came next.

He did nothing to stop it.

—◦◦◦—

Jack opened his eyes, unsure what had awakened him. He turned over and looked at the clock: one in the morning.

Go back to sleep. It's nothing.

Jack tried to accept the advice, but found his thoughts turning to his favorite subject of happiness and heartache: Natalie. His yearning for sleep vanished. He got out of bed and went to the window, pulling the curtain aside. The town was quiet and still. Everyone was asleep—at least everyone who possessed peaceful minds.

Shifting restlessly, his attention was drawn to some movement in the parking lot. Two people stood next to a car. A man and a woman. The man had his back to the vehicle, and the woman pushed her body against—

Jack craned closer. Was that who he thought it was? He shook his head no, but his eyes told him yes.

Lila and Sam.

He let the curtain fall into place and stared into his darkened room. Moving to turn on the bedside light, he sat down. With a jerk, he pulled the telephone into his lap. He had to call Natalie and tell her she was engaged to a cretin; tell her he was in town and he had come to take her away with him. They could start a new life together. She could write and he would teach, and he would never treat her badly, like Sam—

Jack noticed the clock for a second time. He couldn't call. It was one in the morning. Natalie didn't even know he was in

127

town. And maybe she was aware of Sam's dalliances and was determined to live with them.

He returned the phone to its place, then flicked off the light. But sleep was elusive as he battled the fact that Natalie had received two proposals of marriage in her life—and as much as it hurt to accept it, she had chosen someone else.

———∞———

Natalie looked at her watch. She looked at the pizza on her kitchen table. "Oh, Sam. It's one-fifteen…where are you?"

They had a standing date to share a pizza every night when they both worked late. She could always count on Sam walking in at 1:05. So where could he be? Was he all right?

She went to the phone and dialed the hotel. "Hi, Lou. This is Natalie. Is Sam there?"

"Uh…no, uh…he left about twenty minutes ago."

"That's odd, he was supposed to come over—"

"He said he was really tired. Maybe he just went home."

Natalie hung up and dialed Sam's apartment. There was no answer.

She grabbed her coat and car keys.

The parking lot of the Bishop Hotel was dark and still. Natalie cruised down the first row, searching for Sam's truck. She'd already looked at his apartment. He had to be one place or the other…

There it was, at the far end of the lot where employees were instructed to park. She shut off her engine and got out. She went to the truck and checked the doors. Locked. She peered inside. Everything looked normal. She scanned the parking lot. There was no movement anywhere. Except—

Natalie saw something move in a car at the other end of the row. She took a step toward it, then stopped as she realized two people were making out in the front seat. She was ready to turn away when the couple stopped kissing. The woman was the singer, Lila.

She's probably seduced one of the musicians from her band—

Natalie looked closer.

She blinked. She gasped.

And then she ran to her car and backed out of the parking lot.

Natalie slammed the door of her apartment and drilled her coat and keys into the couch. Once in the kitchen, she snatched the pizza from the table and heaved it across the room. Pepperonis spotted a cupboard door like polka dots. Congealed cheese lost its grip. Tomato sauce oozed downward. Natalie melted and beat her fists against the floor.

She cried until sleep took her.

Natalie felt warmth on her face. She opened her eyes and saw a blob of red pooled nearby.

Blood?

She jerked to sitting and was relieved to identify the red as pizza sauce. But her relief was short-lived as she remembered why the pizza decorated her cupboard and floor.

Sam was unfaithful.

Standing, she let her muscles adjust. The sun shining in the kitchen window cut a swath across the floor where she had lain. She reached for a towel, then stopped herself. No. This wasn't her mess. It was Sam's. He'd probably come over this morning, making some lame excuse about why he'd missed their date. Well, she wouldn't be present to hear his lies. The pizza would speak for her.

That and a note.

Natalie took a notepad and began writing. *You selfish, two-timing pig! You want Lila? You can have her! I've gone off to be by myself—which means I'll have far better company than you.*

She hesitated, then crumpled the note and tossed it on top of the pizza.

Let him worry. It would serve him right.

CHAPTER TEN

＊＊＊

A friend loves at all times, and a brother is born for adversity.

PROVERBS 17:17

HE HAD TO SEE HER.

Ben Cranois rubbed a hand over his eyes. Why he *needed* to see Julia—a woman he hated with all his being—was beyond him. But he did. He clenched a fist, feeling like a child mesmerized by a candle flame, warned away but still reaching out to place his hand over the flickering fire.

Get too close and you'll get burned.

Unfortunately, the only way he could see her today, Sunday, was to follow her to church. So here he was.

Ben approached warily, like the beanstalk boy venturing close to the giant's castle. The church even looked like a castle, like some fortress for God, reaching up into heaven. And inside? Would he feel the vibration of God's footsteps? Would he hear a booming, "Fi, fie, foe, fum"?

He had to risk it. He had to see his enemy. His friend.

Ben slipped into the crowd that lined the steps of the church. Between shoulders and heads, he saw the president's limousine pull up and watched as Edward emerged and put a hand to Julia's back.

Following the crowd into the church, he hesitated at the threshold. But the crowd pushed him through, and an embarrassed relief swept over him that he had not been vaporized as he crossed into enemy territory.

While the others moved toward the front, Ben held back and found a place in the last pew, on the aisle where he could watch. And wait.

For what, he wasn't sure.

Hamm would freak if he knew where Ben was. Even the mention of churches turned Mr. Hush Puppy into a pit bull. Ben felt a surge of courage.

What was Hamm so afraid of? After all, forgiveness was a big thing with Julia's God. He was so eager to gain new souls that He would probably order up an angel's chorus just because Ben was sitting in a pew. Too bad Ben didn't intend to be won over.

No, what he wanted was to be on the winning side, and no matter what these Christians wanted to think, believing in a loving God who cared about a person like himself—a God who wanted to offer *him* eternal life—was preposterous. Who wanted to live forever, anyway? It was just another example of the blind leading the blind through the darkness of lies.

The congregation stood, taking Ben with it. A woman in the pew next to him extended the hymnbook in his direction. Ben wanted to shake his head no, but he found his hand taking his half of the hymnal.

But no way would he sing. No way.

The song began. The woman sang in a rich alto voice. "'Christian, dost thou see them on the holy ground? How the powers of darkness rage thy steps around?'"

Darkness? They're the ones in darkness.

"'Christian, dost thou feel them, how they work within, striving, tempting, luring, goading into sin?'"

A shiver started in Ben's midsection and spread to his torso. *Tempting, luring...* It was like they were talking about the urging that grabbed his innards and made him think all kinds of—

He shook the thought away. *No. They're talking about evil. And the energy is not evil. I'm not evil. I'm not luring anybody. I just want them to see the truth.*

"'Christian answer boldly, "While I breathe, I pray!" Peace shall follow battle, night shall end in day.'"

Battle? Christians weren't bold. Christians didn't fight. They were wimps. Patsies. Robotic yes-men. And yet…

Ben looked over his shoulder at the door. Escape. *I should leave now before I begin to doubt—*

"'Well I know thy trouble, O My servant true, thou art very weary—I was weary too…'"

Weary? Sometimes he was so tired. If it weren't for the energy spurring him on, he'd lay down and—

The woman glanced at Ben, her forehead furrowed. She sang the last line to his face: "'And the end of sorrow, shall be near My throne.'"

Ben's eyes filled with sudden tears. *End of sorrow?* He shook his head violently. He couldn't let these do-gooders get to him. They were wrong; their God would lose the battle. Their God didn't care about his weariness. Their Jesus was a weak, ineffectual man who couldn't stand up for Himself. Ben could handle himself. Ben could stand up for Ben.

With an inner explosion, a thought formed and brought with it a stab of pain. *Curse Jesus!*

Ben started when he felt a tug on his suit coat. The woman was seated. Everyone was seated. The hymn was over. He sank into the pew, his mind rattling like a box containing shards of glass. The awful violence of his last thought had been broken. The pain was broken. For the moment…

The pastor moved to the pulpit. He adjusted his reading glasses and spoke, "From 1 Corinthians, we read, 'Therefore I tell you that no one who is speaking by the Spirit of God says, "Jesus be cursed," and no one can say, "Jesus is Lord," except by the Holy Spirit.'"

Ben couldn't swallow.

"From 1 Timothy, 'The Spirit clearly says that in later times some will abandon the faith and follow deceiving spirits and things taught by demons.'"

A softer voice echoed in his mind. *You're being deceived.*

Ben shook his head. The shards of his old thoughts rattled against this new one.

The energy at work in you does not come from good. It comes from—

Ben pursed his lips against letting thought form into a word, but...

Evil.

The pastor closed the Bible, removed his glasses, and looked over the heads of the crowd. The words leapfrogged the rest of the congregation and pierced Ben's heart. "'Repent and be baptized, every one of you, in the name of Jesus Christ for the forgiveness of your sins. And you will receive the gift of the Holy Spirit.'"

"Amen." The word rang out around him.

Ben blinked. The unified power of the word resonated in his chest. *They act as if it's so simple.*

"'Do not put out the Spirit's fire,' for the Holy Spirit is alive in all believers of the risen Christ. He is with you always, but He can be quenched like a fire extinguished with water."

I'm living by another kind of fire...

"When a mind is cluttered and full of complaints, the Holy Spirit will become quiet until we ask for His help. If you don't hear the Holy Spirit or feel His presence, you are under your own control instead of His. His fire has been put out, or He is grieved because you've done something to sadden Him."

He's talking like this Spirit is real.

"Would you pour milk in a dirty glass for your child?"

The woman next to Ben joined others in answering, "No!" She looked at Ben and smiled.

He tightened his jaw. *Don't smile at me, lady. I'm not one of your kind.*

"Of course not. You'd clean the glass first. Jesus Christ cleansed our bodies and souls by dying for us. Then He filled them with the Holy Spirit. Do you believe Jesus is the Son of God?"

"Yes!"

Ben's heart flipped. This was too much. He had to leave.

Soon they'd be shouting "Hallelujah" and "Praise the Lord." He wouldn't be able to bear it. Besides, if he stayed much longer, he would suffer for his weakness. *I shouldn't have come...*

Ben started to stand, but the woman took his hand and held it firmly. He tried to pull away. She held tighter. He stared down at her. Her eyes vibrated with concern.

"Let me go!"

She held on. "Christ died for you, Ben."

How did she know my name?

"He's just waiting for you to say yes to Him. Then the Holy Spirit will come alive within you and banish the energy that's confusing you. You'll be able to do amazing—"

"No!"

The pastor stopped talking. All eyes turned toward Ben, and his breath left him.

What have I done?

He saw Julia and Edward stand in their front pew. *I can't let them see me!* Ben yanked his hand away and ran out of the church. Away from God.

Ben ducked around to the rear of the church building. He didn't want to go back inside, but for some odd reason he yearned—no, he needed—to remain within the confines of the church's boundaries.

He found a back entrance next to a dumpster. A small alcove crowned three steps, and he slipped into it, letting the wall guide him to the ground. No one would find him here. No one would follow him. He was safe. From everything.

He pulled his knees toward his chest and felt the cold of the concrete stoop through his pants. He tugged his suit coat over his bottom, relieved at the instant insulation. He should have worn his overcoat. But who knew he was going to spend any time outdoors?

His car was in the parking lot across the street, and he

thought longingly of its warmth. But it seemed too far away, like an objective across a minefield. He couldn't risk leaving the confines of this hiding place.

This holy place.

He caught the distant strains of the organ and heard voices join voices. He couldn't make out the words but he knew the gist of the song. Glory to God, our Father. The Son, Jesus. *Holy, holy, holy, Lord God Almighty…*

He dug the palms of his hands into his eyes, trying to push some order into the cacophony of forms and ideas. There were two forces duking it out in the center ring of his gut. The gnawing force that had made him flee the church service, and the other force that made him want to stay. Both internal. Both full of power. Both *there*.

But not the same.

Choose.

He shook his head. *The people in the church are wrong. I can't bow to a being who won't let me be me. I can't give in to Julia's God and this Holy Spirit the pastor spoke about. I can't let Him take over, and force me—*

I will not force you. But you must choose.

Ben held his breath, stunned by the clarity of the inner words that seemed to caress him from the inside out. His hands had no strength and he let them drop to his sides. He lifted his face and risked a breath. A sense of peace touched his soul. *I can choose. I don't have to—*

Pain grabbed his stomach and raked across his organs with claws that ripped and tore. His arms instinctively wrapped around his midsection, trying to hug it away; urge it to withdraw. *Stop! Stop it!*

The pain gnawed with fresh intensity. Ben tipped onto his side, a man in a fetal curl, wanting only to die.

The other voice sounded and held no pretense of entreaty or gentle supplication. *You're mine! I'm not done with you yet.*

Ben shivered. He was suddenly consumed with the desire

to do anything to make that voice go away. Give in to it; let it consume him. No more confusion. No more decisions…

That's it, just let go…

And then the pain left. Ben sucked in a breath as he experienced a moment of release that was shocking in its absence from the suffering. But before he could wallow in it, the pain returned as if it had only paused to take a breath. Yet in that brief instant—that brief moment of hope—he decided to fight back.

As the pain swelled with new determination, Ben held up a mental hand, keeping the worst of it at bay. *I have to think.* The part of his mind that was free of the pain frantically tried to find the logic in his situation. *Maybe if I left this place. Maybe if I got away from the battleground…*

He stumbled to his feet and staggered down the steps, heading toward the street. As his feet hit the pavement, the pain eased its grip. *Yes, yes…* He straightened and told his legs to run. At his car, he fell inside. The pain throbbed but he forced a breath. As he fumbled for the keys, one thought ran a tickertape across his mind: *Get away, get away, get away…*

He put the car in reverse and shot out of the slot. When his bumper hit metal, he didn't stop. He put the car in drive and squealed away, entering the street without a look to the right or left. He sped through a yellow light, not knowing where he was going, only caring that it was *away.*

With each block the pain relaxed. He sat upright and tested his lungs. He eased his shoulders into the back of the seat and let his hands loosen their grip on the steering wheel. The memory of the pain faded as quickly as hot breath on a cold day.

He lifted his chin and glanced at himself in the rearview mirror. He wiped the sweat from his brow. What had all that been about? He'd overreacted.

It was nothing. Nothing at all.

Julia sat at the luncheon table with the head honchos of the pastor's convention. Another event, another variation of chicken... The waiter in his white coat began to serve the salad and Julia put her hands in her lap to make it easy for him.

"Hello, Gov."

Julia blinked at the familiar greeting. Only one person in the entire world called her that. She turned toward the male voice. It belonged to the waiter. It belonged to—

"Arthur Graham!" She pushed her chair back, stood, and hugged him, making him balance a salad precariously to his side. "What a wonderful surprise! When did you get into town? How are—"

He raised a hand, looking at the other diners. "Whoa, Gov. You're talking too fast."

Julia put a hand to her chest. "Me? Talk fast? Surely you jest." Arthur was blushing, and Julia saw him looking around the room. Obviously he was not comfortable being in the limelight. She sat down. "I don't want to cost you your job, Arthur. After the luncheon, I want to talk to you. All right?"

"You betcha."

Arthur's smile told Julia he was very aware that he had just repeated her pet phrase. It was good to see him.

They sat in the lobby of the hotel. Arthur looked wonderful. Before Julia had been elected, she and Edward had visited him in prison while he was doing time for robbing the Pump 'n Eat in Haven and car theft and.... But she hadn't seen him since—though she continued to write to him. Arthur had told her he was the only inmate who was on friendly terms with his victim.

"When did you get out?"

"A few months ago."

138

Julia pointed to the cross pendant that peeked out from his collar. "Is that faith or fashion?"

He smiled. "Are you questioning whether my conversion à la Julia stuck?"

"Oh, ye of sticky faith?"

"You betcha. Believe it or not, God and I *are* on speaking terms."

Julia squeezed his hand. "So…what are you doing here?"

"Where? In Washington? Or serving you lunch?"

"Both."

"There's a single answer. I want a job. I want to work for you."

Julia laughed. "If having guts earns points on a résumé…"

Arthur shrugged and traced a finger along the edge of his waiter's jacket. "Prison's been my home for four years. Once I got out, I tried going to my real home, but discovered that all the home ties I had were in knots. I had to start over. I figured I could pick a town at random or I could seek out the one person who ever believed in me."

"Even if she is president of the United States?"

"You're still Julia."

"Yes, I am."

"I bet you talk to prime ministers the same way you talk to me."

She shrugged. "Don't see why not."

"You talked my ear off when you were my hostage in Haven. I was just the one with the gun. You were the one in control."

She remembered her arguments with Edward. "God was in control, Arthur. As for my own controlling nature? I'm working on that."

"Julia Carson, working on giving up control?"

"Not necessarily to man." She pointed upward. "I do know my place—most of the time."

"You know more than most people."

"Why, thank you, Arthur." She was surprised how much his compliment meant to her.

"I've wanted to see you, but I didn't know how to go about it. When I heard on the news that you were going to be at this luncheon…and then I got assigned to serve…I figured it was God giving me the green light."

"I taught you well."

"*God* taught me well."

Julia felt herself redden. Why did she move so easily from right thinking to wrong?

Arthur tilted his head and eyed her through his blond lashes. "Speaking of green lights…how about my offer? Could I work for you?"

Yes. It was perfect. Edward kept telling her she needed to slow down or get organized or…here was her answer. "Yes, Arthur. You can be my personal…something or other."

"Sounds like a challenge. I'll take it."

Art sat on the bus, knowing that his grin made him stick out among the grim-looking people around him. They stared at their newspapers or into the air as if all life had to offer was boring or tiring. He wanted to stand up and make an announcement: *Excuse me? I just got a job as the personal assistant of the president of the United States and I feel great!* They'd probably throw him off the bus. No, most likely they would look up, blink at the interruption, then slink back into their humdrum lives.

He tried to push the grin away. It popped back into place.

It was staggering. Him, working for Julia Carson. The president of the United States.

Although he was good at pretending otherwise, he *was* intimidated by her office. Still, he felt more secure now that she was involved in his life again. He'd never met anyone like her. Feisty, caring, and fearless, she deserved the best—and that's what he vowed to give her. And now that she'd given him a job—a new start—he'd pay her back with his loyalty. His *lifetime* loyalty...for however long that would be.

Art entered the tiny entryway. Two dented mailboxes hugged the wall and a worn stairway greeted him front and center. He climbed the stairs to his apartment, which sat above a pawn shop.

It felt wonderful to put a key in a lock to *his* place. After high school he'd crashed at friends' apartments and had even lived with a girlfriend once, but for the past four years his residence had been the opposite of independent living: the Nebraska State Penitentiary.

Being tried and convicted of armed robbery, car theft, and assault—but *not* kidnapping, thanks to Julia's refusal to press charges—was shocking. In more ways than one. Beyond not liking to face the consequences of his actions, Art kept expecting the legal process to be interrupted by some miracle. After all, hadn't Julia helped him accept Jesus Christ as his Savior? From that moment on, he'd figured everything would be rosy and bright. Bottom line, if Jesus died for his sins, wasn't the price paid? So why did he have to go to jail?

Now Art could laugh at his ignorance—even marvel at the fact that the word *penitentiary* came from the word *penitent*. But during the first few months of being locked up, he'd been one bitter kid. What good did it do to believe in a God who forgave his sins if the world made him pay for those sins?

Only after getting into the Bible Julia sent him did Art see how even God's favorites had been forced to accept the consequences of their actions. Like that King David, a man after God's own heart. But when David committed adultery with Bathsheba—another man's wife—and then had her husband killed so David could marry her, he'd had to pay up. No matter how sorry he was. And because of David's sins, their baby died.

Yet God *did* forgive, and He brought good out of the bad by giving them another son, Solomon, who would become the richest and wisest man ever to live.

That second-chance philosophy kept Art going. Maybe if he focused on the right things, God would bring some good out of *his* mistakes. Actually, God already had. Art knew with his entire being that if he had not been such a nasty kid with a bent for breaking the law, he would not have met Julia Carson...and through her, come to know the Lord. Pretty cool how God worked things out.

Art flipped on the light of his apartment and looked around. Home sweet home...complete with frayed upholstery, stained walls, and plumbing that knocked and groaned. Right now, though, silence engulfed him. The knowledge that there would be no noise unless he made it was heady stuff. The last time he'd been on his own, he'd blown it. It wouldn't happen again.

The smells of the last tenant hit his nose like a right hook: bacon grease, cigarette smoke, and the faint smell of pets long gone. The blinds were pulled off-kilter and he straightened them, adjusting the light and his view of the printing shop across the street. The day was prematurely cold, and Art wrote his name in the condensation on the window pane. He smiled at his Art-work. The apartment properly reclaimed, Art changed clothes and headed out to buy groceries.

Buying groceries—eating what he wanted to eat when he wanted to eat it—what a concept. Maybe after he got his first paycheck from Julia he would be able to afford real meat.

After getting groceries at the corner store, Art juggled the sacks, trying to open the door of the apartment entryway. At that same moment a man burst out of the door, bumping into him. The sack fell to the ground. "Hey!"

"Sorry."

The man stopped to help, and Art studied him. Friend or foe? In this neighborhood, you never knew. The man was clean cut, with a neatly trimmed beard. He smiled and Art made a choice. Friend. "Thanks."

The guy nodded. "I haven't seen you around here before."

Art got to his feet. "Moved upstairs last week."

"I live upstairs too." He pointed to the second floor. "The back apartment is mine. We must be neighbors. I thought someone had moved in."

"Then thanks, neighbor." Art got a hand free and stuck it out for the man to shake. "The name's Art Graham."

The man shook his hand. "Nice to meet you, Art. I'm Ben Cranois." Ben held a can of chili and a container of cherry yogurt a moment longer than necessary as if studying them, using them to judge Art's character.

Apparently Art passed inspection. Ben smiled. "You eaten dinner yet?" He displayed the chili. "Or are you dining in tonight?"

"I don't dine, I eat." Art gave an exaggerated sigh. "But I might be lured away from such gourmet delights as mac and cheese, tuna, and soup." He laughed. "What did you have in mind?"

Ben pointed down the street. "There's a diner on the corner. Great pork tenderloins and fries."

"Now *that's* dining." Art tilted a head toward his apartment. "Let me drop these off upstairs."

It was nice to have a friend.

They got a booth by the window and ordered. Ben wiped his place with a napkin. "So, Art…you got a job?"

Art beamed, feeling like he'd won the lottery. "I just got the job of the century."

Ben looked skeptical, probably remembering their ragged apartments. "Which century?"

Art leaned on the table, knowing that he was grinning like an idiot. He was on the verge of saying, "*I am the president's personal assistant"* when he stopped himself.

Or rather, something inside stopped him. *No! Don't tell him!*

Frowning, Art studied his new friend. Why shouldn't he tell? It was something to be proud of. Things were working out just as he'd planned.

"Art? You going to answer my question? Or is it some huge secret?"

Art laughed nervously. "I'm…I'm a gofer for an executive across town."

"An errand boy."

Art shrugged, feeling an inner calm return. For whatever reason, it had been the right decision *not* to tell Ben his real position.

Ben raised a hand. "Gofer. Been there, done that. It's a thankless job."

"Oh, I don't know…"

Ben sat back while the waitress brought their drinks. Then he leaned over his cup of coffee, fingering the saucer. "Can you keep a secret?"

He's put his trust in me awfully fast. "Sure."

"I used to work for the president."

Art's stomach tightened. "Which president?"

"Do we have more than one? Actually, I don't think the world could take more than one Julia Carson."

At the disgust in Ben's voice, Art fell back against the cushion of the booth. The lack of air in his chest felt like he'd been punched. He searched his memory. *Ben Cranois…* He wasn't familiar with the name. But he *had* been out of commission for four years.

Ben waved a hand. "It's a long story—"

"I've got time."

Ben moved his coffee out of the way, as though his words needed all the space he could give them. "I've known Julia for years. I was her campaign manager when she ran for governor of Minnesota. And I started out as her manager during her presidential campaign."

"But you aren't still working for her?"

"No way. I got out of there halfway through the campaign. She wouldn't listen to me. She talked about God in her speeches. She told the world what that stupid pin stood for—and then all those other pins started to appear." He shook his head. "It was too much. She was poisoning the country with her God ideas."

Art put a hand to his neckline, then relaxed. His cross was safely hidden beneath his turtleneck. "But the country elected her."

"Just because they were duped doesn't mean I fell for it."

"Some of what she says seems pretty logical."

"Excuse me?"

Art paused, considering. He couldn't show his loyalty. If he were reading Ben right, the man hated Julia. How could anyone hate her? She was the most honest, giving, forthright woman Art had ever known. Clearly, though, Ben was waiting for a retraction. Art sipped his Coke. "Maybe I'm wrong. You seem to know a lot about her."

"You bet I do."

Art settled back. As much as he would detest listening to it, he had a strong desire to hear Ben's views. For Julia's sake.

It was worse than he thought. Ben wasn't just opinionated, he was obsessed. And this organization—this TAI—was scary stuff.

Art had never considered himself an actor, yet in the past hour he'd had to do the acting job of his life. He'd had to set aside the man he had become and dig up the man he used to be—the man who could hate and scheme and think of himself first. *That* Art Graham could be of use to Ben Cranois. For as their conversation had progressed, Art had realized he needed to ease himself into this TAI organization.

Go undercover.

Hamm Spurgeon seemed to be the key. Though Ben made him sound like a weakling, the man's position as head of TAI gave him power. Art had to meet him.

Art ate his last french fry and listened as Ben went on and on about the potential of the individual. He reminded Art of his last cell mate—Chuckie Walters could talk the paint off the wall and slap on a new coat of whitewashed bull in its place. Art shoved his plate aside. "I like what I'm hearing. I'd like to join your group."

Ben caught a breath and blinked. "Wow. Yeah. That would be great."

"When can I meet Hamm?"

Ben beamed. Maybe he got brownie points by bringing in a recruit. "Soon. I'll call him. I'll set something up."

Art could hardly wait.

CHAPTER ELEVEN

———⟨∾⟩———

"I am the good shepherd; I know my sheep and my sheep know me.... I have other sheep that are not of this sheep pen. I must bring them also. They too will listen to my voice, and there shall be one flock and one shepherd."

JOHN 10:14, 16

WALTER WAS TYING HIS TIE WHEN THE PHONE RANG.

Addy beat him to it. "Hea-woe?"

"Addy, give it to me." He held out his hand as though she would actually follow directions.

She turned her back to him and said into the receiver. "Uh-huh."

"Addy!"

"Cheerios," she said to the caller.

Walter picked her up, dragging the phone with her. He took the receiver away, and she shimmied out of his arms. He heard the caller's question to Addy. "Did you have any milk on your cereal?"

Walter answered. "Actually, I like mine raw."

"Walter?"

"Who is this?"

"This is Harriet Lane."

Walter inwardly groaned. Why on earth was she calling him? Probably to pass on more negative comments about *Good News*.

"Morning, Harriet. If you care to add this to your breakfast survey, I had coffee, and toast with peanut—"

"I heard a rumor, Walter."

"Huh?"

147

"Drink another cup of coffee and wake up your brain." Harriet's tone was more impatient than usual. "I heard you plan to have a priest come on the show and push a revival meeting."

"It's not a revival meeting." *Not exactly.* "I told him he could talk about a reunion of people who've been to Haven."

"Haven? What's that?"

Walter hesitated. This wasn't Rolf he was talking to; this was Harriet, the woman who made fun of him for reading the Bible. She'd only worked at KMPS nine months. She obviously hadn't heard about his mysterious invitation.

"Walter?"

"Uh...Haven was a place where some other people and I came together and..."

"And what?"

And found God. "And decided what we were supposed to do with our lives."

"According to whom?"

There was no getting around this next answer. Walter took a deep breath. "God."

"Hold up, there." Harriet's laugh was incredulous. "God spoke to you at this Haven place?"

"Well, not exactly spoke to us, but there were these four tornadoes—"

"I don't want to know. Just skip over the God part and tell me what this has to do with some priest who—"

"Father Antonio Delatondo was in Haven with me. So was President Carson."

There was a moment of silence. "Oh...yeah. I guess I do remember reading something about this."

"Actually, there have been many Havens around the country—if not the world—and now Del is organizing a reunion of the Havenites, but he doesn't know how to get in touch with them, so I was letting him come on the program and—"

"Why doesn't God just zap him a list?"

"Very funny."

148

"Not any funnier than a bunch of people meeting in a bunch of towns—all with the same name, mind you—and getting instructions from God. Beam me up, Scotty."

"You're taking it wrong."

"I'm taking it just the way you're presenting it. I'm taking it just the way the viewing audience is going to take it. They are going to think that Walter Prescott—and KMPS—have gone over the edge."

"You're exaggerating."

"No, I'm not. And as the acting producer of *Good News*—"

His stomach clenched. "What did you say?"

"Since Rolf's accident. As a way of showing their appreciation for me finding Rolf in the stairwell, the bosses have assigned me his duties."

"Why didn't they assign *me* Rolf's duties? You don't know anything about *Good News*." *In more ways than one.*

"As I told you yesterday, there have been some stirrings about your preachy ways."

"That's a bunch of—"

"And as the acting producer, there is no way I will allow you to have a priest come on the air to advertise a religious revival meeting."

"You won't...*allow* me?"

There was a moment of silence. "I'm your boss, Walter. Until Rolf recovers, I call the shots."

Walter stood before the interim set. He missed the old one. They'd spent a lot of time making it homey and appealing. Now this replacement would have to do.

What would *not* do was Harriet Lane forbidding him from having Del on the show. He was getting really sick of people overreacting to anything that hinted of religion. If Walter wanted to interview a Buddhist monk he'd have no trouble. A Hindu mystic? Sure thing. A New Age crystal expert? Bring them on. But a Christian? Get out the garlic necklace to fend off the horrifying notion of God and all the people who believe in Him. And don't you dare say the *J* word.

If he weren't the man Haven and Eureka Springs had helped create, he could easily follow Harriet's instructions not to air Del's announcement.

Walter closed his eyes and rubbed the space between them. Oh, to be able to make the easy decisions of his pre-Haven days. He would offer a halfhearted fuss in Harriet's presence, pick Del up at the airport, and then wine and dine him before breaking the bad news that he'd have to find another way to reach the Havenites.

Actually, if he were the pre-Haven Walter, he wouldn't be having this trouble at all. He wouldn't even know Del. He wouldn't be involved in a program like *Good News*. In fact, he wouldn't be living in Minneapolis with his family—

Family. Bette and Addy. If it weren't for the changes Haven had spurred in him, Walter would never have made the commitment to Bette in the first place. He would still be fighting for ratings on the TV news in St. Louis, with a couple girlfriends on the side; living in his bachelor pad; eating frozen enchilada dinners in front of the tube.

He had to concede that the Haven experience had been good for him—*to* him. Yet once he conceded the benefits, he realized there were responsibilities attached, along with constant choices—choices that were complicated because they involved more than me, myself, and I. The decisions that often faced Walter had to be weighed in regard to right and wrong. It sounded simple. Right. Wrong. Black. White. No one ever mentioned the shades of gray that appeared not only in the right or wrong of something, but also in the consequences. Doing the right thing wasn't always easy.

Or clear.

Like now. Harriet was his boss. The right thing in regard to his job and his employer was to follow her directive and blow

Del off. On the other hand, if Walter believed that God's purposes would be enhanced by having a Haven reunion, then the right thing would be to defy Harriet and have Del on the show. The consequences?

No...Harriet wouldn't fire me.

As soon as Walter acknowledged the thought, his mind answered: *Oh yes, she would.* And then what would happen? Rolf might be able to come to bat for him, plead his case. *If Rolf ever regained consciousness—*

Walter shook his head, his thoughts reeling. He'd used a lot of his bonus to get caught up on the house payments. The rest had been used to appease—but not pay off—their many credit card debts. He couldn't afford unemployment. And it wouldn't be easy for him to find another job in television—the secular media often didn't take kindly to people of faith. Harriet was proof of that. The only reason he'd been hired by KMPS in the first place was that Rolf was a strong believer.

That and the fact that God had wanted him hired by KMPS.

Certainly God would understand if he bowed to his boss's instructions? Didn't the Bible state that people were supposed to submit to authority, even if it was in the form of Harriet Lane? And didn't one of Walter's main responsibilities to his family involve taking care of their well-being? If he jeopardized his job by implementing some do-good principle, wouldn't his family suffer? That couldn't be part of God's will.

Could it?

Walter looked at his watch. If he left now, he could stop and see Rolf before meeting Del at the airport. Coma or no coma, Walter needed to talk to him.

—∿∿—

Del loved climbing above the clouds. Although he knew God was with him on the ground; somehow, traveling heavenward gave him the feeling he had crossed an invisible boundary that separated himself from his God. He felt privileged. Who would have thought man could ever fly? Did Abraham, Moses, and Paul look to the heavens and long to be there? Or did the thought never enter their minds because it seemed impossible?

"'All things are possible with God.'"

"Excuse me?"

Del had not meant to speak aloud. He turned to his seatmate. "I was just telling myself that all things are possible with God."

The man raised an eyebrow. "And how did you respond?"

Del laughed. "I never got that far."

The man raised his newspaper. "Good thing. Your statement didn't deserve an answer."

It was Del's turn to raise an eyebrow. "You don't believe in God?"

The man shrugged. "Oh, I believe He's there all right." He waved a hand toward the window. "Somewhere. I just don't buy into the make-me-a-miracle philosophy. We make our own miracles—or messes, as the case may be."

"Ah, a pessimist."

"A realist." The man nodded toward Del's collar. "You're a priest."

"Guilty. And you are?"

"A Jew, by birth, heritage, and non-Christian beliefs."

Del was taken aback. *Why would he feel compelled to tell me that?* "You act as if I'm your enemy."

The man dug a cotton handkerchief out of his pocket, unfolded it, and blew his nose. "Face facts, Father. We're on opposite sides."

"Of what?"

The man stopped blowing and peered over the handkerchief held to his nose. "Of life. It's you against us."

"We have the same God."

"Not from what I've heard."

Del was shocked. *Lord, help me say the right words.* "My God is the God of Abraham, Jacob, and Moses."

"Your God is the God of Matthew, Mark, and those other guys."

"That's true, but—"

"Your God is the God of your...*Jesus*." The word came out like an epithet.

"He's your Jesus too."

The man shook his head adamantly. "I don't think so."

"He's *your* Messiah." Del turned toward him. "Jesus was a Jew. He is the Son of God, the Savior who was prophesized about in the Old Testament. In Isaiah, Jeremiah, and the Psalms."

"I wouldn't know. Like I said—" Some sudden turbulence jolted them. "Hey, what was that?"

Del looked out the window. The clouds were thick but looked benign. "I'm sure it's nothing. Just some crosswinds or some—"

"Attention, passengers. This is your captain. We've run into a bit of trouble with a couple of our engines. We have everything under control, but I'd like all of you to return to your seats and fasten your seat belts. I'll keep you informed as we approach the Minneapolis airport. Thank you for your cooperation."

The man leaned over Del to see out the window toward the wing. "*Two* engines?"

"How many do we have to start with?"

"I have no idea, but two down is two too many."

There was another jolt. The plane dove. People screamed.

Father Antonio Delatondo and the Jewish man prayed to their God.

CHAPTER TWELVE

---※◈※---

"Because he loves me," says the LORD, *"I will rescue him; I will protect him, for he acknowledges my name."*

PSALM 91:14

"ROLF? SHOULD I DO THE SHOW AND RISK MY JOB?"

Walter looked down at his friend and stroked the motionless hand. It was so frustrating having Rolf there…but *not* there. He needed advice. He needed Rolf to open his eyes and put him in his place with some gem of wisdom. Tell him what to do. Insult him, if that's what it took.

He patted Rolf's hand, painfully aware that wasn't going to happen. He'd have to make this decision alone. He moved toward the door. If he didn't hurry, he'd be late picking Del up.

As he passed the nurses' station, he noticed their normal calm behavior had been altered. They were bustling about, talking animatedly on the phone and with each other. Walter's reporter radar kicked in. He moved to the counter. "What's going on?"

A nurse looked up from the phone she was dialing. "Plane crash. They're bringing the victims in now. We're gearing up."

Walter went numb with a sudden knowing. He forced himself to swallow. "What plane?"

The nurse waved his question away and turned her attention to the phone. Walter raced to a payphone. He dialed information for the airline with trembling fingers. While the phone rang, he dug through his pockets looking for the note about Del's flight number.

"Yes! Hello! I'm calling to ask about the crash—"

"We don't have any information—"

"Don't give me that. This is Walter Prescott, KMPS. What flight number?"

There was a moment's hesitation. The woman answered him at the same moment he found the crumpled note. Her voice and the note matched. "Flight 280 from Lincoln, Nebraska."

Walter leaned his head against the wall of the booth and prayed.

Controlled chaos. That was the emergency room. Walter hugged a wall to stay out of the way. He marveled how the triage team made assessments in just a few moments, prioritizing need and treatment. He scanned every victim's face, looking for Del. There hadn't been any reports of fatalities, but surely with a plane crash that produced so many injured, there would be some dead. The odds were in death's favor.

He prayed that God would overpower the odds and produce a mir—

Walter spotted a priest's collar dangling off the side of a gurney. He ran toward it.

"Del?"

Del did not answer. The attendants sent Walter away and pushed the gurney through doors that denied him entrance. Walter backed up until a wall offered support.

Del was alive. Thank God.

—◊◊◊—

Pain.

Del moaned as his mind ran away from the pain. But there was no escape. It was not a dream. The pain was very, very real.

If you wake, the pain will wake. If you sleep, the pain will sleep. Don't wake up...don't wake up...don't wake—

"Del, wake up."

Del's eyelids fluttered, searching for the words.

"That's it, priest man! Come on, you can do it. Open those baby browns. Talk back at me. Yell at me. I don't care which."

Walter.

Del's mind didn't fight anymore. It made a decision. He opened his eyes.

"Atta boy, Del! Nurse! Nurse! He's awake!"

Del practiced opening and closing his eyes a few times. He would never take such a simple act for granted again.

"Water…"

"That's right, buddy. It's me, Walter."

Del closed his eyes, then opened them and tried again. "*Wa*-ter."

"Oh, *water!* Sure. Sure." Walter poured some water in a glass, stabbed a straw into it, and held it to Del's lips.

Ah…life-giving water. Del surrendered to the pillow. The edge of the pain passed, but the bulk of it lingered. A moan escaped.

"Hold on, buddy. The nurse is coming. At least she should be coming. Where *is* that nurse?" Walter moved away from him and Del let him go, amazed that he should relish a moment of quiet so soon after waking. There was something so peaceful in such a sleep. Leaving it was like being torn between two worlds: one he was familiar with, and another that was new, yet inviting.

As the seconds passed, the old world gained control. The sound that had begun with Walter's voice became crowded with other voices, the clatter of dishes, faint music, and foot-steps. Del smelled antiseptic, starch, and turkey with gravy. His eyes moved beyond the edge of his bed to take in a rumpled coat thrown over a chair, a can of Coke on the windowsill, and a crucifix on the wall.

Thank you, Lord. I'm alive!

"There he is!" Walter led a nurse into the room. "He woke up, just like I told you."

"I can see that, Mr. Prescott." The nurse came to Del's bed-side and checked his pulse. They remained silent to let her count. She nodded, smiled, then set his arm on the bed, and patted it. "Hello, Father. Ready to take on the day?"

"That depends on what you have in mind."

"How about some chicken broth, Jell-O, and a sponge bath?"

"Ooh." Walter grinned. "Can I watch?"

Del shook his head. "You're sick."

"Hey, I'm not the one in the hospital."

Del felt for his bandages. There was one above his right eye, spanning his right cheek. He had no casts, but when he moved, the pain zeroed in on his torso.

"You've got three cracked ribs, a few internal organs bruised but not perforated. You're very lucky, Father."

"You crashed, Del. No one was killed. They say it was a miracle." Walter moved toward the TV hanging on the wall. "Want to see? The news is plastered with it."

Del touched the bandage above his eye, trying to remember. Images flashed. He shook his head and looked out the window. A sea of russet trees was broken by an occasional rooftop.

"Where am I?"

"Minneapolis. You made it to the airport but had a rough landing. Don't you remember?"

The nurse raised her hands to quiet him. "Enough current events. Although the patient is awake, I don't think twenty questions is the proper way to ease him into health."

"But—"

The nurse put a hand to Walter's back. "You'll be going now. Come back this evening for round two."

Walter let himself be nudged toward the door. He called over his shoulder. "I'll be back, Del. There's something important I have to talk with you about."

Important? What—? The pain seized him, and the nurse shooed Walter away.

Del had no choice but to let him go.

CHAPTER THIRTEEN

---·◊◊◊·---

"Watch out! Be on your guard against all kinds of greed; a man's life does not consist in the abundance of his possessions."

LUKE 12:15

KATHY SLIPPED HER ARMS IN HER COAT and felt the pocket for her car keys. She had her hand on the doorknob when the phone rang. She glanced at the answering machine, but decided to take the call.

"Ms. Bauer? Randolph Sears here."

Great. Just what she needed. A reminder of the argument she'd had with Roy about the house. She was still smarting at how he'd gotten all defensive...sometimes he took things so personally.

"Hello, Mr. Sears. I'm sorry, but I'm on my way to A Mother's Love. I work there and—"

"I won't bother you long. But yesterday we got a new listing...and I thought of you."

"Why?"

"It's a gorgeous home, up in the hills. A picture window overlooks acres of trees. A real beauty. But what clinched it was that the present owner is a writer, and they'd had an office built in a cupola on the third floor. It has a view that's...let's just say an artist could certainly find inspiration up there."

Oh, elusive inspiration... "That sounds lovely, but—"

"I've arranged with the owner to let me show it to you. I hope you will forgive my presumption, but it is so perfect, I decided to take a risk."

"I don't know. They're expecting me at work."

"But surely you could be a little late? Actually, I'm surprised you have an outside job. I assumed a successful artist like you painted full time."

Dream on. And speaking of dreams…a studio that wasn't in the basement? A studio with a view of the Ozark Mountains, the rolling layers of trees looking like a thousand bunches of broccoli? And in the fall, the magnificent shades of orange, red, and—

"It really is worth a look, Ms. Bauer. I could be over to pick you up in ten minutes. I know an important artist like you doesn't have a lot of free time, but—"

What could it hurt to look? "Come on over, Mr. Sears. I'll be waiting."

Kathy stood in the center of the six-sided cupola. Her throat was tight with the beauty of it. The owner had set his computer front and center, so with just a nod of his head to the left or right he could view the majesty of God's Ozark handiwork. *If I set my easel to the left, every time I reached over to get a new color of paint my eyes would brush over this view. Over and over I would be filled with the magnificence of it all.*

"It's perfect." She said it as a prayer.

"I knew you'd like it." Randolph Sears stood in the background, in the doorway. He was smart; he'd kept quiet, letting her take it in on her own, giving her time to adjust what *was* with what *could be.*

"Shall we see the rest of the house?"

Rest? She didn't need any more than this one room. Once inside the front door, they'd made a beeline for this cupola. Kitchen, bedrooms, baths? Inconsequential. In this little haven, she could be alone with her work. Alone with her inspiration. Alone with her God.

"There's a charming girl's bedroom. I'm sure your daughter…"

160

Daughter. Lisa. Kathy blinked, shame piercing her. She'd been so caught up with this room... She turned toward him. "Yes. Let's go see Lisa's room."

Randolph Sears smiled.

They'd gone full circle and were back in the cupola. Kathy felt a tad more unselfish. She wasn't the only one who would benefit from this house. There was a den with wood paneled walls for Roy, a bedroom with a sleeping loft for Ryan, and Lisa's room...it had a playhouse built into the corner, complete with window boxes populated with silk tulips. And the whirlpool in the huge master—

"So, Ms. Bauer. Shall we write an offer?"

She pulled her eyes from the view. "You don't waste any time, do you?"

"I know when a match is right. You belong in this house."

She nodded. "I do. We do." Reality set in, and the nod turned into a shake. "My husband will never go for it."

"Only because he hasn't seen it." He swept his arm to encompass the room. "This is a home you have to experience."

She sighed. Telling Roy about this house would be like explaining the taste of chocolate versus having it explode on your taste buds.

Mr. Sears pulled out his cell phone. "Would you like to call Mr. Bauer and ask him to join us?"

She shook her head. "He's a doctor. He can't just leave."

His face fell, but he recovered quickly. "Of course. *Doctor* Bauer is an important man. He deserves an important house."

Kathy turned her back on heaven. "Let me see if I can get him out here."

"Would you like me to speak to him?"

"No!" What had Roy called Randolph Sears? Oh, yes, "a slick shyster." The last thing Kathy wanted was for Sears to call her husband. Convincing Roy would take all her talents of negotiation. She softened her tone. "It's best if I do it."

And even then, it would be a long shot.

Roy and Kathy made their way from the hospital cafeteria line to a table. Roy took their dishes off the trays and set them aside, then opened his carton of milk.

"This is a nice surprise, Kath. But I thought you were working with Marcie today."

"I was. I am. I will." *Eventually.* "But I had an errand to do this morning."

"And that errand brought you here?"

Her stomach tightened, and it had nothing to do with the chicken nuggets on her plate. She decided to dive in. "I found us a house."

Roy froze, his hamburger halfway to his mouth. "I didn't know we were looking for one."

She shrugged. "A realtor happened to call this morning and—"

"A realtor?"

There was no way to get around it. "Randolph Sears."

He rolled his eyes and took a bite. "And I suppose he's found us one that's absolutely perfect?"

"Actually…" She met his eyes. "He has." She let go with a detailed description. She tried to gauge his reaction but found it hard to decipher. Roy would make a great poker player.

"So…" She took a cleansing breath and popped a nugget in her mouth. It was cold. "What do you think?"

"It sounds perfect."

She smiled.

"And expensive."

She frowned. He would have to ruin things.

"How much is this castle in the trees?"

His jaw dropped when she told him. He tossed his napkin on his plate. "I'm a baby doctor, Kathy, not a high-priced surgeon. There is no way—"

162

"But my paintings—"

"Are selling nicely. But not nice enough to guarantee that we could handle a mortgage like that."

She fell back in her chair. It wasn't fair. Not fair at all. She crossed her arms. "So you won't even look?"

He reached across the table for her hand. She did not give it to him so he closed his fingers to his palm. "It's too soon, Kath. Maybe someday. I want you to have your dream studio too, you know."

"Do you?"

He pulled his hand back and his jaw tightened. "I'd better get back to work. Gotta keep that money pouring in to keep up with my wife's tastes."

With that, he left her to fume.

"Sorry, Mr. Sears. Maybe…eventually…but not now. Thanks for showing it to me."

Kathy hung up, feeling like a child who'd been told there would be no Christmas, a feeling she knew intimately. When she was six, there *had* been no Christmas. Her dad had gotten laid off and there had not been any money…

She looked at her watch. The kids would be home from school soon. She needed to put this aside. There was nothing she could do about it. She had to snap out of this funk or drive herself crazy.

She smiled as she thought of the perfect remedy.

She went to the basement.

CHAPTER FOURTEEN

"When anyone hears the message about the kingdom and does not understand it, the evil one comes and snatches away what was sown in his heart."

MATTHEW 13:19

JACK STOPPED ALONG THE TRAIL TO MILL LAKE and arched his back. The air at nine thousand feet was far different from Lincoln's oxygen-thick air at one thousand. He found a nearby rock and sat, letting himself look at the scenery, glad to have his attention diverted from watching his feet negotiate the trail.

The woods were perfect—not in an ordered sense, but in the perfection of *disorder*. Fallen branches crossed tiny streams; golden aspen leaves spotted his boulder; bark peeled and hung forlornly from tree trunks. Everything was exactly as it should be. Perhaps nature was the only place where such a statement could be made.

Jack wished he were more perfect. If he were the perfect man, like Jesus had been, he wouldn't be struggling with the temptation to call Natalie and tell her what a heel Sam was. He wouldn't relish her shock. He wouldn't be so quick to want to run to comfort her—or to take over as the love of her life.

But why had he become privy to such information if he wasn't supposed to use it? And why had everything fallen into place for him to come to the conference in Natalie's hometown if God didn't want him to meet up with her again?

He got to his feet and started hiking. If only the woods would supply an answer.

Natalie leaned forward to tackle a steep part of the trail. Her backpack rubbed against her spine, but she did not adjust the strap to ease the pain. The physical discomfort was merely a partner to the mental pain that had spurred her to the mountains to be alone.

She sped up the trail, forcing her lungs to work to their full capacity. The cold air, full of the heady aromas of leaves, damp, and dirt, stung as she grabbed mouthfuls. Sweat slid down her face unchecked; the muscles in her legs burned; her feet stumbled on the rocky trail, rebelling against her frantic pace.

Suddenly, she lurched forward. Forced to stop, Natalie looked up. She was at the boulder she'd been sitting on when she received her invitation to Haven. In a moment of clarity she realized it was no coincidence she had stopped here. She stared at the rock, ran a hand against its surface, and remembered.

She had been writing one of her hack novels then... *Denison's Desire.* She let herself laugh at the memory. Plunging necklines, raspy voices, and swooning—a lot of swooning. She remembered her mentor's pointed question: "Have you ever seen anyone swoon, Natalie?"

Not lately.

If only Fran were here now to offer advice. It was on this very trail that Fran, her red hair flaming against the neutral of her borrowed ranger uniform, had been waiting for Natalie. The supposed ranger had handed Natalie a white envelope, meant just for her. And inside had been the invitation that had changed her life.

If only she could see Fran again...but angels did not appear and disappear at the whim of their charges. Natalie had been blessed with seeing Fran twice in her life—a blessing most people never experienced. Fran's presence had been a gift from God, a special memory she cherished. And now Fran's absence forced Natalie to remember that it was God she was to turn to—not one of His angels. God was very wise. It would have been easy to depend on Fran, even to pray to her...

So much had changed since Natalie had received the invitation. *She* had changed. She was no longer a pregnant, headstrong teenager, bent on fame and fun, unaware her life was lacking anything. With the invitation had come Haven—and a sense of purpose. If only that purpose didn't still seem to be on hold...

No publication. No movement forward. No letting her gift reach the masses with a testimony to God's ways. She hadn't even brought Sam to God—or totally to herself. And now he was with Lila.

She was a failure.

Natalie climbed onto the boulder and lifted her face to the sun. *Help me understand, Lord. Show me where I've gone wrong. Show me the right way.*

Was Sam the right way? She used to think so. But maybe he was just a known commodity. Sam had always been there. Sam never changed—

She lowered her chin at the thought. Was that true? Sam never changed? Then...had he always been capable of unfaithfulness? Had there been other women? She shook her head. Even if his infidelity were a habit, he could change. He could choose to change.

Choose to change...

She'd done it. Changed her life. But what good had it done? Had Haven and the past four years been for nothing?

If it's for nothing, does that mean I am nothing? She shivered against the waves of doubt. *If my writing is part of God's plan, why isn't He making things happen?*

She shook her head, scattering such traitorous thoughts. *Lord, help me...*

Yet, maybe...the timing—the waiting—was for her benefit. It wasn't a punishment. Maybe Sam had been right when he'd wondered if there was more "faith stuff" she had to do, stuff she had to start believing. Was God waiting for her to do something, think something, feel something? Was there some key step she'd left undone? *Show me, Lord.*

She grabbed fistfuls of her hair. She was driving herself crazy. She had to believe she was doing what God wanted her to do. She had to! Though doubt hid like a lurking monster behind every corner, she had to believe. She had to have faith.

She slowed her breathing, relieved when calm followed. *There you go again, getting yourself all worked up. But this isn't about your writing. It's about Sam.*

She'd tried to share with him the wonder of Haven, tried to excite him with the unlimited possibilities God provided. And he *had* listened. But had he heard? Sam had not made any effort to go to church with her—he was full of excuses...

She frowned, giving voice to a new thought. "He never asks questions."

To hear the words said out loud shocked her. But it was true. She'd shared her newfound love of the Lord, and Sam had never asked a single question—or *the* question: *How do I get what you have?*

But what *did* she have? A faith that floundered every ten minutes? A vision of a future that might only be wishful thinking?

I have God.

That was the bottom line. God was constant. He loved her and wanted what was best for her. He didn't expect her to be a perfect example of faith for Sam. He only expected her to turn to Him—repeatedly. Renewing, rededicating, confessing, praising, asking for help. God had the strength. Not Natalie.

"For when I am weak, then I am strong."

She smiled. She'd heard that verse many times, but had never really understood it. Until now.

"When I'm weak, I turn to God—and *He* is strong. I gain strength through Him."

She laughed, enjoying her own private Bible lesson. God was a good provider. He'd provided just what she'd needed; He'd found her even as she sat alone in the wilderness.

Natalie rested her forehead against her knees and let the tears come. Tears of joy for feeling closer to God, and tears of frustration for Sam's ignorance. Would he ever feel what she'd just felt? If only she could find the right words to convey—

It's up to God to reveal Himself to Sam.

She raised her head and stared at the trail, letting the thought sink in. It wasn't up to her to convert Sam. She had planted the seed, but it was up to God to bring in the harvest. She hadn't failed. How could she fail at something that wasn't hers to accomplish?

"Oh, Sam…accept—"

Why did people always talk about "accepting Jesus"? *We should be amazed He accepts us.*

Natalie ran her fingernails through her hair and screamed a prayer—for herself, and Sam. "Help us!"

—◦∞◦—

Jack didn't breathe. He looked down the trail toward the voice. *It's Natalie!* His feet started moving, trying to keep up with his heartbeat. Was she hurt?

He pulled up short—there she was.

He saw her through the trees below him, sitting on a boulder. He looked around for a companion that went with her plea to "Help us." But there was no one else. She was alone.

He marveled at her beauty. She'd let her hair grow and had it pulled back in a band. The wisps around her face moved in the breeze. Her cheeks were flushed.

He began walking again, purposely making noise, not wanting to scare her. She heard him coming. He saw her wipe away a tear, composing herself to meet a stranger. Only he wasn't a stranger…

She looked up. He stopped walking. Her eyes got wide, and

then she slid off the boulder and ran to him.

It was better than he'd imagined.

"Two hours." Natalie picked at a sprig of pine. "All we've had is two hours."

Jack pulled his coat sleeve over his watch, not wanting to see that it was time for him to go. The mountain stream tumbled past their perch on the boulder. The sun cast a mottled pattern on the trail. The chilled air was only an excuse for sitting close.

"Can't you catch a later flight?"

He shook his head. "We've got a few meetings, and then I have to catch the last ride to the airport. I've got school to teach tomorrow."

"Can't you play hooky?"

"Now, what kind of example would I be if I did that?"

She shook her head. "That's what I love about you. You *are* a good example—of so many things."

Jack accepted her compliment but wanted more. They'd caught up on each other's lives as if they had never been apart. Although she'd hinted that things were not great between herself and Sam, she had not said the words that Jack had wanted to hear. And time was running out. "Natalie…are you…content?"

"In most ways."

"I want you to be content in all ways."

She looked at him, a crease appearing between her eyes. "Is that possible?"

He put a thumb on the worry line and felt it ease. "There's a verse, 'The fear of the Lord leads to life: Then one rests content, untouched by trouble.'"

"Hmm. Untouched by trouble…that would be nice."

"It doesn't mean you won't have trouble, it means the trouble doesn't affect you the way it would if the Lord weren't a part of your life."

She squeezed his hand. "There is the essence of my discontent. Not having you to talk to about God and life and…" She faltered. "I need you."

"I need you too." He meant much more than his words implied. "I gave you my address. You have to write."

She nodded once, paused, then nodded again. She slipped her hand around his arm. "But I need…we need…"

Reluctantly, he put a hand to her lips. "We need to do God's will—whatever it is."

"But how do we know what that is?"

"We listen. We seek peace."

She laughed. "I don't think I'm familiar with that state of mind."

"It's the feeling we'll get when we do what God wants us to do."

She frowned.

Jack stood and pulled her up beside him. He dug a hand in his pocket and pulled out a chain, moving it into the sunlight. "This is for you. It was my grandmother's. When I found out I was coming to Estes, I decided to bring it, just in case I saw you."

Natalie turned it over in her hands. A gold cross caught the light. "It's beautiful, Jack. But you shouldn't give it to me. You should give it to your—"

"I should give it to you." He helped her hook the clasp. She put her fingers against the cross.

"Thank you."

He kissed her cheek, then studied her face, committing to memory exactly how she looked at this last moment when she was his Natalie.

It was time to go home.

———∞———

Sam Erickson peered in the side window of Natalie's apartment. He'd already knocked three times, with no answer. Since he had overslept, he expected to find her at the computer, writing about…whatever it was she wrote about.

Oh yeah. Her experiences in Eureka Springs—which no sane person would ever believe or want to read about. A demon and a bunch of angels? Sam had trouble buying into such baloney. Yet she was always after him to believe her, believe God, and believe *in* a God who wanted to have a relationship with him. Yeah, right.

Sam looked for signs of life in the slice of kitchen he could see from the window. Maybe she was hiding, mad at him for not showing up after work. He felt bad about not calling her— and worse for the reason behind his neglect. But he had his excuse all worked up. He'd been late getting off work—they'd had some emergency with the computer records. He was sure he could get Lou to corroborate that part of his story. They'd been so engrossed in fixing the problem that he'd lost all track of time and then he had figured she'd already be in bed, so he'd been nice and decided not to disturb her. After telling the lie, he'd put on his best puppy eyes and plead for forgiveness. "I'm sorry, Natty. I didn't mean to worry you…"

Sam dug out his key and used it. She had a key to his place too. He constantly lobbied for one key to one joint apartment, but Natalie was resolute: No living together and no sex. Another annoying by-product of her Haven conversion. Hadn't he proven himself by sticking with her through the birth of their daughter? And didn't he go back to her after her defection to Lincoln and her fling with that Beau character?

Now *there* was a story he never quite understood. Beau was a demon? Natalie had been seduced by a demon? The story sounded like the script of a horror flick. But the point was, Sam had stuck around—was *still* sticking around and being entirely too patient.

Sometimes, he wondered why. They didn't have much in common anymore. Natalie had her God and her writing, and he had…well, he was still working on that. He'd always been interested in music. Maybe he should work on composing again. Maybe someday, when he had the time, he would.

Sam walked inside and shut the door. "Natty?" He stuck his head in the bedroom. The bed was made. He turned into the kitchen. "Nat—"

He stopped, staring. Pizza remains were strung on the cabinets and floor. The whole kitchen looked as though some crazed kid had pitched one heck of a tantrum.

Great. She was mad. It was going to take all his ingenuity to get out of this one. If only Lila's lips hadn't been so inviting. No man could resist that woman.

Sam spotted a crumpled piece of paper on the floor and retrieved it, smoothing it against his shirt. Then he read it.

You selfish, two-timing pig! You want Lila? You can have her! I've gone off to be by myself—which means I'll have far better company than you.

Sam's knees felt like Jell-O. He leaned against the counter. She knew! But how—

Jack Cummings!

His heart ricocheted within his chest. He wondered how much Jack had seen. Surely not the part when Lila had taken off—

Shame nudged him, only to be shattered by indignant anger. So Peeping Tom Jack had run to tattle to Natalie. He had no right, no right at—

Sam shoved his anger aside and started for the door. He'd better find Natalie.

And quick.

"Natalie!"

She jerked to a halt and looked up. Sam stood at the top of the stairs leading to her apartment. A surge of guilt rushed over her for the time she had just spent with Jack, but it was followed immediately by anger. What on earth was *she* feeling guilty for? Sam was the one who'd been unfaithful. "What are you doing here?"

"I saw your note. I was coming to find you."

She took the stairs two at a time, stopped on the landing, and glared at him. "Find me, huh? How about me finding you and Lila making out in her car?"

His face changed, went white. "You? *You* saw me?"

"Yes, I saw you. Both of you. Hot and heavy. Sam, how could you?"

He hesitated, swallowing, eyes shifting from her to the wall. "Why did you come up to the hotel anyway?" His gaze narrowed. "Were you checking up on me?"

"Don't act like I did anything wrong, Sam Erickson. I was *worried* about you. I called the front desk, and Lou said you'd left twenty minutes earlier. We had a date. You broke it. I thought something bad had happened—" She stopped and realized what she had said. "Something bad *had* happened, though you didn't appear to be suffering much."

"It didn't mean anything, Natty—"

She waved his words away. "That is a totally unacceptable remark; trite dialogue said by a two-timing man in trouble. Surely you can do better than that." She shook her head. "I saw how you looked at her the other night—and how she looked at you." She met Sam's eyes and felt a tear escape. "I thought you were stronger than that. I thought our love was stronger than that."

Sam reached for her, but she stepped away.

"What do you want from me, Natty? I'm not as perfect as you are. I don't hold myself up as this holy man, chosen by God."

"That's not fair. I don't—"

"I'm just an ordinary guy who screws up."

"I'm ordinary too." *And guilty. Spending time with Jack...* She tucked his name safely away.

"You don't act like you think you're ordinary." Sam shoved his hands into the pockets of his jeans. He hung his head, and

Natalie cringed at the stereotypical posture of shame. "I'm sorry, Natty. It won't happen again. Isn't your God big into forgiveness?"

Natalie sighed and closed her eyes. "That's the other problem, Sam. You always call Him *my* God."

"So?"

"He's your God too."

"Yeah...I know, but—"

"No buts, Sam." She moved to the door of her apartment, fishing out her key. "On the trail today I realized it isn't up to me to bring you to God, it's up to Him to bring you to Himself."

"Huh?"

She put the key in the lock, then turned toward him. "God wants to know you, Sam, and He wants you to know Him. Personal. One on one. You can't come to Him on my coattails. You can't find Him through me. You've got to open yourself up so He can come in."

"But I've done that."

She hesitated, then turned the key and stepped inside. Her voice was low—mostly because she wasn't sure she wanted him to hear. "Have you?"

He heard. He stood in the doorway. "Don't go judging my faith. It's personal—you just said so. How I feel or don't feel about God is up to me, not you. Besides, what's God got to do with you and me?" Sam reached for her hand. "Give me another chance."

Natalie pulled her hand to her chest, shaking her head. Spending time with Jack had changed everything. Nothing was clear anymore. Was she guilty of unfaithfulness as well?

Sam put a finger under her chin and raised it. He smiled, and she realized it was the same smile he always used to get his way. "Come on, Natty. We've been together forever. We're a couple. Forgive me and let's go on. We're supposed to be together—I know it."

But I don't know it. Not anymore. Not since—

He took a step toward the kitchen. "I'll even clean up the pizza mess. Things will be just like they were before."

Her voice was soft and full of exhaustion. "But things are *not* just like they were before. Making the pizza mess disappear does not make my image of you and Lila disappear." *Or erase my memories of Jack.*

"But I said I was sorry."

And so am I. She put a hand to her forehead, wishing she could press a clear solution into her brain. "I'm confused right now, Sam. You hurt me, and…" She couldn't name her own indiscretions. "That doesn't evaporate in a few hours."

He threw his arms in the air. "Well, excuse me, Miss Queen of the Grudge. When will you deem me worthy again?"

I've got my own worthiness to worry about. She looked him straight in the eye. "I don't have an answer for you."

He pushed past her out the door. "Until then, believe it or not, I have a life." He slammed the door, and she heard his footsteps fade. A car door. An engine. Then silence.

Natalie closed her eyes. How had Sam turned things around so *he* was the victim? Why did she have the urge to go after him and apologize? Apologize for what? Catching him? For spending time with Jack and not telling him? For caring about—

In one day everything had changed. Like it or not, her life could not play out as always.

Now there was Jack.

CHAPTER FIFTEEN

———◦◦◦———

Declare them guilty, O God! Let their intrigues be their downfall. Banish them for their many sins, for they have rebelled against you.

PSALM 5:10

ART'S PHONE RANG.

"Hamm will meet you tonight. Dinner at Cantigliano's."

Art blinked, letting Ben's words sink in. "That was fast. My lunch hasn't settled yet."

"Yeah…well…he wants to talk to you. We'll meet you there."

Art looked at the door to his apartment. Ben lived right across the hall. "Don't you want to go together?"

"No. I mean…Hamm and I have some talking…things to catch up on before you get there. Come at seven. Sharp."

He hung up.

Art could have used a breather from the TAI philosophy but braced himself to endure it for Julia's sake. And since he started working for Julia tomorrow, he might be able to tell her something about those plotting against her.

If nothing else, he'd get a free meal out of it.

Art met Ben and Hamm at Cantigliano's. Ravioli and revolution. What a way to spend an evening. In the waiting area, he spotted Ben waving him over to a table. Ben was way too excited. Celebrating Art's conversion? The other man seated at the table matched the wimpish figure Ben had described, reminding Art of his eighth-grade math teacher, Mr. Simmons.

Mr. Simmons had related to numbers more than flesh and blood children. Especially flesh and blood children who didn't do their homework and didn't see any advantage to learning how to figure story problems about trains starting at Point A at 10:05 and others starting at Point B at noon.

As Art neared the table, Hamm stood to shake his hand. "Hammond Spurgeon, at your service."

"Art Graham." Art hung his leather jacket on the back of his chair and sat as the point to their triangle.

A tray of antipasto sat at the center of the table. Hamm lifted an opened bottle. "Wine?"

Art declined. He needed to keep a clear head. Hamm topped off his own glass, then slapped his hands on his thighs. "Well then, Art. Tell us about life in prison."

Art's heart dropped to his stomach. "How—?"

"How did I know?"

Ben raised a finger. "What's this about prison?"

Hamm turned to Art. "You'll have to excuse Ben. He's high on passion, but short on research. I, however, happen to know that knowledge is the key to power."

Knowledge…does he also know I work for Julia?

Hamm clasped his hands and leaned forward on the edge of the table. "So…you kidnapped our president when she was in Haven?"

Ben sucked in a breath. "You're *that* guy?" He shook his head. "Art…Art Graham." He looked up, his eyes wide. "Arthur! You're the Arthur Julia spoke about?"

Art resisted the urge to topple the table and run. Instead, he took a drink of water. "That's me." His voice cracked, and he tried again. "That's me."

"Why didn't you tell me you knew her?" Ben frowned. "I told you all about the time I worked for her."

Art shrugged, his mind racing with a plausible answer. "I'd rather forget about my past. I'm not exactly proud of it."

Hamm leaned back, nodding. "You hate her, don't you?"

"What?"

"Julia Carson is the reason you went to jail. You lost four years of your life because of her. It's only natural you hate her."

It's only natural… Art was quick to agree. This was his way out. "Of course I hate her. I despise her." The words felt like poison in his throat.

"Then why did you repeatedly accept Julia and her husband as visitors?"

Art forced himself to breathe. *Lord, help me get through this.* Then it came to him. A logical answer. He smiled a convict's smile. "Why shouldn't I? I'd have been a fool not to accept their money and gifts. All I had to do was pretend to like them and they oozed their forgiveness and good will all over me." He shook his head. "It was a huge joke. They were easy marks."

Hamm studied him a full fifteen seconds, then he raised a finger for the waiter. "Let's order. I hear the manicotti is excellent."

Hamm didn't mention Art's inclusion in TAI until they were enjoying their spumoni and biscotti.

Hamm poured the last of the second bottle of wine into his own glass. "So. Art. I think we could use a man with your background in TAI. Are you interested?"

Art's stomach clenched, which didn't set well considering the amount of food he'd eaten. "What do I have to do?"

"Nothing at the moment. There *is* something looming in the future, but the details are still unclear."

"What kind of something?"

Ben answered. "That's for us to know and you to—"

Hamm waved his words away. "We'll let you know as soon as it's appropriate. Until then, we'll stay in touch." He wrote something on a napkin. "Here's our Web site address. Take a look. Get involved in the online discussions. And be prepared to help when called."

Art cringed at the knowledge that helping TAI would be hurting Julia. He tucked the note in his pocket and decided not to mention that he didn't own a computer. "Sounds like a good start."

Unfortunately his gut said it was just the opposite.

On his first day of work, Art was awake at five. It wasn't that he wanted to spend time primping. No, the problem was that he'd had trouble sleeping. He was walking a tightrope and wasn't sure he liked it. He'd put one foot in Hamm Spurgeon's camp and the other in Julia's.

The butterflies in his stomach dive-bombed each other. One slip and he might lose his job with Julia; another slip, and he'd lose his tenuous position with TAI. He pushed his bowl of cereal aside. The idea of milk hitting his stomach…

There was only one remedy. He closed his eyes and bowed his head. "Protect me, God. I feel like I'm in the middle of a battlefield between Julia and…and I'm not sure what else. But they mean her no good, that I know. Thank you for keeping me from telling Ben I worked for Julia. That would have ruined everything." He took a deep breath and found the butterflies had landed. At least temporarily. "Keep me safe, keep Julia safe, and show me what to do."

That done, he left for his first day on the job.

———

Edward tossed the morning paper on the table, nearly toppling his juice glass. "I can't believe you hired Art without consulting me."

Julia fastened her watch. "He's going to be my personal assistant, Edward. You've been after me to delegate, to cut back so I'll have more time for the important things in life." She kissed his cheek. "Like you."

"That last comment was entirely self-serving and manipulative."

"You betcha."

He felt himself melt. "And as such, totally unfair."

"Absolutely."

He downed his juice knowing there was no way he could win a debate against her. "When does he start?"

She checked her watch. "He should be here around nine."

"How did you get him security clearance so fast?"

"I waived it."

He stared at her, incredulous. "You can't do that."

"I most certainly can."

"But the security…it's for your own good. After all, Art's a…a…" The storm cloud that hovered over his wife's face told him it was in his best interest not to finish that sentence.

Unfortunately, she did it for him. "Because he's an ex-con?"

"Well…"

"We visited him in jail, Edward. We forgave him long ago. He's turned his life around. We've witnessed that."

He could have been faking.

"And no, he was not faking."

"I hate when you read my thoughts."

"Get used to it, bucko."

"Do you mind if I run a check on him, for my own satisfaction?"

"You will do no such thing." She headed for the door leading from their private quarters. She stopped and faced him. "Promise me, Edward."

He hesitated. Julia was far too trusting. If he didn't protect—

"Edward?"

She thought she could handle anything. And she could. Almost anything. But—

"I'll hold my breath until you turn blue," she said.

"It's until *I* turn blue."

"That's what I said."

He knew she would not leave him alone until he promised.

181

He thought of a way out. He raised his right hand. "I promise that I will not run a check on him."

"That's a good boy."

She left him alone. As soon as the door clicked shut, he called the head of security. He—Edward Carson—would *not* run a check on Art. Someone else would. And he'd put a rush on it.

He hoped Julia would forgive him. But more than that, he hoped Art would have a clean slate, and she would never have to find out.

At two minutes till nine, Edward received the security report on Arthur Graham. He was relieved to see that Art had not gotten into any trouble since being released from prison. He'd also been a model prisoner.

Yet there was one disturbing entry, posted just yesterday. Art had been seen in the company of Hammond Spurgeon, an iffy man who was the head of an Internet faction called TAI that instigated annoying anti-Christian harassment. They weren't considered terrorists or even a physical threat; just an organization on the watch list. But to have Art associated with them at all...

Then another name caught Edward's attention. Benjamin Cranois. He'd also been with Spurgeon and Art. Edward and Julia hadn't talked to Ben since he had walked out of their suite in Kansas City two years before. Edward couldn't be sure that Ben was a part of TAI. But he did know one thing: Ben was anti-Julia. All the trouble he'd caused during the campaign, always arguing, wanting Julia to hold back her views. And then leaking the news that Julia had had an abortion when she was young.

Plus the fact that just this week they had seen Ben at church where he had caused a commotion in the middle of the service. He was obviously still a troubled man.

Hamm, Ben…and Art. It was not a good sign.

He had to tell Julia. She would not be happy—and hence, neither would Edward. But it couldn't be helped.

He left his office to find her and take his lumps.

———∞∞∞———

Edward walked into the Oval Office and found Art Graham sitting in front of his wife's desk. Art stood immediately. He looked good. He still had the military haircut he'd had in jail plus some extra muscles developed from the time in the prison gym. But the civilian clothes worked wonders. Dressed in khakis, a navy blazer, and a tie, Art looked every inch the model employee. If Edward didn't know better, he'd think Art was dressed to attend some fancy prep school.

His wife also stood. "Come say hello to Arthur, dear."

Art wiped his hand on his coat in preparation for a handshake. Edward obliged.

"Nice to see you again, sir."

"You too, Art."

Art glanced at Julia and they exchanged a smile. "I'm looking forward to working for Julia—President Carson. I hope I can be of some help."

She piped in. "You can be of great help. Edward is always telling me to slow down, not to try to control everything myself. Isn't that right, Edward?"

Her smile was a challenge. "That's right. But I'm still not sure that Art can—"

"But I can, sir. I can and will do whatever the president wants. I will be her obedient slave."

"I always wanted someone to call me Master."

"Mistress," Art said.

She shook her head. "Nuh-uh. Wrong connotation."

"How about 'oh great one'?"

Julia tapped her lips. "Now, *that* has possibilities."

Edward found their bantering unnerving. Although he

couldn't deny the chemistry between his wife and Art, there was still the security report to consider. It was time to broach the subject. "I have a few ques—"

Julia reached for his hand, extending her other hand to Art. "Why don't we say a prayer and get things started right?"

She stood between them and prayed for guidance, patience, and protection for them all. Edward didn't have the guts to interrupt because he knew when Julia talked, God listened.

And vice versa. With the amen he made a decision. At the moment, he'd let God handle it.

It was safer that way.

CHAPTER SIXTEEN

———⚬⚬⚬———

Be on your guard; stand firm in the faith; be men of courage; be strong.

1 CORINTHIANS 16:13

WALTER STOOD WITH BETTE AT THE DOOR to Del's hospital room. He hesitated a moment, handing the vase of marigolds to his wife. Flowers were girl stuff. Besides, they made him sneeze. He knocked.

"Enter!"

They went in and found Del walking toward them.

Walter rushed to help him. "What are you doing out of bed?"

"Walking, I think." Del had one hand on his ribs and the other on the bed for support. He looked at Bette and smiled.

She smiled back and lifted the flowers as a salute. "We finally meet."

"No thanks to this brute." Walter helped Del back to bed. "For two years now I've told him to bring you down to Lincoln, and he always has an excuse."

"He's good at that."

"A connoisseur of procrastination and excuses. That's our Walter."

Walter hated when people talked about him as if he weren't there. "That is not *our* Walter." He held a glass of water toward Del's face. "Here, drink this. Anything to keep you from telling my secrets."

"They're hardly secrets." Bette put the flowers on the windowsill and sat. She leaned toward Del. "Did you know Walter only likes the potato chips that are curled over on themselves?

185

He digs through the bag searching for—"

Del raised a finger. "Did you know he has a bladder the size of Texas? When I was stowed away in his van on the way to Haven, he drove on and on, never needing to relieve himself, until I had no choice but to show myself so he'd pull to the side of the—"

Walter crossed his arms. "Maybe I should leave, and you two could talk about me in private?"

"Nah, this is more fun. Besides, I'm an injured man. Indulge me." Del's expression turned serious. "But not too injured. I came here to do a television program and I intend to do a television—"

Walter handed Del a glass of water. "Here, have a drink."

Del pushed it away. "This is the second time you've shoved a drink in my face. What's going on?"

Walter took his own sip before setting the glass down. *I don't want to do this...*

"You drank that water like you were a cowboy needing a shot of whiskey before telling the schoolmarm the building's on fire."

Walter cocked his head. "Actually, you're surprisingly close."

"I know the *Good News* set caught fire, Walter. You told me. Has there been a problem setting up a temporary set?"

"Kinda."

"Has there been a delay?"

"Sorta."

Del shook his head. "You're forcing me to add *annoying* and *infuriating* to your list of character traits, friend."

Bette put a hand on Walter's arm. "Just tell him, hon."

"Yes, just tell me, hon."

Walter took another sip of water. Two against one. He was beat.

Del clasped his hands in his lap. "Would you like some lemon Jell-O with your water? The chefs here make a superb bowl of Jell-O."

"I don't like lemon Jell-O."

"I'm sure they have lime."

"Maybe strawber—"

Bette popped out of her chair. "Walter's old boss is in a coma and his new boss is anti-Christian and has forbid him to have you on the show."

Walter flashed her a dirty look. "I would have told him. I was just setting the mood."

"You were discussing Jell-O!"

"I was easing into it. He's just been through a plane crash. I didn't want to upset—"

Del made a *T* with his hands. "Timeout, Mr. and Mrs. P." He pointed to the chairs. "Sit. And only speak when spoken to."

Walter and Bette sat, their hands folded. Walter felt like a chastised pupil in front of the principal. Del put a hand to his bandaged forehead.

Bette touched Walter's arm and they exchanged a look. Her eyes mirrored his own worry. She turned back to Del. "Are you all right?"

He raised a finger. "Only when spoken to, remember?"

She turned an imaginary lock on her lips.

"That's better. Now, Walter. I can't be on the show?"

"I'm working on it." *Trying to conjure up the courage.*

"But I'm here now. Monsignor Vibrowsky won't let me hang around Minneapolis forever, plane crash or no plane crash."

"A heart as big as a walnut."

"Ahem."

Walter locked his lips too.

"Who is this new boss?"

"Harriet Lane."

"Am I to understand by the way you tenderly speak her name that she's not your favorite person?"

"She is against the Bible; against God. That's why she won't let you come on my show."

"On what grounds?"

"On the grounds that you intend to advertise a spiritual revival meeting."

"That's not how I'd bill the reunion, but it is an apt definition." Del leaned against his pillows and studied the ceiling. Then he looked at Walter. "I think we're experiencing some opposition."

"What do you mean?"

"The fire, your boss being hurt and being replaced by a nonbeliever."

"Harriet is more than that."

Del raised a hand. "And the plane crash…"

Walter shivered. "You don't think…?"

"Remember Eureka Springs?" Del said. "'Put on the full armor of God—'"

Walter shook his head vigorously. "No…no way. Not that again. Fighting evil head-on…that was heavy stuff."

Bette took Walter's hand. "Fighting? I don't like the sound of this."

"Unfortunately, it's not up to us to like it or not like it." Del's eyes widened, then he gasped, grabbing his ribs. Walter wasn't sure if the gasp was a reaction to pain or to an idea.

Del took a slow breath. When he let it out, his eyes sparked in a way Walter had seen before. "Actually, we should feel honored."

"Are you kidding?"

"No, I'm not. Satan wouldn't bother with us unless we were doing God's will. And God never gives us more than we can handle. He must think we can handle this."

"But God's not doing it, Satan is."

"I guarantee you, God is in control. He's *allowing* Satan to cause some mischief, but in the end, even Satan's schemes fit into God's plans. God can use everything for good."

"I'd hardly define a plane crash as mischief. Or good."

"Small potatoes in the intricacies of life."

Walter made a face and felt his feet getting colder by the

minute. "Ever get the feeling it would be easier to let someone else arrange this reunion thing?"

"Unfortunately, God didn't ask my opinion on the matter."

"You could say no."

Del shook his head. "You say no enough times and God is going to look elsewhere. In fact, I don't think it's possible to say 'No, *Lord.*' You can't call him Lord—which by its very title is saying yes to him—and then say no to him." He paused a moment. "Don't you ever start your day saying, 'Lord, what can I do for you today?'"

"Not really."

Bette shrugged. "Sometimes."

Walter turned to her. "You say that? Really?"

"Sure. When I feel up to it."

"But I think we're supposed to say it whether we feel up to it or not," Del said.

"What if we don't like what He says?"

"If we rebel and say, 'No, I won't do it,' it's bad. But being arrogant and saying, 'No, I won't even ask' is just as bad."

"So, now I'm arrogant?" Walter crossed his arms. If he wanted this kind of abuse he could call Harriet.

"I'm not accusing, Walter. You're the one who wondered if it would be easier letting someone else arrange the reunion."

"Then how did the discussion get around to my faults?" He shook his head. "This happens way too much. I don't like getting picked on."

Bette and Del smiled at each other, and Walter felt the gentle pressure of his wife's hand on his arm. "We're not picking on you as much as you're picking on yourself."

"Yeah, right."

"It's good you see your own weaknesses, friend. That's a positive thing."

Walter slumped into his chair. "Oh, this is great. The only positive comment said to me all morning is that I'm good at defining the negatives of my life."

Bette kissed his cheek. "Don't pout, Walter."

"See? There's another fault. I pout."

Del shook his head in surrender. "Can we get back to the subject? The reunion broadcast?"

"I suppose." Walter looked out the window. Fun time was over. He couldn't avoid it any longer. "I don't think either of you understand what I'm up against with Harriet. If I let you on my show, I may lose my job."

"You're kidding."

Walter shook his head. "Rolf's out of commission. Harriet's in charge. She's told me I can't do it. She didn't suggest; she gave me a direct order."

"But Rolf approved it before he got hurt," Bette said. "That should count for something."

"But Harriet's made a point of telling me—twice—that our bosses have been complaining about the show being too preachy."

"It's not preachy. It's..." Bette took a deep breath. "It's uplifting."

"Right or wrong, they have the power to lift me up, bring me down, and toss me out." Walter rubbed his eyes. "I've been struggling with this all day. I even went to Rolf for advice."

"But he's in a coma," Bette said.

Del shrugged. "So what did he say?"

Walter stared at him. "Didn't you hear Bette? He's in a—"

"Coma. Yes. I know. But you also know *him*. You went to him already knowing what he'd tell you to do. The fact he was not awake enough to say the words aloud doesn't change the essence of his advice."

Walter leaned his elbows on his knees and stared at the floor.

"Come on, Walter. What would Rolf tell you to do?"

Walter looked up, amazed it was so clear. "He'd say do the show. Do the right thing and let the consequences fall as they may."

"But, hon, you may lose your job. And our finances—"

Walter raised a hand to stop her words. "I know where we stand financially and I take full responsibility, but—"

"Stand. Responsibility. It's all about taking a stand."

"You can't ask Walter to do this, Del. It's too big a risk."

"All acts of courage involve risk."

"But—"

Walter didn't like the panic in his wife's eyes. "You're the one who pushes me to be strong for my faith, Bette. I'm the wishy-washy one. You're the strong one." He softened his voice. "What's going on?"

She clasped both hands under her chin. "Why am I feeling so selfish?" She looked at Walter. "And scared?"

"Because you live an idyllic life." Del kept his voice soft. "Living in a nice house, raising your child, being married to a…a…"

Walter flashed him a look. "Don't finish that sentence or I'll never help you."

"A wonderful, kind, brave-hearted man."

"Weighing those compliments against your earlier cuts brings you back to zero."

Del smiled and held out his hands. "Why don't we pray about it?"

It always came back to this. They held hands.

Walter and Bette got in the elevator. Bette hit the button for the ground floor.

"What do you think?" she finally asked.

Walter was glad they had the elevator to themselves. "I have no idea. I—"

His cell phone rang. He answered it.

"Walter, Harriet here. A change of plans. I have to go out of town for a conference that Rolf was supposed to attend. I'm leaving in an hour. I've talked with Cassandra and Tim about

191

doing that on-location interview with the Habitat for Humanity crew tomorrow."

Harriet is going to be out of town. She wants us to do a broadcast on location... Walter's stomach did the polka. Harriet was still talking.

"I'll be back day after tomorrow. I trust you to handle things—as we've discussed?"

There was an extra stridency in her voice.

"Sure," he said. "I'll take care of everything."

Walter hung up, and Bette took his arm. "What's wrong, hon? You're pale."

He shook his head, resigned. He told her his plan.

<hr />

The next morning, the lights were set, the camera in place. Del saw Walter rubbing his hands together. Apparently Walter's hands were as clammy as his own.

"So. Priest man. Are you ready? Do you know what you're going to say?"

Del took a deep breath, trying to calm his nerves. "Nope."

Walter leaned close and spoke low. "Don't you think a little preparation would be a good idea?"

Del reached for his Bible and opened it to a marked passage. "This is the only preparation I need. 'Do not worry beforehand about what to say. Just say whatever is given you at the time, for it is not you speaking, but the Holy Spirit.'"

Walter rolled his eyes. "He's going to put the words into your head and you'll spew them out?"

"Pretty much."

"Sounds like Charlie McCarthy and Edgar Bergen."

"I'm prettier than Charlie McCarthy."

"You have the same IQ."

Del set the Bible aside. "Don't you understand how the Holy Spirit works, Walter?"

"Sure I do."

"Jesus sent the Spirit to be in us right now. We can either let Him have control or we can stifle Him."

"I'm not stifling anyone."

Del shrugged. "Whatever you say."

The director held two fingers up toward Walter. "Two minutes."

Del took Walter's hand and bowed his head.

"What are you doing?" Walter whispered.

"I'm—we're—going to say a prayer."

"Right here? In front of everyone?"

"You're stifling, Walter."

With a look to the crew to see if they were watching—and of course they were—Walter bowed his head. Del read from the Bible: "'But let all who take refuge in you be glad; let them ever sing for joy. Spread your protection over them, that those who love your name may rejoice in you. For surely, O LORD, you bless the righteous; you surround them with your favor as with a shield.' Amen."

Walter shook his head. "*Shield* was my byword in Eureka Springs; I guess it's appropriate it pops up now. We could use a shield."

Del smiled. "'Ask and you will receive.'"

True, Walter thought. Probably more than they'd bargained for.

CHAPTER SEVENTEEN

Get rid of all bitterness, rage and anger, brawling and slander, along with every form of malice. Be kind and compassionate to one another, forgiving each other, just as in Christ God forgave you.

EPHESIANS 4:31–32

NATALIE BALANCED THE BOWL of breakfast cereal while she got comfortable on the couch. She didn't like the way she felt this morning. She usually popped out of bed at five—sans alarm clock—and ran to her desk to read the Bible, write in her prayer journal, and work on her book. But this morning, she hadn't awakened until seven, and neither the study nor the work seemed inviting.

She found the remote between the cushions and turned on the TV. Mindless babble, that's what she needed. Or news, so the world's troubles might make her forget her own.

There was a knock on the door, and for an instant, Natalie's stomach jumped with one thought: *Jack!*

But no, that was impossible. Jack had left yesterday. Jack was gone.

It was Sam. She opened the door until it stopped against her shoulder.

Sam looked at the bowl of cereal in her hand. "Your cereal's getting soggy."

She didn't move.

"Can I come in?"

She considered saying no, but stepped aside. Sam slipped off his coat and tossed it on the back of the couch. He pointed to her cereal. "Can I have some?"

"Whatever." Natalie went back to the couch, but set the cereal aside. She tucked an afghan around her feet. Sam came in the room carrying a bowl. He sat at the other end of the couch.

"Lose your appetite?"

She shrugged but refused to look at him.

"I take it this lack of enthusiasm means you haven't forgiven me yet?"

"Not yet." She liked the rush of power that flowed with the words. *You're going to pay for hurting me, Sam Erickson.*

Sam ate two spoonfuls. "I'm sorry, you know."

Natalie flipped the channels, liking how the chaos of two-second sound bites mirrored her inner confusion. When the image of a gorgeous black-haired woman flashed on the screen, she turned to Sam. "Did you see Lila last night?"

"Of course I saw her. We both work at the hotel." He dunked his cereal with the back of his spoon.

"Why don't you look at me when you say that?"

He glanced up, then down again.

"Did you talk to her?" Natalie was afraid to ask more.

"Just in passing. *She* came up to *me.*"

"I bet she did."

"We didn't *do* anything, Natty."

"Why didn't you stop by after work?"

"I didn't think you'd want to see me. We had an argument, remember? I thought you'd still be mad."

"But this morning, you thought I wouldn't be?"

He set his bowl on the coffee table, sloshing milk over the side. "Maybe I should go."

"Maybe you—" Natalie did a double take at the television. It took her a moment to register what she was seeing. "That's Del! And Walter!"

"Who are Del and Walter?"

"From Haven! From Eureka Springs!" She turned up the volume.

"Isn't Del the priest?"

"Yes…"

"What are they doing on—"

"Shh!"

The camera zoomed in on Del.

"He looks terrible. What happened to him?"

As if he had heard her question, Del smiled and touched the bandage above his eye. "As you see, I've had a little accident. Actually, I was on Flight 280 that landed hard in Minneapolis yesterday. I thank God no one was killed, for I've come to believe that my death was one of the objectives of that crash."

Walter pulled the microphone toward himself. "That's a pretty harsh statement. Can you explain?"

Del nodded. "Four years ago, I went to Haven. To many of you, that means nothing, but to some of you, that means everything. For you, too, received an invitation to go to a town called Haven. You didn't know why. You didn't know who invited you there. On faith, you went and your lives were changed."

"How?"

Del took a deep breath, holding his ribs as he did so. "In Haven we began a journey—a quest—to find our unique purpose in life. All of us—whether we've been to Haven or not—have been placed in a unique time, a unique place, with unique contacts—a blending of friends, family, and coworkers that is distinct and handpicked."

"Handpicked by whom?"

Del faced the camera. "By God."

Walter played the skeptic. "You expect people to believe that?"

"I do."

"So these people who went to Haven were special?"

"Not at all. I think that was God's point. He chose a few ordinary people to represent everyone. Each participant brought different talents, strengths, and weaknesses to Haven. Yet God planned to use them all."

Sam pointed at the screen. "He talks just like you do."

"Shh!"

"Now that we have the background, why are you here today on *Good News?*"

Del straightened his shoulders. "Now is the time to bring together all the people who went to the different Havens, and there were many."

"How many?"

"I don't know. But there were Havens all around the country, even around the world." Del smiled. "In spite of what we'd like to believe, God is not an American."

Walter changed gears. "So you're planning a Haven reunion?"

"Yes. And since there was no way for me to contact each of you, I am appearing now to issue the invitation. Attention all Havenites, please come to a reunion in Kansas City on Thanksgiving."

"This Thanksgiving?" Walter shook his head. "That's coming up pretty fast."

"Indeed it is. But as most of the people remember, we were only given a few days' notice to come to Haven. I'm allowing a few weeks." He turned serious. "There have been many incidents to stop me from coming before you today for this announcement. A fire and even a plane crash. But God's plans will not be foiled. Therefore—" he held up a sign with a phone number on it—"please contact me at this number. I'll take care of you." He raised a finger as he remembered something else. "And please, bring your families, your friends. Those of you who received mustard seed pins…please join us. The Haven reunion is meant to be a time of thanksgiving—and a time of further instruction and encouragement for all people."

"Who will be speaking?" Walter asked.

There was a moment of silence.

Natalie pointed to the screen. "Del doesn't know! Look at his face; it's as if he hasn't even thought about it before."

Sam yawned. "Doesn't sound too organized to me."

Del's blush faded and he answered sheepishly, "The agenda is yet to be determined. I know that the Havenites understand that God will provide. It's His show, not ours."

Natalie ran to the phone.

"What are you doing?"

"Calling the number. Making arrangements to go."

Sam followed her, took the phone away, and hung it up.

"What are *you* doing?"

"I don't want to go, Natty."

She felt herself redden when she realized she hadn't even thought about him accompanying her.

"It's for Haven people. You. Not me."

Exactly. She tried to find some compassion. "Del said you could come. He wanted everyone to bring family and friends."

"He was just being nice. This is a reunion for the inner circle." He crossed his arms. "I wouldn't want to go. It'll be a bunch of hallelujah-amen types, making the rest of us feel like—"

"We're not like that. We're—"

He shook his head. "I don't belong. I'll never belong."

"That's ridiculous. Haven's not important. God is important. You don't need to have gone to Haven to be close to God."

"But it helps, doesn't it?"

Natalie hesitated. Haven or no Haven, she hadn't exactly excelled in the faith department. Going to Haven hadn't made her life any easier. In fact, if anything, it had made it more diffi-cult. She'd seen miracles, talked to angels, been held captive by a demon. She tended to take it all for granted, to think it was a common experience. Yet, the fact that Haven was special didn't mean *she* was special.

She was relieved when Sam didn't wait for her to answer. "I don't want you to go, Natty."

"Why not?"

"Because Haven's in the past. Going to the reunion will pull you further away from me."

"But if you come with me…maybe it will bring us closer together." *It may be our last chance.* "I'm sure that's what Del had in mind. We all belong to the body of Christ—"

"Give me a break."

"What?"

"That sounds so…" He raised his shoulders, and waved his fingers on either side of his face. "Disgustingly good. You are such a *good* person, Natalie Pasternak."

She felt as if he had slapped her. "Don't be mean, Sam. I've never done anything to make you feel less important than I am."

He raised an eyebrow.

"What? What have I done?" She asked the question as an innocent, while knowing she would be found guilty.

"This waiting for Samuel business you told me about—and the fifteenth."

Natalie straightened her spine. "I'm sure God wants me to wait for His timing about my book. He put the passages about Saul and Samuel into my path so I'd learn to wait. But the fifteenth…" Her spine sagged. "Even I'm not sure about that one."

"Exactly."

She shook her head. "I don't under—"

"Things like that happen to *you,* Natty." Sam began to pace. "You get direction from Him. Guidance. Every time you have a problem, you seem to get it resolved with something God *tells* you. That kind of stuff doesn't happen to me."

It could. If you'd be open to it. "How do you know, Sam? Maybe it's there, right in front of you, but you don't—"

"So it's my fault."

Natalie ran her hands through her hair. "Maybe. Partly. You've got to be open to God's will to be an active part of it."

"Who says I want to be?"

She paused, shocked. "Don't you?"

He shrugged. "Why should I? He hasn't shown any interest in me, why should I show any interest in Him?"

"What a terrible thing to say. God shows interest in you all the time."

"How?" Sam began to pace. "How does He show interest in me? How come I don't know what I'm supposed to do with my life, while you know exactly what you're supposed to do?"

"But I didn't always know. You've seen me go all over the place with my writing. It took two years of trial and error to get it right—and it's been two years since then, and I still haven't gotten anything published."

He took her by the shoulders. "Then how do you *know*? You seem so certain even though God hasn't given you any concrete evidence you're doing the right thing."

Natalie thought back to her conversation with Jack. She fingered the cross necklace he'd given her. "I know by the peace I feel. Peace is the feeling we get when we do what God wants us to do."

"Where did you get that necklace?"

She dropped her hand. "I've had it a while." At the lie, she looked away.

He fell onto the couch. "This talk of peace isn't good enough. I need something real, something specific I can touch and see. And so should you, Natty. You can't live your life driven by gut feelings."

Natalie thought of one of her favorite verses. "'Faith is being sure of what we hope for and certain of what we do not see.'"

Sam shook his head. "Too iffy. I'd believe in God if I could see Him."

"So it's God's fault? You're saying He hasn't done a good enough job revealing Himself to you?"

Sam hesitated. "Well...yeah. I mean, if He's there, why doesn't He just show Himself and make people certain?"

"You're lazy."

"I am not lazy."

"Sure you are. You want God to do all the work, and only then will you honor Him with your belief." She shook her head. "You accuse me of thinking I'm better than other people when here you are, insisting that you deserve a special revelation." She swiped her hand across the air. "Now showing! Limited engagement! God, in all His glory!"

"Fine." He crossed his arms. "Then you do the work. You prove to me that your faith is in something real."

Natalie had a headache. This was ridiculous. "Proving faith is like proving the existence of air. It's not something we can see, it's something that's inside, something we need, something we feel."

"Bad example. I *can* see air; I can see the air moving branches. I can see its effect on things."

"And you can see faith's effect on things."

Sam snickered. "So faith moves branches."

Natalie made two fists and remembered an old saying. "Faith moves mountains. Don't you get it? It's like the verse that was on my invitation to Haven: 'If you have faith as small as a mustard seed, you can say to this mountain, "Move from here to there" and it will move. Nothing will be impossible for you.'"

"That's absurd."

"It's not absurd!"

"But it is." He gave her a leveling look. "I haven't seen you move any mountains, Natty. So what does that say about your faith?"

Natalie tightened her jaw, keeping in all the hateful words that wanted to escape. She walked to the door and opened it. She kept her voice steady. "Out, Sam. Leave."

"Why?"

She reached for his coat and tossed it at him. "You want me to move a mountain? I'm moving one. I'm moving you. Get out."

He stopped at the door, putting his face inches from hers.

202

She looked away. "You're going to have to choose, Natty. Me or God. It's obvious there's not room in your life for both."

She gave him a push and slammed the door on his back.

That night, Natalie called in sick for work. She couldn't push pizzas when all she could think about was her decision to break up with Sam.

She'd spent the day in bed, brooding. Praying. Mourning. And accepting.

It was after ten-thirty when she heard a knock on her door. "Natty? It's me, Sam. Let me in."

Natalie lay in the dark and held her breath.

"Natty, I know you're in there. Open up. I love you. We're meant to be together."

She shook her head. He was wrong.

"Natty…"

She pulled the pillow around her ears. She didn't want to hear any more. Her life with Sam had moved far away, into the past. She couldn't even see its edges in the darkness of her apartment—or her heart.

Finally, Sam gave up.

So did Natalie.

CHAPTER EIGHTEEN

—◦◦◦—

Rescue me, O LORD, from evil men; protect me from men of violence, who devise evil plans in their hearts and stir up war every day.

PSALM 140:1–2

THEY WERE IN THEIR LIMO, thirty minutes away from a charity dinner, when Edward reached for the television on the console in front of them.

Julia shook her head, the weariness of a hard day taking over. "Don't turn that on."

"I think a little death, destruction, and destitution will get your mind off world peace, taxes, and ornery congressmen. Let's try to catch the news."

Edward scanned the channels. The quick shots of sound and pictures matched Julia's fragmented mind. When she saw a familiar face, it took her a moment to comprehend. "Stop!"

The limo driver turned his head. "Excuse me, ma'am?"

"No, no. Keep going. I was talking to Edward."

The driver's eyebrows raised.

"You love doing that, don't you?" Edward whispered. "Making people think we are in a constant state of passion. Not that we aren't, but—"

"Shh!" She grabbed the remote and backtracked one channel, then pointed to the screen.

A moment later, he pointed with her. "Isn't that Walter and Del?"

"It is!"

"What are they—"

"Shh!"

Del was talking. "Since there was no way for me to contact each of you, I am appearing now to issue the invitation. Attention all Havenites, please come to a reunion in Kansas City on Thanksgiving."

Julia clapped her hands. "A reunion? How wonderful." She sighed, suddenly deflated. "How impossible."

They listened to the rest of the broadcast, then Edward shut it off. "I wonder why now? It *would* be good to see everyone, especially under noncrisis circumstances. But thanks to you we're booked for months."

"What do you want me to do, Edward? Put the world on pause?"

He hesitated only a moment. "Yes."

"But—"

"Actually, it doesn't matter. The reunion's on Thanksgiving. We've been invited to Bonnie's. We can't disappoint her."

"But—"

"No buts. You know Bonnie. Our daughter? Our son-in-law, Hank? Our only grandchild, Carolyn?"

"Sarcasm does not become you, dearest. You're acting as if I neglect our family."

"You missed her birthday."

Julia's heart skipped a beat. Her mind scanned a mental calendar. She gasped. "I missed it!" She turned to Edward. "How did I miss it? Why didn't Mary remind me? Or Arthur? I'm sure I had Mary put it on my calendar."

"So it's your secretary's fault?"

"No, but…" She thought of something. "Why didn't *you* remind me?"

Edward looked at her, then away. "It was a test."

"You were testing me?"

"Call it tough love."

She stared at him, and pinched the sleeve of his coat, giving it a shake. "Excuse me, Edward Carson, I don't *need* tough love. I don't *need* to be tested."

He shrugged, obviously unimpressed. "Only someone who fails a test makes such a comment. You're going over the edge, Julia. I had to stop you—or try to stop you."

"At Bonnie's expense?"

"No, not Bonnie's. I called her with birthday wishes. She doesn't know you forgot."

"Then at whose expense?"

"Unfortunately—unavoidably—yours."

Julia slumped on the seat. Anger and shame collided. How could she forget her daughter's birthday? But how could Edward test her? She hated the look of judgment on his face. Fine. So she'd failed the test? She was willing to accept the blame, but people had to cut her a little slack. After all, she *was* president of the United States. She had a lot on her mind.

She shook her head. *I don't have time for this now…*

"You do have time for this now."

She stared at her husband. "How did you know what I was thinking? That's my talent."

"And mine. I know you better than you know yourself."

She crossed her arms. "Okay, hot shot. What else was I thinking?"

He mimicked her crossed arms and gave her a head-to-toe stare. "You were thinking that as president of the United States, you can only be expected to do so much, and that *so much* may or may not include remembering birthdays, doing a daily Bible study, or taking long walks with your husband."

She huffed. "You were only partially right, Mr. Know-It-All. I never thought about the Bible study or walking with you."

"I know."

She took in a breath to speak, then let it out. "You know the strains of my schedule. Something has to give."

"And that something is your family and God?"

He was missing the point. "Not everyone gets the chance I'm getting, Edward. I've been given the ability to change the world."

He raised an eyebrow.

She realized her faux pas. "I've been given the *opportunity* to *help* change the world."

"Good save."

"I aim to please."

"I know. And that's your problem." He took her hand and brought it to his lips. It was a gesture that never failed to melt her, and it took all her power to resist giving in. "In trying to please everyone, in trying to change the world in the time you have in office, you may end up not pleasing anyone. And losing yourself in the process."

She pulled her hand away. "I am not losing myself. I am very adamant about holding onto my convictions, in taking a stand for my beliefs."

"I'm not denying that you're good at the public part of the office, Julia. It's your private life that is suffering. You're so caught up in being the president that you have neglected to be Julia Carson. Wife, mother, friend, and child of God. You've let your position swallow you whole."

She tossed her arms in the air. "I don't know what you expect of me, Edward. I can't do it all."

He applauded. "That's the first right thing I've heard you say."

She looked out the window at the city flying by. Anywhere but at his righteous eyes. "You don't understand. You don't understand at all."

"I understand more than you think, my love."

Time would tell.

"But Bonnie, we *want* you to go." Julia moved the car phone to her other ear. She closed her eyes and listened to her daughter's tirade. She'd thought of the perfect solution: Bonnie and her family would come with them to the reunion.

Unfortunately, Bonnie did not see the plan's perfection.

"Why should we go, Mother?"

"It's a reunion, honey. It would be a nice place for us to—"

"Our *home* is a nice place for us to get together on Thanksgiving. *I* want to cook a turkey. *I* want to set the table with orange napkins. *I* want to sit around our dining room and overeat and laugh and talk, just the five of us. Why should we give up our family reunion for a national one?" She laughed. "Oh. Never mind. Dumb question. I almost forgot. The nation comes first."

Julia's throat was tight. "But—"

"Do what you want, Mother. You know where we live."

The line went dead. Julia hung up.

"What did she say?"

"Oooh!" Julia made two fists by her ears. "She makes me so mad. She's being completely selfish. Can't she compromise? The reunion is important."

Edward's voice was small. "So is she."

Julia closed her eyes and sighed. "Why does she put me in this position?"

"*Us* in this position, missy."

It was no use. Julia couldn't even complain without getting in trouble.

———◦∿◦———

The phone was ringing. Art ran into his apartment and lunged for it. "Hello!"

"Hamm here."

Art tossed his keys on the counter. He didn't feel up to dealing with Hamm tonight. It had been a busy day at work and he was getting more and more frustrated that he was dealing with Julia's secretary—being *her* gofer—more than dealing directly with Julia. He realized his expectations may have been skewed, but his disappointment was still genuine.

"What's up, Hamm?"

"Plenty. I need you over here."

"Over where?"

"My apartment. Got a pen?"

"Now? I had a hard day and—"

"Ooh, I'm crying. Should the world wait while you take a little nap?"

Art sighed. "What's the address?" He wrote it down on the back of an envelope. "Should I bring Ben along?"

"No!" Hamm's voice calmed. "No, not this time. Come alone."

Art didn't like the sound of that.

Hamm opened the door, squinting at the intrusion. He scratched his bare chest. It was not a pretty sight. "Art. Come in."

Art hesitated, replaying the phone conversation in his head. "You asked me over…?"

"I did. I just didn't expect you to come so quickly. Trying to earn brownie points, are you?"

"Hamm?" They turned toward a girl's voice. She stood in the hallway, wrapped in a sheet.

Before he could stop himself, Art blurted out, "How old are you?"

The girl opened her mouth to answer, but Hamm moved between them. "That's none of your affair, boy." He turned to the girl. "Get dressed and go. I've got business."

The girl gave him a pouty look and turned toward the bedroom, the sheet dragging behind her like an unkempt train. "Shut the door." The bedroom door slammed. Hamm leveled Art with a stare. "What? Nothing going on here that concerns you, boy."

"I—"

"Listen, women are drawn to power."

Women? Hardly. Try *girl.* "She didn't look fifteen."

"She's sixteen. I made sure of that."

How considerate of you. "You're old enough to be her father. Grandfather."

Hamm poked a finger at Art's chest, his eyes two flaming flares. "Never question me again. Understand?"

Art took a step back. "Sure. It's none of my—"

"You'd better believe it's none of your—"

The girl came out of the bedroom and edged around them to the front door. The sides of her hair were combed, but the back remained tangled, like the hair of a child who needed the help of her mother. She left without a word.

As the door clicked shut, Hamm moved to the kitchen and turned on a small TV that sat on the counter. He opened the refrigerator and chugged some milk, then extended the carton to Art. "Want some?"

Sharing germs with this man was not an option. Art did his best to hide his disgust, but he couldn't help but make a face.

Hamm fell into a chrome-legged chair, and Art studied him. At their dinner he had looked so prim and proper in his bow tie and white socks. Now, with him sitting so nonchalantly, dressed only in boxer shorts, Art felt as if his own privacy had been violated.

Hamm took a dirty fork and stabbed at a piece of dried meat on a plate. A dead cricket hung in a spider web in the corner. A pile of newspapers teetered on a chair. Hamm noticed Art notice.

"You like my place?"

Art hesitated. "It's not what I expected. The other night… you looked so put together."

Hamm laughed. "A facade, boy. Look like a terrorist, get treated like a terrorist. Look like a nerd, get ignored like a nerd—ignored and passed over, which suits me just fine."

Terrorist?

Hamm rose with a grunt and went in the bedroom. He returned a moment later, zipping his pants. A shirt was tossed over his shoulder.

Art sat at the table and started to lay his hands on the food-encrusted surface, but the layers of stains made him long for gloves. He put his hands in his lap instead. He didn't like it here. He wanted to be gone. "Why did you want me to come over?"

"I want you to explain yourself."

"In what way?"

"Explain why you didn't tell us you were working for President Carson."

Art's heart stopped a moment, then made up for lost beats. "I...I..."

"You look green, boy."

Get a hold of yourself, Art. Calm...calm... Art dislodged a spot of hardened food with his fingernail. He shrugged. "She offered. I said yes. What can I say? The woman likes me. It's to my advantage to play up to it. She thinks of me as her pet project. The poor ex-con helped by the gracious and forgiving president. It's good PR." He looked Hamm in the eye. "Would you say no to the job?"

Hamm considered this a moment. "No, you're probably right. So what do you do?"

"Whatever she wants. I'm a gofer."

"And you see her? You know her schedule. You have access to...things?"

"What kind of things?"

Hamm rubbed his stubbly chin. "I don't know yet. But your position may come in handy."

"How?"

Hamm ignored the question and pointed to a game show on television. The contestants were jumping up and down, clapping. "Fascinating, isn't it? How excited people get about *things.*"

Art glanced around Hamm's apartment. "Apparently you don't have that vice?"

He gave a sly smile. "Not that one."

Art thought of the girl and felt his stomach turn. "You didn't answer my question. How can me working for Julia come in

212

handy? How can she help TAI spread the truth that you and Ben talk about?"

"There are different versions of truth. Certainly you know that?"

"Well, sure…but—"

"To get people to change their minds; to get them to think how we want them to think, we need to confuse them, torment them, make them look for something better."

"Why not just show them something better?" Art tried to remember the lingo Ben had used. "Show them that individual power, that truth is—"

"Will you lay off the truth bit? You sound like Ben. Like an idealistic dreamer."

If this was how Hamm talked about his friends… "But don't we have to teach people in order to make them change?"

"Absolutely not. When we try to teach, we risk having logic taking over. God argues as well as we do. Forget enlightenment. Befuddlement is far more effective. People are used to being confused; used to having contradicting ideas floating through their minds. Most wouldn't know truth if it bit them, so there's no need to argue. Just add our views to the jumble. The mish-mash will lead to bewilderment, bewilderment to apathy, and finally apathy to our greatest ally: inaction. To have a thousand people do nothing is better than risking the chance of a single person doing something good. People are patsies."

Hamm's logic was sound—and that was frightening. Art glanced at the TV screen and noticed the game show had given way to something new. He saw a man in a hospital bed talking and heard a word that was familiar to him.

"…Haven. To many of you, that means nothing, but to some of you, that means everything. For you, too, received an invitation to go to a town called Haven."

Art pointed at the screen. "That's the priest from Haven!"

"You know him?"

"I knew of him. He was with the others when I kidnapped

213

Julia. I shot him, but his wound was healed. Instantly."

"But how—?"

Art shushed him, wanting to hear.

"In Haven we began a journey—a quest—to find our unique purpose in life. Each one of us has been placed in a unique time, a unique place, with unique contacts—a blending of friends, family, and coworkers that is distinct and hand-picked."

"Handpicked by whom?"

The man in the hospital bed faced the camera. "By God."

"That interviewer guy was there too! He was the guy I was aiming for when the priest jumped in front of him."

When the broadcast was over, Hamm turned off the television, and Art noticed that his face had paled. The older man pointed at the screen. "How dare they get airtime on national television to endorse their do-gooder propaganda. And a reunion?"

"It makes sense. Those people are close. Julia and Edward said—" Art stopped himself from saying more.

"What did they say?"

Art resumed his tough-guy routine. "They brag about the experience. How God brought them together so they'd dedicate their lives to such and such. Big talk."

Hamm stared at the floor, his fist at his mouth. "I'd gotten some information about an upcoming event instigated by the other side. We were trying to stop it, but…" He looked up. "I wonder if this reunion is it, and our attempts to stop it have failed?"

"What attempts?"

There was a foreign tightness to Hamm's voice. "It's none of your business—yet. But if this reunion happens, we'll have believers coming out of the woodwork. We may be forced to whip up some big-time opposition."

Opposition. Battle. Art shivered. "What are you talking about?"

Hamm tossed a dirty plate in the sink. "You ask way too many questions. Especially for an untested rookie." Then a grin formed, starting at Hamm's eyes and moving down to his jaw like a disease conquering a weaker organ. "But maybe…if you're willing to be tested."

Art's muscles tensed. This could be the end of his association with TAI. He was only willing to go so far… "What did you have in mind?"

Hamm stared at the blank TV screen a moment before slapping his hands together. "Steal her pin."

"What?"

"Steal President Carson's mustard seed pin."

"What will that prove?"

"That you can do it. That you're that close to her. That you're willing to take a risk for us."

"She likes the pin. It's sentimental to her. But it's just a pin. Losing it won't hurt her."

"Maybe not. But it will help you gain favor with me—and with my boss." He leveled Art with a look. "Isn't that enough?"

"Who's your boss?"

Hamm raised an eyebrow. "You really want to know?"

Art hesitated. It was the logical next step. "Sure. I mean, shouldn't I meet him if I'm going to risk my job for—"

A thump sounded in the bedroom. Hamm spun toward it, and Art could swear the man was holding his breath. Art followed suit. Neither one moved. After a minute with no other sounds, Hamm grabbed his shoes. "Let's go."

"What was that?"

"Now!"

"But I want to meet—"

Hamm hurried out the apartment door, his shoes in his hands. He shut the door behind them. "Don't worry. You'll meet him soon enough. You can count on it."

CHAPTER NINETEEN

I will turn their mourning into gladness; I will give them comfort and joy instead of sorrow.

JEREMIAH 31:13

RYAN BAUER COULDN'T TAKE HIS EYES OFF the television set. Images of yesterday's plane crash in Minneapolis flashed across the screen. The damaged plane teetered to one side, the wing broken. The lights of the emergency vehicles pulsed. And the people. The hurt, scared people.

Ryan pulled his knees to his chin. His insides ached. How awful it must have been for them to feel the plane falling. He'd gone on a roller coaster once—a kid's roller coaster—but he'd felt the drop in his stomach just the same.

But this was different. These people hadn't known if they were coming out safe at the bottom of the drop. They'd been afraid.

Ryan didn't like being afraid. There hadn't been many times in his life, but the times he *had* been scared were enough for him. Like the time during the tornadoes in Haven when his dad had been swept away, and when his dad came back and then died again...

Then there was the time Lisa disappeared, and the time she got appendicitis, and the time his friend, Willie, cried 'cause his Dad had spanked him too hard...

Nope. Ryan didn't want anyone to be afraid.

"Now, for local news..." The news switched to the scene of a house fire in Eureka Springs. A family huddled in blankets against the cold, their eyes sad—and afraid.

The front door opened and Ryan's mom and dad came in.

They'd been to dinner, but his mom didn't look happy. He'd heard them talking about a new house. What was wrong with the one they had?

The baby-sitter met them at the door, as did Lisa. Ryan stayed where he was.

"Hey, buddy-boy." His dad ruffled his hair. "Isn't there something happier on TV?"

The baby-sitter broke in. "I asked him if he wanted to watch cartoons, but he said no, he wanted to watch the news."

His mom hung her purse on the hat tree. "That's his newest thing."

"I thought it was morbid, but—"

His dad stood behind him and rubbed Ryan's shoulders in the way Ryan loved. "Ryan doesn't watch it for the thrill. He's our conscience in the world. Aren't you, buddy?"

Ryan didn't answer because he wasn't sure what *conscience* meant. All he knew was that he watched the news because he *had* to. The people needed him to see their pain.

How else could he pray for them?

Ryan sat next to his dad and Lisa watching TV. His dad held a huge bowl of popcorn.

Ryan made a face when Lisa grabbed a handful and stuffed it in her mouth, spilling half of it. She also insisted on pretending to feed her stuffed toy, Bunny Bob, though Ryan noticed she ate what he spilled too. Lisa did everything fast and messy. He'd show her how to do it. He took a few kernels and held them in one hand while he fed himself the kernels, one by one, with the other. Lisa noticed but she stuck her tongue out at him. *Gross.* It was covered with half-chewed popcorn.

Ryan was glad his dad had kept the news on in spite of Lisa's complaints. He knew his dad was proud of his interest in the news. Once Ryan had heard him tell his mom, "How many eight-year-olds care about anyone other than themselves?" That had made him feel good. And he liked when they watched it together, because then Ryan could ask questions. His dad usually had good answers, but Ryan hadn't asked the really hard stuff yet. Like "Why is there war?" or "How come God lets bad things happen?" He didn't ask the questions because he didn't want to hear his dad say, "I don't know."

Lisa took the remote and switched channels.

"Don't grab, honey."

"But I want good stuff, not icky stuff."

"It's not icky, honey. It's the—" Their dad stopped talking. "Hey!" He took the remote away from her and backtracked.

"You said don't grab, Daddy."

"I know but…" He stopped on a station. "Kath! Come here! Del and Walter are on TV!"

Ryan's mom appeared from down the hall, shoving an arm in a sweatshirt. "On TV?"

"There." His dad pointed and his mom sat on the arm of the couch, right next to Ryan. They listened to Del's speech.

"Well, I'll be. Del was in that plane crash."

Ryan tugged at her pant leg. "I saw that on TV. I saw it."

Lisa curled into the cushions. "Turn to cartoons. This is boring."

Ryan couldn't look away. "No, it's not, Lisa. That's Del. He's the man at Haven who was shot and the bullet hole went away. Like magic."

His mother touched his shoulder. "Not magic, sweetie. It was God's doing."

Lisa dug her head under their dad's arm. "I don't remember. I was too little."

"I remember." Ryan nodded solemnly. "I remember all of it."

He saw his mom and dad exchange a look and knew they didn't believe him. It didn't matter. He remembered. It had been a very special time in his life. He remembered the trip on the bus with his mom and Lisa, and the motel room with the Arkansas Razorback bedspread meant just for him. He remembered running a car up and down his daddy's leg, and his daddy shooing him away when all he wanted was a hug. He remembered Lisa's rubber-toed tennis shoe found in the grass; grape Kool-Aid and mashed potatoes tossed onto Walter's shirt…

"Are we going to the reunion, Mom?"

His dad answered. "Sure we are. Del has asked your mom to paint a picture to use on the programs. The original is going to be raffled off."

His mom walked away. Her head shook back and forth like the ticker on the clock. When she spoke, her voice sounded tired. And sad. Really sad.

"I'm not sure, Roy. I don't feel much like painting anything inspirational—or going to a reunion."

"Don't be silly." His dad went to her side and put a hand on the back of her neck, stopping its swing. "You have to. Del's depending on you."

She brushed his hand away and faced him. "I don't want people to depend on me. I've had people depending on me my whole life. I don't want to *be* dependable anymore. I want to enjoy life."

"If this is about the house—"

"The house is only part of it. The point is, when is it my turn?"

Her turn to do what? Ryan hated to see his mom so upset. He went to her side and hugged her. He heard her heartbeat in his ear. "Don't be upset, Mom. I'll help you."

She started to cry. Ryan felt her pain.

CHAPTER TWENTY

Resentment kills a fool, and envy slays the simple.

JOB 5:2

MONSIGNOR VIBROWSKY SHUT OFF the television and scowled at it. His anger vexed him because he was sure it stemmed from some deeper vice that he preferred not to think about. The truth was, Father Del bugged him.

Del's luck was unbelievable. How many people could be in a plane crash, survive, and have it fit perfectly into his plan? Not even just fit, but *enhance* his plan.

The national media had picked up on Del's *Good News* broadcast, zoning in on the fact that a survivor of a plane crash was calling together a religious revival. The monsignor had already seen one interview with Del where the interviewer had asked, "Are you planning this revival because you survived the plane crash?" To which Del had adeptly answered, "Actually, I survived the plane crash because I'm planning this revival." It was a classic case of "Which came first? The chicken or the egg?" The press walked in to what they thought was a crisis-provoked decision, only to find the opposite was true.

The monsignor sat up to get blood flowing through his body. Perhaps movement would dispel his anger and jealousy. But perhaps not. Those traits had been with him for serveral years—ever since Antonio Delatondo had come into his life with mystical talk of being sent to the St. Stephen's parish by divine intervention.

Divine intervention. Nonsense. Such things only happened in the Bible or to saints who lived hundreds of years ago. They did not happen in Lincoln, Nebraska, to ordinary people who had trouble getting up in the morning and who wore ponytails. Actually, the removal of Father Del's ponytail had been the monsignor's one victory—even though he had nothing to do with it. One day, Del had simply shown up properly shorn. "It was time," he had said.

Who was Del kidding? It was *past* time.

There was a knock on his office door, and Mildred came in with a stack of pink notes.

"Excuse me, Monsignor, but the phones...people are calling about the reunion. What should I tell them?"

Monsignor closed his eyes and rubbed his temples. "I knew this would happen when Del gave our telephone number. He had no right to—"

"I don't mind, Monsignor. Really, I don't. It's just that I don't know what to tell them. Father didn't leave any instructions."

"I'm sure he didn't."

She ruffled through the pink notes. "Do you know what hotel it's at? What time? The cost?"

"No, and I doubt Del knows either."

"What?"

"Never mind." Monsignor rose and walked to the window. He clutched his hands behind his back and looked upon the peaceful fall day. Had anything been peaceful since Del had come into his life?

"Monsignor? What should I tell people?"

He took a deep breath and turned toward her. "Tell them Father Del will call them back. Personally."

"But he's in the hosp—"

"Tell them."

"Yes, sir."

She left him alone with his jealousy.

The monsignor's phone rang. He had barely gotten out the word, "Hello," when the caller cut in.

"Since he isn't there, they told me to talk to you."

"Who is *he?*"

"Del. My brother."

"You're Del's sister?"

"The one and only."

"I didn't know he had a sister."

"Ah." She took a breath. "Black sheep are seldom given the credit they deserve."

"You're the black sheep?"

"The very blackest. I'm a wild, irresponsible, flighty woman who can't hold a job—or a man." She gave a throaty chuckle. "The name's Alexa Margaret Delatondo. Lexa for short."

The monsignor leaned back in his chair and closed his eyes. *Two of them. There are two of them.* "What can I do for you, Lexa?"

"I saw Del on TV. I want to talk to him."

"He's not here. He's still in Minneapolis. I'm not sure when he'll be flying back, considering he's in the hospital."

"He looked okay to me. Del has always lived through close calls. Why, there was the one time on our bikes when we went over the edge—"

"I'm quite busy, Lexa. Would you like to leave a message for your brother?"

"Message?" She laughed. "No, no message. I think I'll take a little trip and grace him with my presence."

"You're coming *here?*"

"Is *here* off limits?"

"No, no…it's just that—"

"I won't be any trouble—or no more trouble than usual. You'll have to ask Del exactly what that means. But I figure there was a reason I saw Del on TV after all these years. I'm afraid I haven't kept in touch with my family—estranged for being strange, you know how that goes. There's just my mother and Del now, but I've been…busy with my life. More than busy."

"And you're not now?'

"Let's say there's been a sudden lull. I have the time, and Del's given me the excuse. Lincoln, Nebraska, here I come."

Monsignor hung up and wondered why he was being punished.

CHAPTER TWENTY-ONE

Those who suffer according to God's will should commit themselves to their faithful Creator and continue to do good.

1 PETER 4:19

WALTER PAUSED OUTSIDE Harriet Lane's office. He put the piece of paper he was holding between his teeth and tucked in the back of his shirt. This would be great. Although he'd taken a chance by going ahead with Del's broadcast, the response coming into the station was encouraging. People were interested in Del, the reunion, and of course, the plane crash. There was nothing that piqued the public's interest more than people on the threshold of death—especially if they survived. It gave them hope and pushed their gratitude button because it hadn't happened to them. He and Del had discussed just that point on the way to the airport that morning.

Walter removed the paper from his teeth and tried to press the marks out of it. This was his insurance policy. He'd had his secretary type up some of the positive phone comments. Added to that was his mental list of the national coverage they'd received. He felt ready to face any opposition. After all he had right on his side.

He knocked on Harriet's door and opened it. "May I come in?"

Harriet took off her reading glasses and indicated the chair in front of her desk. She did not smile. Walter's stomach did a one-eighty. Something wasn't right.

He decided to take the offensive. Before he sat down, he placed the page in front of his interim boss. "Pretty good ratings, don't you think? National coverage too. We've been mentioned on the big three, plus CNN, plus—"

He stopped when she did not even touch the paper. He scooted it an inch closer and pointed to the leading comment. "See there…a woman from Pipestone, Minnesota, said it was wonderful to see proof of a miracle. She'd been in a plane crash once, and all the press reported about were the wounded and dead. She's also interested in the reunion."

Still no response.

"Then there's the man from Aurora, Colorado, who thought it was a great idea to have a revival on Thanksgiving, since that is the day we're supposed to say thanks to—"

"You disobeyed me." She leveled him with a look. "You waited until I was out of town and then you disobeyed me."

Walter retracted his hand as though she might slap it." Technically…yes, I did. But I figured with the tie-in of the plane crash, and the fact that—"

"The fact that *you* wanted to do it."

"Well, yes." Walter scooted his bottom into the back of the chair. "Rolf had already approved it. It was all planned. If he hadn't gotten hurt—"

"But he did get hurt. And I was appointed to take over his position. I was in charge."

But you were wrong! "It worked out great." He tried to keep the whine out of his voice. "We were planning an on-location shoot anyway—"

"You did it to spite me."

Walter realized she might be partially right. "I did it because I thought it was the right thing to do." His mind scrambled for a good excuse. "Did you hear Del's interview with ABC? The one where he said he was saved from the crash because he was planning the reunion?"

"He sounded cocky and egotistical."

"If you knew Del you wouldn't say that."

"But since I don't know Del—as is the case with the rest of

226

the audience—I'm sure my opinion is shared with the general public. I thought you people were supposed to be humble."

You people? Walter's jaw tightened. "We are. But we're also supposed to tell the truth and take a stand, even if we get flak for it; even if there are consequences."

Harriet didn't answer. She stared at Walter until he had to look away or burn from her gaze. Why on earth had he mentioned consequences?

"So are you willing to accept the truth? Are you willing to get flak—"

"I wore my flak jacket, just for the occasion." When she didn't smile, his own smile faded.

Harriet raised her chin. "You didn't let me finish."

Walter's heart beat in his throat. "Sorry. Go on."

"Are you willing to accept the consequences of your actions?"

Walter swallowed. "Sure. As long as they're fair and reason—"

"You're fired."

Walter blinked once for each shocking syllable. "You can't do that."

"I just did."

"But it was a good segment." He pointed to the paper on her desk. "It got good response; it got national attention; it—"

"Was totally against my directive." She shoved the paper toward Walter with one disdainful finger. "I told you not to air your friend's agenda. I made clear to you the consequences of going against me."

"But I didn't think—"

"Exactly. You didn't think it mattered. You thought that just because I'm your interim boss, you could do what you wanted. You thought that just because I wasn't the producer of the great *Good News* that I didn't mean what I said. You thought that just because I am a woman—"

"Hold it." Walter raised his hands. "Your being a woman had nothing to do with it."

"But the rest? What about the rest?" Walter didn't answer. He moved to the edge of his chair and put his hands on her desk. "Harriet…I'm sorry if you're offended that I made a decision against one of your directives, but you *are* new to *Good News*, and Rolf *did* approve this segment, and there were so many circumstances that told us this was supposed to happen."

"Us?"

"Del, myself…and my wife."

"Three against one?"

"We're not against you, Harriet. We were simply forced to make a decision based on factors that…you may not have been able to…" He was digging himself a hole.

"I may not have been able to understand?"

"Well…you *could* have understood them if you'd wanted—" The hole was getting deeper. He took a deep breath and ran a hand over his head. "I've got a little girl, Harriet. A wife. House payments. Bills…"

"You need this job? Is that it?"

"Yes." Walter was relieved she understood. "I need this job."

"Then you should have done more to keep it."

He was stunned. He wasn't sure how he'd gone from relief to panic in ten short seconds. "But—"

Harriet picked up a pen and looked to her work. "That will be all, Mr. Prescott."

"But—"

She glanced up at him, and he noticed the frown lines around her mouth. "That will be *all.*"

Walter stood and found his legs wobbly. "But what about Rolf? He'll be mad when he wakes up and finds me gone."

"*If* he wakes up."

He's got to wake up!

"Good-bye, Walter. Please have your office cleared out by noon."

Walter tightened his jaw to keep it from trembling. "You're a cruel woman, Harriet Lane. May God help you."

She gave him a sickly smile. "Don't bother getting God to help *me,* Walter. You're the one without a job."

Touché.

Walter heaved a box containing his personal belongings into the back of his van. He slammed the door, capturing a shoot of a philodendron. He let it be. Its strangulation mirrored his own feelings. Harriet had slammed the door on his life but good.

Walter wished he were a drinking man so he could hide away in some darkened bar where no one knew him. Drown his sorrows in a river of booze. Pass out so he wouldn't feel the pain.

But he wasn't, so he couldn't.

Walter pulled out of the parking lot of KMPS. For the first time in a week he did not slow down to take note of the progress of the construction crews repairing the fire damage. Such things didn't affect him anymore. For all he cared, the entire station could burn to rubble. Since they didn't want him, he didn't want them.

But that wasn't true, and he knew it. He liked his job. He liked Rolf and Cassandra and Doug; he liked finding stories that lifted up instead of pulling down. TV was all he knew. But who would hire him now? What recommendation could he expect? None. Rolf was in a coma. Harriet was his enemy. And the news of his firing would be around the Twin Cities by tomorrow morning—if it wasn't already item number one on the gossip list. He had been disgraced. He had been humiliated. He had been wronged.

Or had he? He had disobeyed his boss. No matter what had been his justification, he'd done wrong. Doing wrong for the right reasons…such decisions were never clear-cut. Nor were their consequences easy to take.

But the consequences he'd been handed went far beyond the intangibles of humiliation and shame. They affected his livelihood. They affected his family. It wasn't fair.

Walter got on the interstate leading home, the rush of traffic pulling him along like a lemming following its leader to disaster. Maybe if he just stayed on the highway and drove and drove and drove…

No. He had to go home. And once home, he had to tell Bette—admit he was a failure. He could see it now…he would walk in during the middle of the day, and she would look up with questioning eyes. "Why are you home, hon?" He would have to tell her. She would cry and try to comfort him. After fifteen minutes, the practical implications would sink in, and she would begin to ask him all sorts of annoying questions about house payments, charge card bills, and other points of failure.

It was a no-win situation.

Walter's attention was drawn to a brightly-colored billboard. *WIN! WIN! WIN!* He craned his neck to get a better look. Such a happy sign, so full of hope…

Hope. Just what he needed.

Hmm…maybe there was a way he could win after all.

Walter sat in his car and looked at the bank balance in their savings account book. Beyond miniscule. The checking account was worse. Before using his bonus to pay down bills, he'd been robbing savings to cover expenses. Their nest egg had diminished to a few broken shells. The only money they had was money his father had left for Addy's college fund. A thousand dollars. If only he'd held onto the bonus a little longer…

"Sir? May I help you?"

Walter whipped his head toward the drive-through teller. She smiled sweetly.

Don't do it, Walter. There are other ways. Bette will under—

There was a thud on the roof of the car, and Walter jumped, looking around. *What on earth?* But there was nothing there. No more sounds.

"Sir? May I help you?"

He turned back to the teller with a start. Yes, she could help him.

"I need a withdrawal slip please."

The Emerald Casino drew Walter in as if it knew he had a pocket full of money and a heart full of high hopes. Walter didn't hesitate in the parking lot. He didn't want to give himself time to think. Get in, get out, go home with the cash. Having money in his hand would soften the news that he'd been fired. *See, Bette? I can still provide for us.*

Walter walked under the glittering marquee and traded sunlight for the glow of decadence. The interior of the casino assaulted his senses. Royal blue, red, and purple lured him with promises that he deserved to be treated like a king. False gold curlicues and candelabras proclaimed that more was best. Carved cherubs teetering on chubby toes made him forget that vice was encouraged here. Bells, mechanical music, and whoops of joy drew him in with promises that he too could make the clappers of riches ring.

He turned toward the cashier's cage. The man inside smiled and waited for Walter to hand over the first hundred dollars of his money—Addy's money. Walter looked at the man's eyes, hoping for confirmation or some acknowledgement of the importance of this money. But the man's eyes did not change. Pocket change. As the bills were drawn into the cage, Walter's fingers twitched. *Get them back!*

It was too late.

The cashier shoved a tray of dollar coins toward Walter. This was all he got? It didn't seem a fair exchange. But he didn't need to worry. He wouldn't be touching the rest of Addy's money. This first hundred would become a thousand and the thousand would become…

Walter stepped away from the cage. Then he hesitated. It

wasn't too late. He hadn't lost anything. He could cash in his chips and leave. Walk away.

An elderly woman sitting at a slot machine nearby jumped out of her seat and squealed. Bells clanged. Coins shot into the metal receptacle, announcing the victory one at a time, for all the world to hear. *Ping-ping-ping-ping-ping-ping-ping...*

"I won! I won!"

Walter walked deeper into the casino's cavern.

A car honked.

Walter swerved to the safety of his lane. The sudden rush of adrenaline jarred him back to the moment. He sat straighter in the driver's seat and placed both hands on the steering wheel. If he wasn't careful he'd end up—

So what? I've lost everything. I've lost my job, our money...isn't the next step losing my—

Walter's attention was drawn to a passing billboard. A laughing couple toasted each other. The sign read, *Give in to the feeling.*

There was no feeling. Life had drained out of him. Everything he'd worked for was gone. All his time had been wasted...

Another billboard proclaimed: *The time is now!*

To do what? He had nothing. He was worth nothing. He'd destroyed their future. He didn't deserve to have a fu—

"No!" Walter sucked in a breath, jolted by the fatalistic thoughts. He pulled onto the shoulder of the interstate and put the car in park. Cars sped by, making his car shudder in their wake. Walter's breathing was short and shallow as he leaned his head against the steering wheel and squeezed his eyes shut. "God! Help me! I'm sorry, I'm really sorry. Everything's gone wrong. And now I'm feeling...I'm feeling..."

Walter raised his head and opened his eyes. He shook his head in shame; left, right, left, right—

Next to the highway was another billboard. He read its message. He read it again. Then he began to laugh, his tears of despair turning into tears of joy. Walter sniffed loudly, shaking his head again—this time in awe. "Thank you, Lord."

He wiped his face dry, took a cleansing breath, and pulled onto the highway. He tooted his horn at the billboard for a credit bureau, which had unintentionally proclaimed the word of the Lord.

Don't give up!

———✦———

Bette sat on the couch and stared at the floor. She wished she could cry. Tears had always been a comfort to her. But in this situation they would be a waste. What good would it do to cry? Or speak.

Ever since Walter had explained the situation and confessed his stupidity at the casino, she had remained silent. It hadn't been because she didn't have anything to say—she had *too much* to say. She feared if she let the words out, the polluted water of her anger, bitterness, and fear would flood the space between them and wash their marriage away. Walter had lost his job—by doing the right thing. And he had lost all their money—by doing the wrong thing. If only the right could outweigh the wrong. Why had doing right brought such dire consequences?

She blinked as she was reminded of another man who had done the right thing and had suffered unfairly for it. Joseph. Fresh words came to her. Words devoid of anger and disappointment. She took a breath and spoke. "God was with Joseph."

Walter looked up, his obvious relief at her saying something quickly replaced by a look of puzzlement. "Who's Joseph?"

"Joseph in the Bible."

"Joseph and Mary?"

Bette put her hands on her cheeks. They were warm. "No...the other Joseph. I didn't mean to say it out loud. I was

233

just thinking of Joseph, the boy who was sold into Egyptian slavery by his brothers. While he was a slave, he rejected the advances of the wife of an Egyptian official, but he was still accused of rape. Even though he did the right thing by resisting her, he was punished. He was put in prison for years."

"And I suppose he accepted all this with a smile."

"Not really. He was confused. He'd always felt that God had a special purpose for him. In fact it was his cocky certainty that had egged his brothers on in the first place. But as a slave in prison, he wondered why God was doing this to him."

"A logical question." Walter hugged a pillow to his chest. "But I'm not a slave in prison."

"No, but you are being punished for doing the right thing."

Walter shook his head. "Is there a happy ending to this story, because I don't—"

"There *is* a happy ending. While he was in prison, Joseph's talents were recognized and eventually he became the governor of Egypt—second in command under the pharaoh. He saved thousands of people's lives—including his brothers'."

"Okay…" Walter scratched behind his ear. "I seem to remember this story now. And it's interesting, but the last time I checked, Minnesota was fresh out of pharaohs."

Bette closed her eyes trying to find some patience. Sometimes Walter took things so literally. "Look beyond the details of the story, hon. Look at the lesson."

"The best politicians have spent time in—"

"Walter!"

"Sorry. Why don't you explain it to me."

"The lesson is, sometimes there are consequences to doing the right thing. If you resist temptation by making a choice to do right—like you did by airing Del's segment on *Good News*—you have to accept those consequences." Walter opened his mouth to speak, but Bette stopped him with a hand. "And… God can bring good things out of your struggles, if you keep your eyes on Him."

Walter poked his fingers through the fringe on the throw pillow. "That takes care of me doing the right thing…but what about me doing the wrong thing by gambling away our savings?"

"There are consequences to that too."

"Don't I know it."

"You can get another job. I could work—"

"But our plan was for you to stay home with Addy, at least until she starts school."

"Plans change." Bette looked around the living room. She knew what she was going to say next would not go over well. Maybe she shouldn't say it. Maybe she wouldn't *have* to say it. Maybe Walter could appeal to the administration of KMPS and get his job back. Maybe he'd get another good paying job right away. Maybe Rolf would come out of his coma right this minute and make everything okay.

But maybe not. Maybe there would be more downs before they would be able to climb back up. She closed her eyes for a moment. *Lord, show us what to do.*

She opened her eyes and said the words that had been on her mind. "We need to sell the house, Walter."

He sprang to standing, waving the pillow in the air. "Uh-uh. No way."

Bette nodded, feeling a new confidence after hearing the words said out loud. They'd been living on the edge a long time. Over the edge. She'd tried to ignore Walter's financial irresponsibility, but by allowing it to continue…

She'd worked hard at submitting to Walter as head of the household—and God knew it wasn't easy aiming to be that Proverbs 31 woman. But it did make sense that someone had to have the deciding vote on things, and she had been willing to let that someone be Walter. *Willing or eager?*

So what about the times when the decision-maker was wrong? What happened to submission then? Wasn't she also his partner? His equal partner. *"And they will become one flesh…"*

Had she neglected her own responsibility in their family unit, using submission as a way to escape blame? Avoid confrontation? Pass the buck? She'd seen that Walter was on a downhill slide for a long time, like a willful child on a sled heading down an icy hill toward destruction. Yet clothed in her safety net of submission, she'd let him zip on by. *It's not my job. He's the one messing up.*

Her silence under the guise of submission had been a part of the problem. And now it was time to face the music, discordant as it might be. She moved to his side, placing a hand on his shoulder. He flinched. She did not remove her hand. "We can move into a smaller house, Walter. Maybe an apartment? Just until we get squared away."

He whipped around to face her. "But this house was perfect for us. It was the only house I looked at. It called to me. It felt right."

"It was right. For two years it *has* been right. But circumstances change. It's just a house." *A house that I love.*

Walter drilled the pillow into the couch. "I said no! God can take my job away, and I can lose our money, but I will not give up our home."

"You may not have a choice, Walter."

He stormed out of the room. She heard their bedroom door slam. She didn't go after him.

CHAPTER TWENTY-TWO

———◦◦◦◦———

"But we had to celebrate and be glad, because this brother of yours was dead and is alive again; he was lost and is found."

LUKE 15:32

DEL WAS MET AT THE AIRPORT by a sympathetic Father Caspian, and met at the front door of St. Stephen's by a frenetic Monsignor Vibrowsky.

"A moment of your time, Father?"

Caspian pointed toward Del's room. "He needs his rest, Monsignor. I don't think—"

"Which he will get as soon as he addresses the current problem."

It was then that Del noticed the stack of pink message slips in the monsignor's hand. He put a hand on Caspian's arm. "I'll be okay."

Caspian glanced at the monsignor, then picked up Del's suitcase and disappeared down the hall.

Del put a hand to his ribs and faced his superior, hoping they could do this sitting down. "It's about the reunion, isn't it?"

Monsignor locked his knees and raised his jaw. He brought the messages front and center. "It's getting out of control, Father. You've put the parish in an awkward position. Mildred has been swamped with phone calls from people asking questions we aren't prepared to answer. You left us running blind."

Duly chastised, Del realized he hadn't thought things through well. He turned toward the parish office. "Let me go apologize to her—"

"You can do that later." He took Del's arm and led him

down the hall to an empty office. "Here. This is your space. Use it and let the rest of us get back to normal." He slapped the messages on the desk. "Understood?"

"Yes, sir."

The monsignor strode down the hall, leaving Del alone. It was charitable of him to supply some office space, but that meant Del should get to work. And he didn't feel up to that. Not at all.

He eased himself into the desk chair and fanned the messages before him. Area codes he didn't recognize. Surnames from Smith to Stancowsky. They made him happy—and relieved—that he wasn't going to give a reunion and have no one come. But they were also a discouraging reminder of the enormity of the details left unsettled.

He ran a hand over the bandage on his face. The wound throbbed, as did his ribs. He should be in bed. But how could he rest? People demanded answers to questions for which he had no answers.

Not yet.

He covered his eyes and bowed his head. "Lord, I believe this is supposed to happen, but I'm still not sure I'm the one to do the job. I'm not good at this type of organizing. I have no clue where to begi—"

"You always were clueless."

In the span of a few seconds, Del recognized the voice, let his mind register disbelief, and looked up to confirm the impossible. "Lexa!"

His sister leaned on the doorjamb and crossed her arms. Father Caspian stood behind her, grinning. "I found her wandering through the rectory living room."

"I think back doors offer a much more interesting viewpoint of the world. Actually, I was hoping to catch a priest in his Skivvies." She shrugged. "Maybe next time." She clapped Caspian on the arm. "Thanks for saving me from myself, Father."

"I figured Del would appreciate a friendly face." Caspian looked around the office. "I thought you'd be drawn and quartered by now."

"Our beloved leader had better things to do; I think he's on the planning committee of a new Inquisition."

Caspian raised an eyebrow. "My, my…you must be tired. You're absolutely caustic. Touché, Brother Del." Caspian saluted and left them alone.

Lexa turned to face Del. "So. Then. What have you gotten yourself into, brother?"

Del pushed himself away from the desk and moved to greet her. At the last moment, he hesitated, unsure she would accept his hug.

She waved him close. "Come on. Hug me. I know you won't think it's a proper reunion without a hug."

He hugged her as fiercely as his injuries would allow, then pulled away to look at her. She hadn't changed much in five years. Still solid and athletic with a short no-nonsense haircut that mirrored her no-nonsense approach to life.

She looked behind him. "Where's the ponytail?"

He reached for it. "I cut it off in a fit of conservative frenzy."

"Don't give in to them, Delly. It was hard enough letting them take you away from me, but to have them take your ponytail too." She shook her head.

"Who exactly is *them*?"

She shrugged and fell into a chair near the desk. "The church. The world. God."

"Yikes, it's a conspiracy."

"Absolutely."

Del returned to his seat and placed his hands on the desk. He studied her. "You look wonderful."

"That's never been a problem."

He noticed the catch in her voice. "But something else is?"

She shrugged and looked at her manicure. "Just the usual. Another month, another man."

239

"Last I heard you were living with Pat—"

"Pete. And that was—" she counted on her fingers—"six live-ins ago."

Del nearly choked. "You've lived with six men in five years?"

"Seven counting Pete."

"Does Mother know about this?"

"Mother would prefer not to hear about her wayward daughter. That way she can still think of me as her saintly little girl."

Del had to smile. "You were never a saintly little girl."

She raised an eyebrow, conceding the point. "Anyway, I've been going through a bad time and when I saw you on TV—"

"What bad time?"

She moved to the window, and Del braced himself. It must be pretty serious if she couldn't say it eye to eye. He thought about going to her, but he could tell she needed space.

Silence settled between them.

Finally, she spoke. "I'm tired of men leaving me." She turned to look at him. "You were the first."

"I didn't leave you. I became a priest."

"You left me. God took you, then He took Dad."

These were old arguments; they weren't what bothered her now. "Ancient history."

She shrugged and looked back to the window. "How come everything can be going along just fine and then suddenly you get this...this *feeling*, this discontent that pops up and won't leave you alone."

"This *you* is you?"

She nodded and returned to her chair. "I've never led a conventional life."

"I hadn't noticed."

She smiled. "Being different was expected of me. It was my duty."

"According to whom?"

"I don't know…maybe it's because you became a priest—"

"You can't blame everything on my decision."

"I'm not. But when you made the choice, I knew what you were giving up…" She looked to her lap. "It's like I decided to grab onto the aspects of life you'd discarded."

"I didn't discard anything. I chose."

She sighed. "So you say. But I've never understood that choice. How can you choose God over what's real?"

"God is real."

She leaned forward, putting her arms on the desk. "But that's what I don't get. How can a life talking to some being we can't even see be more real than dealing with flesh and blood people?"

"I'm not a hermit, Lexa. I deal with flesh and blood people every day."

"Trying to lead them to God."

"To the One who made us. We owe everything to—"

"Then why did He make me such a mixed-up woman?"

Ah. The truth finally surfaced.

Del reached across the desk for her hand. "Sometimes God stirs us up for good reason."

"To drive us crazy?"

"To draw us closer to Him, to make us leave behind our sinning ways."

She squinted an eye at him. "You saying I'm a sinner?"

"No worse than I."

Her laugh was bitter. "Oh, that's a stitch. Delly, the kid who was God's gift to childhood, who fulfilled his parents' dream by becoming a man of God, is as big a sinner as his sister who has drank, drugged, and dallied."

Del pulled his hand away. "You forgot about Mellie."

Lexa bolted from her chair. "Don't give me that, brother dear. You made one mistake by trying to help a hooker get out of the life. It turned out bad—"

"She was killed."

"But *you* didn't kill her. Her pimp of a husband did that."

"There have been other things—"

Lexa raised her hands. "I don't want to hear it. Whatever you've done, you've paid back tenfold. What happened to the forgiveness of sins, Father Del?"

"I know I've been forgiven."

"Well, I don't!"

Her declaration echoed in the room. Del watched her chin quiver, and he reached for her a second time, but she shook her head and looked away. When she spoke her voice was soft. "I haven't prayed in years, Delly. I figured God wouldn't want to hear from me when I was so blatantly living a life against Him. But lately, I'd gotten the urge to begin again. Yet I didn't know how. And then I saw you on TV…" She looked at him, her face pathetic. "I want to start over, Delly. I want a fresh start."

Del went to her side and pulled her close.

And this time, she let him.

It took an hour for Del to fill Lexa in on what had happened to him in the past five years. The voluntary homelessness, the invitation to Haven, the bullet wound healed in a miraculous moment, the move to Lincoln, the battle with a demon in Eureka Springs… He could tell she was skeptical, but he knew it was important to lay everything out in the open. What he wanted her to do, he had to do.

When he stopped his story, she shook her head. "So, that's it?"

"Pretty much."

She snickered. "And to think I thought the priestly life was boring."

"God keeps me on my toes."

She pointed to the pink messages on the desk. "Forget toes. It appears you're up to your eyebrows in work."

Del hated to be reminded of it. The immensity of the task threatened to pull him under. "It's work I have no idea how to do. Like I said when you came in, I haven't a clue—"

She slammed a hand on the desk. "But I do!"

"What?"

Her eyes flashed in that way he'd seen a hundred times during their childhood. Something was cooking in that brain of hers.

"In between living life in the fast lane, I, Lexa Delatondo, worked as an event coordinator for a multimillion-dollar corporation."

"Worked?"

She gathered the notes together. "I quit my job a week ago because of that annoying begin-again urge. I'm a free agent." She looked up at him. "You need me."

"I do?"

She waved the stack of notes in his face. "This is why I'm here. To help you organize this reunion."

Del felt a flood of relief. It was too good to be true. His prodigal sister's return corresponded with an answer to his reunion problems. "You'd do that?"

"This is what I do best. Organize. Mobilize. Prioritize."

"Terrorize?"

She slapped the notes against her palm. "You ain't seen nothing yet."

Del laughed. "Promise?"

Del knocked on the door to monsignor's office.

"Come in."

Del took Lexa's hand and led her into the lion's den.

The monsignor looked up from his papers. "So. I see she found you."

"Monsignor, I want to introduce you to my sister, Alexa Delatondo."

When the monsignor didn't offer a hand, Lexa did. "I'm afraid I'm out of the loop, Monsignor. Should I kiss your ring or something?"

"That won't be necessary."

Del noticed they weren't asked to be seated. Oh well, they could do their business just as well standing up. "Besides seeing my sister again, her coming is a godsend. She's going to help organize the reunion for me."

Monsignor raised an eyebrow.

"It's what I do—did—for a living, Monsignor. Del's never been very good at organizing things, so I'm glad to—"

"We'd appreciate getting Father Del back to his regular duties. He made a promise that this reunion would be handled in his spare time and—"

"And now it will, Monsignor." Del took a step forward. "However…I plan to ask one of my students to help Lexa—in her spare time."

"Did you have someone in mind?"

"Actually, yes. Carrie Peterson. She's worked with me at the food bank and she's very good with the sort of tasks Lexa needs help with."

"So you're robbing the food bank for your own purposes?"

Del was ready for this one. "The food bank has plenty of help. And Carrie has agreed—" As soon as Del said it, he realized he shouldn't have.

"So you've already asked her?"

Del took a deep breath. "When I was showing Lexa around we happened to see Carrie in the halls. Actually, she volunteered."

"Hmm."

"Would that be agreeable, Monsignor?"

"It appears that what I agree to matters little, Father—"

"That's not true. I want—I seek—your approval on all—"

The monsignor leveled Del with a look, then flipped a hand

in dismissal. "Go do your stuff, Father."

Del turned to leave and held the door for Lexa. As he shut it, he heard Monsignor's final words: "But watch it."

CHAPTER TWENTY-THREE

*"You did not choose me, but I chose you and appointed you
to go and bear fruit—fruit that will last."*

JOHN 15:16

NATALIE WAS AMAZED TO FIND HER EYES OPEN. How long had
she been awake, staring into space? Her dreams had edged into
reality without crossing a distinguishing line. Both were filled
with sadness.

Sam was gone. It had happened so fast…

It was odd to wake to the thought of no Sam in her life.
She'd left him behind once before. Would she stay away this
time, or run back to him again? And again? Could she ever
completely sever the tie that bound them together? Should she
sever it? Or could it be loosened, allowing each of them to
move and live, separate but forever linked?

"I hope so."

Her words hung in the empty apartment like an unin-
tended benediction. She sat up in bed and swung her feet to
the side. The air nipped at their warmth. She moved to the
kitchen and saw that it was snowing. She stood at the window
and watched the flakes parading past, calm, silent, and unhur-
ried. When they reached a flat surface, they joined other flakes
that had come before, blending their unique characteristics
until they formed a larger mass. Stronger, more imposing, yet
still full of individual beauty.

Like people? Each unique, yet stronger together than apart?
Stronger together…coming together…
The reunion!

Natalie whipped her head toward the phone. It was suddenly clear. She would go to the reunion and gain strength from being with others. She found the telephone number from Del's television show. She dialed, almost giddy with a renewed purpose that was consummated when she asked for Del and finally heard his voice.

"Del? Is that you?"

"Natalie?"

"Yes, it's me. I'm coming...I mean I want to come to the reunion."

"It wouldn't be the same without you."

"Is everyone else coming?" *Please let everyone be there.* "Is Kathy...and Roy? Walter? Is Julia speaking?"

"Julia speak—"

"I just assumed."

Del laughed. "What a great idea. Do you think she would?"

"Is she coming?"

"I haven't heard from her yet, and she is kind of busy running the country. She's not just our Julia anymore."

"She will always be our Julia." Natalie experienced a sudden certainty as if her hope for togetherness was already a reality. "And she'll be there. I know she will."

———

Julia. Speaking at the reunion. It was a wonderful idea, but Del had no clue how to bring it about. Surely he couldn't just dial the White House and get through?

The thought dogged him during his first period history class, making him say, "President Carson" when he meant to say, "President Lincoln" and "reunion" when he meant to say "union." After class, he decided to talk to Lexa about it. He stopped by the reunion office. She was on the phone but as soon as she saw him she waved an excited hand. "Hold on just a minute, Madam President, my brother is right here." She put a hand over the receiver, her eyes wide. "It's *her!*"

Del shook his head in amazement. *Thank you, God, for perfect timing.* He took the phone. "Julia! Milady!" He noticed Lexa raising an eyebrow. He shrugged and continued. "I wanted to call you, but wasn't sure how."

"You put the fingers on the buttons and push, Antonio. It's not hard."

He laughed. "You know what I mean."

"Yes, I do. And I'll give you a direct number. But why did you want to call? To give me a personal invite to this reunion of yours?"

"Sure…I mean, of course—"

"You're hedging, Father."

Del turned his back to escape his sister's incredulous glare. He lowered his voice. "Would you be willing to speak at the reunion?"

She hesitated only a moment. "I'd love to."

"You would?"

She laughed. "Edward's always telling me I can't say no, so how can I make you the exception? And since when have I not liked to talk?"

"Let me think about that one."

"Who else is on the program?"

Del looked at his sister and said another quick prayer of thanksgiving for her arrival. "Actually, since my dear sister has shown up—"

"I just met her. Bit of a wildfire, isn't she?"

Del smiled at Lexa, and she stuck her tongue out at him. "A wild godsend. Since she's taken over the reunion, things have started popping. Never one to be shy, Lexa has been asking for volunteers when people call in. So far she's booked quite a lineup of volunteer musicians, workshop leaders, and speakers—of which you are the crowning glory."

"Are you trying to wrap me around your little finger, Antonio, because I—"

"You wrap with the best of them. Right?"

249

"I'm a regular corkscrew. Just ask Edward."

"How is your Rock of Gibraltar?"

"Flinty and fine."

"I've always envied you two…"

"For what?"

"For your relationship. The love you have for each other. Your feistiness."

"Thou shalt not covet another person's feistiness, especially if you're a priest who made a vow—"

"I know, I know." Del didn't regret his vow never to marry—at least not too often. But Julia and Edward had something beyond marriage. A bond that was stronger than any he had ever witnessed. "I'm so glad you're coming, Julia. Somehow your participation makes it seem…real."

"I'm not sure I want that kind of credit—or responsibility—but I'm looking forward to it too. It's a grand idea."

"His grand idea."

"Aren't they all?"

Del hung up and was forced to face his sister. Her arms were crossed. "You said you knew the president, but I thought you were joshing. You? My ornery brother? And you call her Julia?"

"She was my friend Julia before she was president."

Lexa slapped her hands on the desk. "Well, I am now suitably impressed. Any other famous people coming to this Haven thing? Any wayward movie stars, talk show hosts, royalty?"

"I don't know. I suppose there could be, but God didn't invite people to Haven because they were famous. Actually, I think we were invited because we were so terribly ordinary."

"Julia Carson is hardly ordinary."

"She may be famous now, but she has the heart of an ordinary woman."

Lexa straightened her desk. "You're right. That's why I voted for her." She pointed to the clock on the wall. "Don't you have a class to teach?"

Del ran out the door, then backtracked. "I'll come help you over the lunch break. Let me know if anyone else famous calls."

Lexa shooed him away. "Won't matter none to me. I am hereby immune to being starstruck. With one exception—if Mel Gibson calls, you'll have to scrape me off the floor."

Jack put his hand on the phone but he did not lift the receiver. Although Del had said that anyone could go to the reunion, he wasn't sure that meant him. He hadn't been one of the original Haven disciples. He'd received a mustard seed pin in the mail—as had so many others—but did that make him a second-class invitee or on equal footing with the rest? With Natalie.

Just call.

Jack picked up the receiver, dialed, and asked for Del.

"Del…it's Jack Cummings."

"All hail Jack, the prayer warrior of Eureka Springs."

Jack felt himself redden even though there was no one to see his blush. "I wasn't the only one who prayed, Del."

"But a mighty good one. You coming to the reunion?"

Jack felt a surge of relief. "I was thinking of it."

"Do more than think, young chum. Come join us. Julia and Walter will be there. And Natalie. She called this morning."

Jack's stomach danced. "She'll be there too?"

"Ah…your voice reveals that your feelings for her haven't changed."

"Stronger than ever, I'm afraid."

"And hers for you?"

"She's engaged."

A pause. "But not to you?"

"Not to me. To Sam Erickson, the father of her—"

"Baby. Hmm. Old ties are strong ties?"

"Apparently." He wanted to save face by saying that Sam

251

was a sleaze and there was a chance that Natalie would eventually come to her senses, but he didn't. As pleasant as the backbiting would be, he had to take the high road. "I saw her. I saw Natalie at a convention I went to in Estes Park."

"So you've already had a reunion."

"Too short." *And too inconclusive.*

"They usually are."

Suddenly Jack thought of something. "Did Natalie make a reservation for two? I mean…is Sam coming with her?"

"She made a reservation for one, so maybe you still have a chance."

Maybe. With God's help, maybe.

━◦◦◦◦━

Roy raised a hand, stopping Kathy's words. In his other hand, he held the phone, waiting for someone to answer.

"But Roy…"

"Shh. Hello. This is Roy Bauer. My wife, Kathy, and I want to sign up for the reunion. Two adults and two children."

He exchanged information. Then the woman on the phone asked, "Is this the Kathy Bauer who's painting the picture we're going to raffle off?"

Roy looked at Kathy who sat across the table from him with her head in her hands. He didn't think she'd even started the painting. "She's the one."

"Not to hurry her, but since Del put me in charge—by the way, I'm his sister, Lexa. He'd never push, but time waits for no artist. I need a photo of the painting ASAP if we're going to use it on the front of our program. Del probably didn't make the timeline very clear because he didn't have a timeline, but now—"

"I understand. And I'll tell Kathy. She'll get right on it."

He hung up the phone and stared at his wife. She peeked out from between her fingers. "I assume the *she* you're referring to is me?"

252

"Yup."

She lowered her hands. "Del wants the painting, doesn't he? Was he mad?"

"I spoke to his sister and no, she wasn't mad, just adamant."

"Sister?"

Roy shrugged. "Her name's Lexa. She's in charge." He reached across the table and patted Kathy's hand. "How much do you have done?"

She pulled her hand away and stood. "None. I've been preoccupied, what with the art showing and then…" She didn't finish the sentence. "I'll get to it."

"Now's a good time."

Her eyes flashed. "I can't just conjure up inspiration, Roy."

She can be so annoyingly self-absorbed. Yet he was forgiving. He had to be. She'd been forgiving of him when she'd wanted to have a baby of their own and he hadn't. He couldn't. He'd been an abortionist. He didn't deserve his own child. And all Kathy's talk of a new house? Although he hadn't spelled it out to his wife as yet, he knew the real reason behind his reluctance. He felt like he didn't deserve a bigger, better house. How ironic that Kathy wanted things to make up for her past, and he *didn't* want things to atone for his.

She waved a hand in front of his face. "Oh, Roy…am I boring you? Or do you simply not care about my predicament?"

Roy sighed. When Kathy had a problem, the rest of the world had better be willing to wait. He held his anger in check. Anger was not the way to deal with his wife. If he yelled she would raise the wall, batten down the hatches, aim the muskets… He kept his voice on an even keel. "You have a terrible habit, dear lady, of acting as if you are the only one to feel overwrought. Do you think I always feel like doctoring? Patients don't care if I feel like dealing with them or not, it's my job. And painting is your job." He braced himself before his final volley. "Now, go do it, whether you feel like it or not."

"It's not the same."

"Sure it is. What's the old saying? Work is 10 percent inspiration, 90 percent perspiration?"

"But—"

"Go perspire. The inspire part will come."

He was greatly relieved when she didn't argue with him.

———∿∿∿———

Lexa looked up from her work. A wispy teenaged girl stood in the doorway. Lexa recognized her as the one Del had asked to help with the reunion. "Carrie, is it?"

"Father Del told me to come help you now." She smiled and blushed. "Actually, he said I was supposed to come save you from yourself." She pointed to the growing piles strewn across the desk. "I'm a good organiz—" She stopped talking to look down the hall, then stepped into the room. Del entered behind her.

Del put a hand on Carrie's shoulder. "How are my favorite girls?"

Lexa and Carrie exchanged a glance, and Lexa winked. She'd take care of this. "First off, brother dear, only one of us is a girl and since she's doing the work you have absolutely no talent to do, I suggest you cool the condescending flattery—*boy*."

Del clicked his heels together and offered a crisp salute. "My apologies, captain, sir!"

Carrie giggled and Lexa groaned. She'd forgotten what a charmer he was. Where Lexa got herself in trouble by being too brusque, Del had a talent for getting himself out of trouble by using his wits. "Yeah, yeah, cut the baloney. You're forgiven. Maybe. This time."

He bowed low. "So…how are things going, *ladies?*"

"This lady is swamped and relieved to see this younger lady come help." Lexa flipped through a pile to find a tally sheet. She held it to her chest. "Do you want to know how many people we have coming so far?"

"I don't know…do I?"

"You do."

His eyes widened and he sucked in an exaggerated breath. He took Carrie's hand and closed his eyes. "Okay, we're ready. Let's have it."

"Dramatic Delly…" She lowered the sheet. "The current number coming to the reunion is…a drum roll please…"

"Lexa!"

She shrugged. "Two thousand four hundred and thirty-two."

Del opened his eyes and his mouth dropped. Then he let out a whoop. "I had no idea…I wasn't sure anyone would come…I mean I hoped but—"

"Ahem."

Del looked to the doorway. Monsignor Vibrowsky placed his hands behind his back. "What's going on here?"

Lexa stood and moved toward the door carrying the tally sheet. "We were celebrating, Monsignor. The reservations have hit nearly two—"

The monsignor's raised hand stopped her progress and her words. His face was hard. *As was his heart? His jealous heart?* She took a pen from the desktop. "Can I add your name to the list, Monsignor?" His head inched back as if she'd asked him to go to a hippie love-in. "It's just a reunion. A reunion of God-fearing people, of which—I assume—you are one?"

The monsignor raised his chin, did an about-face, and left.

Del fell into a chair and put his head in his hands. "Oh, Lexa, why did you have to do that?"

"Do what?" She gave him as innocent a smile as she could muster.

"I battle with him enough without you provoking him."

She returned to the safety of her chair and placed the tally sheet on the desk with a confident slap. "I tell it like I see it, and I see that Monsignor Vibrowsky is green in every shade, color, and hue. Plus he has it in for you."

"No, he doesn't…not exact—"

"Yes, he does." Carrie's voice was small.

Lexa pointed. "See?"

Del looked up at the girl. "Has the monsignor said something to you?"

Carrie looked at the floor. "He warned me…"

Del and Lexa exchanged a look. "Warned you?"

She looked up, her eyes nervous. "He said you were… unstable. That all your visions and signs were the mark of a crazy man."

"That's it!" Lexa shoved her chair back and stormed toward the door. "I'll pulverize the guy."

Del grabbed her arm. "You will not."

Lexa stared at him. How could Delly be so nonchalant? "He's slandering your name. He's working against your project."

"He *did* tell me I could work with you," Carrie said. "I was just supposed to be careful and report—" She put a hand to her mouth.

"You're a spy?"

Carrie reddened. "Not a spy, I'm just supposed to—"

"Report back to him." Lexa shook her head in disgust. "I rescind my invitation for him to come to the reunion. He doesn't deserve to come. In fact, I will insist he does *not* come."

"Lexa…"

She threw her hands in the air. "I mean it. If he shows up I'm calling the police."

"Lexa, stop it."

How could Delly be so blind? "If he shows up it will be to no good. He'll try to hurt you, brother."

"He wouldn't hurt me."

"He *is* hurting you."

"He is entitled to his opinion. And he *is* my superior."

"In rank only." She took a deep breath to try and calm herself. "It's his pride. 'Pride goes before destruction, a haughty spirit before a fall.' See? Even I know that one."

Del leaned his elbows on his thighs and tented his fingers under his mouth. "'If a man digs a pit, he will fall into it; if a man rolls a stone, it will roll back on him.'"

She shook her head. He was so naive. "The Bible may have outlined the way things are supposed to be but human nature usually has a different idea. I certainly hope you're right, Delly. Otherwise, I may have to give justice a little push."

Lexa had looked everywhere for Del. The school was quiet. She stuck her head in the door of another classroom. At first she thought the room was empty. She started to move on when she heard Del's voice.

"Whatcha need, Lexa?"

She took a step inside and saw him in a far corner, getting to his feet. He had a piece of paper in his hands. She flipped on the light, adding detail to the twilight coming through the windows. "Do you do this often, brother dear?"

He arched his back. "Do what?"

"Crouch in the corner of an empty classroom?"

"I wasn't crouching, I was kneeling."

"Oh…well, then that explains it." She made a face.

"I was praying." He looked down at the paper, then extended it toward her. "This is the list of the people who've signed up for the reunion."

Lexa knew it well. "You've been praying for—"

"I didn't get through the entire list, but I will."

She looked at him incredulously. "You were praying for each one of them? There are over two thous—"

He shrugged and brushed off his knees. "I figure if God is good enough to get these individuals to come, I need to pray for them."

"What if we get tons more?"

"Then I'll need to pray tons more."

She was newly amazed at her brother's goodness. Most

people—if they decided to pray at all—would do it the quick and easy way, en masse. But not her Delly.

Yet she still had one question… "You pray in an empty classroom because it's filled with the spirit of learning and open minds?"

He grinned. "Actually, I pray in my classroom because it's quiet and no one can find me—especially a certain monsignor."

"But I found you."

He took her arm and shut off the light. "You always could."

<hr />

"But we've got to go to the reunion."

Walter avoided Bette's eyes. He shook his head and fingered his mug of coffee. It was cold. There was no way he was going to a reunion and suffer the indignity of his humiliation. He could just imagine the conversations that would brand him in the opening minutes of seeing his friends:

"How are things going, Walter? How are things at the station?"

I was fired.

They'd blush and look to the floor. "Oh…well…how's the house coming? You finished off that attic space yet?"

We're selling it. I overspent. I got behind on payments. I gambled away what little cash we had—even my daughter's college fund… I'm a failure. I don't belong here.

They would filter away, uncomfortable with his defeat. People didn't want to hang around losers. The reunion was about God. And what had Walter done for God lately?

Not much.

Bette wiped Addy's face and hands, and then the tray of her high chair. "I know you're worried about money, Walter. But it will show up. I know it will. This reunion may be just what we need right now. A revival of our faith where we can be with friends and remember what's important."

"We know who's *not* important anymore."

Bette gave him a look that both acknowledged and condemned his self-pity. "The least we can do is sign up. Reserve a spot."

Walter shrugged. Maybe they could come up with the funds. He was scheduled to go to a job interview in a half hour. A radio station needed someone to sell ads. If he got the job, he would start getting a paycheck. But that would be at least two weeks away...

"I'm sure Del would give us credit."

Walter blinked. "No, you don't! You don't tell Del anything about our misfortune. Not Del, not anybody."

"But, Walter, they're your—"

He shoved his bowl of cereal away. The spoon did a back flip over the edge. "They're my friends whose lives are going along fine. Friends who are doing what God wanted them to do."

"How do you know?" Bette took Addy out of the high chair and set her down. Addy ran into the living room, oblivious to her father's pain.

If only I could run away...

Bette refreshed his coffee. "Maybe they're struggling too. Maybe you can help each other if you go and talk together."

Walter didn't want to think about it anymore. He *did* want to see his friends. He *did* want to go to the reunion. But he didn't want to be humiliated. *I have to get a job. I can't go as a failure.* He pushed his chair back and stood. "Do what you want, Bette. I don't want to deal with it."

He left for his interview.

———※※※———

"Bette! I've been waiting to hear from you." Del's voice was full of excitement. "If you hadn't called me, I would have called you. I assumed the three Prescotts were coming to the reunion, but my sister, Lexa, says it doesn't count until she gets a tally on her sheet. Did she get all the pertinent information from you?"

"All signed up. She's quite a dynamo."

"*Dynamite* most of the time, but yes, she is."

A voice sounded in the background: "I heard that, brother."

"See what I mean?"

Bette hesitated. She wasn't sure she should say any more to Del. Maybe she should just leave it be. Let Del think that everything was fi—

"What's wrong, Bette? Your silence is shouting."

Bette took a deep breath. *Help me, Lord.* "Walter lost his job, Del. He got fired for doing the reunion broadcast against the directive of his boss."

"He got fired because of me?"

She hadn't thought of it stated so bluntly, but it was true. "Yes."

"Oh, Bette…how is he taking it?"

"Guess." She knew she wouldn't have to say more.

"That bad."

"That bad." Bette covered her eyes. "That's not all."

"Spill it."

"I don't know if I should be telling you this but—"

"I love Walter, Bette. You know that. I want to help."

And I want your help. "You see…we were behind on bills, and when Walter lost his job…he wanted a quick fix. He gambled away our savings hoping to hit it big. We have nothing. We're selling the house."

"Ahhh…I don't know what to say."

"You don't have to say anything to me, Del. But I'd—we'd—sure appreciate your prayers."

"You've got 'em. And don't worry about the cost of the reunion. We'll absorb—"

"No, no. Don't do that. At least not yet. I've been praying for a way to come and I'm not giving up on God yet. Save the charity for someone who really needs it."

"Bette…"

"We'll be fine, Del. Somehow, we'll be fine."

She hoped it would be true.

Lately, Bette hated getting the mail: bills they couldn't pay, advertisements for trips and goods they couldn't afford, and offers for credit cards they didn't want. But today, the letter at the bottom of the pile got her attention. It had the return address of the homeless shelter where she volunteered. That was odd. She never got any mail from them. Perhaps they needed her to help with a special project—but why didn't they call like they usually did?

She slipped her finger through the flap and pulled out a letter. The first word grabbed her eyes: CONGRATULATIONS! She scanned the page, then went back and reread every word. After it finally sank in, she held the letter to her chest and looked toward heaven. "Thank you, Lord."

She could hardly wait until Walter got back from his job interview.

———∿∿∿———

Walter knew he should be happy. He'd gotten the job at the radio station and was now officially an ad rep. Not a bad job title. But it wasn't TV, it wasn't an executive position, and it wasn't the kind of job he wanted to be doing.

My new job is a consequence.

He turned into their driveway and scowled at the For Sale sign in the front yard. If only they didn't have to move. His paycheck *would* be enough to make the house payments—if they didn't eat, wear clothes, or drive anywhere.

The sale of the house is a consequence.

He shut off the car and let the silence settle around him. The first thought from his mind was, *It isn't fair.* But he quickly reined in the words, hoping God hadn't noticed. He bowed his head and tried to make amends with a proper prayer. *Lord, I blew it. I know there are consequences to what I did. But I'm sorry, really, I am. And I do thank You for the new job—such as it is.* He sighed and wished he could keep the asides to himself, even though he knew God heard all of them, one way or another.

He tried again. *It just kills me to have to sell the house.* He squeezed his eyes shut and tried to draw his next request from deep within. *Please help us get through this and I promise I'll never...* He hesitated. He'd never be a jerk again? A snicker escaped. Being a jerk was second nature to Walter. He could only pray to be less of a jerk. He was glad God's love was big enough to encompass his many faults.

Walter looked up to see Bette standing at the front door. She waved at him. "Walter! What are you doing sitting out there? Come in! Come in! Something great has happened."

She couldn't have heard about his job—besides, his job deserved a *good*, not a *great*. He got out of the car and let her enthusiasm draw him inside. She hurried to the coffee table, snatched up a paper, and put it behind her back. He braced himself for a guessing game. He hated guess—

"Guess what came in the mail?"

He sighed. "A massive tax refund from 1982."

"Guess again."

"An inheritance from my rich Aunt Irma."

"You have an Aunt Irma? So do I...I haven't seen—"

"Bette..."

She took a deep breath and brought the paper front and center. She read it like a proclamation. "'CONGRATULA-TIONS! You have won Liberty Shelter's charity raffle! Your prize is two round-trip airplane tickets to any city in the continental U.S. Please contact...'" She looked up, her face beaming. "We can go to the reunion! I was praying for a way and God's given us one."

Tears threatened. He looked to the floor.

"Walter? Honey? What's wrong?"

Everything. Nothing. He looked up in spite of the tears. "How come He's so good to me—us—in spite of everything?"

She wrapped her arms around him. "Because our God is an awesome God."

He shook his head, still amazed. "Amen to that."

She slipped her hands around his arm. "How did the job interview go?"

Walter smiled. Then he told her about his new job—the job that suddenly seemed less like a consequence and more like a blessing from a God who gave him so much more than he deserved.

CHAPTER TWENTY-FOUR

"Freely you have received, freely give."

MATTHEW 10:8

KATHY SAT IN FRONT OF A BLANK CANVAS. Nothing was happening. Nothing. *If I were sitting in my cupola studio, overlooking the mountains, I bet I'd feel some—*

Ryan came running down the stairs; an elephant in hightops. "Mom! Mom! You got a special letter. Dad had to sign for it." He jumped the last few stairs and ran to her side, waving the envelope. He took one final hop in front of her and handed her the letter. She saw Roy coming down the stairs, his eyes full of questions. Lisa scrambled past him.

With her audience waiting, Kathy didn't have time to ponder the possibilities. But when she saw Sandra's return address, she guessed its contents. She ripped it open, then grinned and held the check to her chest. "It's a check from the showing. It's my portion of the money from the sales."

"How much is it for?" Lisa tried to bend back the edge of the check so she could see the amount.

Kathy held it out of her reach. Roy tried to snatch it. Kathy laughed and walked away from them. "Greedy little things, aren't you?"

Roy put his hands behind his back, feigning indifference. "I'm merely curious."

"Do you always drool when you're curious?"

"Do you always torture your message-bearers?"

She'd made them wait long enough. She turned the check around while stating the amount out loud. "Six thousand two hundred and fifty-three dollars."

Lisa pulled on her sleeve. "That's tons, isn't it?"

"Not quite, but it's plenty for now."

Roy pointed at the blank canvas. "Maybe the money will give you inspiration."

Kathy took one look at the white expanse and was surprised to find he was wrong. The check was a nice reward, but it did not elicit any spark. If compensation didn't incite her to paint, what would?

Yet the money *would* come in handy. She turned to Roy. "With this money we could..." When he gave her a look, she didn't finish the sentence as she intended. "We could put the check in savings like good, boring, middle-class people."

Before Roy could respond, Lisa took the check and stared at it. "But what do we get to buy, Mommy?"

Ryan plucked the check away from her. He handed it to his mother. "This isn't our money, Lisa; this is Mom's."

Shock jolted Kathy at her son's words. She'd never given the impression her earnings were earmarked for herself any more than Roy implied his earnings were for his use alone. Why would Ryan say such a thing? Then she got an idea... "Get your shoes on, family. We're going out."

"Where we going?"

She only smiled. "It's a surprise."

They went to the bank, and Kathy insisted on going inside. She didn't want to reveal her surprise prematurely. She put the bulk of the check in savings, but the rest...

Kathy returned to the car.

"What did you get, Mom?"

"Did you get me a sucker? I wanted to go through the drive-through to get a—"

Kathy handed each of the kids a sucker.

"Where's mine?" Roy asked.

Ryan pulled his out of his mouth and reached toward the

front seat. "You can have mine, Dad."

Roy politely declined. He started the engine. "Where to, Miss Moneybags?"

It was time. Kathy reached into her bank envelope and pulled out two crisp one-hundred-dollar bills. She handed them to the kids in the backseat. "To the toy store, chauffeur!"

Both kids held the bills in front of their faces, their mouths open. Ryan was the first to snap out of it. "We get to use this all on toys?"

"All on toys."

Lisa's eyes were wide. "Can I buy tons and tons with it?"

"Tons and tons."

Ryan lay the bill in his lap reverently, while Lisa waved hers like a flag. "Faster, Daddy! Let's go, let's go, faster!"

Lisa did not enter the toy store, she assaulted it like a soldier raiding an objective. Roy hurried after her, leaving Ryan with Kathy.

Ryan stood near the entrance, looking down at the hundred-dollar bill. From the crease between his brows, Kathy could tell he was thinking hard. He was so different from his impulsive sister. "Where to, Ryan? Do you want to look at that video game you've been wanting?"

Ryan shook his head, still deep in thought. Then he turned to his mother. "Could I do this alone, Mom? I'm big enough."

"Why sure, sweetie. Go ahead." Kathy watched him walk into the rows of toys, disappointed that he wasn't letting her come along. Part of the fun of giving them the money was seeing their excitement in using it.

Oh well. She turned left and followed the sound of Lisa's voice. Hopefully, Lisa had enough enthusiasm for them both.

Lisa, Roy, and Kathy were at the checkout. "I sure wish I could have gotten the doll car, too." Lisa looked to Roy, showing her best pleading eyes. "Can't I have it, Daddy? It's just a few dollars more."

Roy looked to Kathy, then shook his head. They both—they all—knew that Roy was the softer touch. He never objected to money they spent, even when Kathy occasionally got carried away.

"If you take something back, you can have—"

"But I want it *too!*"

Kathy's patience ebbed away. Lisa could be such a sweet girl—and such a selfish one. "You act this way, sweet cakes, and next time, I won't give you any money. Do you understand?"

Lisa's lower lip popped front and center. "Yeah. I understand."

Kathy looked up to see Ryan coming toward them. His cart overflowed with toys. She was relieved he had found something he wanted.

Then she noticed what was in the cart. There was a doll, a pink stuffed bunny, toddler trucks, and various boy toys he already owned.

Lisa pounced on the cart, taking the doll. "Is this for me?"

Ryan took it back. "No, it's not for you."

Roy took it and gave it a hug. "Then it's for me?"

Ryan smiled, but patiently took it back a second time. "No, it's not for you, either."

Kathy shook her head. "I don't understand your choices, sweetie. Most of this stuff is for girls, and the boy toys are things you already have. It's very nice to get more for Lisa, but she doesn't need—"

"I told you, it's not for Lisa." He looked at the floor. "This stuff is for those kids who lost everything in the fire."

"What fire?"

Roy nodded as if he understood. "The fire that's been on the news. A family on the other side of town lost everything in a fire." He turned to Ryan and put a hand on his head. "You want to give all this to those kids?"

268

Ryan nodded.

"That's dumb."

"Lisa!"

Kathy let Roy reprimand their daughter. She was busy looking at their son, a huge lump growing in her throat. She looked at the toys accumulating on the checkout counter. "Didn't you buy anything for yourself, sweetie?"

He looked her straight in the eye. "I don't need anything. They do."

Kathy put a hand to her mouth, trying to stop the tears. She was so ashamed. She'd never once thought about doing anything charitable with the money. Her first thoughts had been of herself. Even the money for the kids had been an afterthought, the product of a guilty conscience.

"What's wrong, Mom? Isn't it okay?"

Roy looked at Kathy and she could tell he knew her thoughts. He put a hand on Ryan's shoulders. "It's more than okay, son. It's wonderful. Your mom's just moved by your generosity."

Kathy could only nod as she ran from the store.

Kathy heard her family's footsteps as they approached the car. They weren't talking, and she felt bad that her quick retreat had put a damper on their outing. Roy put the sacks in the trunk, though Lisa insisted on bringing her doll into the backseat with her. Three doors shut. Kathy sniffed.

"Why are you crying, Mommy? Do you want to hold my doll?"

Kathy blew her nose, shaking her head. "No, thanks, sweet cakes. The doll is all yours."

"I'll give the doll to the people—well, maybe not this doll, but I'd give them the..." She thought a moment. "The checkers game. They could have the checkers game. I don't really like checkers *that* much."

Suddenly, Lisa's words melded with Kathy's own actions. Lisa's offer to give something she really didn't care about meant little and cost her nothing. Just as Kathy's thoughts about giving the reunion one of her lesser paintings meant little—and cost her nothing. Either she had to give Del one of her best paintings or she had to create a new one with an equivalent investment of time and emotion.

"Mommy? I'll give the checkers."

"No, Lisa."

"Why not?" Lisa's lip threatened. "Why does Ryan get to give all the stuff, and I don't? His stuff's not better than mine. I said I'd give the checkers."

Roy didn't start the car. He glanced at Kathy, then turned around in his seat to face Lisa. "Ryan's gift *is* better than yours."

"Roy…" Kathy was afraid he was being too harsh.

"She has to be told." Roy reached under his seat and pulled out his ever present Bible. He flipped the pages. "There's a story…here it is. Luke 21: 'As he looked up, Jesus saw the rich putting their gifts into the temple treasury. He also saw a poor widow put in two very small copper coins. "I tell you the truth," he said, "this poor widow has put in more than all the others. All these people gave their gifts out of their wealth; but she out of her poverty put in all she had to live on."'" He closed the Bible.

Lisa slunk into the seat. "But Ryan's not poor."

"But he gave all he had." Roy continued. "Ryan gave everything he had—the best he could find. You giving the checkers—something you really don't like in the first place—is not the kind of gift God wants us to give."

Kathy nodded, finding comfort in the confirmation. "Let's go home." She turned to Roy. "Now."

"Why the big hurry?"

"Thanks to a very special boy, I've just found the inspiration I needed." Kathy looked back to her little boy who had given all he had—to the children from the fire, and to her.

Kathy stood before her blank canvas for the second time that day. But before she got started, she bowed her head. *Forgive me, Lord. Who needs a house with a magnificent view? I have a magnificent family. Help me always to give my best—with no thought of reward.*

When she opened her eyes, the ideas rushed in.

CHAPTER TWENTY-FIVE

—⟨ଵଵ⟩—

"But if serving the LORD *seems undesirable to you, then choose for yourselves this day whom you will serve."*

JOSHUA 24:15

ON HIS WAY TO WORK, one fact commandeered Art's thoughts: He still hadn't stolen Julia's mustard seed pin.

He justified his inaction all sorts of ways, telling himself that the opportunity had not arisen, the time had not been right. He'd even considered spilling everything, asking Julia to loan him the pin so he could show it to Hamm.

But then she'd had that health care bill to worry about, and some Middle Eastern head of state was coming to visit, and Edward had just gotten back from a speaking engagement in Arizona. They both were preoccupied. Consumed. Julia and Edward didn't need to worry about TAI. He'd do the worrying for them.

And for himself. Truth was, Art was scared. Scared of getting caught—and scared of *not* getting caught, of letting the theft propel him deeper into the bowels of TAI.

He'd worked so hard to climb out of the hole he'd created in his life. From punk kid to the president's personal assistant. Not bad. So why risk it all? Maybe his fears about TAI were absurd. Maybe he'd read too many suspense novels in prison. Maybe he saw threat where there was none.

Maybe he was risking everything for nothing.

Hamm Spurgeon gave him the creeps. Forget Hamm's penchant for minors, or the fact he dressed like a Sunday school teacher and lived like a slimeball. Forget his loyalty to TAI, which fluctuated oddly from being a protective king of the hill to mocking the organization. Hamm wasn't stable. Fine. Art could handle all that.

But then there was the strange way his gut grabbed when Hamm talked to him…as though Hamm's words flowed into Art's consciousness on a river of evil. Hamm could say, "Good morning," and Art's skin would tingle like he'd been slapped. With the sound of the words he'd find himself shrinking inwardly—cowering in a mental and spiritual corner—until Hamm's influence withdrew and it was safe to come out again.

Art had felt this way before, a long time ago…when his father's drunken rages had the power to turn Art's family into flinching, wincing weaklings, afraid to say boo for fear it would set off the monster.

Add to this Julia's excitement about the reunion… Every time she talked about it, Art got a different kind of glitch in his stomach. She and Edward had invited him to come as their guest. The joyful anticipation he should have felt was tinged with fear—Hamm had implied something big was coming down at the reunion. And Hamm wanted Art to be a part of it.

He was a rubberband being pulled in two directions. Sooner or later, he'd snap.

Today, Art *had* to steal the pin. No outs. No delays. Last night Hamm had made it perfectly clear he was not going to share any more information about TAI's plans until Art proved himself.

So this was it. Today was the day he hurt Julia in order to save her.

"Yoo-hoo? Arthur?"

Art blinked and realized he'd been staring at nothing. But not nothing. He'd been staring at Julia's blazer, which was draped over the back of the couch. The mustard seed pin was on the lapel, calling to him.

Take it, take it…

But Julia was standing close. Any minute now, she'd put on the jacket and be off to the Oval Office.

"Arthur?"

He forced himself to look at her. "Sorry. I've got a lot on my mind."

Julia slipped a pile of papers in a folder. "What's her name?"

Art felt himself redden. "There is no woman in my life." He forced himself to smile. "Except you, Madam President."

"Oooh, flattery first thing in the morning. Keep it up and I'll let you bow to my briefcase." She pulled some photos from an envelope, moved to the coffee table, and turned them in his direction. "Christmas card time. We had these taken for our personal cards, and I need you to get things going at the printer. Which one do you like?"

Art leaned over them. Both Edward and Julia were photogenic, especially sitting in the White House rose garden. He picked his favorite and handed it to her. "I like this one. You have a glint in your eye, like you're up to something."

She held it close. "I think that was taken right after I goosed Edward."

"Gov!"

She tenderly ran a finger across the photo, then snapped a finger on Edward's head. "He got me first." She looked at her watch. "Speaking of the goosed gander, where is he? I need him to see these before I—"

Art jumped when his cell phone rang. He wasn't used to such perks.

Julia smiled at him. "She's calling you."

Art felt himself blush even though he knew there was no "she." He answered the phone.

"Did you do it yet?" Hamm.

Art's skin crawled even as he covered the receiver and whispered to Julia, "Excuse me a minute."

She nodded and left to fetch Edward.

She was gone. He was alone. Art's heart banged against his

throat. He looked at the pin on the coat. *Do it! Now!*

Hamm's voice intruded. "Art? Answer me."

"No, I didn't take it yet." He glanced toward the bedroom. "You shouldn't call me here."

"I can call you anywhere I want, boy. Especially when time is running out."

"What does that mean?" Art's mind was a jumble. Time was running out for him too. Any minute now, Julia would come back and take her jacket… He didn't have time to think. He made a beeline for the blazer. His fingers touched the pin. It was like a tie tack with the clasp on the back side. He shoved the phone against his shoulder and fumbled to get ahold of the pin.

"We have things to do, Art. People to stop."

Art's stomach executed a somersault. He wished he knew more. *"How* do you plan on stopping Julia?"

"You really want me to go over this on the phone? How dumb do you think I am?"

"Hamm…"

"Don't Hamm me. Prove yourself, boy. Steal the pin and get back to me. Today. This is your last chance."

Hamm hung up. Art shifted the phone to the crook of his neck, reached down to pinch the back of the pin's clasp, and pulled—

"Art? What's going on?"

Edward stood in the doorway. Julia was beside him. She looked at the jacket. The pin. His hands. She looked at his face, her own brimming with questions.

"Arthur?"

Edward stomped into the room and ripped the jacket from his hands. The pin and its back fell to the carpet with a soft *pooh.* All three stared at it a moment before Edward picked it up and handed it—and the jacket—to his wife. Julia held the pin in the palm of her hand as if waiting for it to talk, to tell her why.

Art took two steps back, wishing the floor would swallow him up so he wouldn't have to face the disappointment in Julia's eyes.

"Explain yourself," Edward said. "Explain why you would take Julia's pin. Then explain about the person you were talking to. What's this about 'stopping Julia'? And who is Hamm?" His eyes narrowed. "Would that be Hamm Spurgeon, the dissident the security check uncovered?"

Julia closed her hand on the pin and stared at her husband. "Hamm Spurgeon? What are you talking about, Edward?"

Edward flipped a hand at Art. "Ask your personal assistant. Ask him to explain why he's consorting with people on security's watch list."

The excuses that surfaced were lame and useless. "I'm…I'm sorry. It's not what you think."

"So you don't know Hamm Spurgeon? You weren't talking with him on the phone about stopping Julia?"

"Well…yes, but—"

Edward took a step toward Art; Art compensated. "You're a plant, aren't you? You got hooked up with some criminal types in prison and decided to take advantage of our friendship to get in good with them. What's your scheme, Art? What are you up to?"

Art felt relieved to finally be able to say it. Maybe this was for the best. It was time they knew what was going on. "Actually, I *am* a plant. But not for—"

Edward clapped his hands. "All right. That's it!" He thrust a finger in Art's face. "We trusted you. Julia gave you a fresh start, even though I told her not to. It was all a sham, wasn't it? All the high and mighty talk about changing your life, turning it over to God? A con to see what you could get out of us. To get close to us. To steal from us." He cocked his head. "To hurt us?"

This was going all wrong. "No, it's not like that. I—" He saw Julia clutch the pin and the blazer to her chest. She closed her eyes, her head shaking *no, no, no…*

Art wanted to fall at her feet. *Don't think badly of me, Julia. I wasn't stealing it for me, I was stealing it to help you.* "I wouldn't hurt—"

Edward continued. "You already have. You're involved with questionable characters, and we catch you stealing…" He shook his head. "The mustard seed pin of the president would fetch a good price, wouldn't it? Or was it merely the crowning trophy? Were you going to sell your story to the tabloids? 'How I Duped the President.' Did you and your con friends get a good laugh after our prison visits? Did our trust and forgiveness entertain you?"

Art wanted to die as Edward's accusations collided with the story he'd created for Hamm. The lie seemed sickeningly real.

Edward seized Art's arm and dragged him to the door. Although Art could have easily muscled his way out of the grip, he surrendered, letting Edward propel him into the hall like a bum being thrown into the streets.

A security guard hurried to Edward's aid and another came running.

"Get him out of here! And make sure he's never allowed near the White House again."

"You've got to listen to me!" Art yelled.

Edward shook his head. The guards sandwiched Art with rough grips and led him down the hall. He looked back and saw Julia standing at the door, her face drawn with sorrow and disappointment. A tear streamed down her cheek.

Art looked away. It was hard to breathe. His life was over. He'd done the unthinkable.

He'd made his Julia cry.

~~~

Julia sank into a chair. "I can't believe this is happening. There has to be some explan—"

Edward shook his head. "You are blind, and I am dumb."

She looked up. "I'm afraid you're going to have to explain both of those comments."

Edward placed himself in front of her. "Art's not the repentant follower you think he is. He's been seen with some questionable people. That Hamm he was talking to is a known troublemaker, and Ben Cranois—"

"Our Benjamin?"

"He stopped being our Benjamin two years ago, missy. When I had the security check done on Art I found out that the three of them were—"

"A security check? I told you not to do one on Arthur. I told you—"

Edward threw his hands in the air. "You told me you could handle it. You had things under control. But you don't, and it's about time you realized other people have a job to do too. You are not omnipotent, omnipresent, or even very bright sometimes. Especially when your own safety is concerned. What good is having a calling from God if you're dead?"

"You're overreacting. I'm sure there's an explanation. You didn't give Arthur time to explain himself."

"He didn't deserve time. He was caught."

She shook her head. Why had Arthur tried to steal her pin? And was he involved with this Hamm character? It didn't make sense. "I don't understand what's going on, Edward, but I'm sure Arthur wouldn't do anything to jeopardize my safet—"

"You don't know that. You bypassed the system. You took control—and I let you. Nothing serious happened this time, but what about the next time Julia Carson wants her way? What's it going to take to get you to relinquish the reins?"

For once in her life, Julia had no answer.

—◈—

Art's success had been his failure.

He'd proven himself to Hamm. Even though he didn't have the pin, he'd lost his job because of the attempt. Surely that would be proof of his loyalty to TAI? But at what price?

Art sat in the subway car and stared straight ahead. He let the *whoosh-whoosh-clatter* of the speeding train take him deeper into the underground of his heart. He'd escaped to this subterranean labyrinth to ride anywhere and nowhere. He had no idea what station they were approaching. He had no idea if he'd missed his stop. He had no stop. He deserved to stay in this tunnel forever, to never see daylight or smell air that wasn't heavy with damp and sweat and dirt. To never enjoy silence. To never feel steady on his feet, but to go through life enduring the sway and rock that could lull him to sleep. To sleep to forget. Oblivion.

But there was no forgetting. His conscience screamed, unrelenting. He'd betrayed the person he admired the most—or he *hadn't* betrayed her, but she *thought* he'd betrayed her.

Maybe that was worse.

His plan to help Julia by infiltrating the bad guys' camp seemed ludicrous. Who did he think he was? James Bond? When he'd first suspected TAI's intentions, he should have contacted the police or the FBI or Arnold Schwarzenegger. Someone with clout and big guns.

It's not fair.

Art blinked at the thought. The old lady across the aisle looked at him funny and adjusted the shopping bag at her feet. Had he said the words out loud? He looked past her to the blackness of the window. In it, he saw the reflection of himself. Art Graham. The hood. The thief. The child of God.

Art watched his forehead buckle. His chin quivered. He was a broken child. He bowed his head and put a hand over his eyes, hiding his grief. *Lord, I thought this was what You wanted me to do! I even felt proud that You trusted me with this assignment. But Julia hates me. She thinks badly of me. She thinks I betrayed her. I can't bear it! Isn't there another way? Can't I keep my honor and still save Julia?*

He opened his eyes and looked up. The old woman was

studying him. The trained slowed. She smiled and stood. But instead of heading toward the door, she crossed the aisle. Toward him.

She handed him a postcard before walking away. "Jesus loves you."

He flicked his tears with the back of a hand. He looked at the card. It had a picture of Jesus on the front; the picture he'd seen a hundred times with Christ dressed in a purple robe, kneeling in the Garden of Gethsemane moments before his arrest. A verse was inscribed at the bottom: "'Father, if you are willing, take this cup from me; yet not my will, but yours be done.' An angel from heaven appeared to him and strengthened him."

And suddenly, Jesus' prayer was Art's prayer. He read the words again and added an amen.

As the train came to a stop, Art looked toward the exit doors. The old woman returned his gaze. She smiled. She nodded.

And then Art realized that even more of the verse applied to this moment.

For the old woman had appeared to him—and strengthened him.

He laughed at God's mysterious ways.

———— ∾∾∾ ————

Ben heard steps in the hall. *Art.*

He rushed to catch him before Art went inside his apartment. He had something on his mind. He swung his door open just as Art put the key into the lock.

"I thought I heard you."

"Hey, Ben." Art opened the door and took a step inside.

"Aren't you home early?"

"Not really."

There seemed to be more to Art's words than he was letting on, but Ben didn't have time for it. He had his own problems. He dug his hands into his pockets. "I...I..." Finally given the opportunity, Ben didn't know what to say. *The energy is draining out of me, and I'm scared that I'm losing my way. The drive is weakening. The urgency is gone and I want it back. I want to feel a part of things again. I want—*

"I was wondering if you'd seen Hamm lately."

"Why do you ask?"

Ben shrugged, trying to keep it casual. "I haven't talked to him since we went out to dinner. Before that, we'd talk every day. And last I heard, he thought something important was brewing that TAI would be dealing with and…"

"The reunion."

"The what?"

Art blinked. "You don't know about the reunion of the Haven people?"

It was worse than Ben thought. "That proves it. Hamm's shutting me out." He leveled a look at Art. "Ever since he met you, I haven't seen him."

Art dropped his keys. "Listen, I'm not trying to snatch up your position with TAI or with Hamm. Believe me, I'm not that desperate for friends. He's weird."

"A little."

Art snickered and picked up his keys. "A lot. Did you know he likes young girls?"

"What are you talking about?"

Art cocked his head, and his expression said he couldn't believe Ben was so ignorant. "Never mind. Just rumors."

"From whom?"

Art waved the question away and backed further into his apartment. "I'm beat. I'll talk to you tomorrow."

Ben took a deep breath and let it out. "I'm not going to take this, Art. You can't usurp my position in TAI. I worked hard to be a part of—"

Art held up a hand. "You're not listening to me. I do not *want* your position. And I'm sure Hamm was going to tell you about things."

Ben's breathing was heavy. He felt like a petulant child whining, *But Dad likes you best.* "Then he's going to tell me now. I'm going over to Hamm's and have it out with him."

Art hesitated. "I wouldn't do that if I were you."

"Why not?"

Art shook his head adamantly. "Hamm is not the type of guy you want to rile."

Ben was confused. Although he'd witnessed a few flashes of Hamm's anger, there was nothing to fear. Hamm was still the fat-bottomed weakling who even Ben could flatten with one hand tied behind—

Art looked toward the door, suddenly pensive. "Actually… I have to see Hamm myself. Care if I go with you?"

Considering you're probably the cause of my demotion… "I don't need a bodyguard."

Art stepped into the hall. "Wanna bet?"

⟞◦⟝

Hamm opened the door, then leaned on the jamb. "Well, well. Two for the price of one. To what do I owe this intrusion?"

Art was in no mood to play games. "Ben has something he wants to tell you."

Ben's face was stricken. "I…I…"

They both waited for Ben to finish, but nothing more came out.

"Uh-huh." Hamm stepped aside. "Well, come on in and let's see if Mr. Eloquence can find his voice."

Art was relieved that another jailbait tidbit didn't come trailing out of the bedroom. But it was obvious by the way Ben's upper lip curled that he had never graced the halls of Hammdom before. The housekeeping was worse than normal. Dirty laundry covered the couch and the carpet was littered with popcorn and newspapers. There was the distinct smell of burned oil.

"I see Cranois does not approve."

Ben pulled his eyes from the mess. "I just expected—"

"Me to be as squeaky clean as you?"

Ben reddened. Art regretted bringing up the fact that Ben had something to say. He tried to change the focus. "I passed my test today, Hamm."

Hamm tossed dirty underwear to the floor to clear off the overstuffed chair. "Where's the pin?"

"I don't have it."

He stopped his body on its way to sitting. "Then you passed nothing."

"I got caught."

Hamm fell into the cushions with a laugh. "I would have loved to see that."

"Such a sympathetic soul."

"What are you two talking about?" Ben asked.

"A little test of loyalty." Hamm told Ben about stealing Julia's pin. Art did not miss the look of satisfaction that passed over Ben's face.

Art straddled a kitchen chair. "I was caught—and fired."

Hamm laughed louder, slapping the armrest. "Oops."

"Yeah. Oops. Thanks to you."

"Hey, don't sweat it. Actually, it's probably best you distance yourself from our dear president. A low profile is in order."

Art heard Ben take a breath before he said, "The reunion?"

Hamm swung his attention in Ben's direction and hesitated. At that moment Art knew that Ben's ignorance about the reunion was not an oversight. Why wouldn't Hamm want Ben involved?

"Who told you about the reunion?"

Ben pointed to Art.

Art jumped in. "I assured him that you were going to tell him." Hamm's face didn't change. "Weren't you?"

Hamm's eyes continued to scrutinize Ben.

"Don't look at me like that."

"Like what?"

"Like you're judging me."

"But I am judging you."

Ben looked away, then lifted his chin in a show of guts Art would have been wary to risk. "You have no right—"

Hamm raised an eyebrow. "The energy's weakening in you, isn't it?"

Ben reddened and Art frowned. What were they talking about?

"That's none of your business."

Hamm rose from his chair and circled Ben like a Gestapo officer interrogating a prisoner. "As head of TAI it is my business. If you're not one of us anymore, if the force has withdrawn due to some act of disloyalty—"

Ben's eyes panicked. "I haven't done anything against—"

Hamm stopped in front of him. "What about the church?"

"I…I was stalking Julia."

"That's the problem. You're obsessed with Julia. Your focus is too narrow. All your talk of truth and the individual is just a guise to cover your passion for—"

"That's not true!"

Art moved between them. "Hey, you two. We're on the same side."

Hamm spun toward him. "And you, Arthur Graham. I am getting no readings on you at all."

"Readings?"

Hamm smiled and looked Art over from head to toe. "We— I—have a very jealous boss who requires complete loyalty. He reveals things to me about the people who work for me. Like good old Ben here…the wavering, waffling Mr. Cranois, who wants to be a big man but who holds back from tapping into the full power of…"

When Hamm let the words trail off, Art retreated toward his chair. "Of what?" *Lord, thank you for your protection from whatever power Hamm's talking about. Stay with me. Don't leave.*

Hamm didn't answer. His eyes glazed a moment, and then he nodded to himself and let out a little laugh. "Sometimes even *we* have to proceed on faith. You lost your job for us. That will have to be enough. Time is running out."

Art found it hard to swallow. "You said that before. Explain."

Hamm shuffled his shoulders and seemed to discard the seriousness of the last few moments. "The reunion, dear boy." He glanced resignedly at Ben. "I guess, whether *I* like it or not, we are a trio." He laughed. "A terrible trio, off to a reunion."

Ben smiled like an idiot. "Thanks, Hamm. That's great. But what about the other members—"

Hamm scarred him with a look. "A trio is plenty."

"But I was already going," Art said. "With Julia."

"That was before you lost your job." Hamm grinned. "Want to room with me?"

I'd rather eat nails. Art sighed. He hoped all this was worth it. "So, what's the plan?"

Hamm raised a finger, making a proclamation. "Loose lips sink ships. There's only one captain on this boat, boys, and I'm him. And until you need to know, you will *not* know." He crossed the room and plucked a book from a shelf. He held it to his chest, closed his eyes, and raised the other hand to the sky. "But what I can tell you is…praise the Lord, brothers! We're going to a revival!" He opened his eyes, gauging their reaction. Neither Ben nor Art moved.

Hamm tossed the book on the couch, walked to the door, and opened it. His voice regained its edge. "Now, out. Both of you. I have a victory to plan."

As soon as the door closed behind them, Ben clapped his hands, then took the stairs in a broken rhythm, each step corresponding to a word. "This will be great! We'll be in the middle of things. Going to their meetings, having a chance to share the truth with them. Proving to them how wrong they are."

Art had had enough. "Give it a rest, Ben."

Ben's eyes narrowed. "What's with you?"

Oops. "Nothing. I'm just mad that I lost the cushiest job in the world."

Ben put an arm around his shoulders. "Don't worry, Art. You'll get another one. Or you could come work at the shipping company with me."

Joy.

"Cheer up. We're both in. And we're all going to the reunion."

But not with Julia. Not with Julia.

Once outside, Art glanced up at Hamm's apartment. The man stood at the window, looking down at them. He did not wave. He did not smile. He just stared.

Art felt his soul shiver.

———∿∿∿———

Ben did a little jig across his living room. He was back in. He was not an outsider any more. The Three Musketeers were going to the enemy's reunion—to do what, he wasn't sure. But that would come.

For the moment, Ben had to be satisfied with being a follower instead of a partner. A demotion of the pride, but not the intellect. He still had a lot to contribute. And he would contribute, spreading the cause of truth to all individuals who—

Cut the baloney.

Ben stopped his dance as the thought slapped him.

You're a hypocrite. It's Julia you're interested in.

Had Hamm been right? Was all his interest in TAI a cover for his obsession with one woman?

Is this about truth or do you merely want to stop Julia because she hurt your feelings by believing in the direction God was leading her rather than the direction you wanted to lead her?

Ben fell onto the couch and pulled a pillow to his chest. If that were true, then the last two years of his life had been a joke. He'd pursued a hatred born of hurt pride.

Give it up.

He shook his head against the thought. And yet...

If he could work through this Julia thing, he wouldn't *have* to be a part of Hamm's roller coaster. After all, the urgency *had* eased. Lately, he'd actually been able to breathe easily. He'd taken the departure as a bad thing, but maybe it was good. Maybe it was for the—

He tossed the pillow on the floor and stood. "I don't need Julia. Or Hamm. I won't go to the reunion at all. I'll think of my own way to tell the world my message."

A pain sliced through him like a machete hacking through a jungle, doubling him over. He toppled onto the couch and mumbled an answer. "Okay, okay…I'll go."

The machete was sheathed. But Ben knew the urgency was back, and with it something deeper, stronger. The energy took control as if it didn't really need Ben at all, and certainly didn't need his permission to exist or not exist. It spread its fingers through the sinews of his body, grabbing hold, staking claim. Ben was aware of a shift: the energy had changed from a vital— if misunderstood—presence to a weight that was tired of messing around.

Ben took one breath. Then another. He surrendered and in his surrender found an exhausted relief.

He didn't move for a long time. He felt the weight's presence, long after the pain had withdrawn.

What he'd said was true. He was back in. For better or worse, he was not an outsider anymore.

God help him.

———⟩⟨———

Art answered the phone.

"Arthur?"

"Julia!" He sat up straight as if she were in the room.

"I just wanted to call to tell you how sorry I am that all this…" She seemed at a loss for words. Julia was never at a loss for words.

"I'm sorry too, Gov. I didn't…I wish…"

"Me too, Arthur. Me too."

"It's not what you think." The words came in a tumble.

"Then tell me…"

A pause. "I can't."

"Why not?"

"It's complicated."

"I can handle it."

"I know."

"Then—"

"But *I* can't."

There was a moment of silence. Art's throat was so tight he thought he would die from the pain of holding the words of explanation in. *Please, Lord, help me! Let me tell…*

"I don't understand any of it, Arthur. And if you can't tell me then I can't… Take care of yourself. Keep in touch. I'll be praying for you. I love you, son."

Art nodded to the phone and hung up. He fell over on the couch and pulled his legs close.

His mind screamed. His heart wailed. His soul sighed.

And God held him very, very close, appreciating his obedience.

CHAPTER TWENTY-SIX

———◦◦◦———

Come and see what God has done, how awesome his works
in man's behalf!

PSALM 66:5

ART AND BEN SAT IN HAMM SPURGEON'S KITCHEN. Art's stomach
bolted and churned, like he was on a spinning carnival ride.
Maybe it was the smell of the eggs Hamm was cooking…or,
more likely, from the fact that the reunion was in two days.

Nerves and Hamm's cooking were not compatible.

The previous month had been hell. Although Ben had gotten him a job at the shipping company, Art had far too much
time to think. Loading boxes utilized the muscles, not the
brain. And the two issues that consumed his thoughts were
Julia and his sacrifice.

To be truthful, he'd come to terms with the latter. Art was
sincerely—eternally—grateful God was tolerant because in his
frustration Art had let Him have it, every ounce of his anger—
R-rated words and all. In return, he had received a small sem-
blance of peace. Or was it resignation?

Either way, Art was ready for this reunion business to be
over. If all happened according to his much prayed for scenario, Julia would be saved from harm, Hamm would be
arrested, Ben would fade away to wherever obsessed idealists
went to brood, and Art would have his job back with all sins
forgiven. He would be a hero. No penalties, no fouls. Business
as usual.

He was both pleased and appalled that Julia called him
weekly. But after her first contact, he'd used his answering
machine to screen his calls. He couldn't talk to her. Not again.

Not until he could vindicate himself.

Unfortunately, Hamm hadn't divulged any more of their plans. And according to Ben, the Web site was eerily quiet, as if everyone had been told to shut up. Art had even threatened to quit TAI a few times, hoping Hamm would give in and share what he knew. But somehow Hamm always managed to pull Art back into the fold without leaking a thing. And Ben was no help. He'd become the compliant follower, oddly willing to bow low and kiss Hamm's tootsies.

And Art's further questions about this mysterious boss had been greeted with sarcastic laughter on Hamm's part. If Art heard the line, "In time..." once more, he'd give Hamm's jowls a jiggling they wouldn't forget.

But now...they were leaving tomorrow. Hamm had to tell them something. Why else the invitation to breakfast?

Art balanced his kitchen chair on the rear two legs. "So, Hamm. What's Plan *A*? *B* or *C* too, if you've got them."

Hamm served the eggs. He didn't speak until the plates were set before them. He wiped his hands on his pants. "We, dear sirs, plan to make a big bang at the reunion."

"Bang?"

Hamm slammed a hand on the table, making the dishes clatter.

Ben froze, the salt shaker poised over his eggs. "You plan to kill people?"

Hamm's lips formed a sarcastic sneer. "What do you suggest? Talking them to death?"

"But—"

"It's time for action, Cranois."

Art cleared his throat, hoping his voice would sound normal. "Exactly what kind of action are we talking about?"

Hamm put his hands on Art's shoulders and pushed him forward until all four chair legs made contact with the floor. Then he leaned into his ear. "Death, destruction, and mayhem, Art my boy."

"But how——"

Hamm shoved against Art's shoulders to stand upright. "Do you have any experience with explosives?"

"No. Of course not."

"You will."

Ben stared at him. "You're going to set a bomb?"

Hamm took a seat at the table, putting his face above the plate of eggs to catch a whiff. "It's going to be a psychological *and* physical battle, Cranois. I told you that weeks ago."

"But a bomb...people will be killed."

"We have to make a statement that will get the attention of the country. The world."

Art's head began to shake. Everything in his entire being was repeating one word: *no, no, no, no...*

Hamm took a bite, waving his fork. "This is going to happen whether you two help me or not. You're both expendable."

The nausea returned, and Art forced himself to speak evenly. "Sure, sure, Hamm. Take it easy. We're on your side, remember?"

Hamm pointed the fork at Art's face. At his eyes. It was too close and Art blinked as a counter against its position and the opaque wall of Hamm's stare.

"Have no doubts," Hamm said. "It *will* happen."

Art pushed the fork away. "Don't treat me like an underling. I'm a partner, not a peon."

Hamm shrugged and speared another bite. "Whatever you like to believe." He ate and wiped his mouth with the back of his hand. "The plans go beyond the three of us. These next few days are extremely busy. Schemes for sabotage and setbacks are rampant. Ben, you will be pleased to note that your beloved Julia's presence is required at the reunion—at this point we would even work to *get* her there. But the others will have a harder time of it. Our forces are primed and ready. Actually, I'm jealous of the fun they will have." He sighed. "But I can't do it all. We each have our assignments."

Art traced the edge of his plate. "Some of the Haven people won't get to the reunion? Are they going to be killed?"

"Killed sooner or killed later, what's it to you?"

"I was just wonder—"

"Probably not killed. Unfortunately, God has His armies on the alert. I've heard reports…but we can still make it difficult. Oddly enough, God allows His people to experience obstacles— He seems to think it makes them stronger." Hamm shook his head. "It's totally illogical."

Art's head was spinning. What kind of talk was this? "How do you know what God's doing?"

Hamm winked. "Demons spread the reports, dear boy. The winning side makes a point of knowing. How else can evil triumph over good?"

Demons? Uh-uh. No way. This stuff doesn't happen. "You're not a—?"

Hamm waved a hand. "No. I'm not. But I've made my choice, just as Ben has." His eyes blackened. "Just as you have. Right, Arth-ur?"

Lord! Help! Art forced a laugh, though it came out rough and raw. Then he took a bite and chewed, forcing his tone to be casual, as though they were discussing baseball scores. "I've got my own agenda. I don't need anyone—any*thing*—else muddying my plans."

Hamm shrugged. "Think what you like, but you *are* working for him."

No, I'm not. I'm working for Him. Art sipped his coffee. It burned his throat, but he did not react. "But if, as you say, God has His armies…what makes you think we can do anything against them?"

"We have legions on our side, Graham." Hamm's eyes were dead; his smile cruel. "Legions. Do you understand?" He looked at each of them in turn. "Do you both understand?"

They nodded.

It was showtime.

Loud claps sounded in Kathy's dream but the sound didn't fit with the story line. Confused, she opened her eyes, leaving the dream behind. She raised herself on an elbow to check to see how much time they still had until the alarm would wake them. They had to get up at 7:00 A.M. to leave for Kansas City. With the four-hour drive, they figured they could just get there in time for Kathy's noon meeting with Del. If only Roy hadn't had to go in for that emergency last night they could have—

She blinked once. Twice. *No...it can't be...* In one motion she sat up and shook her husband. "Roy! We overslept! It's 7:15!"

Roy bolted upright and took the clock radio into his lap. He stared at it as if it were an alien machine. "I set it for seven. I know I—" He looked to the hallway. "I set the kids' clocks too. Why aren't they up?"

Kathy was already in the hall. "Kids! Up! Up! We've got to get going!"

The house erupted in chaos, but they got dressed and in the car in record time. As they pulled out of the driveway, Roy said, "Lucky you woke up, Kath."

Luck had nothing to do with it.

—⚬⚬⚬—

Lexa moved her suitcase forward in the check-in line at the airport. Although Kansas City was less than four hours from Lincoln, Lexa had insisted they fly. It was her treat since the chintzy monsignor wouldn't spring for it. Lexa did not understand why such a man was given authority. Monsignor Vibrowsky was an arrogant, annoying—

She didn't let herself finish the apt description. Once again, Delly's good influence was having an impact on her character. Shucky-darn. It had been such fun being a rebel.

"Next."

She and Del moved to the counter and presented their tickets. The agent unfolded the computer printout that represented their electronic tickets and smoothed the pages against the counter. She typed on the keyboard, made a face, then typed some more. She ran a finger under some numbers on the sheets of paper, then painstakingly typed them in one at a time.

Lexa tapped her fingers against the counter. "Is there a problem?"

The agent looked up, then back to the screen. "Well…actually…let me check one more thing."

Lexa watched her fingers fly, but her stomach clenched. She looked at her brother and tried to give him a reassuring smile.

"I knew we should have had the old-fashioned tickets," he said. "It just didn't seem right to only have a printout."

"I do this all the time, Delly. And I've never had a prob—"

The agent looked up, meeting their eyes for the first time. "We have a problem."

"Then fix it," Lexa said.

The agent looked to either side as if scouting for reinforcements. "I'm afraid it's not that easy. We have a full flight and we can't just add—"

Lexa grabbed the tickets and pointed to the flight number. "Add nothing. We already have tickets. We have seat assignments. I've paid for—"

The woman escaped into the keyboard, though Lexa wondered if she was actually typing anything relevant. "I'm sorry, but for some reason your names do not show up on the passenger list. Now, we do have a later flight this evening, if—"

"This evening is too late," Del said. Lexa noticed his face was pale. "My sister and I are responsible for a reunion in Kansas City that starts tomorrow. At noon, we have a meeting with the convention people to make final preparations. The first participants are coming in today. We have to be—"

"I'm sorry, sir. Maybe another airline can assist—"

Lexa had had enough. She grabbed the worthless tickets. "Let's go, Delly."

"I'm sorry, ma'am. I don't know what happened, but there's really nothing we can—"

Lexa didn't want to hear it. She wheeled her suitcase toward the exit with Del following behind.

"Where are we going, Lexa? We *could* try another airline—"

Lexa stormed through the exit doors. "No, we couldn't. Not unless you want to fly to Kansas City via Chicago, Dallas, or Timbuktu. And arrive considerably later than we need to. Personally, I prefer not to zigzag across the country unless absolutely necessary."

He scrambled after her across the street. "So what are we going to—"

She hoisted her suitcase up the curb and faced him. "We're going to drive."

"But we only have four hours until the meet—"

"Then we don't have a moment to spare, do we?"

For once he didn't argue with her.

———

Natalie tried calling Sam one more time. In the weeks since their breakup, she had stayed away from him as much as possible—though he hadn't made it easy. Because they'd known each other so long, he knew her schedule—as well as nearly every detail of her life—so he'd shown up after work or called her within moments of her getting up in the morning. He'd wanted forgiveness for Lila; she'd given him that. He wanted to reinstate their engagement. That she could not do.

Not that she and Jack had taken up again. She'd been thoroughly tempted to call Jack and tell him she was a free woman, but if she did that, she felt it would be like cheating on Sam—as if their breakup were an emotional reaction rather than a rational conclusion.

297

If she were honest, she'd admit it was both. Seeing Jack again *had* stirred her emotions, which had also made her think things through. She and Sam were meant to be friends. Period. She loved him and always would. But she did not feel the bond that she assumed—she hoped—would be a part of a marriage partnership. It wasn't about their tastes being different; the fact he liked action movies and she liked mysteries, or the fact he liked butterscotch and she liked chocolate. Those were details that meant little to the depth of a marriage. But the fact that he could be tempted by Lila...that scared her.

It scared her, but she understood it. She'd felt the same lure with Jack. That realization had been a shock, in more ways than one. She had never considered herself a sensual person and she had certainly never dreamed she would be attracted to someone as plain as Jack. Didn't passion need a handsome face to thrive?

Apparently not. For with the reappearance of Jack in her life, Natalie realized the spark of a new depth of love she hadn't known existed. She was falling in love with Jack—all of him. She loved his gentleness, his insight, his way of looking at her when she was talking that told her he was truly listening. She loved the way he encouraged her and didn't laugh at her confusion or insecurities. She loved the way he would hold her hand as if it were the essence of intimacy. She even loved the way his smile dipped to the left, forming a crooked line across his face.

But most of all, she loved him for his faith—that intangible element of his character that made his eyes shine from within. Where she and Sam had shared a life of concrete events, she and Jack shared a life of endless possibilities that continued into eternity. Sharing an infinite God forever was better than sharing finite space for a limited physical lifetime.

She felt guilty for not being able to reach Sam's heart during their years together. But she'd come to realize she wasn't the keeper of his soul.

So in these weeks between her breakup and leaving for the reunion, she had stayed away from both men in her life, hoping for a divine clarification of what she should do next. She didn't want to blow it this time. God had been very patient with her, but now it was time to wait and listen. She had spent her life trying to do things her way in her time. Now, it was time to do things the right way, in God's time.

It was time to trust Him—and surrender. Surrender Sam and Jack and her writing…surrender everything that she kept trying to figure out and make right.

Either her life—every aspect of it—was God's or it wasn't. She couldn't say the content was His, but the details were hers. It was all or nothing. She had to set the offering at His feet and walk away…

Natalie suddenly realized the phone was still ringing and Sam hadn't answered. She hung up. She'd wanted to say goodbye before leaving for the reunion. But it was not to be. She grabbed her suitcase, shut off the lights, and left her apartment.

Why did she have the feeling it was for the last time?

As she drove down Interstate 76 and neared the Colorado–Nebraska border, Natalie wished she'd had the money for a plane ticket to Kansas City. It had not been an option. The hotel room and meals were going to take most of her savings. If only she had a book contract then she'd have the money to fly—

Stop that! Stop complaining. I'm going to the reunion. That's enough—even if it is a twelve-hour drive.

Natalie sat straighter in her seat and wondered if she would ever reach the point where she was content with the moment. Why did her thoughts constantly betray her selfishness? Good intentions meant little against a traitorous mind.

"Concentrate, Natalie. Concentrate on getting—"

A tire blew.

Natalie struggled for control of the car. She felt and heard the flap-flap-flap of the blown tire as she eased herself onto the shoulder of the interstate. She stopped the car and let herself breathe.

"Not again!"

Natalie could not believe her luck. What was it with her and eastern Colorado? Four years ago, on the way to Haven, she'd blown a tire. The route leading to Nebraska had it in for her. She should have taken I-70 through Kansas.

She flipped on her emergency flashers and got out. At least it wasn't two in the morning like it had been the last time. And at least Natalie was four years smarter and knew how to fix a flat. She looked up and down the interstate, hoping that maybe a pickup would pull behind her, and John, one of the Haven mentors, would pop out and help her, just as he had the first time she'd been in this predicament.

But there was no pickup. There was no John. Just a string of cars that moved into the far lane to give her room to handle her problem. Alone.

She opened the trunk and pulled out the jack and tire. Lucky for her she'd checked the spare before she'd left home. It had been a whim that had paid off—for the spare *had* been completely flat.

As she rolled the tire to its intended spot, she stopped. It was not luck that had made her check the spare. Not luck, not a coincidence, not a fluke. It was God. He'd been looking out for her and had given her a nudge to check it. Thank goodness she had taken it. But with every nudge she took, she wondered how many she missed.

She looked to the wide expanse of skies and took a deep breath. "Thanks, Lord. Thanks for taking care of me."

Natalie sat in her car in front of the old house near the capitol building in Lincoln, Nebraska. She looked up at the attic window and remembered her many hours at the desk beneath its panes, torn between writing her now discarded novel and her books about Haven. Beau, the demon, had pushed her toward the novel, and Jack had pushed her toward God's will in writing her testimony about Haven. Such was life: the pull between God and the world.

She took a cleansing breath, relegating the past to the past and the future to God. It did no good to dwell on either segment of time. Right now she was in Lincoln on her way to the reunion in Kansas City. That's all she needed to know.

Natalie glanced at her purse and found her hand moving to open it. She pulled out a slip of paper with another Lincoln address on it. Jack's. She'd battled with the idea of stopping by—she knew that was the main reason she'd chosen to drive through Nebraska rather than Kansas. She'd even considered calling him but had decided against it. She didn't want to push. She didn't want to take matters into her own hands. She was into trust. And if God wanted her to meet up with Jack in Lincoln, then it would happen. She would swing by his house and let God take care of the rest.

She put the car into drive.

—◦◦◦—

Jack closed his suitcase with a satisfying zip. He couldn't believe he was actually going to the reunion. He wasn't a Haven alumnus, yet twice now, God was allowing him to be a part of that group. It was strong evidence that God was gracious.

Jack looked at his watch. It was time to leave—especially since he was being forced to take a bus to Kansas City. He couldn't believe the bad timing with his car's transmission going out. He yanked the suitcase off his bed and headed to the front door. But as his hand reached for the knob, he hesitated, suddenly overcome by the need to pray. This need had been present off and on all day, as if someone were repeatedly tapping him on the shoulder saying, "Now, Jack. Pray now." He knew better than to ignore such promptings. Jack set his suitcase down and bowed his head, leaning it against the door.

His short prayer for a safe trip turned into five minutes of thanks, a request for the safe journeys of the others, and the hope that those attending the reunion would come with open hearts ready to receive whatever God wanted them to receive.

"Amen." Jack opened his eyes, grabbed his keys, and went outside. He checked to see if the door was locked, and turned around as a light blue Volkswagen drove up.

No...it couldn't be... But it was.

The engine shut off. The car door opened. Natalie got out and looked at him over the top of the vehicle. She smiled, but he could see the hesitancy in her eyes.

"Hi, Jack."

Jack tossed his suitcase to the ground and ran to her, engulfing her with a hug. "Thank you, Lord!" When he let her go long enough to look at her face, he saw she was crying. "Natalie, why the tears?"

She laughed and wiped them away. "I didn't know if you'd be here. I didn't know if I should stop. I didn't know if you *were* here, if you'd be happy to see me. I didn't know—"

He ran a hand along her cheek. "You knew, Natalie. You *know.*" He glanced at the car, needing to confirm one last time that she was alone. "Where's Sam?"

"Back in Estes. We're not engaged anymore."

Jack knew it wasn't proper to grin, but he couldn't help himself. "That's too bad."

She laughed at his clear duplicity. Then her face grew serious. "Actually, it *is* too bad that I've led him on for so long. He is—and always will be—a good friend, but that's all."

"How's he taking it?"

She shook her head and looked to the ground. "I don't want to talk about Sam. I want to talk about us."

He took her hand. "I've been waiting for you, Natalie. I didn't want to press after seeing you in Estes, but I've never given up hope. And when Del told me you were coming to the reunion, I—"

"Del told you?"

"I pried it out of him." He turned her hand and ran a finger across its palm. "It's such a miracle you're here. I was just headed out the—" He stopped as he thought of something. "In fact, I would have been five minutes gone if it hadn't been for an intense need to pray that came over me at the door. We would have missed each other. I'd just gotten back from taking my car in to be fixed and was ready to walk to the bus station when—"

"Your car...you have to take a bus?"

He shrugged. "My car was running fine until last night. I had to take it in this morning. Luckily, there is a bus that goes to—"

"And you haven't been at home?"

He didn't understand what that had to do with anything, but he nodded.

"How long have you been gone?"

Now he was really confused. "An hour. I just got back and was leaving—"

She smiled, her eyes radiant. "I had a flat tire that delayed me thirty minutes. If that hadn't happened, I would have shown up at your door when you were out. I would have left without you."

He kissed her hand. "God is good."

"Indeed He is." She looked at her car. "And there will be no bus for you, Mr. Cummings. Your chariot awaits."

He looked at her rusty vehicle, which was no better than his own. But none of that mattered as long as Natalie was at his side.

———

"We can't go, Walter. Not when Addy has a fever."

Walter knew she was right, but he didn't want to admit it. He sat at the kitchen table in their new apartment and ran his

303

hands through his hair. Everything had fallen into place for them to go—what with winning the raffle tickets, selling the house, and moving just the weekend before. And even his job...although he didn't like working at the radio station, he'd come to accept it. At least he was bringing home a paycheck, even if it was for selling soda pop and oil changes to the world. As soon as they got back from the reunion, they would look for another house—a smaller one. Although it didn't come easily, Walter was learning to live one day at a time.

But missing the reunion? That didn't seem right. Certainly there was a way? Bette sat beside him, fingering her mug of coffee. He put a hand on hers and she showed him disappointed eyes. "I really want to go, Bette. I felt so sure we were supposed to go."

She nodded. "Me too."

Walter let out a breath. "Let's pray about it."

He regretted that her eyes revealed how rare it was that he suggested such a thing, but thankful when she didn't verbalize it. "That's a wonderful idea, Walter." She turned her hand over and squeezed his. She bowed her head.

He did the same, still feeling awkward about praying out loud. This was not his thing, but desperate times necessitated desperate actions. Walter cleared his throat. "God, our Addy is sick. We don't fear for her life or anything like that. It's just the flu or something, but whatever it is, it's keeping us from going to the reunion." He opened one eye to see Bette. Her eyes were closed and there was a crease between her brows. He closed his eyes again and continued. "We want to go, God. But more than that, we think we're supposed to go. We don't understand why this had to happen now, why—"

Bette suddenly pulled her hand away. Walter opened his eyes to see her eyes wild with a new idea.

"What's going on?"

She blinked twice, then looked at him. "It's opposition, Walter. Don't you see? Satan wouldn't want us to go to the reunion to gain strength by being with other believers, so he's putting an obstacle in our way."

Walter tried to swallow, but found his throat dry. "Del's talk of opposition's got to you."

"This has nothing to do with Del. Think about it."

Walter stifled a shiver. *"He* caused Addy's sickness?"

Bette shrugged. "Could be. There's no way that we can ever know for sure, but I think we should act as if it's a fact."

"By doing what?"

"By praying for God's protection for our little girl."

Walter had lived through a direct confrontation with a demon in Eureka Springs, but he didn't like the idea that evil was out there doing its stuff—especially not to his little Addy. "So go ahead. Say it. Pray it for both of us."

Bette nodded and closed her eyes once more. "Lord, we don't know what is causing our little girl to be sick, and if it is Your will, then be with her as she recovers, but if it is evil opposition that is trying to prevent us from going to Your reunion...Lord, protect Addy, protect us, and protect all those who are trying to get to Kansas City. Keep us safe and use Your awesome power to get us where we're supposed to be. Amen."

They looked at each other and took a synchronized breath. "That should do—"

"Mommy?"

They looked up and saw Addy standing in the doorway to the kitchen, her hair tousled from sleep.

Bette scooped her up and took her back to the table, setting her on her lap. "You shouldn't be out of bed, honey. You need to rest and—" Bette put a hand on Addy's forehead. She reached for Walter's hand and pulled it over the table. "Feel her forehead, Walter."

Walter knew his hand was not as expert in gauging a fever as Bette's, but he did it anyway. And even his hand could tell that their daughter was not feverish.

Bette beamed. "It's gone! The fever's gone!" She waved a

hand toward the bedroom. "Go get the thermometer to check for sure."

Walter hurried down the hall to get it. Bette put the thermometer in Addy's ear. A moment later she read the number. "Ninety-eight point six!" She began to laugh. "She's well! Praise God, she's well!"

Walter shook his head, incredulous.

Addy squirmed out of Bette's arms. "Toast, Mommy. I want toast with peen-butter."

Bette stood to get it. After taking a step, she turned back to Walter. "Don't just sit there, hon, get the suitcases ready. We have a plane to catch."

Walter began to laugh, his mind swimming with shock and gratitude. They were going to the reunion after all. Thanks be to God.

CHAPTER TWENTY-SEVEN

They cried to you and were saved; in you they trusted and were not disappointed.

PSALM 22:5

DEL FELT TOTALLY CONFIDENT WITH LEXA at the wheel. As he studied her profile, he saw determination tighten her features. She would get him to Kansas City on time and nothing would stop her.

She must have felt his scrutiny because she glanced at him. "The scenery is that way." She pointed out the windshield.

"You are much more fascinating than scenery."

"Since when did you become a flatterer?"

He shrugged. It wasn't flattery. What he'd said was true. She was something special. "I've missed you all these years."

"I've missed you too, Delly."

"I worried about you."

"I worried about me too."

"*Worried.* Past tense?" She shrugged, and he knew he was asking an impossible question. His sister was not one to make plans past the hours in the present day. The fact she was jobless and manless at the same time was proof she hadn't thought through the consequences.

"After the reunion is over, I will throw myself to the wind and see where it blows me."

"You're not sticking around?"

"Maybe."

"I like having you close."

"You say that now, but we both know our lifestyles grind like sand on glass. If I stuck around you'd just get mad at me."

"You don't have to go back to your old ways, Lexa. You said you came here to get a fresh start."

"Maybe I've reconsidered. Old ways are known ways. I am who I am. Isn't that acceptable?"

"Yes, but…"

"Ah…the *but* that said a thousand words."

"Everyone can improve on his or her life. It's a continuing process."

"Right. You get one area squared away and another character project comes up. I'm tired of struggles. Is there anything wrong with gliding for a while?"

"But you came here to—"

"To help you." She repositioned her hands on the steering wheel. "Although that wasn't my first intent it turns out to be a virtuous excuse—and I'll take virtue wherever I can find it."

"Don't you think it's time to settle down? Have kids? Mother would sure love a grandchild."

"So? Don't blame me. You didn't give her any either."

"You'd make a great mother."

"You'd make a great father."

He laughed. "I *am* a great Father."

"Cute." She reached into the backseat and retrieved his jacket. "Enough talk. Let me drive in peace. Use this as a pillow and sleep."

He scrunched the jacket into a wad by his head. "Gee. At least airplanes give you a real pillow."

"Watch it. Complainers don't get peanuts and ginger ale."

"Then I'll have to be good."

"Do try, Delly, though I know it's a stretch. Now shh! Sleep."

Del slept. And dreamed.

"Oh, no."

At his sister's low exclamation, Del pushed himself straight in the seat, letting the jacket-pillow fall into his lap. It took him a moment to remember where he was.

"There's an accident." Lexa pointed to the flashing lights in the near distance.

"Let's say a prayer for them."

"You go ahead. I'll say ditto."

Del prayed for those injured. He and Lexa turned their heads as they passed. Ambulance personnel were working frantically on a man lying on the shoulder. His car was in the ditch.

Lexa shivered. "Uhhh. Death scares me."

"Not me."

"You're kidding."

Del turned in his seat, her words bringing him fully awake. She had to understand. "There's nothing to fear in death."

"There's everything to fear in death. It's the end. Game's over. Lights out."

"It's not the end. It's moving on."

She sighed. "Here it comes…"

"What?"

"That eternal life junk."

"It's hardly junk."

"It is if you don't believe in it."

How could they have grown up in the same household and gone to the same schools, yet have such differing views of life—and the afterlife? "Why don't you believe, Lexa?"

"There's no proof. I need proof."

"The apostle Paul said, 'To die is gain.'"

"Then Paul was crazy."

Del shook his head. "The struggles are here, in this life."

"Don't I know it."

"In heaven there will be no struggles. No tears. No sorrow. No lights out. The light will be on full blast. His light."

"Words, Delly. Just words."

"Words from the Bible."

She shrugged.

His heart fell. If she didn't believe the Bible held truth, then how could he prove eternal life was true? One belief led to another. "Lexa, you know the Bible is the Word of God, don't you?"

"Maybe."

Del rubbed the bridge of his nose, his mind swimming. *Lord, please help me reach my sister.* He tried to order his thoughts. When one finally loomed clear, he began. "The events in the Bible have been proven by scientists and historians as real. They happened."

"Okay...I'll give you that."

"And thousands of prophesies in the Bible have come true. More facts."

"Another point for you."

"You've read the Bible, Lexa. I know you have."

"Some of it."

"Has any of it sounded false? Wrong? Should we murder? Should we hate? Should we live only for ourselves?"

"No, of course not."

"So the principles of a good life laid out in the Bible sound absolute and ideal, right?"

"Well...yeah."

"Then why believe part of it and not all of it? Why believe Jesus lived—as historians can prove—and not believe that He was the Son of God, He died for our sins, and He rose from the dead, promising us eternal life in heaven? There are eyewitness accounts. John, Matthew, James, Peter..."

"Well..."

"What proof do you have there is no heaven?"

"I didn't say I had any proof."

Del touched his sister's leg. "Then why not open your heart to the idea? We have a choice to believe what we want. Good things and bad things. I see no advantage in believing the bad things, and great advantage—and peace of mind—in believing the good. The evidence is there if you let yourself see it. Let the

Holy Spirit do His work in you. He'll help you believe."

She shook her head. "Don't get into that Spirit stuff. I find that creepy."

Del nodded. He knew there was a proper time. To push now would hinder God's work. The seed of Lexa's faith had been planted when she was a child. Today she'd opened the door to let him feed and water that seed. But too much water would drown it. It was time to stop, to let the Holy Spirit take over.

"I can't make you believe anything, Lexa. I can only tell you what I believe and show you how it has affected my life in ways beyond my imaginings. The rest is up to you. Be open to God. He'll do the rest. In His time. In whatever way is best for you."

He saw Lexa struggle to swallow. "I want to believe what you do, Delly."

"Then let it happen."

"You make it sound so simple."

Del smiled. For this, he had an answer. "It *is* simple—with God by your side. You can't will yourself to believe. You have to let Him do the work. He *wants* to. Jesus said, 'Come to me, all you who are weary and burdened, and I will give you rest. Take my yoke upon you and learn from me, for I am gentle and humble in heart, and you will find rest for your souls. For my yoke is easy and my burden is light.'"

"Sounds good."

"It is good, Lexa. Very, very good."

—⁓—

Roy nudged Kathy and whispered in her ear. "It's beautiful, Kath."

She followed his gaze to her painting, which sat on an easel next to the reunion registration desk.

She opened her mouth to thank him when the couple in front of them turned to join in their conversation. The wife spoke. "I hear they're going to raffle it off. I'll certainly buy a chance."

The husband cocked his head, studying the painting. "So many faces…I wonder if they're real people."

Roy nudged Kathy again. She wasn't sure she liked this situation. If God wanted her to be humble about her work, why was she constantly tested with praise? *Lord, I want to do things right. Especially here. Let me start out right at the reunion.*

Roy answered for her. "They *are* real people. This is the artist right here. My wife, Kathy Bauer."

The couple's eyes widened. "Harry, she's the artist."

"I heard, I heard." Harry held out his hand. "Harry Bennett and my wife, Dorothy. We've never met a real artist before."

Kathy shook their hands. "This is my husband, Roy, and our children, Ryan and Lisa. And what do you two do for a living?"

Harry smiled at his wife. "We own our own paint store in Arizona. We—"

Kathy laughed. "Then we have plenty in common. We both work with paints."

It took Harry a moment to get the connection. Then he laughed too. "I guess you're right. *Artistes,* all."

As they moved up in line, Dorothy pointed to the painting. "So…the faces are real people? That woman on the right looks like the presi—"

Kathy's attention was drawn to a man standing a few feet in front of Dorothy. He looked so familiar…

"Art!" She hadn't meant to speak out loud, but as she did so, all heads turned toward her, then to him.

Art tensed, and Kathy had the strong sense that he wanted to flee. He looked around, then walked toward her, hand extended. "Hi."

She didn't do it on purpose. It was more of a knee-jerk reaction: She put her hand behind her back. Her tone, when she spoke, was low and resentful. "I thought you were in jail."

Out of the corner of her eye, Kathy saw Harry and Dorothy do a double take.

Art stuffed his hands in his pockets. "I did my time. I got out."

But you held my child captive with Julia. You held her in front of you as a shield against the police. You—

Kathy was appalled when Art turned to her daughter. "Hey, Lisa. Remember me?"

When Lisa cocked her head and squinted at him, Kathy's heart began to pound. *You leave my daughter alone, you kidnapper, you…criminal!*

Art nodded at Lisa's uncertainty, then pulled his billfold out of his pocket. "Maybe this will help you remember." He unfolded a paper and held it for Lisa to see. It was a child's drawing of a dog.

Lisa's face lit up. "I drew that! In the school!" She looked at Art a second time. "You're him? The guy who drew pictures with me?"

Kathy blinked. *That's what she remembers? Drawing pictures? Not the gun battle or—*

"That's me." He took the picture back and carefully refolded it.

"Why do you still have it?" Lisa asked.

Kathy wanted to know the same thing.

He glanced around quickly—was he hiding from someone?—then smiled. "Because I like to be reminded of Haven. My whole life changed there. I did some pretty bad things…I'm really sorry, Lisa. I was a different person back then. I didn't know—I didn't care—about doing the right thing. I just wanted to do my *own* thing."

Kathy yanked Lisa back against herself. "Why are you here?" She knew the words were hateful, but they escaped anyway.

"Kathy!"

Roy's expression made her feel it would be better to evaporate than to take another breath. She knew she should have

313

forgiven Art by now—in fact, she thought she had. But clearly knowing and doing were two different things.

No one said anything—which was a blessing. *I should apologize. I should—*

Before she could force the words, Lisa stepped forward and tugged on Art's sleeve. "I remember you. And it's okay. It's all okay now."

With her child's forgiveness, Kathy's humiliation was complete. Any words of reconciliation now would seem insincere and convenient. She glanced at the registration table. She and Roy hadn't signed in yet; they could turn around and go home, where she could wallow in her character defects. She didn't deserve to be at the Haven reunion. She was no better a person now than she was four years ago. She avoided everyone's eyes, wishing she could run away.

Art turned toward the painting. "Did you do this?"

"Yes."

"It's beautiful. The people joined together around the cross...there's Julia's face."

Roy intervened. "Everyone who was at Haven is there—and other people who've been important in Kathy's life."

Here was a chance to redeem herself. "I figured if I was going to draw a multitude of faces, I might as well have them represent people who have touched me."

Ryan pointed. "See? There's Del and Walter. Natalie and the mentors. And even our daddy."

Roy put a hand on his shoulder. "Uninvited but loved by God."

Kathy nodded. Although her marriage to Lenny had not been great, every once in a while, she still missed him. She knew God had His hands full with Lenny up in heaven.

She felt Lisa take her hand. "Where's Art, Mommy?"

Kathy's heart dropped into her stomach. She'd thought her humiliation was complete? She'd been wrong. "I...I..."

Art put a hand on Lisa's shoulder. "I don't deserve to be a

part of the picture, Lisa. I was working against God back then."

Lisa looked up at him. "But you're here now."

He nodded, but a crease formed between his eyes. "God's good about second chances."

With a mumbled "Excuse me," Kathy ran out of the room. She certainly hoped Art was right.

"Mommy?"

Kathy looked up from blowing her nose and saw her daughter in the rest room doorway. "I'll be there in a minute, sweet cakes."

"Art left, Mommy. You can come out now. He won't hurt you."

Kathy felt like a fool. "I know that, honey."

"I do bad sometimes, Mommy."

Where was this coming from? "You're a good—"

Lisa shook her head. "I do bad, but you forgive me." Her eyes were worried. "Don't you?"

Kathy bent down and pulled Lisa close. "Of course I do."

Lisa pushed away. "Then why don't you forgive Art?"

"It's more complicated than—"

"But why?"

Why indeed? God didn't make any distinction. Forgiven was forgiven. The slate was wiped clean. Jesus died for all.

Kathy ran a finger along her daughter's cheek. "Would you pray with me, sweet cakes?"

Lisa nodded and bowed her head. That simple act tore through Kathy's pride. She confessed her sins.

And was forgiven.

Kathy exited the rest room feeling rejuvenated. It wouldn't be easy to face Art or Roy's condemning gaze or even the strangers. But it had to be done. It was part of the process of redemption.

But Art was gone, as were Harry and Dorothy. Life had moved on while Kathy dealt with her shortcomings. That in itself was a good lesson: The world was not waiting with bated breath for Kathy to get it right. People had their own struggles to contend with.

Thankfully, Roy and Ryan were there. Waiting and ready to forgive. Roy stepped toward her, holding out a hand. What had she done to deserve such a man?

The answer came to her in a flash: *nothing*. She had done nothing to deserve Roy, her children, her painting talent, her friends, her home, God's forgiveness, eternal life…the list went on.

Only one statement described her feelings at the moment, as Roy took her hand and kissed her cheek: God was merciful—and very, very good.

Art dug his hands in his pockets and walked toward the hotel gift shop. He'd grab himself a bag of chips and a Coke, go upstairs, and hide out. He didn't want to meet up with any of the other Havenites and endure that *look*—as though he were dog doo they wanted to scrape from the bottoms of their shoes.

Of course, he couldn't blame them. They only knew him by his actions in Haven, which had been less than admirable. Robbery, kidnapping, a hostage standoff with police, and a shooting. He was not going to get the key to *that* city.

But he wasn't the same man who'd done those things.

It sounded trite, like a cop-out. But it was true. Sometimes he felt like he'd led two lives—or three. His life as a child before he'd gotten into trouble, his life full of crime and bad choices, and his life with God leading the way.

Maybe if he got on the hotel PA and made one blanket announcement, he could rid himself of his past once and for all: "Listen up, people! I was a bad guy. I was scum. But God set me free of all that. I'm on His side now. I'm working for—"

Hamm Spurgeon.

Art grimaced. Scrap that idea. He couldn't tell anybody anything because as far as they could see, he hadn't changed a bit. Not a—

There was a commotion by the front door. A crowd of suits came in, their wary eyes scanning the lobby. It could only mean one thing...

Julia!

People drew together in small groups, whispering, pointing. Art slipped behind them, wanting to see, not daring to be seen.

She came through the doors with Edward by her side. She looked beautiful, her gray suit matching her hair.

A sudden realization slapped Art: He could have been coming through those doors with Julia if he hadn't got drawn into this ring of espionage. He could have come to the reunion in a position of honor instead of slinking along the sidelines, waiting to hinder Hamm in his plot of death, destruction, and mayhem.

It wasn't fair. Not fair at all.

Suddenly, Julia hesitated, like a doe in the forest alerted to a sound. She looked in Art's direction...

Their eyes met for a moment, then he looked away, not sure what to do.

He risked a second look. Julia was talking with Edward. Discussing *him?* Secret service agents looked in Art's direction, scoping him out.

Then Julia walked toward him. Smiled at him. The bystanders in front of him fidgeted nervously, not sure what to do. The president was coming close. Then they saw that her eyes were not focused on them, but on someone behind...

They parted and let her through. Art stood alone. His feet would not move. His hands clenched and unclenched. At least he managed a smile.

She stopped in front of him, though Art saw that Edward's hand held her upper arm, ready to pull her away. She held out her hand. "Hello, Arthur."

"Uh…hi, Gov…Madam President."

She took a deep breath. "You came on your own."

"Yes."

She patted his hand and leaned toward him. "I'm glad."

Edward spoke. "We have to go, missy."

She nodded. "Maybe I'll see you later?"

"Maybe."

And she was gone.

Art slipped away from the questions of the curious and escaped into a stairwell. That was close. Hamm had told them that it didn't matter if they were seen by people they knew. They were participants in a revival. All were welcome. But still…to come face-to-face with Julia…

Art leaned on the railing and closed his eyes. *Help me through this. Help me stay focused on my mission. Keep me safe and—*

The door to the stairwell clanged open. Art looked up to find Hamm had burst in, shutting the door.

He glared at Art. "What was all *that* about?"

"I was getting something to eat. I didn't know Julia was coming in."

"But now she's seen you."

Art shrugged. "You said it was all right if people saw us, we could just say that we—"

Another stairwell door clanged. They both looked up, listening. But there was no other sound.

"So did you give her your alibi for being here?"

"I didn't have a chance." He forced a shrug. "It's no big deal. It doesn't affect what we're doing."

"What *we're* doing?"

"I…I was looking for you. I wanted to see if I could help with the explosives. You said I'd learn about them and you haven't—"

"No need. It's done."

Art's heart bounced off his toes. "It can't be!" *I wanted to help; I wanted to mess it up; I wanted to know what you were up to so I could tell—*

Without warning, Hamm shoved Art against the wall, squeezing his neck with a viselike grip. Art's toes grappled for the floor. *Where was the man getting his strength?*

Art didn't want to know.

"Don't you ever tell us what can and can't be!" Art saw the veins in Hamm's eyes and smelled the man's fetid breath. "I am the one who has received his power! I am the one in control. You will do what I want, when I want you to do it. You have no say, no voice, no rights."

Art coughed, gasping for breath. He tried to pull Hamm's hands away, but to no avail. "Stop…" It was all he could manage. A surge of terror grabbed hold. Was this the end? Death in a stairwell?

Hamm blinked, seeming to notice Art's predicament for the first time. He eased his grip, and as Art's feet found the ground, Hamm backed away, smoothing his shirt and adjusting his bow tie. "Well. There. That's done. We'll see you later, right, Brother Graham?"

He gave Art's cheek a friendly pat and left the stairwell.

Art sank to the floor, using the wall as a guide. This was worse than he thought. The bomb was set, and he had no idea where. He couldn't help. Couldn't stop what was going to happen. And Hamm's weird dual personality was becoming more pronounced. More frightening. It wasn't just Julia's safety Art was worried about anymore. This was a spiritual battle; the stakes had been raised. *Lord, I'm scared. Protect—*

Footsteps sounded on the stairs above him. He pushed his way to standing and coughed, trying to clear passage through his aching throat. He did not expect the person on the stairs to be Ben.

"Are you all right?" Ben studied him slowly.

"You saw?"

"Heard. I was afraid to come any closer." He looked at the door nervously. "What's gotten into him?"

Art rubbed his throat. "I think you know the answer to that question."

Ben shook his head. "This isn't what I had in mind. None of it."

"Then why have you gone along?"

"Haven't you felt...it?"

"Felt what?"

Ben lowered his voice. "The weight. The force. The evil."

Art put a hand on Ben's arm, all thoughts of keeping his cover fading. "You don't have to give in to it, Ben. Hamm's wrong. What he's doing is wrong."

"But you...you joined us."

Art hesitated. "Let's just say I've changed my mind. Hamm can't go around killing people, no matter what his cause is."

"I know. I despise what this has turned into. I hate Julia, but I don't want her dead. But it's too late."

"No, it isn't. You and I can band together against him. We can—"

Ben pulled away, shaking his head violently. "I can't risk it. You don't know. The pain. The power. It's got me. *He's* got me."

"No, he doesn't. Or he doesn't have to. God is stronger than—"

"No!"

Ben ran into the hall. The stairwell echoed in defeat.

—◦◦◦—

Lexa walked toward the main registration desk and looked over the workshop room assignments. So many people had signed up at the last minute that they'd had to get larger rooms for most of the workshops. It was a good problem to have. They'd gone from two thousand registrants to eight thousand, with people coming in from all fifty states. She'd even heard about reunions being held in six other countries. All evidence of God's global call. Astounding.

Lexa saw her brother mingling with incoming guests. He was hugging a chubby man who looked slightly familiar, while a pretty woman and a little girl looked on. Lexa couldn't keep from smiling. Del had always been a hugger.

Del turned in her direction, and his face lit up. He motioned her over. "Lexa! I want you to meet Walter Prescott, his wife, Bette, and their little Addy."

Walter. Now she remembered where she'd seen him. She shook his hand. "You were on TV with my brother. And you went to Haven with him."

Del blushed. "Technically, *I* was with Walter. I stowed away in *his* van."

"Ah, yes," Walter said, "we were quite a pair. The priest and the pompous pain."

A woman's voice came from the left. "How about adding a precocious purveyor of prose to the bunch?"

Everyone turned around, and Lexa saw a pretty young woman walking toward them. She was accompanied by a man Lexa pegged as plain—until his smile added depth to his looks, the way a tuxedo made an ordinary man look special and important.

"Natalie! Jack!"

More hugs and introductions.

"So you're the author? I've always envied people who could use words well."

Natalie shook her head. "I write the words. As for the *well* part...?" She shrugged.

Jack slipped his hand through her arm and patted it. "She's an author-in-waiting. Because of her, the whole world will know what happened in Haven and Eureka Springs."

"Here, here!" Del put an arm around Natalie's shoulders and gave them a squeeze. "It's so wonderful being together again. In fact, I've been thinking that we need more time to churn over old memories. I want all of you to join me for dinner tonight. My treat. I'll get in touch with Kathy and Julia and we'll have our own special reunion. A party."

Lexa raised a hand, shaking her head. "But Delly, tomorrow's a huge day. Wouldn't you rather take it easy tonight?"

He stared into the space between them, a crease forming between his eyes. "No. I want to do this. I want all of us to be together. Tonight. Before the rush of events starts in the morning. Before..." He shook his head as if dispelling a disturbing thought, then smiled. "Agreed?"

"Sure." Walter grinned at his wife. "We never turn down a free dinner, do we, hon?"

Bette's eyes widened for just a moment, then she nodded. "We'd love to, Del."

Jack looked to Natalie. "We're in."

Del clapped his hands together. "Seven sharp. We'll meet here."

Lexa wished he wouldn't push himself, but she knew it was a done deal. Besides, she couldn't worry about this evening. She had work to do now. "You're in television, right, Walter?"

He hesitated and looked at his wife. "Right."

"Then maybe you can help me handle the TV and video crews. I'm dealing with aliens. I don't speak their language." She took a step away, but he didn't follow. "You coming?"

From the looks exchanged between Del and Bette, she guessed something was being left unsaid. But the last thing she had time for right now was deciphering her brother's cryptic looks.

Walter moved to her side. "Sure. I'd be glad to help."

<hr />

Ben spotted Hamm standing with a couple near a huge, potted plant. He turned to slip away in the opposite direction, but it was too late.

Hamm waved him over. "Brother Ben, come on over here and meet these nice folks from Texas."

The contrast between Hamm's actions in the stairwell and his down-home, best-friends act was disturbing. Hamm was dressed in his usual chinos, but today, they looked a tad too short. He'd added a plaid shirt, buttoned at the neck, which made his chins more prominent. In his shirt pocket, he had a pen with a cross on the clip, and a shiny new Bible was clamped under his arm. He looked like the Christian character from a low-budget movie—and sounded like one too.

Hamm drew Ben under his arm, grinning at the Texans like a goon. "This is my best buddy, Ben. Ben, this is Julie and Matt Clydesdale from Midland. Julie went to the Haven in New Mexico, praise the Lord!"

From the look the couple exchanged, they would rather be talking with a cactus than Hamm Spurgeon. Ben understood the feeling perfectly. He shook hands, then excused himself and fled to the elevators.

Maybe he should consider Art's offer.

Fumbling for his card key in front of his room, Ben's spine tingled. He turned around to see Hamm sauntering down the hall toward him.

"You can run, but you can't hide, Cranois."

Hamm grabbed the key from Ben and slipped it in the door. He motioned for Ben to enter.

Ben grappled to take control of the situation. This was *his* room. Hamm had no right… He turned to face him, lifting his chin—he hoped defiantly. "You're making a fool of yourself, Hamm."

"Watch it, Cranois."

Ben resisted the urge to crumble. "You look like a Bible-thumping moron from the sticks."

Hamm preened in front of the mirror. "I think I look pretty good."

"You're a cliché. If you want to blend in, you should dress more…normal."

"Like you?" Hamm's eyes gave Ben the once-over.

"Sure. I may not approve of these people's philosophy, but I'm smart enough to realize their image has been maligned. And you're not helping."

Hamm unbuttoned his collar. "Ben Cranois, defender of the faith." Hamm looked around the room. "You've unpacked."

"So?"

"Tomorrow our mission will be accomplished. And once it is, you won't want to be lagging behind, repacking your under-wear."

Ben's stomach knotted as he remembered what he'd heard in the stairwell. "So... you've done it? You've set it?"

Hamm sat at the foot of the bed, bouncing on the mattress. "A fake ID, some construction tools, and a condescending smile got me right where I needed to be. That, and some help from our boss."

"Where did you put it?"

"It's a secret."

"You're shutting me out again."

Hamm shrugged. "Live with it. Just be assured that all is ready. When the time is right, all I do is push a button from the safety of my seat. That's all you need to know."

"This is bu—"

Hamm moved to the door. He looked back, giving Ben a smile that could only be described as evil. "Got a complaint? Take it up with the boss. Happy Thanksgiving, Cranois."

Ben ate dinner in his room in the company of a football game. He didn't want to risk seeing Hamm or Art or Julia or anyone. He wanted to hide. Let it be over so he could go home.

He shoved his dirty dishes aside and set his laptop on the table by the window. Maybe Hamm had posted something about where he set the bomb. He got on the Internet and called up the site.

A message appeared: "Unable to connect. Unknown host." He tried again with the same results. And again. Each time, the computer gave the same response. Unknown host.

What in the…? Ben's mind swam with possibilities—none of them good. He reached for the phone and called Hamm's room. "What's with the Web site? It won't come up anymore… has someone discovered us? Should we be worried?"

"It's gone. It isn't necessary anymore."

"Of course it's necessary. Tomorrow is the culmination of our work. We should be in contact with the other members, get their input, share our success." There was a moment of silence. "Hamm?"

"There are no other members."

"What?"

"There is no TAI. It was all a sham. I dismantled the Web site as soon as we got here."

"What are you—"

Ben heard Hamm's sigh of exasperation. "You're an organization man. I needed you to help me, so I created an organization. TAI. But now that you're committed, now that you and Art are here, I can let it go."

"But the other members…the chat rooms…?"

"All me, myself, and I. Actually, I'm glad it's over. It was quite exhausting."

Ben's mind flitted through past online conversations. Those people…his friends and colleagues…they were all Hamm? How could that be? How had he been so gullible? Stupid? Blind? Had there been some clue he'd missed? "You tricked me."

"Hey, you do what you gotta do. I had my orders."

Ben slammed the lid of his computer. "I'm going home. Now."

"No, you aren't."

Ben shoved the laptop across the table, knocking a mug of coffee on the floor. "Why shouldn't I leave? You don't need me.

You tricked me into joining a fictitious group, then you got me involved with a bombing where people will get killed—yet you won't tell me the details. Or is that a farce too? You act like you need me, but then you don't trust me." He ran a hand over his face. "If I'm important enough to woo, I should be important enough to be in on things. Why am I here with you? Why me?"

"I asked the same questions. Why you?"

Ben's throat went dry. "Did you get any answers?"

"Rumors are rampant in the spiritual world."

"Which means?"

"Our side heard that you are wanted by their side."

"Isn't everybody *wanted* by God? At least that's what they say."

"Yes. To some degree. But there's something more with your case. There's been a special interest in you, which made you a more appealing target. Our boss wanted first dibs."

Ben stifled a shiver. "I feel like the biggest piece of pie at a church dinner."

"At least you're wanted."

For what? "Don't I have a say in any of this?"

Hamm hesitated. When he laughed, the sound grated like fingernails on a chalkboard. "Yeah, right. What do you think?"

He knew what Hamm was saying. He didn't have a choice. Not a bit.

Still, what *did* he think? He remembered the times he'd gone against Hamm, done what he thought was best, listened—if only for a moment—to that other voice... *Maybe I do have a say.* Ben felt a slice of hope lighten the darkness of his thoughts. Maybe—

Hamm's voice was quick to fill the silence. "Leave the thinking to me, Cranois. You can't say no. You've felt his power."

Ben sat straighter in the chair, a burst of bravado taking over. "I can handle a little pain."

"It won't be a little."

But maybe it would be worth it...

"He's spent a lot of time on you. You should feel very honor—"

Ben hung up. His hand hovered above the phone, shaking.

A choice. Free will…it couldn't be that easy. Hadn't Ben made a choice that was irrevocable?

A fearful inner turmoil gripped him.

Hamm had said that God was interested in him? What exactly did that mean?

An ache shot into his temples, veiling his questions. He felt as though a shadow had moved front and center, pressing down on him, on his heart, on his spirit…

Ben fell onto the bed and leaned against the pillows. A commercial came on the television, and he reached for the remote to gain some silence.

Lose the weight now! the voice on the commercial exclaimed. *Lead the life you want to live! It's easy. All you have to do is ask for help. That's why we're here…*

Ben sat up in the bed, staring at the screen. Lose the weight now…could it be? Was it really that simple? He grabbed onto the idea. He could do it. He could lose the weight now. All he had to do was ask—

Ask whom?

He knew the answer. His chest heaved. Could he do this? He scanned his memories for a time in his life when he had prayed. He remembered one time…when he was a boy. He'd been sitting in church next to his grandmother…

He took a breath and smelled her floral perfume and the aroma of oak and polish. He saw the worn corners of the hymnal in the slot in front of him, the gold letters embossed on the burgundy cover. He heard the murmur of adult voices speaking together. He heard his own child's voice. *Our Father, who art in heaven…*

Ben tossed the remote on the bed and bowed his head. He placed his hands under his chin, readying himself to concentrate hard. *Do it right, Ben. This is important.* He took a deep breath and began. "Our Father...I want to lose the weight. I want to—"

The lights went out. The television zapped off.

Ben stopped breathing. He waited a few moments to let his eyes adjust to the darkness. A blackout in a hotel full of guests. What a mess that would be.

He slid off the bed and moved to the exit, planning to enter the hallway where there might be emergency lights leading to the lobby. He opened his door. The hall lights were on. He heard the ding of the elevator. A couple across the hall opened their door. Their room was bathed in light.

Ben looked back in his room. It was dark.

It's him! Stopping me before I prayed.

Run, Ben! Run away. Escape evil's presence.

His muscles tensed. He took a step into the hall.

The lights of his room came on.

"Sir? Is there a problem?" A bellboy walked toward him from the direction of the elevator.

"I...I..." Ben looked right, then left, then back into his light-filled room.

The bellboy stared. "Are you feeling okay? Can I help you? Get someone?"

Yes! Get someone? No. Ben grabbed the doorjamb for support and scanned the hall. He half expected Hamm to round the corner, grinning at the parlor trick. *How'd you like it, Cranois? Why don't I show you something really amazing...*

Ben took a step back and found the door in his way. He glanced into his room and was relieved to see the lights had stayed on. *Did I imagine everything?*

Yes or no, the only place he would feel safe was within the four walls of his room. Behind a locked and bolted door. Alone.

"Sir?"

Ben looked up. "No...I'm fine." He shut the door in the bellboy's puzzled face. He turned the lock. Leaned against the solid feel of the door. Fear snatched every cell, taking him captive.

One more day. He could tolerate the weight one more day. Tomorrow it would be over. Then maybe, having done his duty, he could truly escape.

He slept with the lights on.

CHAPTER TWENTY-EIGHT

Blessed are they whose ways are blameless, who walk according to the law of the LORD.

PSALM 119:1

DEL LOOKED OVER THE PREPARATIONS in the private dining room. The room was aglow with candles, their light reflected in the dishes. Royal blue napkins spilled out of the water goblets like linen fountains. A lovely room, good food, and trusted friends. Perfect.

The fare was going to be simple as befitted Del's budget. Although he usually wasn't impulsive, after getting the idea to have the dinner, he'd reserved the room, chosen the menu, and made a long-distance phone call to make a withdrawal from his retirement fund to pay for it. The banker had not been very pleased with him—Del had caught him just moments before closing for the Thanksgiving holiday. But they'd wired the money to Kansas City so the dinner could go on.

Del grinned, surveying the scene. Being spontaneous could be fun, albeit expensive.

Of course, Lexa would object to his spending—and normally Del wouldn't think of robbing his future to pay for a dinner, but somehow…when he'd seen his Haven friends, he needed to hold on to the moment. He'd never given them anything. Tonight, he would give them the gift of fellowship and food. And something more.

Something very meaningful…

"Speech! Speech!"

Del stood at his place and waved down the friendly applause. He pretended to be embarrassed at Julia's words, but inwardly, he was pleased. He wasn't one to speechify, but tonight was different. Tonight he felt an intense need to say what was in his heart, and Julia had paved the way. "Now, now, people. The applause isn't necessary—"

Kathy laughed. "You love it."

Del shrugged. "I don't have a speech prepared—"

"Thank God for that!"

"But I do have a request. And I want you to do what I ask without a word. Without protest." He looked at the faces around the table. "Agreed?"

Walter shook his head. "I will not do the hokeypokey and turn myself around. Friend or no friend."

"There will be no dancing involved."

Lisa raised a hand. "I like the hokeypokey. And the bunny hop. We did those at your wedding, right, Mommy?"

Kathy slipped an arm around Lisa. She smiled at her husband. "Roy does a mean bunny hop."

"I could teach everyone how to line dance," Natalie said.

Walter made a face. "Ewww…country music? No way."

Edward put his arm around his wife. "Julia and I are waltzers from way back."

"It took me months to get Edward to count to three instead of four."

"Not months, just a few weeks."

Del enjoyed their bantering, but wondered how he was going to turn the conversation from dancing to—

Jack stood, calming the talk. "Come on, everyone. Let Del make his request. We owe him that much for this delicious dinner."

The room quieted, and Jack sat down. Del cleared his

throat, thankful for Jack's help. "I would like each of you to remove your socks and shoes. Women with hose can remove shoes only."

"Now I *know* there's going to be dancing."

Del smiled at Walter. "No dancing. I promise."

They did as he asked.

———∽∽∽———

Within moments, Julia guessed what Del was going to do. Her heart swelled with the immensity of it. Looking around at the others, she wondered if they understood. Or had they been distracted by the joking?

She felt Edward's hand on her arm, and by the look in his eyes, he knew what was coming. She had to bite her lip to keep from crying. When she saw Del move to a cart in the corner and pull out the basin and the towel, the tears came. *Thank You, Lord, for the perfection of this moment.*

Lisa looked in her direction. "Mommy, she's crying."

Everyone turned toward Julia. *No, no! Don't give your attention to me. Look to Del. Look to his sacrifice and humility.*

Del solved the problem by coming to her first. He knelt in front of her, placing the basin of water on the floor between them. Gently, he took her feet and set them in the bowl. He washed them, then dried them with the towel, following Jesus' ultimate act of humility when He washed His disciples' feet.

She looked down. Kneeling before her was her friend, Antonio, who had attained such humility. How far she had to go…

When he was finished, Del looked up at her and smiled. His face beamed, glowing with an inner light. There was not a hint of selfishness or artifice in his features. She placed her hand over his. "'Having loved his own who were in the world, he now showed them the full extent of his love.'"

Del nodded and offered his own verse. "For you Julia: 'Blessed is the nation whose God is the LORD, the people he

333

chose for his inheritance.' 'Blessed are they who maintain justice, who constantly do what is right.'"

Julia rested her hand on Del's head. "'Blessed are the meek, for they will inherit the earth.'"

Del smiled and moved on to wash Edward's feet. "'Blessed are the peacemakers, for they will be called sons of God.'"

"Thank you, Del."

Del picked up his basin and took it to Walter's feet. Walter shook his head. "You don't have to do this, Del."

Del put a finger to his lips, quieting the protest as he washed Walter's feet. "'Blessed is the man who perseveres under trial, because when he has stood the test, he will receive the crown of life that God has promised to those who love him.'"

Walter ruffled Del's hair, and Julia knew it was the warmest form of affection Walter could offer.

Bette was next. When Del was finished with her feet, he looked up at her and winked. "'But blessed is the man who trusts in the LORD, whose confidence is in him.'"

"Amen to that." Bette picked up Addy and set her feet in the basin.

"Wa-er, Mommy. Keen feet!"

Del wiped off the tiny feet and wiggled Addy's big toe. "'Blessed are the pure in heart, for they will see God.'"

Lisa ran toward Del. "Me next!"

Del nodded and washed her feet. "'Blessed is the man who fears the LORD, who finds great delight in his commands.'"

"I'm not a man."

Del smiled and touched her cheek, then moved to her brother. Ryan's expression was so solemn. Could a child so young understand the humility and obedience Del was displaying?

"'Blessed is he who has regard for the weak; the LORD delivers him in times of trouble.'"

"Thank you, Mr. Priest."

Del looked to Kathy, who was crying and shaking her head.

"Ryan's verse…he *does* care for the weak. You wouldn't believe what he did with the money I gave him." She blew her nose. "But me…I don't deserve this, Del. I don't—"

"Shh." He took her feet and placed them in the basin, drying them as if they were delicate porcelain. "'Turn my eyes away from worthless things; preserve my life according to your word.' 'Cast but a glance at riches, and they are gone, for they will surely sprout wings and fly off to the sky like an eagle.'"

"I've let my love of things take over."

Roy put a hand on her shoulder, and she leaned toward him. "Shh, Kath. It will be all right."

Kathy nodded, but Julia felt her anguish. The material world was a mighty lure.

Roy was next. He held Kathy's hand as Del worked. "'Blessed are those who hunger and thirst for righteousness, for they will be filled.'"

Julia remembered Eureka Springs and their armor of God verses. Hadn't Roy's involved righteousness?

Only three more left. Del walked to Jack's feet. Jack, the newcomer to their group, the one who had been the able prayer warrior during their battle with the demon.

"'Blessed is the man who listens to me, watching daily at my doors, waiting at my doorway.'"

Jack put a hand on Del's shoulder and quoted a verse of his own. "'Blessed is he who comes in the name of the LORD. From the house of the LORD we bless you.'"

The basin was transferred to Natalie's place. "Hi, Del."

He smiled up at her and washed her feet. "'Blessed is she who has believed that what the Lord has said to her will be accomplished!'"

She put a hand to her mouth and her forehead furrowed. "It will be?"

Del nodded.

"Oh, Del…I needed to hear that. I've tried to hold on to His promise, but…." She shrugged.

335

Natalie had told Julia about her books over dinner—and the promise she felt God had made in her heart. For Del to quote such a verse…it was not a coincidence. Julia understood the struggle in waiting. Their whole society had turned into a land of instant gratification. To learn to wait was an art.

Finally there was only one person left. Alexa. Del's sister. He walked to her, leaned down, and hugged her.

"I love you, Delly."

She didn't need to say more. He washed her feet, dried them, and kissed them.

"'Blessed is the man whose sin the Lord will never count against him.' 'Blessed rather are those who hear the word of God and obey it.'"

"Oh, Delly…" Lexa began to cry and shook her head. "So many sins…"

Del drew her hand to his lips and kissed it. Then he stood and spread his arms to encompass them all. "I love all of you. You've changed my life."

Julia's throat tightened as she looked at all the people in the room. Her Haven friends and their families…they were all family now and she loved them as she loved her own blood—in spite of their flaws and because of their blessings. The family of God, united by their desire to do God's will; united this evening by a humble friend who had reminded them of their call.

There were hugs all around. Del always had been a hugger.

———————

Del walked Lexa to her room. He unlocked her door for her. She put her hand at the back of his neck and pulled his forehead to hers. "Did you have fun, little brother?"

"Immense fun."

"If you promise not to tell anyone, I did too."

He laughed and kissed her hairline. "Sleep well, sister. Tomorrow's a big day."

"Don't I know it." She shucked off her shoes before she got

inside the doorway. She dug her toes in the carpet and threw out her arms. "Ahhh! I am in heaven!"

"Not even close."

"Mmm…you've got your heaven, and I've got mine."

"Actually, I was hoping we'd be there together someday."

She stopped her ritual and put her hands on her hips. "You mean you want me to torment you for eternity?"

"Absolutely." He could think of nothing better.

She kicked her shoes out of the way so she could close the door. "You're a sick man, Father Del. A very sick man."

Del went to his adjacent room. He hadn't realized how tired he was until he got in bed. His muscles rebelled at the comfort. Within minutes, the drone of Lexa's television in the next room shut off. He heard a soft tap on the wall their headboards shared. "Night, Delly," she called.

He smiled and tapped back. "Night, Lexa."

It was just like when they were kids. He hugged his pillow and fell into a contented sleep.

CHAPTER TWENTY-NINE

———◦◦◦———

And we know that in all things God works for the good of those who love him, who have been called according to his purpose.

ROMANS 8:28

ON THE FIRST FULL DAY OF THE REUNION, Art awoke with one thought embedded in his mind: *Tell someone.*

He sat up in bed and realized it was the only solution. There was a good possibility that he would never know where the bomb was located, so that shouldn't stop him from telling. He'd taken this as far as he could. He was out of his league. He had to tell security. Warn Julia. Edward. Someone. He didn't want the reunion to be ruined by some bomb scare or an evacuation, but he couldn't see any other alternative. People's lives were at stake.

He glanced at the clock. 6:45. He'd get dressed and call Julia. Meet with whomever he had to meet with. Spill everything.

A smile spread over his face. By spilling everything, he would be vindicated. He would be Julia's friend again. He popped out of bed with new purpose.

There was a knock on his door. *At this hour?*

Art pulled a T-shirt over his gym shorts and looked through the peephole. It was Hamm. *Not now!* Art held his breath. Maybe if he didn't answer...

"Come on, Art. It's early. I know you're in there. Open up. I've got food."

But I don't have time to eat. I have to see Julia.

Hamm pounded on the door and Art thought of the other

339

guests who might be sleeping. Just one more meeting, and Art would never have to see Hamm's ugly mug again.

He opened the door.

Hamm swept into the room carrying a breakfast tray. "Good morning, fellow terrorist! How are you this morning?"

Art stuck his head into the hall. "Where's Ben?"

"Probably boning up on existentialism, ready to wow the masses with his superior knowledge."

Art closed the door. Hamm was already setting the tray on the table by the window. He removed the silver cover from a plate of eggs and bacon. The aroma was intoxicating. Toast, juice, milk, and coffee. A vase with a white carnation completed the tray.

When Art didn't make a move, Hamm tossed the plate cover on the bed and flourished a napkin over his arm like a waiter. He motioned toward the chair. "Your seat, sir."

It smelled too good to pass up. Art sat, and Hamm laid the napkin in his lap. He poured the coffee.

"Where's yours?" Art asked.

"I ate already."

Art ate a strip of bacon and shoveled two scoops of eggs into his mouth. It had been a long time since he'd had a big breakfast. He slathered his toast with grape jelly and bit off a corner. He downed his juice, and sipped the coffee. Hamm sat in the other chair and watched him.

Art devoured the last strip of bacon. "So what's up for today?"

"A little preventative medicine."

"Huh?"

The sarcasm in Hamm's grin was like the clang of a warning bell. Art stopped with the glass of milk halfway to his mouth. Hamm looked at the food, then at Art. His grin intensified.

Art stared at the nearly empty tray of food and drink. *No…Lord…* He did a quick mental scan of his body. He wasn't hurting anywhere. He just felt a little—

Then it hit him. The glass was suddenly a weight. It slipped out of his hand, and milk sloshed over the remains of his feast. Art jerked to his feet, nearly toppling the table. He grabbed the edge for support. "You...drugged me?"

Hamm twiddled his thumbs. "Poison was my preference, but I was told not to go overboard. Apparently, the boss thinks you might still be of use to us. Sometime. In the future."

Art lunged for him. "You—"

Hamm slipped out of the chair, letting Art fall into it. He checked his watch. "A few more minutes, and you will be out of commission for the rest of the day. Sorry, Graham, but we couldn't risk you succumbing to a stab of conscience. Apparently others have seen evidence of your betrayal, even if I haven't."

Art's eyelids were leaden. He leaned against the armrest for support. "O-others?"

Hamm grabbed a triangle of toast and headed for the door. "The forces of evil, dear boy." He took the Do Not Disturb sign from the knob and held it for Art to see. The words blurred. "Have a good nap, Graham. I hope the police cars and ambulances don't wake you."

He left.

Art slept.

—⁓—

Edward covered the receiver and turned to Julia. "It's for you."

Julia shook her head. She was running late. Del's opening remarks were scheduled to begin in ten minutes, and she couldn't find her other earring. "Take a message."

"No way, missy. You'll want to take this one."

Julia raised an eyebrow and took the phone. "Hello?"

"Mother?"

"Bonnie! Happy Thanksgiving, honey."

Edward moved away to answer a tap on the door to their suite. *Oh no, not someone at the door when she wanted to talk with—*

Edward swung the door wide, and Julia saw Bonnie standing in the hall, a cell phone to her ear. Hank was behind her, their lovely Carolyn tucked under his arm.

Julia threw down the phone and ran to her. "Bonnie!"

They hugged. They cried. They laughed.

"Happy Thanksgiving," Bonnie said.

Julia couldn't stop smiling. "The very happiest."

<hr />

"You're not nervous, are you?"

Del looked at his sister as though she were crazy. "Me? Nervous? Whatever for?"

At his sarcasm, Lexa pinched his ear, then consulted her clipboard. "Take comfort in the fact that the television crews are ready and the conditions of the print media have been met."

"It sounds like they've given you ransom demands."

"They have. If I didn't do what they asked, they threatened to take *you* captive. Actually, I was their first choice, but after intense negotiations, I made them settle for you. I told them one priest was worth much more than an ex-everything."

"Ex-everything?"

"Ex-girlfriend, ex-employed person, ex-obnoxious know-it-all."

"I didn't know that last one had made it into the ex-category."

"Don't test me." She flipped a few pages and checked her watch. "Enough of the compliments. You're on."

Del's stomach dove to his toes. "Now?"

She got behind him and pushed him toward the stage where a podium had been built. It looked like an expansive stone altar, with ledges and nooks on the front that held ivy and pots of mums. A Havenite from D.C. had offered to create something special for the stage, and Lexa was pleased with the result. Del had said the design was quite appropriate—reminiscent of the altars built for sacrifices in the Old Testament.

"I can only distract you so long, Delly. Step up to the podium, say your how-dee-dos and Happy Thanksgivings, and tell them where to go when. Then the music service starts, and you're done for the day."

"Until I have to introduce the President of the United States."

"A piddling detail." She kissed his cheek. "Now go. Knock 'em dead."

It was nearly time for lunch, and Del stood along the edge of a corridor, watching people. The morning's activities were going great. The flow of participants from one workshop to the next went off without a hitch. Even the children's activities were a success—though there had been a temporary deficit of orange construction paper until Lexa convinced the teachers that God created yellow squash as well as orange pumpkins.

Del didn't attend any of the sessions, but floated from one to the next, marveling at how God had made it happen. Sessions on "How to Listen to God," "Prayer 101," and "Sharing the Faith" were packed with intent people taking notes and asking questions. The breaks were spent in the corridors, talking, discussing, making new friends—and seeing old ones.

Del saw Kathy and Roy. Roy was hugging an older woman and introducing her to Kathy. Del had nearly forgotten that Roy had his own Haven friends to see.

Havenites, family, friends, believers of all kinds... Mustard seed pins were everywhere, and stories of their mysterious deliveries could be heard amidst the tales of Haven invitations. All were welcome. All were invited in one way or another.

Del spotted Walter and waved him over. Addy held Bette's hand and carried a yellow something-or-other. "Are the Prescotts having a good time?"

Addy held up her picture. "Cosh."

Bette interpreted. "Squash, honey. And yes, they are. My mind is swimming with new ideas. If I can remember half of what I've heard, I could conquer the world."

Walter made a face. "Forget swimming, my mind is soggy. Drowned. And it isn't even noon."

"Maybe food will help." Del pointed toward the main floor of the auditorium, which was set with tables for lunch.

"That depends. What are we having?"

Del tried to remember. "Some kind of sandwiches, fruit something, salad stuff, and some sort of bars."

"That's specific."

"Lexa's the detail person. I just go where she sends me, sit where she tells me, and chew with my mouth closed."

"Play the part of a peon. That's what I do best."

Del studied his friend. He'd noticed at dinner the night before that Walter hadn't told anyone he'd lost his job or that they'd given up their house. When asked, Walter had handily changed the subject. Or, when pressed by Julia, downright lied. And now...his flip comments might be Walter just being Walter, but they might also be Walter covering a damaged self-esteem. If only there were something Del could do to make him feel more impor—

He got an idea. "I was wondering if you would help me this afternoon."

Walter looked suspicious. "Maybe. Depends."

Bette swatted her husband's arm. "You be nice. After all Del's done for us."

"Yeah, yeah, sure. I'll help. What do you need?"

"I'm supposed to introduce Julia's speech—it's the last event of the day. Would you like to help me? It could be a joint introduction."

"What would I say?"

"You could tell them how Julia got herself kidnapped, how—"

He shrugged. "I suppose I could work something up."

Del was willing to allow Walter some of the attention. No matter what the monsignor liked to believe, Del preferred to be in the sidelight rather than the limelight. He saw Bette look at her watch and knew it was time to let them move on. "I'd really appreciate it, Walter. Meet me in the wings backstage fifteen minutes before her speech. I'll clear it with the Secret Service people. Just give them your name."

"Sure. No problem." He turned to walk away.

Bette looked back to Del and mouthed the words, *Thank you.*

You're welcome.

———※———

Kathy cut Lisa's sandwich in half.

"I don't like ham," Lisa said, slumping into her chair.

Natalie stood at her seat across from them. "I saw peanut butter and jelly. Would that do?"

Lisa nodded. Natalie went and got one. Lisa beamed and quickly bit off the corner of the sandwich.

"Say thank you, Lisa," Roy said.

"Frank you." A crumb tumbled from her mouth, and Kathy resisted the urge to say, *Don't talk with your mouth full.* She owed her daughter a little slack.

Natalie laughed. "You're welcome. She sure is getting big. How old is she now?"

"Six," Kathy said.

Natalie nodded, looking down at her plate. Suddenly, Kathy remembered. Natalie had a daughter. She'd been pregnant in Haven. Kathy had been influential in helping her make the decision against abortion and for adoption. "How's your daughter?"

By the poignant relief on Natalie's face, Kathy knew that her guess about her friend's thoughts had been right. "She's fine. I think. I get pictures and a letter twice a year."

"I'm sure that's nice—but hard too."

"Giving her up was the right thing to do. But still…every time I see a little girl…" Natalie shrugged.

Jack put a hand on her arm. Kathy could see the bond between them, as if words weren't necessary. She wanted to ask…*should* she ask?

She asked.

"Where's Sam?"

Natalie swallowed with difficulty then pushed her plate away. She turned to Jack. "I'm not feeling very well. I need to go up to my room. Will you take me?"

Jack stood immediately and led her away.

"Oops," Roy said.

Kathy watched them go. "That about covers it."

———

Natalie headed toward the elevators, but at the last moment detoured to a couch in a quiet corner. She fell into the cushions. Jack slipped beside her.

"Spill it, Natalie."

She crossed her arms.

"Don't pout."

"I'm not pouting. I'm thinking."

"I accept your distinction. Now tell me what you're thinking about so intently."

"Sam."

Jack had thought he was ready for that answer, but he wasn't. At the words, doubt assaulted him from every side. Did she regret coming to the reunion with him? Was she wishing Sam were sitting beside her right—

"I don't miss him at all."

Jack blinked. "What?"

She sighed and relaxed her arms. "Shouldn't I miss him? Shouldn't I feel guilty for leaving him behind? Shouldn't I feel bad for having such a great time here with you?"

Even as relief swept over him, making him feel almost

346

light-headed, Jack knew Natalie was asking loaded questions. "I'm not sure how to answer without digging myself a hole of trouble."

Natalie stood and headed for the elevators. "I have a headache. I need to lie down a few minutes."

Jack followed her, putting a gentle hand at her elbow. He pushed the button to summon a car, wishing there were some way to help. There was. He said a quick prayer.

In spite of her moodiness, Natalie couldn't help but smile at what she deemed the "elevator phenomenon." Once inside the small box, people looked not at each other, but at the numbers lit above the door. The close proximity of shoulder to shoulder tested the comfort level of space-loving Americans. And the poor children, crammed into the crannies around people's waists and hips...

"Mommy, see what I made?"

Natalie glimpsed at the dark head of a little girl standing behind her to the right. There was a shuffle of paper as the craft project was shown.

"It's a beautiful rainbow, honey."

"God made rainbows 'cause He loves us. It's His promise He won't flood us ever again."

Natalie nodded to Jack and smiled. It was amazing how children grasped the simple truths of God.

"See, Daddy?" More shuffling.

"That's beautiful, Grace."

Natalie sucked in a breath. *Grace?* That was her daughter's—

The mother spoke. "Karl, do you think we'll have time for Grace to take a nap? She really needs..."

Karl? Sally and Karl? The people who adopted Grace?

Without intending to, she squeezed Jack's hand. Hard. He flinched and gave her a concerned look.

What should I do? Should I turn around and introduce myself?

As whom? As Natalie Pasternak? As Grace's biological mother? What if they haven't told her about me yet?

"I don't wanna take a nap. I'm not tired."

Karl spoke. "But you've got a big afternoon ahead of you. Later on, they're having a special session for the three- and four-year-olds. A 'Jesus loves me' parade or something like—"

Grace began to sing. "'Jesus loves me, this I know...'"

Natalie stifled a sob. Her daughter knew who Jesus was! Her daughter knew about Noah and the ark, and probably David and Goliath, and Mary and Joseph... Grace had two parents who loved her and cared for her enough to bring her to the reunion.

Natalie started at a thought. Had Karl and Sally gone to Haven too? Before Grace was even born, had God set in motion the family that would one day take care of her? It was too perfect.

"Excuse us."

Natalie hadn't even noticed that the doors to the elevator had opened. She and Jack moved to the side to let the family exit. Natalie's heart was in her throat and her eyes darted, trying to take in every detail. The dark straight hair that mimicked her own, the slim build that mirrored herself and—

Jack squeezed her hand. "Natalie? What's wrong?"

Natalie shook her head, not taking her eyes off her child. As the little girl walked down the hallway holding her mother's hand, she glanced back at the elevator, and Natalie saw her daughter's face in person for the first time since her birth. She recognized the dark baby eyes that had looked into her soul, making an instant connection that time or place could never break.

The elevator doors began to close, but Natalie's hand shot out to stop them.

Another passenger said, "Hey! Make up your mind!"

Natalie ignored him. She held the door and with her other hand waved at the little girl.

Then, in a moment Natalie would never forget, Grace smiled and waved back.

And their souls embraced.

"That was your daughter?"

Natalie paced up and back in her room. "My Grace!" She clapped her hands, raised them to heaven, then clapped them again in an alternating rhythm with her stride. "She's actually here!"

"Why didn't you say something to them?"

She sat on the foot of the bed. "It all happened so fast. When I first heard Grace tell her parents about her picture, I just thought she was a cute kid. Then when I heard her name, and Karl's name, the cute kid became *my* cute kid and my mind took off and I thought of what their conversation was telling me about their family." She looked up at Jack. "They love each other. They're raising my little girl to know the Lord. What more could I hope for?"

"You could have introduced yourself."

This was her inner battle. "I don't know. It was lucky we were standing in front, with our backs to them. I've sent Grace pictures of me. They might have recognized me."

"The reunion's not over. They still might recognize you. Is that so bad?"

Is it, Lord? Is it okay for me to meet Grace?

"It might happen, Natalie."

It might happen!

Natalie felt a wave of excitement wash over her. It was quickly followed by a wave of peace. "If they recognize me, I'll know it's because God wants us to meet. Just seeing her was a gift. I won't grab any more."

"But what if God wants to give you more?"

She laughed at the thought of it. "I certainly won't reject it."

Jack sat down beside her. "There's a good possibility

they've been to Haven."

She took his hand and looked at him. "I know. It's perfect." She looked away. "I wish Sam could have seen her."

"More regrets about him not being here?"

She shrugged. "Sam made choices. So did I. Mine led me here, his led him..." *To Lila.*

"I've never asked, and you can tell me it's none of my business because I really don't have to know but—"

"Just ask."

"Does Sam take much interest in Grace's life?"

Another regret. "No. Which has always reinforced my decision to give her up. I would have been raising her alone."

"You would have been a great mother. You *will* be a great mother."

"Someday. But Grace deserves a full family, not a part of one. A lot of people don't have a choice about raising a child alone. I did. I chose to give her two parents and a better future. God's my Father and Grace's. As a parent I was only the caretaker of *His* child." She shrugged. "I merely relinquished care to a couple who could do better."

She felt Jack's hand on the back of her neck. "How's your headache?"

She stood and faced him, offering him her hand. "Gone. Completely gone."

"And your regrets about Sam not being here to see her?"

"I can't worry about it. I can't try to second-guess God or live in the agony of what-ifs. I am here. You are here. I feel with my entire being we're supposed to be here. Together. That is enough."

"And Grace is here."

She kissed his cheek. "Which is more than enough."

———— ༄ ————

"Can I talk to you a moment, Del?"

Del turned around to see Kathy standing near a meeting

350

room. "Is something wrong, Kathy? Why aren't you in a work-shop?"

"There's something I have to do before the raffle. Two things actually."

She looked to the floor, and Del could tell whatever it was, it was hard for her. "Name them."

She lifted a paper sack between them. "After lunch, I went out and got some paints. I want to change the painting."

"Isn't it a little late to be—"

"Yes, it is. But this is important." She took a deep breath. It caught a few times on the way out. "It was wrong of me to omit Art from the painting. I don't even know if I did it on purpose or just forgot him. I'd like to think it was the latter, but I don't know. I thought I'd forgiven him, but when I saw him...I disappointed myself—and God. I need to make it right."

Del nodded. "You had a second thing you wanted to do?"

"I want to ask Art to pick the raffle winner."

"Are you sucking up?"

She blushed again. "I'd prefer you call it making amends."

He gave her a hug. "It's a wonderful idea."

Kathy hesitated. "Can't you ask him for me?"

"Nope."

Kathy had expected as much. Doing the right thing was so hard sometimes. She let out a huge sigh. "Then...do you know where I can find him?"

"Actually, I haven't seen him."

Why do I feel so relieved? "Well, if you do, tell him I want to talk to him. Okay?"

Del's smile was kind. "I'll do that."

———◊◊◊———

Ben hesitated at the door to the workshop, "Living Your Purpose." He stepped to the side to let others in.

Hamm stopped beside him. "What's wrong?"

"I don't think I'm up for another one. Can't Art do it for a while? Where is he, anyway?"

"He has his own assignment. You're the philosopher. Art's better at other things."

Ben felt a sudden tug at his insides. Hamm had been so mad at Art yesterday, and today Art was nowhere to be seen. Was there a connection?

He shoved the thought aside. He couldn't get between the two of them. His job was to attend the workshops, do what he could to dispel their ignorant notions about the importance of God, and let Hamm do his stuff later. Hopefully much later. After Ben had slipped away, free and clear of the entire affair.

Ben smiled as the people passed, but lowered his voice. "This is harder than I thought it would be. The other workshops didn't go so well, Hamm. They shot down your arguments that God only spoke to people in biblical times, and I refuse to be proved wrong one more time by some old lady who knows the entire Bible backward and forward. I didn't know that God *wanted* Jesus to die on the cross. I thought it was a tragedy, not a victory."

Hamm pulled him away from the door. His eyes flashed. "Don't let them get to you, Cranois. It *was* a tragedy. That's the sneaky way God works. He tries to get people to think that something bad is good, that suffering and trials have some greater purpose. It's a lie to make people accept the bad stuff."

"But—"

"And I don't appreciate you offering the information that Satan can't read their minds."

"He can't. You told me he can't."

"But *they* don't know that. At least, some of them don't. Remember, we're here to confuse, not to teach."

Ben nodded, but inside he felt his own confusion. It was disconcerting to realize that he was learning something at a Christian reunion. The people were eager and most were willing to listen to other opinions. They were knowledgeable and open. And he'd never heard so many people admit their faults—not in a ploy to gain sympathy, but in an honest way that made Ben admire them—even made him look to his own weaknesses. Obviously, he couldn't share any of this with Hamm.

Hamm nodded to an older couple as they passed. "I sure liked your point about Moses, Mrs. Kern. Praise the Lord."

The woman smiled and went into the meeting room with her husband.

Ben leaned toward Hamm. "Would you stop with the 'praise the Lord' business at the end of every sentence? You don't hear anyone else talk like that."

"I've heard them say 'praise the Lord'—and worse."

"But they don't throw it out casually. When they say it, it means something."

"It does, does it?"

Ben felt himself redden. He wanted to go up to his room, grab his suitcase, and leave. Since their psychological warfare wasn't going very well, it might be best to call it a wash. Besides, he had this terrible feeling in the pit of his stomach...

Hamm pulled Ben toward the door. "Come on, it's starting."

"I don't want—"

"I don't care what you want. It's the last workshop. Deal with it. And see if you can do some good this time—for our side."

Ben was enthralled. The speaker of this last workshop was good. Very good. Ben had even taken notes, readying himself for the open discussion at the end. But it was going to be another tough one.

The speaker paced in front of her audience. "As I've said, God has placed you in a unique place, in a unique time, coming in contact with unique people. He's put you in a place that is like no other. Haven made us realize this. The mustard seed pins reinforced the idea. But what have we done with this knowledge?"

"Messed up," said a man named Walter.

There was laughter. "Certainly—for most of us—that *has* been part of the process. An important part."

Ben shook his head. Here they went again, saying that trials were good. He looked up and found the speaker pointing at him. "Ben. You disagree?"

He looked at Hamm, who raised an eyebrow. "Well, maybe. It just seems that if—since—Christianity is such a positive thing, shouldn't it be easy?"

A tittering of laughter. Ben felt himself blush, but the speaker was kind. "Please know that we're not laughing at you, but with you. You ask a question that plagues us all. God's promises are grand, but often the process of attaining those promises is rough."

The woman next to Walter raised her hand. "I've found that I learn more from the dark times than I do the good times. The good times are like frosting. They taste good, and they're pretty, but when you think about it, they really aren't necessary. And you seldom eat just frosting. You put it on top of the cake—a base mixed, and beaten, and poured out, and baked, and—"

Walter added, "And sometimes burnt."

She smiled at him. "The point is, the trials and the lessons make up the cake of our lives. They are the body. They are what fills us up. If we only ate frosting, we'd be sick to our stomachs."

"A wonderful analogy, Bette." The speaker turned to Ben. "Does that help?"

Ben opened his mouth to answer, but Hamm interrupted. "So if everything is ultimately good for me—because I learn from my mistakes—what's the big deal with sin? Why fight it? Do it, experience it, and ultimately learn from it."

A pretty young woman at the end of the row raised a hand. "This morning in my quiet time, I read a passage that answers your question." She looked down to her Bible and the man next to her helped her find the verse. "Romans 6:1–2, 'What shall we say, then? Shall we go on sinning so that grace may increase? By no means! We died to sin; how can we live in it any longer?'"

A man behind them spoke up. "I found some different verses this morning, also in Romans. 'But now that you have been set free from sin and have become slaves to God, the benefit you reap leads to holiness, and the result is eternal life. For the wages of sin is death, but the gift of God is eternal life in Christ Jesus our Lord.'"

A teenager popped out of her seat, holding her Bible. "This is so cool! I read stuff in Romans this morning too. From chapter 8: 'Those who live according to the sinful nature have their minds set on what that nature desires; but those who live in accordance with the Spirit have their minds set on what the Spirit desires. The mind of sinful man is death, but the mind controlled by the Spirit is life and peace; the sinful mind is hostile to God. It does not submit to God's law, nor can it do so. Those controlled by the sinful nature cannot please God. You, however, are controlled not by the sinful nature but by the Spirit, if the Spirit of God lives in you. And if anyone does not have the Spirit of Christ, he does not belong to Christ.'"

Ben shook his head. All these answers, given to all these different people on the same day, to be remembered and used to counter a question meant to confuse. A coincidence? Somehow, he just didn't think so. He risked a look at Hamm. His face was red and his lips kept opening and closing as if he wanted to say something but couldn't find the right words.

Maybe there are no right words to counter God's Word.

The speaker looked at her watch, then opened her arms to the group and smiled. "It's time to go. We are all sinners—and continue to be even after being shown the truth. Sin is like a weight upon us, pushing us down, making us doubt and be fearful."

A weight? The weight? The weight is sin?

"We have choices to make. Constantly. Some will be the

right choices and some will be wrong. The joy comes from the fact that if we try to do right, if we confess our wrongs to the Lord, then we will be forgiven to start fresh another day. And hopefully, if we learn from our mistakes, we will not have to suffer under the same weight again."

She gave Ben a special smile. He bit his lip, experiencing a surge of emotion more powerful than he had ever felt before.

"I'm going to close with another reading from Romans—which I also was given as a gift this morning for just this purpose." She opened to a marked page. "'Who shall separate us from the love of Christ? Shall trouble or hardship or persecution or famine or nakedness or danger or sword? As it is written: "For your sake we face death all day long; we are considered as sheep to be slaughtered." No, in all these things we are more than conquerors through him who loved us. For I am convinced that neither death nor life, neither angels nor demons, neither the present nor the future, nor any powers, neither height nor depth, nor anything else in all creation, will be able to separate us from the love of God that is in Christ Jesus our Lord.' Amen."

As soon as they got in the corridor, Hamm sidled next to Ben, his words warm on Ben's ear. "What's wrong with you, Cranois?"

Ben shook away Hamm's attention and headed toward the elevators. He needed to be alone. To think.

Hamm yanked him aside, causing a few concerned looks. "Oh no, you don't." Hamm pasted on a smile, but his words were venom. "It's nearly showtime. You're not going to hide away in your room and get all touchy-feely on me. We're here to do a job and we *will* do it. *You* will do it."

It was an effort for Ben to push out the words. "You don't need me."

"No, I don't. We don't. But we have you, Cranois. We own you."

"Ben? Are you all right?"

They looked up to see the speaker from the last workshop standing close. Her brow was furrowed.

"He's fine. He's just moved by your workshop."

Ben didn't say anything, yet a part of him wanted to grab the lady's arm and run down the hall with her, where he would beg her to tell him more about sin and forgiveness and—

"If you have any questions about what we talked about—or about anything else—please feel free to contact me."

Ben risked a look. She was holding out a card. He took it and quickly pushed it in his pocket, fearful that Hamm would grab it away. "Thanks."

It was time for the predinner raffle. People sat at the round dining tables, the white linens a bright contrast to the cornucopia centerpieces overflowing with gourds and fall leaves. Kathy stood backstage, looking for Art. The light reflected off the portion of the painting that was still wet. What good did it do to add him into the picture if he wasn't around to see?

She stopped the thought. That wasn't the point.

"You're on, Kath." Lexa extended an arm toward the podium.

Taking a deep breath, she moved onto the stage. The crowd quieted, and Kathy tapped the microphone. "It's time to raffle off the painting. If you would all get out your tickets."

She gave them a few minutes to find their stubs. Roy and Ryan carried a box on stage with Lisa tagging behind. She turned to her son. "Would you pull out a name, sweetie?"

Ryan pulled out a name and handed it to her to read. "Sally Witherston. Would you come up here, please?"

A young woman squealed and popped out of her seat. She dragged a man and a little girl to the stage with her. They were accompanied by applause. When the family arrived, Kathy and Roy shook the parents' hands, but the little girl held back, standing in front of the painting.

"Come here, Grace," the mother said.

Grace shook her head and pointed at the painting. "That's Natalie…that's my other mommy!"

Sally blushed and rushed to Grace's side. "No, honey, I'm sure—" She stopped and looked at the picture, then turned to Kathy, eyes wide. "That's Natalie."

Kathy stepped toward them. "Why yes…it is. It's Natalie Pasternak. She was with me in Haven."

Karl picked up Grace and balanced her on his hip. His eyes were locked on the painting. "Natalie is Grace's natural mother."

Kathy felt a lump in her throat. Standing in front of the entire reunion was Natalie's—

There was a shout, and Kathy shielded her eyes to see into the crowd. "I'm here! I'm here!"

"There she is!" Kathy pointed. "Natalie. Come up! Come up!"

Natalie snaked around the tables and nearly ran to the stage. But when she came face-to-face with her daughter, she stopped a few steps short.

Grace looked at her daddy, then her mom, then Natalie. She pointed a pudgy finger. "You're my other mommy?"

Natalie did not wipe away her tears. She nodded. "Hi ya, Grace."

Grace scanned her parents' faces one more time as if asking permission. Both parents nodded and smiled.

"Hi, Natalie."

Natalie took a step forward. She held out her hand. After a moment's hesitation, Grace shook it. Natalie drew the tiny hand to her lips and kissed it.

The audience rose to their feet.

CHAPTER THIRTY

Let us discern for ourselves what is right; let us learn together what is good.

JOB 34:4

BEN DRILLED A SHIRT INTO HIS SUITCASE. It was too much. The audience applauding for a girl who'd been an unwed mother? And then they were having a Thanksgiving dinner where they'd hold hands, pray, and get all gushy? It was sickening.

And yet…

A part of Ben wanted to stay and let their goodwill wrap around him until he was swallowed up in their hope and faith. And a part of him wanted to see Julia.

Back in D.C. he'd gone to great lengths to catch a glimpse of her, but here at the reunion, he hadn't—and couldn't—bring himself to see her, knowing it might be for the last time. Yet…he *would* love to hear her speak. No one could speak like Julia. Even her enemies had to give her that.

And he *was* her enemy. Wasn't his presence here proof of that? But that didn't mean he wanted to see her die.

So he was leaving.

The reunion had been a waste of time. He'd come ready to change the world and found that if anything, this world of believers was changing him. And he didn't like it. Not one bit.

Hamm didn't need his help. Hamm was on his own mission, fed by a frenzy Ben had experienced but didn't want to know any better. And Art? Where was he? Ben had called Art's room but had gotten no answer. Maybe he'd checked out too. Smart guy.

Ben zipped his suitcase. In a few hours he would be home.

359

Safe, but confused. He needed time to think. Away from these people. Away from Hamm. Maybe he'd move so Hamm couldn't find him. Or would Hamm and his kind *always* be able to find him?

Ben left his room and hurried down the hall.

There had to be a way to start over. There had to be.

———

After their Thanksgiving dinner, Del pushed himself away from the table and moved behind Julia's chair. "If you'll excuse us, I believe it's just about time for Madam President to wow us with her wisdom."

Lexa turned to Julia. "Do you get nervous before you give a speech?"

Julia put a hand to her midsection. "Usually no, but this evening…" She shook her head.

Edward squeezed her hand. "Too much turkey and dressing."

"You can never have too much turkey and dressing." Julia turned to her granddaughter and winked. "Right, Carolyn?"

Carolyn beamed. "Right, Grandma."

Julia straightened her suit jacket. "Well, here goes. Take notes everyone. There will be a quiz later."

Bonnie smiled. "Always the teacher."

"Always the ham," Julia corrected.

As they walked to the exit, Del scanned the room, looking for Walter. His seat next to Bette and Addy was empty. He was probably waiting for them backstage, pacing the floor, getting nervous about his introduction.

Good ol' Walter. This was going to be just what he needed.

———

Walter couldn't believe his luck. In the rest room he'd run into Olly Davis, a reporter friend from St. Louis. Former reporter, that is. After covering the reunion, Olly was moving to Chicago to take a producing job. In television.

"Tell me about your new TV station in Chicago, Olly."

As Olly talked, Walter's mind ran ahead to meet the possibilities. Chicago might be a nice place to start over.

—◦◦◦—

Julia and Del turned down the corridor leading to the backstage entrance. A man bumped into Del and both pulled back.

"Sorry."

"Excuse—"

The man looked up, and Julia saw his face. "Benjamin!"

Ben's eyes flashed with recognition. He side stepped around them and hurried away, carrying a suitcase.

"Benjamin! What's wrong? Come back. I want to talk with—" *What is he doing here?*

A Secret Service agent pointed after him. "Do you want me to get him for you, ma'am?"

Yes. "No…"

Del touched her arm. "Do you know him?"

"That's Benjamin Cranois. He was my campaign manager when I was running both for governor and president—until he quit before the presidential election." She continued to look down the empty corridor where Ben had fled.

"I think I saw him coming out of one of the workshops," Del said.

"You're kidding." If only she could believe that Benjamin had experienced a change of heart and was at the reunion for inspiration—but that was a long shot. She shook her head. "That was rude of me. Miracles happen every day."

Del looked at his watch and took her arm. "It will be a miracle if my sister doesn't explode because we're late."

"We wouldn't want that."

They hurried off—but for some odd, inexplicable reason, Julia's stomach was more tense than it had been in a very, very long time.

Ben stood in line at the checkout desk. His heart raced. He couldn't believe his luck. He'd managed to avoid Julia the entire reunion until the moment he was leaving?

Oh well, it didn't matter. In a few minutes he would be gone and she…she…

Would be dead?

"Are you checking out, sir?" The desk clerk smiled and positioned her fingers on the keyboard.

Checking out. Giving up. Running away.

"And you are…?"

Good question. Who was he? A coward? A patsy for an organization that didn't exist? A dupe for a demon-of-a-man who didn't care whether Ben lived or died—didn't care whether anyone lived or died? A has-been, who could have been, but now wasn't…

Ben had been proud to be a champion of truth. But *this* truth?

Leave!

Stay.

Ben blinked with a new thought. "Has Art Graham checked out?"

"Let me check." She typed in his name. "No sir, he hasn't."

"Are you sure?"

She looked at the screen again. "Positive. Would you like me to call—?"

Ben shoved his suitcase over the top of the counter. "Keep this for me."

"But sir…your name?"

Ben called back over his shoulder. "Cranois." He ran for the elevator. He needed Art. He needed reinforcements.

Before it was too late.

—⁓—

Art had the sensation of aching muscles. He tried to move. But when he did, he fell onto the floor.

Some floor. Somewhere. He couldn't remember where.

Julia...

The drugs pulled him back under.

—⁓—

Ben knocked on Art's door. He listened. No sounds. He knocked again. Louder. "Art? It's me, Ben. Are you all right?"

He hadn't seen Art all day. Art hadn't checked out. Had Art been put out of commission?

I have to get in that room!

He continued pounding. Guests at the far end of the hall exchanged nervous whispers before escaping into their rooms.

Julia would be introduced any minute. Most likely, soon after, Hamm would detonate the bomb. People would die.

Ben banged his forehead against the door, leaving it there, closing his eyes. *Please, God, please...help me.*

—⁓—

Wake up!

Art opened his eyes. It was dark except for a stripe of moonlight cutting across the bed above him.

The bed *above* him? Why was he on the floor? *Hotel floor. Reunion.*

He pushed himself onto his forearms. His head pounded. He searched the room for a clock. 7:03? In the morning or the evening?

He tried sitting, but his muscles rebelled. He moaned.

"Art? Are you in there?"

He looked toward the door. A slice of light marked it. The voice was outside. It sounded familiar.

"Art? It's me, Ben. Open up! It's an emergency. We're running out of time!"

"Just…just a minute." He wasn't sure if his voice carried.

"Hurry!"

Hurrying was not an option. He stumbled to his feet and staggered across the room, balancing against the furniture and walls. Finally, thankfully, he reached the door and opened it. Ben pushed into the room, backtracking to switch on the light.

"What happened to you?"

Art tried to get his bearings. A breakfast tray sat on the table by the window. He pinpointed what he was feeling: "Hamm drugged my breakfast."

"You've been out all day?"

Art rubbed his head. It didn't feel attached to his neck. "What day is it?"

Ben grabbed Art's arm. "It's Thanksgiving. They've just had the dinner. Julia is going to speak at any moment. Hamm is going to detonate the bomb." He pulled Art into the hall. "We have to stop him!"

Art's questions—and recovery—would have to be handled on the run.

———✀———

"Delly…"

His sister glared at him. Del looked toward the stage entrance. They couldn't wait for Walter any longer. The audience was well into their after-dinner cup of coffee. It was time to introduce Julia. Now.

Julia leaned close. "You look nervous, Antonio."

"I'm not used to speaking before throngs or teeming masses. And twice in one day…"

She patted his arm. "They're just people. Well fed and a little drowsy after a full day. You don't have to worry about rebellion or hecklers nearly so much as nappers. The trick is to keep them awake."

"No one sleeps when Julia Carson talks."

"Except Edward. He snores."

"Brave man."

She shrugged. "Luckily, his attributes far outweigh his faults." She clapped Del on the back. "Now let's do this thing before the mashed potatoes settle, and your sister attacks."

Del looked one last time for Walter. So much for good intentions. He took Julia's hand and they bowed their heads. "Give us the words that need to be said, Lord."

He went onstage to introduce the president.

———

Julia strode out to the podium, giving Del a hug as they passed. She was ready. She was more than ready. These were truly her people, and she had something important to say to them.

"Good evening, ladies and gentlemen." The crowd roared at her first words, and Julia quieted them with a hand. "I am so pleased to be speaking to you today. We have much in common. One God, one goal to bring Him glory, and one struggle to make ourselves better. If we don't achieve this goal or surmount this struggle, then we are of little use to the world. Without God we are as effectual as an inanimate object, as distasteful as a drink of lukewarm water."

She smiled. "Lukewarm...that is what I want to speak about today. Let's say you are working hard around the house, cleaning the attic, going through the old boxes, hauling stuff outside to be given away. It's hot in the attic; the entire heat from the house has risen to smother you. You're sweating. Your mouth is dry. What would you like?"

She saw the audience's surprise when she waited for an answer.

"Help from my husband," a woman blurted out.

There was laughter.

"I was thinking of what kind of *drink*."

"Iced tea."

"Lemonade."

"A soda with lots of ice."

Julia nodded and raised her hands, fending off more answers. "Exactly. All these drinks have something in common: They are cold." She raised a finger. "Now a different scenario: It is cold and rainy outside, it's a Saturday afternoon, the house is quiet, and you've started a fire in the fireplace. You grab your favorite book and settle in for a cozy hour of silent indulgence. What drink do you make yourself?"

The crowd was quicker to respond this time. "Hot chocolate."

"Tea."

"Cappuccino with hazelnut creamer."

"Ooh, now that sounds good." She leaned forward on the podium. "The point is, when you really want to relax on a cold day, you want to drink something hot."

There were nods of agreement.

"When do you want to drink something lukewarm?"

The audience shook their heads. Finally someone said, "Never!"

"Exactly. In fact, there is nothing more distasteful than a lukewarm drink. We want to spit it out." She waited a moment, scanning their faces. Finally, she presented her punchline: "Our lives are lukewarm."

Del stood in the wings watching Julia. How lucky he was to know her. No...luck had nothing to do with it.

He closed his eyes. *Dear Lord, thank You for letting me be Julia's friend. Thank You for this reunion and for making it come off so smoothly. It's been a glorious day, Lord. A glor—*

"A glorious day indeed."

Del's eyes shot open, and he looked toward the voice. "John!"

Del's angelic mentor smiled and accepted Del's hug. "You always were a hugger."

"What are you doing here? The last time we saw each other, we were battling it out with a demon."

"I come with a message."

"From whom?"

"From the Father."

Del found it hard to swallow. Of course. God did not let His angels be seen on a whim. They were His messengers. They came at His command. Del took a calming breath. "Give it."

John nodded and looked at Del intently. His eyes were serious but full of compassion. "And Jesus said, 'If anyone would come after me, he must deny himself and take up his cross and follow me. For whoever wants to save his life will lose it, but whoever loses his life for me and for the gospel will save it.' 'Do not be afraid of those who kill the body but cannot kill the soul.' 'So do not fear, for I am with you; do not be dismayed, for I am your God. I will strengthen you and help you; I will uphold you with my righteous right hand.'"

Del looked away, trying to assimilate the words. *Lose a life? Kill the body? Do not be afr—* He turned to John to ask a question.

But he was gone.

Ben heard Julia's voice. He rushed to the door of the auditorium and cracked it. "She's already on!"

Art leaned against him. He still hadn't recovered. Ben wasn't sure what kind of help he would be. Through the door Ben saw the back of Hamm's head where he sat at a table, a cup of coffee in his hand, an empty dessert plate pushed aside. Enjoying the evening like everyone else.

Ben shivered. Somehow Hamm's ordinary facade was more terrifying than if he'd been hunched on top of the table, foaming at the mouth. There was something bone chilling about watching evil laughing. Evil making jokes. Evil putting a hand across the back of his neighbor's chair.

Evil stalking. Waiting. Ingratiating itself in a haze of normal. Earn their trust. Get their defenses down. Then pounce on the unsuspecting victims.

Have I been a victim too?

Ben suddenly felt as if he were straddling a fence so precariously that the brush of a breeze could push him one way or the other. And though he wasn't sure he had control over which way he'd fall, he knew which way he *wanted* to fall.

Toward God. And away from the weight.

Art leaned against the door. "What's going on?"

Ben pulled himself out of his thoughts. "Julia's talking. I see Hamm. Should we tell somebody? Secret Service? Security?"

Art shook his head and closed his eyes. "By the time they question us and requestion us it will be too late."

"But how can we stop him? We don't even know where the bomb is."

With difficulty, Art positioned himself to see in the door. After a few seconds he pulled back. "That stone thing. That altar. It has to be in the altar. It's central. It has nooks and crannies where a bomb could be hidden. I should have thought of that before."

Ben took a look. "Hamm mentioned passing himself off as a construction worker. That's the only thing that looks as if it's been built new."

Ben saw Hamm put his arm around the woman next to him and whisper in her ear. They laughed softly.

He disgusts me. He's so terribly wro—

Suddenly, Ben lost his breath as if all the air had been sucked out of the room.

"Ben? What's wrong?"

He pressed on his chest, wishing he could force air into his lungs. A familiar pain clutched his insides, preventing air easy access.

"Ben?"

He raised a hand and tried to remain calm, fearing that if he gave into his panic—or gave any further indication of what he was about to do—the weight would clamp down with one final viselike grip and kill him.

Do not defy me! A voice raged inside his head.

Warn someone. You can stop this thing! Another voice, a calming voice, echoed.

Ben made his choice. He fell off the fence. With an intake of breath, he tried to pull the door to the auditorium all the way open.

The pain sliced through him and he grabbed his chest.

Then suddenly, he saw Hamm pull something from the pocket of his suit coat. He put it in his lap. He extended a finger—

Ben wanted to yell, but the pain silenced him. Then he saw Hamm jab at the box. Again and again.

The detonator wasn't working!

Ben used a surge of energy to laugh.

The pain retaliated.

———⟊∿∿⟊———

Julia paused a moment, allowing the audience to think about what she'd just said.

"Too many of us are guilty of living our lives drowning in a river of lukewarm water. We float through the days and years, not jumping onto either shore, never standing on the muddy bottom and wading through the currents to one side or the other. We are content to drift downstream.

"What we don't realize is that the river contains rapids, whirlpools, waterfalls, and hidden obstacles. If we don't make our way to shore, we risk being pulled under. We risk destruction. We have to choose the hot or the cold, one shore or the other. We can no longer drift, expecting others to save us.

"Being lukewarm threatens to bring us down as a nation. We have become hardened, self-satisfied, and self-sufficient. Complacent. What people can see and buy has become more important than the riches that are unseen and the treasures they can give away. But material things will waste away to nothing. The unseen things of life—faith, hope, and love—are eternal. What we *take* pales compared to what we can give away. Have we forgotten that it is more blessed to give than to receive? All of us, whether churched or unchurched, have heard this—have learned this—through personal experiences, large and small. Truths like this are indisputable.

"Then why have we forgotten such truths? Why do we concentrate on taking instead of giving? On ignoring instead of acting? On being lukewarm instead of hot or cold."

She scanned the faces in front of her. *Please, Lord, let them understand…give me Your words.*

"There was an ancient town called Laodicea. It was thriving and successful in all material ways. It was rich, but oh, so poor. Its people said, 'I have everything I want, I don't need a thing.' They didn't feel the need to be hot or cold about life. They were content in the mediocrity of lukewarm. Their true purpose and worth was stifled by their own indifference. They felt they didn't need anybody.

"Do we feel that way? We can't. We don't dare! For with that self-satisfied complacency comes destruction. There is more to life than the riches we enjoy in the flesh. What about the riches of the mind? The heart? The soul? If we are lukewarm in these segments of our lives, we are not truly living. And we will be held accountable. There are consequences for apathy. The heavenly Father we all share speaks these words to the people of Laodicea—as He speaks them to us: 'I know your deeds, that you are neither cold nor hot. I wish you were either one or the other! So, because you are lukewarm—neither hot nor cold—I am about to spit you out of my mouth…. Those whom I love I rebuke and discipline. So be earnest, and repent.'

"We can't let evil win because we did nothing. We can't mind our own business anymore. Our business is each other.

We can't keep values and morality to ourselves; they must permeate our work, our play, and even our government. Can you have the church without virtue? Can you have the state without ethics? 'From everyone who has been given much, much will be demanded; and from the one who has been entrusted with much, much more will be asked.' We've been given much. It's time to ask of ourselves—to *demand* of ourselves—much, much more."

Julia stood upright, but an agitated man to her right caught her attention. He seemed to be poking at something. He was murmuring under his breath, but his words grew louder, drawing attention—

Suddenly, a door to the auditorium swung open and Julia saw Benjamin stagger inside. Arthur was right behind him. Benjamin looked at her for a moment, his face contorted with pain. "He's got a bomb!"

Who's got—?

Julia glanced to her left and saw Antonio running toward her with two Secret Service agents close behind. Del shoved her away from the podium.

And then the world around them simply…exploded.

CHAPTER THIRTY-ONE

—◦◦◦—

The smoke of the incense, together with the prayers of the saints, went up before God from the angel's hand.

REVELATION 8:4

"COME AWAY, MADAM PRESIDENT." A Secret Service man pulled on Julia's arm.

"Leave me alone!" She cradled Antonio's head in her lap.

"But you're hurt—"

It didn't matter. She didn't care.

Julia saw people running and screaming, their faces contorted in panic. Chairs were overturned. Water glasses were toppled with puddles forming on the carpet. Linen napkins were strewn like clothes in a teenager's room. But oddly, there was not a single piece of stone on the main dining floor, as if the explosion had only blown itself backward.

On the stage, people stood amidst the debris, speaking into cell phones and walkie-talkies. Roy ran toward her. A woman carrying a doctor's bag was close behind. Their eyes were on Antonio.

Antonio.

Julia looked at the dear friend who had saved her life. There was way too much blood. Roy's first act was to pry her hand away from a wound in Antonio's chest. She hadn't realized she'd instinctively pressed against it. She heard Roy and the other doctor talk to each other, making quick decisions. Roy barked toward the throng of people nearby. Someone nodded and ran to obey his order.

Julia wanted to stroke Antonio's head and comfort him, but his face was pocked with cuts from the exploded stones of the altar. Bits of gravel-sized rock intermixed with skin and blood. Her fingers zoned in on an uninjured spot above his right eye where she touched him gently.

A sudden drop in the decibel level drew Julia's eyes to the dining room floor. There was no more running. No more chaos. Although security kept people along the perimeter of the room, their eyes were on Antonio. They sought each other's hands. People began to kneel together. Some bowed their heads; some raised their faces. Some prayed silently, and some called out.

And there was Benjamin. He looked as though he had been unwittingly drawn into the room, confused and dazed. He held a hand to his chest, clutching at it as if in pain. He staggered a step, then dropped to his knees with the others. Julia's heart leapt. Could it be true? Had Benjamin become a believer?

Julia blinked and added her prayers to the rest...

"Julia!"

She looked up and saw Arthur coming toward the stage. Secret Service barred his way. He raised a hand toward her. She acknowledged him. She could do nothing more. Not now. Not—

She heard a moan.

"Antonio!"

His eyes shot open, and Julia gasped at their intensity. He did not look at her, or Roy, or the other doctor. He looked toward the ceiling. But his gaze was not unfocused. He *saw* something. All three of them turned their heads to see what he was looking at.

———◦◦◦———

Del heard himself moan, but not in pain. Rather, he uttered moans of ecstasy as, *full of the Holy Spirit, [he] looked up to heaven and saw the glory of God, and Jesus standing at the right hand of God.*

Del could not take his eyes off the Lord. Jesus looked upon

him, and those holy eyes held a kindness and serenity that was all encompassing. Although Jesus was not alone—although thousands upon thousands of angels surrounded the Christ for as far as the eye could see—Del knew that Jesus cared for him—for Antonio Delatondo, priest, brother, son, sinner—with a love that was utterly unfathomable.

"'Look!'" Amazement, humility, and wonder pulled the words from Del's raw throat. "'I see heaven open and the Son of Man standing at the right hand of God.'"

Del tried to raise his arm to touch the Lord, but his limb was heavy and would not move. He heard voices around him and felt hands press and prod. There was pain, but it was unimportant. If only he could keep his eyes on the Lord...*his* Lord.

Then without warning, he felt an inner rupture, as if what was old had been ripped away. His focus threatened to turn inward, and he fought it. He couldn't bear the thought of losing his connection with the divine. *No! No! Don't pull me back! Help me, Lord! I cannot bear to be without You!*

Jesus held out His hand. The pain was silenced, its grip severed. When Christ spoke, Del knew there was no greater, no more glorious sound in all creation: "Come, Antonio. Well done, good and faithful servant! Enter into the reward that is yours."

Del smiled, and his heart—his soul that could never be injured by worldly violence—began to soar at the words he had longed for a lifetime to hear.

It was time to let go; Del was ready. "Lord Jesus, receive my spirit. Lord, do not hold this sin against them."

And when he had said this, he fell asleep.

—◦◦◦—

"*No-o-o-o-o!*"

Ben cringed at Julia's scream. He watched as she drew the priest into her arms and rocked him. Then those people kneeling around Ben joined in the cry, and oddly, their prayers grew more fervent.

Why are you praying now? The priest is dead! God didn't hear you the first time.

"Take Your servant, Father Del. Comfort him, love him…"

"Help us understand, Lord…"

"Thank You for sparing the president…"

"Show us what to do next…"

"Please, God, remove the evil that did this terrible thing…"

Ben swallowed hard, trying to find a way to breathe between the stabs of pain in his chest. The evil who did this? Himself. Hamm. *But I tried to stop it. I called out. I warned—*

All done too late. Someone had died.

He got to his feet and headed for the door.

"There he is! There's the man who yelled, 'He has a bomb.' And the other one…"

Ben ran.

—⁓—

"Let go of us! Let us through!" Walter pushed at the people gathered in front of him. If they didn't move, he was going to pick them up and *make* them move!

He looked to Julia and Roy, hoping one of them would help him, Lexa, and Edward get close.

"Let them in." Julia's voice was raspy; she was covered with blood. As Walter drew close, he saw some of the blood was from her own wounds, but most was Del's. Edward ran to her side.

Walter and Lexa sidestepped the debris, and Lexa sank to the floor beside her brother. Julia lowered his body so she could see him.

"Oh, Delly…no, Delly. Don't leave me now!"

Walter felt as though he were choking. Angry, desperate, he shoved Roy on the shoulder. "*Do* something! Bring him back! Make a miracle like the one that happened in Haven!"

Roy shook his head. "I can't make a miracle, Walter. No man can. And there is no *back* anymore. Del has moved on."

Lexa looked up, her eyes wild, and said what was screaming in Walter's mind: *"No!"*

There was a commotion in the wings. Natalie grappled with security. "Let me thorough!"

Julia raised a hand. In her allowance, Natalie, Jack, and Bette streamed through. Walter saw Kathy standing with the kids in the safety of the wings, shielding their eyes from the blood. He also saw Julia's daughter and her family.

Natalie collapsed at Del's feet. She touched the hem of his pant leg. "He can't die! He was the only good one among us."

"He was pure."

"Good."

"Sincere."

"Godly."

"He was my Delly."

They turned to Lexa. It all came down to that. Although Del was their brother by friendship, he was her brother by blood.

She stroked his face, her tears blackened trails down her cheeks.

"He was so brave," Natalie said.

Lexa sucked in a breath, putting a hand to her mouth.

"What?" Jack asked.

She looked at all of them, her eyes wide, brimming with tears. "On the drive down here, we talked about heaven, and Del said he wasn't afraid, that death wasn't the end, it was just moving on."

Walter got a shiver. "As if he knew…"

Julia put a hand on Lexa's arm. "When Antonio was dying he looked to heaven and—" Her voice caught in her throat, and Walter saw her swallow hard. "He…he said he saw Jesus. He was so peaceful."

A sudden, stunning certainty sped through Walter's mind, making him gasp for air. He pointed to Del's body. "That…that should have been me!"

"What?"

Walter felt tears streaming down his cheeks, but he didn't care. He wasn't sure if he would care about anything again. "I was supposed to help introduce you, Julia. But I was out schmoozing, playing the big shot, trying to get a job—"

"A job? I thought you were working at—"

Walter shook his head. "I *lost* it. I lost my job, our house. I gambled away our savings." Bette took his arm, but he shook her away. He needed to face this. Maybe if he had faced his humiliation earlier…

He saw his friends exchange a look. Whatever their thoughts were, it was better than he deserved. "If I'd been where I was supposed to be, I would have been the one to jump in to save Julia."

"Are you sure?" As soon as Edward said the words, he raised a hand, apology in his eyes. "Sorry. That wasn't fair."

Walter shook his head with the burden of the truth. "You're right. Who knows if I would have sacrificed myself for Julia. Back in Haven, it was Del who jumped in front of a bullet for *me*. It's in his character, not mine."

Julia looked up at him. "You don't know that, Walter."

He shoved his hands in his pockets. Who was he trying to kid? "I know. We all know." He leaned down, took Del's hand in his, and kissed it. "I love you, priest man. I'm so sorry."

As the weight of grief pressed in on him, he couldn't take any more. Dropping Del's lifeless hand, Walter scrambled to his feet and ran off the stage.

—⧡—

Edward patted the cushion next to him.

Julia shook her head and continued pacing.

"Sit down, missy."

"I don't have time, Edward. I have to—"

He got off the couch, took her hand, and pulled her to the edge of the cushions. He put his hands on her shoulders and pressed her to sitting.

She tried to get up.

He pushed her back down, pointing a finger at her. "Stay."

She gave up.

He sat at the other end of the couch and pulled her feet into his lap, making her bottom pivot on the cushions. He began his massage.

Although it felt heavenly, she resisted the comfort and started to pull her feet away. "Edward...I can't. I have impor—"

He shoved her feet to the floor, his eyes flashing. "What's it going to *take* to make you slow down, Julia? If the Second Coming were to happen right now, I'm afraid you'd tell Christ, 'Can you hold on just a minute? I have important work to do.'"

"That's not true." She reached for his hand and smiled. "I promise I'll behave when Jesus comes again."

He tucked his hand away, unappeased. "But what about now? You nearly get killed—" his voice broke on the word—"yet you won't allow yourself ten minutes to relax."

"I'll get myself another personal assistant. Like Arthur. That will help—"

"This has nothing to do with another person helping you! You have *hundreds* of people willing to help you. The problem is not arranging your schedule, the problem comes in arranging your heart."

"My heart is fi—"

"Your heart is *not* fine. God's given you plenty of time to do what needs to be done. The minutes and hours are ample. It's your priorities that are skewed."

"But my work—"

"Is secondary to your relationship with God. And with me, for that matter."

"But I'm the—"

"President. I know. And you have a responsibility beyond the rest of us. But the basic priorities of Mr. and Mrs. Public are the same as yours. God and family have to come first, whether you're the president, a teacher, or a truck driver."

She clutched a pillow to her chest. "But I took time out to be here—for God. I took time out to see Bonnie."

"I'm the one who called Bonnie and pleaded with her to be here. She was the one who took the effort to do it. You did nothing."

She opened her mouth to speak, then shut it again.

His eyes were forgiving. He sat beside her, and she laid her head on his chest. Everything he said was true—and was so hard to change. "I need you, Edward."

"Yes, you do."

Edward turned on the news. Julia listened with her eyes closed. A drone. A mass of words that meant nothing in light of the evening's—

Edward moved the pillow that was his chest. "Julia! Listen! They're replaying parts of your speech. A speech for a Christian audience is now blanketing the world."

"Hmm." She heard him turn the channel. *So what? What did one speech matter? She'd given hundreds of speeches.*

"Listen…there's more…"

"A Christian rally turned into a rallying cry this evening when a terrorist's bomb cut through the stone podium where President Julia Carson was giving her speech. Father Antonio Michael Delatondo of Lincoln, Nebraska, pushed the president out of the way and was killed in the explosion. The president received cuts and bruises but is said to be resting comfortably in—"

She opened her eyes. "Turn it."

Edward flipped the channel.

"…from Sandusky, Michigan. Tell us about the terror of the bombing. How did people react to the carnage?"

A pretty woman smiled nervously at the camera. "There was no terror—and no carnage. There was the heroic sacrifice of Father Delatondo who gave his life for the life of the president—who was also his friend."

"How many others were injured?"

The woman squared her shoulders. "None. It was a miracle. Although there were people seated at tables not twenty feet from the stage, the explosion went backward. Only the good father and the president were injured. Not a pebble rained down on the rest of us."

"We've been told they've held two men for questioning. What do you—"

"There has always been—and will always be—evil in this world until Christ comes again. We've already had one prayer meeting to pray for those men."

"Pray for—"

She nodded vigorously. "This was a reunion of people who believe in God; people who know that everyone has a unique purpose on this earth. Those men have gotten sidetracked. They've chosen wrong. But God can use them too. Hopefully, that will be the good that will come out of this tragedy. Men who allow their lives to be changed."

The reporter swallowed as if he didn't know what to say next.

"Ha!" Edward clapped his hands. "Way to go, Sandusky!"

Julia nodded. "Way to go, Antonio." Then she realized something. She sat up, took the remote from Edward, and shut off the television.

"Hey—"

"Forget that. Listen to me. Antonio accomplished more in his one act of sacrifice than I have ever accomplished in all my speeches and actions."

"I wouldn't say—"

"It's true. His brave act was the antithesis of a lukewarm life. He took a stand. He made a choice. And he backed it up with the ultimate offering. His life. And because he gave his life, I have mine."

They shared a moment of silence. Then Edward pulled her back into the safety of his arms.

The phone rang while Julia was in the shower. Edward answered it.

"We've got two of them in custody."

"We heard. Who are they?"

"A fellow named Hamm Spurgeon and another named Arthur Graham."

Arthur!

"The Graham fellow keeps asking for Julia. Says he knows her personally."

"He does. But how is he involved?"

"According to him, he isn't. Not really. He says he was trying to infiltrate the group Spurgeon worked for—a group called TAI. Says he was trying to uncover their plot." The man snickered. "He didn't do a very good job of it, did he?"

But Edward didn't share the officer's sarcasm. *Oh, Arthur, have I misjudged you?*

"Edward?"

He turned toward the bathroom door. Julia stood in her bathrobe, drying her hair with a towel. He hadn't heard the shower turn off. He spoke into the phone, "Hold on a minute." He put his hand over the receiver. "The two men held for questioning…one was Arthur."

"Arthur?"

"He claims to have gone undercover to stop the bombers. He said—"

She threw the towel on the bed. "I have to go to him."

"Julia! He may have been part of the plot to kill you."

She was at the closet. "No, he wasn't." She swung around and glared at him. "And you know it."

Edward sighed. Yes, he did. He spoke into the phone. "We'll be right there."

"You've got a visitor."

Art sprang to the door of the cell. "Who is it?"

The guard laughed. "They say it's the president of the United States, but I think they're pulling our—"

"No, they're not. It's her."

"Sure it is, buddy."

It did no good to argue. The guard would know the truth soon enough.

Julia and Edward sat on the other side of the glass. The visitor room was empty of all other prisoners and visitors. Secret Service lined the perimeter.

Art cringed when he saw the cuts on Julia's face. He picked up the phone at the same time Edward and Julia did and watched as they held the receiver between them so they both could hear. "Are you all right?"

She exchanged a look with Edward. An I-told-you-so look. "I'm fine. But Del…"

"I know. I'm so sorry."

Edward took the phone. "So you *are* involved?"

Julia grabbed it back to the shared space between them. "No, he's not." She faced him. "No you're not, are you, Arthur?"

The opportunity to finally tell the truth, to finally be vindicated was overwhelming. But Art held back the tears. Those could come later. When everything was all right. When they were friends again.

"Let me tell you what happened…"

⸻

Ben leaned his head against the window of the airplane. His heart pounded with the frantic pace of the past four hours. And then there was the pain, which only made his agitation worse. It was still present, but in an odd way had eased…perhaps because he had stopped fighting it, accepting it as punishment. His indecision had betrayed God and Satan both. The pain was proof of that. And so Ben ran. From man, God, and from the weight of the evil which had been a part of his life for too long.

Unfortunately, he knew the odds were good that all would find him and he would pay the consequences. The consequences of man were a known commodity, but the consequences of betraying good and evil? He cringed at the thought. But he was sorry…so terribly sorry.

Ben had heard on the news that Hamm and Art had been taken into custody, and he was 100 percent certain that Hamm Spurgeon would not take the rap alone. It wasn't in Hamm's character to be magnanimous or merciful. If only Ben could get home before Hamm ratted on him. Yet what good would that do? *You can run, but you can't hide.*

Art's arrest was regrettable, but the truth would come out.

The truth…

He'd done all this to promote his version of the truth. The power of the world was in the individual. One God over all was a ridiculous concept of the weak. Wasn't it? Or was it? What was the truth? The real truth?

Ben dug the headphones out of the seat pocket, hoping the music would help his mind—and the pain—fade. As if in answer to his thoughts, a new pain sliced through him. A reminder… A moan escaped.

"Are you okay?"

Ben opened one eye to look at the man seated on the aisle. "I'll be fine."

"Want me to get the flight attendant?"

"No…no…" Ben sucked in a breath and felt the claws of the pain ease their grip. The passenger did not look convinced, but shrugged and unwrapped his headphones. "Channel three is good classical. Soothing. Maybe it will help."

Ben nodded and put his own headphones over his ears. He turned to channel three. The strains of Barber's "Adagio for Strings" drifted into his brain. Perhaps if he concentrated on the beauty of the music, he would forget about—

Ben jerked as a sudden burst of light flashed. It was as if a huge photographer's flashbulb had gone off. He blinked, trying to adjust his eyes back to normal. He pulled the headphones off his ears and turned to his seatmate. "What was that?"

But the man's headphones were on and he fiddled with his blanket as if nothing had happened. Ben saw an attendant coming down the aisle. He raised a hand. "Miss?" She stopped at his seat, handing him a pillow. "No thanks, I have one…but what was that flash of light?"

Her eyebrows dipped. "Excuse me?"

"That big flash of light a moment ago?"

She shook her head. "I'm sorry, sir. I didn't see any flash of light."

"But—"

"Would you like me to get you a blanket?"

"No…no blanket." Ben fell back in his seat. *What's going on? I didn't imagine it. It was real.* He tried to look outside, but all he saw was his own reflection in the glass. *The stress…it's the stress.* He replaced the headphones and closed his eyes.

Suddenly, the strains of the violins stopped. Ben reached to adjust the volume. Would he never get any peace?

"Why do you persecute Me?"

Ben's eyes shot open. He looked at his seatmate a second time, but the man was resting comfortably. *He* wasn't hearing strange voices. *Who spoke to me?*

The answer was immediate. *"I am Jesus, whom you are persecuting. Now go into the city, and you will be told what you must do."*

Jesus! Without further thought or rationalization, without forcing himself to explain the unexplainable, Ben acknowledged the instructions as real and vital.

And he said yes.

The music returned, and the strings swelled to their climax, matching the swell that was taking place in Ben's heart. He drew in a breath. He let it out. He did it again. Only then did he realize the immensity of what had happened.

I have been released!

He laughed. He cried. And with the liberation of these emotions, his mind filled with praise and thanksgiving, not in the form of words, but in a stronger essence that flowed through every cell and vein.

Benjamin Cranois lifted his face and smiled. And with each passing moment, he celebrated the revelation that the pain was gone—and the mercy of God had taken its place.

CHAPTER THIRTY-TWO

---ⁿⁿ---

LORD, you establish peace for us; all that we have accomplished you have done for us.

ISAIAH 26:12

LEXA STOOD AT THE EDGE OF DELLY'S GRAVE, her arm around their mother.

"My son…"

Lexa drew her mother close, knowing there were no words to counter their loss. Especially since the favored son had died, and the sinful daughter still lived. Her reconciliation with her mother would not be easy. But Lexa had the time, and since coming back to Del, the inclination. The bridges of her life needed to be mended and her brother—and this God she was just beginning to know—had provided the tools.

As the monsignor finished his benediction, Lexa said her amen and looked at the crowd who had gathered at the gravesite: Julia, Walter, Natalie, Kathy, and many others who had been at the reunion. Strangers who had seen a glimpse of her brother's character and wanted to pay their respects.

Lexa smiled to herself. Martyrs are not born—they die.

The press was there too, but they had kept a considerate distance. Actually, Lexa didn't mind their presence, as the coverage her brother and the reunion had received since his death had been positive and enlightening. People were excited about the ideals her brother emulated: sacrifice, love, and a heart full of God. Del's death had made people think about their own lives—and their faith.

Her smile broadened. Del would have been pleased.

As the crowd turned back to their cars, Lexa spotted Carrie.

When their eyes met, Lexa surrendered her mother to Bette for a moment, and the girl ran into Lexa's arms.

"He's gone!"

Lexa put a hand on the girl's head and kissed it. She pulled back. "But aren't we lucky to have known him?"

Carrie nodded and Lexa brushed away one of her tears. A man approached, standing a respectful distance away. Carrie turned and held out her hand to him. "Dad, this is Lexa Delatondo, Father Del's sister. Lexa, this is my dad, Charlie Peterson."

Lexa shook his hand, noting that the blue of his eyes matched his daughter's. "You have a wonderful young lady here."

"I think so too." He pulled Carrie under his arm. "She sure enjoyed working with you and Father. Being a part of the reunion—even just the planning of it—was very special to her."

"I told her she could have gone with us, but she said it wasn't possible." Lexa had always wondered about that.

Charlie looked down at his daughter. "She's protective of me. Ever since her mother died, she's been handling the house and school and her work at the food bank—"

Lexa shook her head. "Plus helping with the reunion." She tweaked Carrie's nose. "Why didn't you tell me? I wouldn't have worked you so hard."

"I wanted to help."

"And that, you did."

Carrie blushed then looked up. "What are you going to do now, Lexa? You're not leaving town, are you?"

It was a good question. "I don't know. There's nothing to keep me here. I don't have a job, my savings are running low, and since Delly's not here anymore..."

"What kind of work do you do when you're not organizing reunions?"

"I organize other people's lives—but rarely my own. Give

me a clipboard, a calendar, and a decent budget, and I'm in heaven."

"Really?"

She smiled at him. "That *really* sounded chuck full of possibilities. You have something in mind?"

He extended his elbow to both females. "Let's walk and talk about it."

It was a wonderful idea.

Lexa cleaned out her desk. She smiled at the slips of paper that were decorated with her brother's doodles. Curlicues, faces, dogs wagging their tails. She put them in the keep pile.

Looking up, she saw the monsignor walk by in the hall. Sneak by, if she was any judge of the quick and quiet way he slid past her doorway. *Uh-uh. Not so fast.* There was one more piece of business to take care of.

She hurried into the hall to catch him. "Monsignor? Do you have a minute?"

He stopped walking and paused a full five seconds before he turned around. "Yes, Ms. Delatondo?" He did not come to her.

Fine. If you want to do this out in the hall, I can handle that. She walked toward him, locking onto his eyes. He looked away. *Can't take the heat, can you?* When she reached him, he finally looked up and she saw him swallow. *Before I'm done with you, you'll be swallowing more than your spit, you bitter, egotistical man.* She took an extended breath, making his curiosity suffer just a moment—

"I'm…I'm sorry, Ms. Delatondo. About Del."

All the words of bombast left her. "Thank you."

"He was a good man, and I regret…" He looked to the floor.

She finished the sentence for him. "You regret giving him a hard time?"

His jaw tightened with a retort, then with effort, relaxed.

The place between his eyebrows dipped and he bit his lower lip.

Is he going to cry?

"I...I should have—"

Lexa put a hand on his shoulder. "We all *should* have, Monsignor. Should have done better deeds, thought kinder thoughts, and appreciated Delly when we had him. He was—and continues to be—an inspiration."

The monsignor put his hands behind his back and nodded. Then he walked away.

Lexa watched him go. She was familiar with the shame in his drooped shoulders; she recognized the confusion in the shake of his downcast head. And she identified with the remorse in his lifeless shuffle. She'd been there. She *was* there.

At that moment, she let the anger go and in its place discovered something new.

Forgiveness.

As the monsignor turned the corner, leaving her sight, Lexa Delatondo forgave him.

And then, she forgave herself.

———※———

Natalie sat in her car. Jack stood beside the window.

"I can't believe you're going again." He leaned down to her level. "We did this once before. I didn't like it two years ago; I don't like it now."

She reached through the open window and took his hand. "But this time is different. This time I'm coming back."

"I'm glad you're giving us a chance."

"I have to. I have to quit running away and start running *to* something."

Jack grinned. "Me?"

"Don't get cocky on me, Jack Cummings."

He kissed her. "I wouldn't think of it."

"I know. That's one reason I love you."

He pulled back. "You love me?"

Funny how she'd felt the emotion for quite a while but had never said it aloud. "I love you."

Jack pumped his fist in the air and did a three-sixty. "Yee-ha! Natalie loves me!"

Natalie laughed and noticed a boy on a bike giving them a strange look. "Shh! Your neighbors will think you're crazy."

"Crazy in love."

Natalie rolled her eyes, though inwardly, she loved his romantic gushing. She started the engine. "Find me an apartment, Jack. Close to you. And cheap. I'm still a struggling writer, you know."

"But not for long. Remember what Del told you at the dinner: 'Blessed is she who has believed that what the Lord has said to her will be accomplished!'"

"I think I need to put that in perspective. I looked it up. That was said by an angel to Mary when she believed she would conceive a child by the Holy Spirit. A far grander job than the one I've been given."

"Don't belittle your purpose. Mary had hers, you have yours, and I have mine."

She loved how he always made her feel better. "And what's yours?"

He kissed her one more time. "To love you the best I can."

Natalie tossed her keys on the coffee table and slumped onto the couch with a stack of mail in her lap. She was exhausted. The drive had been long and her emotions high. She'd cried for Del, stewed over what she'd tell Sam, and battled the urge to turn the car around to be with Jack. She felt as if she'd done a week's worth of work in an eight-hour drive.

She sorted the mail, tossing the ads on the floor, the bills on the coffee table, and the—

She stopped short as she noticed the return address on one

letter. Capstone Publications. *It's a letter. It's not my manuscript returned.* She started to rip open the envelope, then stopped herself. She pulled the letter to her chest and closed her eyes. "Lord, I hope, I hope…but whatever it says, I want to thank You for a reply. At least I can go on with my life. I trust You. I—"

She couldn't wait any longer. She tore open the envelope and unfolded the letter. *"We are pleased to offer you a contract for Seeking Haven…"*

She scanned the rest of the letter, then slid off the couch to her knees. She touched her forehead to the floor, sobbing.

It had finally happened. She was done waiting for Samuel. Samuel had finally come, and God had accepted her offering.

"Praise the Lord!"

Natalie laughed at Jack's proclamation. "I still can't believe it. I've waited and waited…"

"How long was it?"

Natalie did the mental calculations. "Exactly fifteen months today since I first heard from Capstone."

She heard Jack suck in a breath. "Fifteen, Natalie! Fifteen!"

Her dream. The fifteen glowing on the pillow. "It didn't mean the fifteenth; it represented fifteen months!" She began to laugh. "I'm so glad God didn't let me in on the months part from the beginning. I don't think I would have taken fifteen months kindly."

"But you *did* take fifteen months kindly. You waited. You had faith. You were patient for God's timing."

"Actually, I was rather *impatient*. I wasn't gracious about it. God witnessed all my emotions: anger, bitterness, frustration, giving up…"

"Giving *it* up. Surrender."

"Eventually."

"Maybe that's what God was waiting for, for you to surrender your work to Him. He waited for you to let it go."

Natalie thought back to the day before the reunion when she'd finally offered her writing to God. Totally. Completely. Without restriction. It had been the twentieth. She looked at the postmark on the letter. "Jack..."

"What's wrong?"

She began to laugh. "Nothing. Nothing at all."

———

Ryan and Lisa raced into the house, obviously relieved to be free of the car and eager to play with the toys they hadn't seen in four days. Kathy felt the same—at least about the car part. She hated long drives. And after Del's death, they had traveled up to Lincoln for the funeral, and then all the way back home today. What she really wanted was to prune in a hot tub.

Roy carried the suitcases inside. "I'll check the messages, then I need to stop in at the hospital. I'm sure they aren't pleased with me taking off two extra days."

"It's not like you could help it, Roy." Kathy hung up her coat. "I really wanted to be at Del's funeral, and if those slave drivers at the hospital can't have a little compassion—"

He put a hand on the back of her neck. "Down, girl."

She rubbed her eyes, knowing she was testy. She pointed toward the bathroom. "Bubbles. I need bubbles."

Roy pushed the button on the answering machine. "I plan to do the same when I get home."

The machine started. "*Kathy? You don't know me, but I was at the reunion, and I saw your wonderful paintings. I was wondering if you have any others for sale? Please call me at...*"

Roy wrote down the name and number. "You have a sale."

"It appears so."

They were quiet for the second message.

"*I was at the reunion and saw your lovely painting. Lexa Delatondo gave me your number. I would like to know where your work is available. My name is...*"

Roy's grin was huge. "A star is born."

They listened to nine more messages from people wanting Kathy's paintings. She sank onto the desk chair, staring at the notes. "This is too much."

"You mean you can't do it?"

She shook her head. "I *will* do it. Whatever it takes. What I mean is, it's too good. Too generous of God to give me all this success after all I've done wrong."

Roy kissed the top of her head. "Our God is a forgiving God."

She could only nod in humble amazement.

Roy emerged from his bath, looking quite cuddly in his terry cloth robe. He must have felt cuddly too, because he snuggled next to Kathy on the couch.

"It's good to be home."

"Yes, it is."

"Speaking of home..." He sat up straighter and looked at her. "I was thinking...maybe it *is* time we look into buying a new house."

"What brought this on?"

He shrugged. "With all this new business coming in... maybe I was wrong in discouraging you. Tomorrow, why don't you call that Randolph Sears and make an appointment to see—"

"No." Kathy was amazed at the adamant tone of her voice.

"Why not?"

It took a moment for the reasons behind her answer to materialize enough to share. She turned to Roy, tucking her feet beneath her robe. "I don't want a new house—not yet. I'm not ready for it. I may have the material means to get it, but I don't have the spiritual means to handle it. Having a bigger, better house still means too much to me. Having *things* means too much to me. In fact, I have a whole passel of things to return to stores."

"I said you could keep the other dresses—"

"Stop it!"

She bolted from the couch, amazed at her own outburst. She turned to face him. "Stop letting me get away with it! I've got an addiction that is just as strong as drugs or booze. I'm addicted to *things*, Roy." She thought of her stash in the basement closet. "It's not just the dresses…" She shook her head. She'd show him the extent of her vice later. "And when you go along with me…let me…" She tried to find the words. "I can't depend on you to keep my ethics and faith in line. I can't use you as a scapegoat: 'If Roy doesn't mind then it must be all right.' It's not all right! I am not a better person than I was as an unwed teenager because of the things I have purchased. I am a better person because of my relationship with God."

He held a hand to her. She shook her head and did not take it.

"I have to learn to be content…" She sighed at the immensity of her thoughts. "Maybe when I don't want a house so much, it will be time to get one." She shook her head in frustration. "Does that make any sense?"

Roy reached for the Bible sitting on the end table. She smiled at him. "There's a verse to confirm all this, isn't there?"

He flipped through the pages, grinning. "There is *always* a verse." His finger pegged it. "And here it is. The verse for the day, especially for Kathy Bauer: 'Keep your lives free from the love of money and be content with what you have, because God has said, "Never will I leave you; never will I forsake you."'"

She fell onto the couch and hugged him, resting her head on his shoulder. "What more do we need?"

———⟨∿⟩———

Ryan couldn't sleep. He lay in his bed, looking at the poster of the Arkansas Razorbacks his dad had taped to the ceiling. He'd always wanted to be a football player.

Until now. Until Father Del.

He would never forget how Del had burst across the stage to push the president out of the way. Then the explosion. His mom had pulled him under the table. But he'd peeked out. He'd *seen.*

There had been no sound. He could see people running and screaming, but all Ryan could hear was his own breathing. And then the light had shone on Del, and Del had looked into it and smiled. And talked. There'd been a communication going on that Ryan couldn't hear. But he could feel it.

The peace. The joy. The total contentment of knowing God and Jesus.

"I want that," he said aloud.

You will have that.

Ryan blinked. He smiled. And he knew.

It was true. It was possible. Even for an eight-year-old boy. God had called him. Now he needed to do his part. "Yes!" he said aloud.

He bolted upright in bed, wanting to run to his mom and dad to tell them the news. But when his toes touched the floor, he changed his mind.

He couldn't tell anyone. Not yet. He didn't want them to talk him out of it or say he was too young to make such a decision. They'd be wrong. The decision was made. Ryan could not undo the calling if he wanted to. The deal was done. The promise sealed.

Ryan glanced at the ceiling. The members of the football team were not his heroes anymore. He only had room for one hero in his life. He smiled with a new idea.

He went to his desk and found a book he'd gotten for Easter last year. He flipped the pages, looking for one picture in particular. He found it and carefully ripped it out.

He dug through a drawer until he found some tape, then took his desk chair and placed it on his bed. He climbed on top of it, setting his feet to keep it steady, and put the tape dispenser in his teeth. Ripping down the poster, he let it float to the floor, unneeded. Obsolete.

In its place he taped the picture of his new hero. His new role model.

He smiled, satisfied with his work. He got down and put everything away.

Then Ryan Bauer got back in bed, pulled the covers under his arms, and looked up at the face of Jesus.

He would be just like Father Del. He would accept the sacrifice. No matter what the cost.

—◈—

Bette tied an apron around Walter's ample belly. "I'm so proud of you, Walter. The shelter can always use another helping hand."

Walter didn't want Bette's compliment. It only proved what an egotistical, selfish boor he had been before. His change of heart was Del's doing. Del had repeatedly tried to get him to do the right thing in life, and was finally getting through to him in death.

His throat tightened. How was he going to get along without him?

Walter had been through hell since the reunion. His reactions had ping-ponged all over the place, from his declaration that he was going to become a priest in Del's honor—which Bette had quickly nixed for a myriad of reasons—to his declaration that he would not rest until the creeps who murdered Del were hung on the nearest yardarm.

He realized Bette may have taken advantage of his condition when she'd suggested he come with her to serve a meal at the shelter. But in his befuddled state, he was in no shape to think up any good excuses.

Bette took the stainless steel covers off the serving trays, and another woman dipped a spoon in each. Walter was assigned the mashed potatoes. *One glob or two?*

The homeless people formed a line. It was clear they'd done

397

this before. They were each given a plate of meat loaf, and they moved down the line to be served the potatoes, corn, roll, and oatmeal raisin cookies.

Walter got the hang of it and only spilled one scoop of potatoes on the table. He heard the people's thank-yous and glanced up once in a while. But he found it awkward to serve them. Even though he and Bette had lost most everything, he was still a *have* and they were the *have-nots*.

"How are you doing today, Gwen?" Bette said.

"Doing better, Bette. Got my ankle looked at down at the clinic."

Walter looked at his wife. She knew these people by name? And they knew her?

Bette and Gwen continued to chat as Gwen moved down the line and Walter filled two more plates. Then a man spoke to him. "'Blessed is the man who perseveres under trial, because when he has stood the test, he will receive the crown of life that God has promised to those who love him.'"

Walter knew that verse. It was the one Del had given him at the reunion dinner. He looked up and saw a man holding a plate, staring at him. The man had long dark hair pulled back in a low ponytail. His features were Italian. He looked an awful lot like—

The man smiled and leaned toward Walter confidentially. "Forgiveness. Forgive yourself."

Walter felt his mouth drop, and the spoonful of potatoes hung in the air.

"May I have some of those, please?"

Walter blinked and dropped the scoop on the man's plate. He winked and walked away. Walter had to concentrate on serving the line of people behind him. When they were finally through, he scanned the dining room.

"Who are you looking for?" Bette asked.

Walter continued looking. "Did you see that man who looked like Del?"

"No, I don't think so…"

"He had a ponytail and he even quoted the verse that Del gave me at the dinner."

"I didn't hear anyone quote a verse."

Walter took off his apron and gave it to her. "I'll be right back. I have to find him." He walked up and down the rows of tables, looking at each face, receiving a few questioning glances.

Bette came up beside him. "Did you find him?"

Walter shook his head, making one last pass over the room. "He's not here." He pointed to the empty space where dirty dishes would be placed. "And he hasn't left. No one has left."

"I don't know, Walter. I have no explanation for you."

Walter stopped searching. He put a hand to his mouth.

"Now you're smiling?"

It was so simple, yet so profound. "I won't have to get along without Del, Bette."

"You won't?"

Walter shook his head. "His words are with me. What he tried to teach me is with me. The memory of his life is with me. And I won't forget him. Not ever."

Bette put her arm around his waist. "Amen to that."

The phone was ringing when Walter and Bette got home. Walter lunged for it before the answering machine picked up. "Hello?"

"He's awake, Walter! Rolf's awake!"

"Marion?"

"He opened his eyes this morning. Just like that!"

They both knew it wasn't just like that. Rolf had been in a coma for over a month.

Her voice softened. "He can't talk. He can't walk. The doctor says he's going to have to learn everything again."

Walter swallowed hard. "Can we see him?"

"Please. Please come."

Walter knocked on the hospital door.

"Come in."

He and Bette found Marion standing next to Rolf's bed. Rolf's external injuries were long healed, but he didn't look all there, as if he were asleep while awake.

"Hey, Marion. Hey, boss man. Have a nice nap?"

Marion put a tissue at the corner of her husband's mouth. "Look, honey. It's witty Walter, come to torment you."

Rolf offered no reaction.

Walter felt tears threaten. He forced a smile, then took Rolf's hand and squeezed it. "It's great to have you back, guy."

Rolf blinked a few times, and there was a hint of recognition in his eyes. Then slowly, deliberately, the corner of his mouth raised in the hint of a smile.

"He remembers you!"

But would he ever be the Rolf Walter remembered?

Walter fell into the driver's seat, staring at nothing. Bette's hand touched his arm.

"He'll get better, hon. I know he will."

Walter didn't nod.

"He will. We'll continue to pray for—"

Walter blinked and turned toward her. "I wasn't worried about that, Bette. Don't you get it? I wasn't worried about *that.*"

"I don't understand."

He looked into her trusting eyes—eyes that still looked for the best, eyes that failed to see what a selfish heel he really was. "When I went into Rolf's room and saw firsthand that he can't talk...my first thought was that he won't be able to help me get my job back." His heart felt like it was crumpling under the weight of his faults. "I didn't think of *him;* I thought of me." He fell toward her soft shoulder. "When am I going to change, Bette? Really change."

"You have changed, hon. You're a good man."

"Who constantly takes one step forward and two steps back."

She kissed the top of his head. "But you stop yourself sooner now, Walter. You recognize what's happening. And I'm here to push you forward again. And God's here."

Walter nodded, his cheek rubbing against the rough wool of her coat. "But will I ever get it really right, have the good thoughts, do the good deeds without being tempted to do otherwise? Will God ever be proud of me?"

She ran a hand along his face. "Oh, hon...He's proud of you right now."

Walter took in a breath and held it. Maybe she was right. For right now, God had Walter exactly where He wanted him. At His feet, asking for help, forgiveness...

And unconditional, patient love.

Ben sat at the diner, reading a newspaper. He shook his head in disbelief. The paper reported that Hamm Spurgeon had been indicted for his bombing of the reunion, for the death of Father Antonio Delatondo, and for the attempted murder of the president. Ben had scanned the article twice, looking for his own name—or Art's—but found nothing.

How was it that Hamm had not squealed on him? It was a mira—

"It's a miracle, isn't it?"

Ben looked up and shock jolted through him. It was Art! They'd not seen each other since the reunion. Someone else had moved into Art's apartment.

Art indicated the empty seat opposite Ben. "Can I sit down?"

He swallowed. "Sure."

Art slid into the booth and clasped his hands on top of the table. He looked at Ben. Finally he said, "Is it over for you?"

The tears appeared unannounced. Ben put his hands over his face. "When I think what a close call it was for so many people, I—"

"He got to you, didn't he?"

"He?"

"God. He did the same thing to me in Haven, through Julia."

"And you changed."

"Not by my own doing—except for the act of giving Him the chance, it was all God. *He* changed me."

Ben thought of the light in the airplane, the words, and the final lifting of the weight. He'd felt a glimpse of God's power then. But in the days that had followed, he'd held it at arm's length, living in a kind of limbo between good and evil. A no-man's-land of indecision.

Art touched Ben's arm. "Do you want to change too?"

Suddenly the limbo was over. With that one question, Ben knew. It was time. He bit his lip and nodded.

Art took a deep breath. "I never thought I'd be doing this for someone else."

"So what do I do?"

Art thought a moment. "You tell God you're sorry. You tell Him you want to know Him, and you tell Him that you believe in all that His Son did for you."

"The cross?"

"Yeah. The cross."

Ben looked around the diner. Not exactly an auspicious place to change one's life. But it was good enough.

Ben sat on his couch, a Bible in his lap. It had been a present from Art. He'd suggested Ben start with the gospel of John. He'd said that Ben would find out about Jesus there. And since Jesus was the key...

The phone rang. "Hello?"

"Benjamin!"

Ben recognized the voice immediately. "Julia!… Madam President, how are you?"

"I'm fine."

"Oh, Julia…I'm…I'm so sorry. I was so wrong."

"I know. Arthur told me. It's all right. You're forgiven. You know that, don't you?"

His throat tightened. "I know that."

"What can I do to help?"

He couldn't believe it. Julia Carson offering to help *him*. After all he'd done. "You could pray for me."

"I have been praying for you, Benjamin. Don't you understand? I've been praying all along. And now, God has answered my prayers. We'll keep in touch, okay?"

He couldn't even say good-bye. He gently hung up the phone. It wasn't supposed to turn out this way. Ben Cranois was supposed to live a life full of conflict and be consumed with a quest for power. His life should be full of anger and bitterness. So…where was this love coming from?

He looked at the Bible in his lap and knew the answer. He opened it to the page Art had marked and began to read…

In the beginning was the Word, and the Word was with God, and the Word was God. He was with God in the beginning.

And the Word was Jesus.

Now to him who is able to do immeasurably more than all we ask or imagine, according to his power that is at work within us, to him be glory in the church and in Christ Jesus throughout all generations, for ever and ever! Amen.

EPHESIANS 3:20–21

Dear Readers,

Lead us not into temptation...

Wishful thinking. It seems that the closer we get to God, the more determined we are to do His will, the more we are faced with temptation. Or maybe we simply get better at recognizing it? When we are sure about what's right, what's wrong takes on a neon glow.

But that doesn't mean we aren't drawn to it. *Flash, flash, blink, blink. Look over here! Come closer! One little touch won't hurt...*

It seems I am destined to learn as my characters learn. At one time or another, I have experienced most of the temptations addressed in this book. And survived, thank God. What I find fascinating is that as I get closer to Him, most of my temptations come from within myself rather than from a third party or the world. They are the temptations of my own character flaws: greed, impatience, pride, control, the yearning for the praise of men more than God. Definitely been there, done that.

As in the previous Mustard Seed books, many of the characters' experiences stem from my own. I, too, had a vision for the "fifteenth" in regard to the first book in this series (and it did indeed symbolize fifteen months!). I fought the battle Natalie fought to force an answer from the publisher, and found comfort—and self-control—in the "waiting for Samuel" verses. And I was given the word *Laodicean* just like Julia—having no idea what it meant.

I have found that with the temptations I am given, I learn great things—or at least have the chance to take a decent shot at it. I learn more from my struggles than the good times—an annoying fact that got easier once I accepted its truth. And now, those struggles are...*different* than they were before I got close to God. Or maybe I'm different. I have fewer crises, fewer events that I designate as emergencies. I go with the flow, knowing He's in control; it's for my own good, and things will go better if I stop fighting the situation and learn from it—do my lessons, struggle through the tests, and take my lumps. I take solace knowing that the next time will—or at least *can*—be easier. It's pretty much my choice.

As with my other novels, this book has endured a huge metamorphosis. I've asked God why it can't come out right the first time, why the drastic changes. I feel a discontent in the process I am forced to go through. I want to accept what seems to be my lot and then I remember what a very wise author friend of mine (Angela Elwell Hunt) once said: "The human part of each of us constantly struggles with the Spirit part. The word *contentment* carries a connotation of passivity; yet it's a real active struggle." And so I resist the temptation to feel discontent. God knows what He's doing. Another day, another struggle…

But on to giving thanks to three people who are always a blessing and never (okay, rarely) a struggle. I want to thank my sister Crys Mach, and my fifteen-year-old daughter, Laurel, for reading the manuscript and offering much needed insight. And of course, my editor, Karen Ball, for having the amazing talent of spurring fresh ideas with just a few pointed questions of "What if…?"

What if…we could be the kind of people God wants us to be? Think about it. Aspire to it. Resist the temptation to think that it can't be done. It can. With His help.

"You were taught, with regard to your former way of life, to put off your old self, which is being corrupted by its deceitful desires; to be made new in the attitude of your minds; and to put on the new self, created to be like God in true righteousness and holiness… Be kind and compassionate to one another, forgiving each other, just as in Christ God forgave you" (Ephesians 4:22–24, 32).

In that hope,

Nancy Moser

Bible Verses in *The Temptation*

Prologue:
Temptation/Hebrews 2:18

Chapter 1:
Seeking/Psalm 14:2
Armor/Ephesians 6:18

Chapter 2:
Listening/Proverbs 19:20–21
Truth/John 8:32
Lukewarm/Revelation 3:15–16

Chapter 3:
Grace/2 Corinthians 12:9
Temptation/Matthew 6:13
Deliverance/Matthew 6:13
Gifts/James 1:17
Waiting/1 Samuel 13:11–14*

Chapter 4:
Listening/Zechariah 7:13
Worry/Philippians 4:6
God's plan/Job 42:2

Chapter 5:
Wisdom/Daniel 12:3
Protection/Psalm 121:5–6

Chapter 6:
Motives/1 Corinthians 4:5
Pride/Proverbs 16:18
Praise/John 12:43

Chapter 7:
Sin/Romans 6:12
Foundation/1 Corinthians 3:11–15
Obedience/Deuteronomy 4:29–30

Chapter 8:
Treasure/Matthew 6:21

Chapter 9:
Temptation/1 Corinthians 10:13

Chapter 10:
Friendship/Proverbs 17:17
Holy Spirit/1 Corinthians 12:3
Deception/1 Timothy 4:1
Repentance/Acts 2:38
Holy Spirit/1 Thessalonians 5:19

Chapter 11:
Belonging/John 10:14,16
Possibilities/Mark 10:27

Chapter 12:
Guilt/Psalm 91:14

Chapter 13:
Greed/Luke 12:15

Chapter 14:
Understanding/Matthew 13:19
Weakness/2 Corinthians 12:10
Contentment/Proverbs 19:23

Chapter 15:
Protection/Psalm 5:10

Chapter 16:
Courage/1 Corinthians 16:13
Armor of God/Ephesians 6:11
Speaking/Mark 13:11
Protection/Psalm 5:11–12
Asking/John 16:24

Chapter 30:

Right/Job 34:4

Commitment/Mark 8:34–35

Fear/Matthew 10:28

Comfort/Isaiah 41:10

Giving/Acts 20:35

Apathy/Revelation 3:15–16, 19

Responsibility/Luke 12:48

Chapter 31:

Prayer/Revelation 8:4

Heaven/Acts 7:55

Jesus/Acts 7:56

Praise/Matthew 25:21

Surrender/Acts 7:59

Forgiveness/Acts 7:60

Persecution/Acts 9:4

Calling/Acts 9:5–6

Chapter 32:

God's will/Isaiah 26:12

Faith/Luke 1:45

Contentment/Hebrews 13:5

Trials/James 1:12

Jesus/John 1:1

Glory/Ephesians 3:20–21

* paraphrased

Excerpt from book four in The Mustard Seed series,
The Inheritance.

WALTER PUSHED BACK IN THE RECLINER, his feet rising with the footrest. He put his hands behind his head, ready for a Saturday nap. "Go get the mail for me, Addy."

Walter's four-year-old daughter pinched her father's big toe. "Say *please.*"

"Please."

"Say pretty please."

"Pretty please, thank you, glory glory hallelujah with whipped cream and a cherry."

"Say—"

Walter pointed toward the door. "Go!"

Addy shrugged and went outside, letting the screen door slam. Walter closed his eyes, knowing he would have approximately thirty seconds of peace before his daughter blew back into his presence.

The door slammed a second time. Walter cracked an eyelid and extended a hand. Addy stood just out of reach.

"Give it to me, please."

She shook her head. "Mom says whoever gets, gets to open. It's a rule."

"Since when?"

"Since always."

"How come I've never heard of such a rule?"

"'Cause you're usually at work when the mail comes."

Good point. Then he thought of something. "But it's Saturday. I'm here. I get—"

She turned her back on him, flipping the mail against her chest as if she were expecting a windfall of letters addressed to Addy Prescott, child extraordinaire.

"Addy…"

She sighed and handed it to him. "Mom says the grass needs cutting. I'm going over to Tenisha's. Bye."

And she was gone.

Walter flipped the footrest down and dropped the mail onto his lap. He was constantly amazed at his daughter's knack for slipping in an instruction of what he should be doing—or what his wife Bette thought he should be doing. But the difference between his wife's methods and Addy's was that Bette had tact—or brains enough to know that the way to get Walter Prescott to cut the grass was *not* to tell him to do it. He was a big boy. He knew it needed to be done. And he'd get to it. Eventually.

Walter looked through the mail. Bills, tempting offers of credit cards they shouldn't get, a mailing stuffed with coupons they would surely use, a catalog for women's clothes and…what was this? An official-looking letter from an attorney's office in Wisconsin?

Walter isolated the letter from the pile. He stared at it a moment, racking his brain. *What did I do now?*

He shook the ridiculous thought away. He hadn't done anything. He'd been a good boy. Annoying, exasperating, and stubborn, but certainly good enough to keep lawyers and the law indifferent. Walter ripped open the letter. The heading was embossed in glossy black letters: Sylvan and Schuster, Attorneys at Law. Walter scanned the text, his eyes zeroing in on certain key words: *great aunt…died…will…*

The letter got to its point. He sucked in a breath. *An inheritance.*

Aunt Irma had died and left him some money? His heart began to race. He went back to the beginning of the letter and read every word, hoping a dollar sign would jump out at him, shouting exactly how excited he should be.

But there was no dollar sign. No amount listed.

He tried to remember the deceased. *Irma…Irma…she was Pop's older sister.* Old maid older sister. No kids. No kin? Pop was gone. So was Pop's brother. There might be a cousin out East somewhere, but Walter had lost touch. Was Aunt Irma's estate going to be divided two ways?

He forced his breathing back to normal. Half of piddle is piddle.

He tried to remember what Aunt Irma had done for a living. The smell of pizza came to mind. Pizza places...that was it. Irma had started a chain of pizza parlors. He remembered going there as a kid. Good pizza. Layered with pepperoni and deep with cheese. At one time she'd had lots of locations. But that had to be thirty years ago. Had she sold out? Or was she still reaping the proceeds at the time of her death?

Walter and Bette could sure use the money. Although Walter had a decent job as a salesman for a radio station, Bette had put them on a budget. Walter often wondered if she was a descendant of Ebenezer Scrooge. After one of his spending sprees, she'd even hidden the checkbook. He knew it was for his own good, but still...

Six months ago, they'd managed to buy a house—a far smaller house than the first one they'd purchased in Minneapolis, the one they'd had to sell when Walter had lost his job at the TV station and had gambled away their savings. But now with an inheritance... They could use a new vehicle. Walter's van had contests to see who could be more temperamental, it or Walter. And the refrigerator only made ice when—

Stop dreaming, Walter. Call!

Walter shook his daydreams away and pulled the phone to his lap.

He had an inheritance to claim.